WORLDS A
WORLDS APART 2

Also by Terry Jackman

WORLDS APART COLLECTIVE
HARPAN'S WORLDS: WORLDS APART

WORLDS ALIGNED:
WORLDS APART 2
[Concludes Harp's story?]

TERRY JACKMAN

Elsewhen Press

Worlds Aligned: Worlds Apart 2
First published in Great Britain by Elsewhen Press, 2024
An imprint of Alnpete Limited

Copyright © Terry Jackman, 2024. All rights reserved
The right of Terry Jackman to be identified as the author of this work has been asserted in accordance with sections 77 and 78 of the Copyright, Designs and Patents Act 1988. No part of this publication may be reproduced, stored in a retrieval system or transmitted in any form, or by any means (electronic, mechanical, telepathic, quantum entangled, or otherwise) without the prior written permission of the copyright owner.

Elsewhen Press, PO Box 757, Dartford, Kent DA2 7TQ
www.elsewhen.press

British Library Cataloguing in Publication Data.
A catalogue record for this book is available from the British Library.

ISBN 978-1-915304-46-9 Print edition
ISBN 978-1-915304-56-8 eBook edition

Condition of Sale
This book is sold subject to the condition that it shall not, by way of trade or otherwise, be lent, re-sold, hired out or otherwise circulated in any form of binding or cover other than that in which it is published and without a similar condition including this condition being imposed on the subsequent purchaser.

This book is copyright under the Berne Convention.
Elsewhen Press & Planet-Clock Design are trademarks of Alnpete Limited

Designed and formatted by Elsewhen Press

This book is a work of fiction. All names, characters, places, planets, aliens, pirates, militia, navies, governments and events are either a product of the author's fertile imagination or are used fictitiously. Any resemblance to actual events, benign dictatorships, ruling families, armed forces, extra-terrestrials, planetary bodies, places or people (living, dead, or missing assumed dead) is purely coincidental. No laws of physics were broken in the making of this book.

CONTENTS

1 1
2 13
3 25
4 35
5 49
6 61
7 67
8 81
9 89
10 97
11 105
12 117
13 127
14 137
15 145
16 161
17 175
18 193
19 201
20 211
21 219
22 227
23 235
24 247
25 259
26 265
27 271
28 277
29 285
30 295
31 305
32 317
33 323
34 329
35 331
36 337
37 341
38 347

Dedicated to all the writers who encouraged me to continue, most obviously Jacey Bedford, Juliette McKenna and my tutors at Milford and Arvon weeks, who definitely stopped me abandoning more writing [and so politely pointed out where I failed, just as helpful].

And of course to all the Oncology doctors, surgeons and staff in the north-west who've given me the *time* to write this. Go Clatterbridges!

Thanks everyone.

Terry Jackman

1

The new uniform with its captain's bars fit like it was made for him, which this one was. And *Defiant* was on final approach to World Orbital. He hadn't been required till now, being VIP and all, but now he was sat near the rear of the bridge in a cushy visitor chair, flanked by his new cousin Emika, his boss Colonel Ngow and the other two members of Hawk flight crew, all in their own high-collared, fancy dress. He'd argued it wasn't right jumping him from private to captain like he was the same as Emika and his crewmates, who'd earned it, but that hadn't stopped them adding the curved lines to his shoulder.

And now real-captain Emika reckoned she was acting as his "aide", which was ridiculous. He'd even dared to say so but that hadn't changed things either. The Navy weren't saying what *Raptor* was or how she'd won the battle but they had made it public their prototype had saved the day against the massed attack of pirates. And alas identified her crew, including the unwelcome detail that the gunner was a Harpan, from the Founding Family, a real-life hero. Everyone seemed very pleased about that. Everyone bar him.

So now he sat, surrounded by *Defiant's* Execs, to watch World's Orbital grow larger on *Defiant's* screens and listen to the to and fro between *Defiant* and this new Orbital Command.

There was to be a special welcome for them. Del laughed at it, while Yentl shrugged it off and called it "downside". Mac had shook her head at both of them and patted Harp's hand. He was really glad Del and Yentl were getting medals, and the medics who'd supported them were getting commendations on their Navy records. He just wished they'd leave him out of it.

Not the first time he'd made that wish. Nor probably the last?

+++

World Orbital must be a lot bigger than Moon's, cos *Defiant* could drift in close enough to dock, even if it was at the end of a longer strut. Despite her mass she docked so smoothly only the viewscreens and com confirmed it. They also confirmed rows of Navy uniforms making lines out there right up to the mouth of *Defiant's* umbilical. By the time the umbilical was connected a *Defiant* marine guard was marching through it to join the fun, and out on the dock, a long walk off where the lines ended, a less orderly collection of bodies was arriving, clumping underneath a temporary canopy back there, presumably to dodge the intermittent drip of dockside condensation. Most of those appeared to be in uniform as well, with lots of glitter.

Harp lined up behind Del and Yentl in the umbilical, waiting for the word to disembark. Ngow and Emika flanked him, pretty much boxing him in. Even here he could watch the scene outside evolving on his flash new wristcom, patched into *Defiant's* bridge screens. 'Emika, are there civs out there to meet us?'

'Yes, a few.' He saw her share a look with Ngow. 'They decided to hold the award ceremony here on the dock. They felt it was appropriate, and it's a more controlled environment. You know, less crowds.'

If he had to do this he supposed a smaller audience was better. 'But no talking yet, right?' She'd promised.

'No 'casters even close enough to shout,' Emika said firmly. 'It wasn't easy but I'm the best aide you've got.' She grinned at him then shifted back to solemn. 'Show time. Wristcom off, Captain?'

It was now. 'Thanks.' He could admit her presence helped. So many new rules: do this, don't do that, pretend you're real-Family.

Someone ahead snapped orders. Del and Yentl marched forward. Harp fell into step, told himself he could do this at least. After all he wouldn't have to say anything, just march, halt, make a nod, back off and done. Easy.

Especially with Emika to stop him making a total fool of himself. So he'd shot a few pirates with the Navy's new toy. *Raptor's* weird tec had done most of the work; they should be pinning a medal on her hull instead. It wasn't as if anyone here knew *Raptor's* weapons system wouldn't so far work to its capacity without him.

Emika had diverted him from his original question. Deliberate? Crip, he should have zoomed in before he shut down his com, but too late now. Forward march onto the dockside, to the clack and smash of all these bodies standing to attention. Ignore that. Keep going, keep going, parade halt in front of the low platform under the big umbrella, a platform full of brass, and civs, one of whom even Harp could recognise now. Maxil Cho Harpan, the current Founder.

Cold panic, heated by a stab of anger. This was Emika's notion of aide? Because she'd known, hadn't she. And Ngow. Everyone always knew, except him.

His comrades in arms were stepping up to collect their medals. A part of Harp heard the exchanges. The Founder – his new-found grandfather for landsake – greeted Del as 'Pilot', Yentl as 'Navigator', nodded formally and thanked them for their service. Ngow's turn now. 'Commander, we congratulate you on a stellar operation.' Ngow stepped away. That made it Harp's turn. Up a step.

The eyes were darker than his, a small relief, but it was still too much like looking in a time-distorted mirror. Desperately Harp picked out more stuff that didn't match. Older, obviously. A thicker waist. Still tall but just a little shorter. But the rest... the red-gold hair was maybe paler but the almost-ochre skin tones and the sharply slanted eyes and cheekbones; they were blatantly related, who would doubt it.

Only now he was supposed to accept he was a 'direct descendant' as they'd called it. Not a bastard after all. He'd just had to wait twenty odd years to find out. No, scratch that, even that was wrong, cos he was barely twenty now according to his 'real' records. Even had a different birthday. It was like he was a stranger.

Oops. The older man hadn't waited for him to reach the designated spot this time but taken a step to meet him. 'Captain.'

'Sir.' He stuttered to an untidy halt, thrown off his game by the change. One of the hovering brass jumped forward too, nodded and passed his boss the medal. Harp figured he'd better stay put and let them decide what to do.

Maxil Harpan stepped in closer, snapped the shiny morsel to his collar; didn't step back. Didn't formal-nod the way he had with others. No, he laid a gloved hand on Harp's shoulder and gripped, hard. 'Welcome home, boy.' Were those actual tears glistening behind the lashes lowered for a second? 'This is a great day for the Family.'

Yeah, but was it for Harp?

Harp pulled himself together. 'Thank you, sir.' When the hand fell away he took the backward step Emika had coached him for then nodded quickly, Navy-style, like the rest. The space between them widened further when the Founder stepped away as well. And nodded back, much slower. Harp thought about breathing again and beat a retreat.

Any hope of real escape was of course forlorn. There was a "reception". Emika *had* warned him about that; a drink and a snack, she'd said. He planned to stick close to his team.

Turned out to be Navy grunts in white jackets carrying small trays round a room in the Orbital's core. Harp supposed the tortured scraps on them must be the food. Other grunts took orders for drinks then fetched them, like these folk were too important to walk to the bar at the far end. Harp wanted a beer but he wasn't sure they'd have one here in officer country so he asked for wine like Emika; figured it was safer. That recalled his fancy meal with Hissack in the capital; so not too bad then, though he hadn't drunk it since. But the snacks, no, didn't fancy those, even if his stomach would stand it.

Only Emika murmured, 'Try the little crackers, that's what I choose when I'm nervous.' And the funny little triangles turned out OK and helped to calm his stomach. Or the thought that even Emika got nervous.

A steward came to take his empty glass – the things were barely three swallows anyway – and offer him a fresh one. He would risk one more if only cos it gave him something to hang onto. Different sort this time, much sweeter. Not his thing. He held it like a shield for a while then tried another sip – his mouth felt dry as Moon dust – still too sickly. Looked for somewhere he could dump it but the steward saw, appeared with his tray and took it.

By that time the crowd had got noisier, his head ached something fierce and people kept on talking to him, even when he didn't say much. But Emika stuck to him like caulking gum, and the Founder – *Grandfather* – was off at the other end, surrounded by a mob, so that was better than he'd feared. Looked like he could stay here in his corner. He suspected Del and Yentl were deliberately talking for him, shielding him a little from these strangers. Only then they turned to face him, cutting off the others for a moment. 'Figure you'll be off soon,' Del said softly.

'Really?' Thank the stars.

But then he spoiled it. 'You can cope with all this, kid. You know that, right? Anyone who can handle *Raptor* can walk rings round civs, however flash. You'll be all right.'

'Yeah.' Yentl nodded gravely. 'Go down there and wow 'em, Captain Harpan.' Both the Hawks… saluted formally, the jerky nod, a hand against their breastbones?

Yentl must have seen his disbelief, the man smiled gently. 'Fake it till you make it, eh Harp? You've the Founding Family behind you now, so use them?'

But the Founding Family were strangers while the ones he wanted at his back right now were going back to the *Defiant*. While he – his stomach rolled – stars knew what waited in *his* future.

Emika stepped in while Harp was swallowing. 'Looks like Ser Maxil's Security are preparing to leave, that means us. OK?'

OK? If he said it wasn't would that change anything?

Ser Maxil – might as well learn to talk about people the way Emika did – and his aides, hangers-on, whatever, were indeed drifting toward the farther exit, some of the shinier brass still trying to have the last word. Harp figured two lowly captains would bring up the rear but as soon as he and Emika approached they were gulped into the centre of the bunch, right next to Maxil.

'Ah there you are. Said your farewells, I assume?' The Founder sounded friendly. Harp supposed he likely was, with Emika. The mob closed in, effectively shutting the rest out. 'I hope Emika is looking after you, Maxil?'

'Yessir,' came on auto, but…

The Founder must have seen him freeze a moment. 'What? Ah, your name, eh? I expect we'll cause some confusion, there haven't been two of us for some time.'

That. Didn't. Help.

Perhaps the Founder saw that too. 'I suppose you find being called Maxil rather strange anyway.'

'I. Folk usually called me Harp, sir.'

The sudden grin was shocking. 'Harp, eh, a nickname? Well, why not, it's yours and no one else's. When we're not in public anyway?'

'Yessir. Thank you, sir.' At least something might stay the same. Except he spotted Emika had frowned, for just a moment.

+++

It was a private shuttle this time with wider aisles and bigger chairs. Family – turned out that meant Ser Maxil, Emika, Harp and a young guy waiting for them – sat in state at the wider rear. The rest kept themselves to the front – there was even a gap – and tried to pretend they weren't there. The separation made Harp feel he was still on show even though there was less of a crowd.

A woman offered drinks. He declined, figuring the second wine hadn't been wise. Ser Maxil promptly ordered him a brandy instead, wanted or not. He'd heard of the costly drink but never tasted one, amber stuff it was; he sipped experimentally, the shivers faded and he realised Ser Maxil was talking to him again. 'Well... Harp.' That grin resurfaced. 'That's the first hurdle over. Now, Emika is going to get you settled into your apartment but I'm afraid you'll still have quite a full schedule the first few days – Jontig here has the details Emika – but we'll try to give you time to breathe.'

'Schedule,' Harp said carefully. Maybe the crackers had been off too?

'Yes. There's been no chance to get you outfitted, except your uniform for the ceremony. That'll work for some of the interviews but-'

'Interviews?'

'Don't look so panicked. I realise it's a lot to adjust to but we have to live a portion of our lives in public, and the public are very keen to see you and get to know you a little. If we give them a few opportunities right away it'll dull the fever, as it were, and you'll be able to relax and find your way about much better.'

'Yessir.' He was going to be on show, was what the man was saying. He supposed some part of him had known it, but...

Emika looked sympathetic but didn't argue and this Jontig – more Family? – had no expression, maybe busy trying to size up Harp the same way Harp was him. He figured the guy could make his new life easier or harder; question was which.

Ser Maxil – who'd at least given Harp an out on the same-name thing – maybe – wasn't finished. 'Jon's cleared to stay with you for the first couple of days but then he goes back to his usual job, assisting my son Feldin, your uncle. Once you feel comfortable we'll arrange interviews for your own staff and the like.'

Apartment. Staff? Now he did feel sick. 'Sir, Colonel Ngow's expecting me to report back for duty. He said something about other projects...'

'The colonel wasn't then aware who you are, boy, was he? If you still want the Navy after the dust settles I'm sure we can arrange something but there'll need to be a period of adjustment, yes? Acclimatisation? You can see that?'

'Yessir.' Yes he saw. Retraining, again. He shut up and tried to face it but his vision blurred. They weren't going to let him hide in a corner, as he'd naively thought they'd prefer. No, they were going to throw him to the sliders.

+++

'Here, are you all right, boy? I realise it must be a lot to take in but everyone will help. Maxil? Harp?'

Ser Maxil's voice buzzed. The man's face wavered, tilted. Crip he was, he was. 'Sick,' he tried to say, tried to stand, found himself flat on his back with people shouting over him. Hands tugged his collar, pulled his jacket open, but the shuttle shuddered, and everything spun. Shouts. Thuds. Under attack? Needed to arm his turret.

'Uh.' Harp tried to rise. Couldn't. But *Raptor* needed her gunner. Where was he hit this time? Stomach wound?

'Easy, Captain.' Hands pressed him into... pillows? A bed? The guy bent over him was even loosening restraints.

'What th'hell?' No wait, he'd seen this face before. With Maxil. Not the Jon guy, Daichi was the name he'd heard, in Maxil's Security. But they'd been... on a shuttle.

This wasn't the shuttle.

Nor a cabin. A fast recon said bedroom, surface-style, huge, and shadowed cos two big privacy screens, coloured a soft purplish blue, were down over the wall opposite the bed. Which was also huge and also purplish, only several tones of. One, two, darker, smaller panels. Maybe exits? Fancy art. Was that a holo of the Founder?

The man was still close. 'How do you feel, ser?'

Nauseous. And heavy. Harp considered lying but what the crip. 'Daichi, right? What happened?'

'If you don't mind, ser, Ser Feldin wishes to discuss that with you in person. I've sent word you're awake.'

Ser Feldin, that was... Maxil's son, his new-found uncle? He wasn't tracking fast enough yet, was he? 'Caffee?'

'Certainly, ser.' While Daichi's back was turned Harp got himself as far as sitting up, decided he felt washed out, and starved, but otherwise still in one piece. No obvious wounds anyway.

The caffee was black and strong, another reminder how much these folk knew about him now. 'Where am I?'

'Your apartment, ser.' Humouring him? Though Maxil had said something about an apartment. So they were down on World. With World's nastier gravity; that explained why he felt heavier. Maybe. But it didn't explain how he'd got here.

A soft chime. The other man reached out then offered him a wristcom. 'An internal call, ser. Will you take it?'

'Yeah.' Relief; Daichi left him to it. Harp took an extra breath then tapped. Another half-familiar face looked up at him, an office sort-of setup in the background. 'Maxil? Daichi sent word you were awake. How are you feeling?'

"Maxil..." Harp's brain scrambled. This guy looked a lot like older-Maxil, smiled like him too, but...?

'Oh of course, we haven't met yet. I'm your uncle, Feldin.'

The – 'Ser Maxil's son.'

'That's right. Bit of a challenge all this, eh?'

'A bit, yessir.'

'Call me uncle, boy. At least in private.' Harp stayed silent; Maxil made the self-same comment; looked like even names would be a minefield here. And this Feldin wasn't finished. 'I'm glad you're all right. I'm tied up right now, for another hour, but after that I'd like us to meet, if that's OK with you?'

Of course it only sounded like a question.

'Yess – fine. That's fine.' He couldn't get his tongue round uncle.

'Good. Don't overdo it, try to eat, take a shower, whatever. I promise I'll explain things when I get there.' Feldin's image vanished.

Daichi reappeared in one entry. 'The facilities are

through that panel, ser. Would you like breakfast before or after?'

Breakfast, in bed? Oh no. But food soon, definitely, when had he last eaten? 'I'll get up first.'

'Very well, ser. If you need anything please call.'

'Yeah.' Not if he could help it.

Getting out of bed reminded him he was subject to more gravity again, he felt heavier with each step he took, like those first days here in the Navy's training facility. It also reminded him he'd need to up his exercise regime again, to build the extra muscle to withstand it. Times were he really missed Moon's lesser grav – missed Moon, despite its drawbacks. But at least such changes weren't too odd now after time on Orbitals, and the *Defiant*. Where he'd stay if anyone would let him. Ah well, best foot forward, make an effort.

The second dark panel was indeed a head – washroom. The only thing he could say was it wasn't as big as the bedroom. The shower unit was a glassite walk-in, room enough for six and they still wouldn't knock elbows. When he dropped the thin pants someone had changed him into – not a thought he wanted to dwell on yet – and stepped behind the rippled wall a voice inside, embarrassingly female, asked what settings he required. When he guessed 'default' six jets sprayed lukewarm mist. There was a word for this. Decadent? But he couldn't resist experimenting, a hotter temp, heavier spray. When he called 'off' the voice even asked for drying instructions.

At the same moment the outer panel slid aside and Daichi hovered. 'Your naval gear has arrived, ser, would you prefer uniform or a robe?'

He'd prefer privacy, but he'd survived worse. 'Uniform. Thanks.'

'No trouble, ser. I ordered your standard shipboard menu. I hope that's acceptable.'

'Uh, yeah, fine.' Was he going to have to start talking like this too? 'I'm on my way.' Maybe he could hide in here till the guy was gone.

Navy pants and tee and a Navy style breakfast made him feel calmer, and fuller; he'd been starving. The new wristcom said he still had time to kill before his uncle – Feldin, practise that – arrived. He opted for a recon.

Turned out there was hidden storage all around him, in the bedroom and the washroom. Towels if he didn't want to air dry, several robes and softsoles. One whole bedroom wall slid open when he walked toward it to reveal another room behind with racks and shelves and cubbies, very obviously empty bar his meagre gear from *Defiant*. There were actual, static mirrors in there and a padded bench, and other stuff he couldn't even guess at. This was how real-Harpans lived? He took a breath and dared another foray.

More space through the other door, for sitting. Well, there were some fancy seats, another area for meals and a fancy desk face-on to several wall screens, blanked out at the moment. It looked like a whole area around the desk could screen off like a private office, and he thought those screens, set up to slide out of the walls, were seriously soundproofed. Very private, if you wanted.

Somebody had chosen mauves and creams in here too but lighter shades. More daytime suitable, he guessed. He liked it, though it didn't feel like his – but then why would it?

He was contemplating a strange contorted object on a low table when another chime announced incoming and Daichi popped up again. 'I believe that will be Ser Feldin, ser.'

'Oh?' The man was waiting... 'Oh, yeah, how...'

'Access is voice activated, ser.'

Of course it was. 'Door, open?'

2

Ser Feldin Harpan – ser, not sir, remember – was yet another variant of himself. Not as old as Ser Maxil – duh – though oddly greyer haired, a mix of grey and yellow. Did Ser Maxil fake it? Other than that the man looked as fit as a steer; wide shoulders and washboard abs under that thin civ tunic. Regular workouts? Maybe to deal with all this gravity? A straight back suggested either Navy training, or a bossy mother figure. He'd had one like that in PreEd.

Daichi organised more caffee, set it on that lower table then vanished again. Harp and Feldin sat. At least the man got straight to the point, and without all the long words. 'Well, Maxil. Or Max sounds younger – would you prefer that? Or, Emika said something about Harp?'

Harp thought about his options, since he had some. Sure, Harp was familiar, but this guy didn't look comfortable with it. Nor was Emika? Maybe it didn't sound as Harpanish as they'd like, but if he was a Harpan now he guessed he had to let folk see that. And it wasn't quite as bad as people saying Maxil, like he was the Founder. 'Er, Max would work, I guess.'

'Good choice. A little strategy.' What Harp was starting to think of as the Harpan smile. 'Won't do any harm to remind people who you're named after, eh?'

'Yeah. Yessir, I see that.' Looked like he'd been neatly roped and branded.

'Max it is then. But you must be wondering what happened.' Feldin carried on when Harp nodded. 'Security's best guess is the second glass of wine. Unfortunately there were no traces left to analyse and the steward has vanished. Mz Chan, our Head of House Security, is very unhappy about that. But Maxil's medic was onboard as usual so he took charge at once and here you are in one piece. My father and Mz Chan send their apologies for not keeping you safer. I'm afraid we underestimated the danger. We assumed you'd be safe on

Navy territory.'

'Danger.' Was this Feldin saying what he thought?

'Yes. That's what we need to discuss.'

Harp's brain caught up. 'Emika said Regis's family might not be friendly.'

'But you weren't expecting to be poisoned, eh, before you even got here. Frankly we didn't either but now we'll be a lot more careful.'

'But…' *Poison?*

'I should fill in some background.' Seeing another nod the other man continued, 'As the ruling Family we're always going to attract some level of threat. I'm afraid that's going to be part of your life now too. In some ways your time on Moon might help, you've experienced dangers most of your kin haven't. But from now on you'll receive regular confidential briefings to update you on any Family concerns, as we all do. I understand you were already privy to Navy secrets.'

'Right.' Crip. Secrets on top of secrets.

'Our primary focus at the moment is of course the Regis aspect. Komar Regis, if you weren't aware, is one of Eleanora's grandsons. She's the current head of House Regis.'

'Komar?'

'Yes, the traitor you uncovered?'

'Ah. Never knew his given.'

'Oh? Well, at one time rumour had it she was looking at Komar as a possible heir. She'd never made any bones about doubting her first son's suitability and it looked like young Komar had ingratiated himself. But then he got into a scandal over money, embarrassed his House and cost them a fortune in bribes and restitution. Word was Eleanora was the one who shipped him into Moon Militia in hopes the talk would die down. Maybe she thought he'd come back older and wiser.

'Of course now she and her House have a much worse problem. She's taken a big hit to the House's reputation, and her own, being so closely related to a traitor. Several of her investors have fled so the Regis businesses are taking hits as well. Perhaps more significantly, Eleanora herself has been publicly embarrassed and someone like her will take the loss of face very seriously. Our reading is she's now weighing brute revenge – on us or Komar is a toss-up – against more diplomatic solutions. The fact it was a Harpan who brought the treachery to light was guaranteed to hit her harder, and that goes double now that everybody knows you are a hero. With me so far?'

'Yessir.' Oh yeah. He'd blackened her family's name, made her lose considerable face and ended up the white Harpan knight to … Komar Regis' black. A public comparison, with Harpans winning hands down.

'Plus, Eleanora has another problem.' There was more? 'Komar's parents. Medam Sirena, his mother, is Eleanora's eldest daughter. She argued long and loud against banishing her beloved child to Moon, and blames Eleanora for her loss, for leaving him without family support, and thus *causing* him to go completely off the rails.' Feldin didn't try to hide his disgust. 'Three days ago Sirena made some very damaging remarks to that effect, in public. Word got back to Eleanora, who wasn't pleased.' Sudden grin. 'We may have had a little to do with that. But it might possibly have prompted this attack on you. On the other hand we feel it's more likely it was down to Komar's mother losing her temper, not uncommon.' Poisoning wasn't uncommon? 'Unless there's anyone else we should know about with a grudge against you?'

'I don't know any.' Harp tried to sound calm. 'I hardly know anyone on World outside the Navy– oh.'

'Oh?'

'There was a professor, Simshaw. He didn't like me much.'

'Involved in the Flashback mission, yes?'

'Yeah, in charge of the medical side. He pushed. I got so tired I could have got myself killed so Colonel Ngow took over. Simshaw wanted to do a lot of tests, cos of my, our, bloodtype being different? But I don't see why he'd want to kill me.'

Feldin nodded. 'We have him on file but no, I agree. Over-ambitious, self-serving, but hardly a large enough motive. He'd be more interested in studying you alive than dead.'

They'd looked? 'Er, is there anyone else *you* considered, ser?' He'd got this time; might as well know the worst while he was at it.

His new-found uncle sighed. 'A few. You've had quite an eventful life haven't you? But most of your past relates to Moon or the Navy, as you said, so we can probably eliminate those. Bottom line; we're concentrating on the Regis aspect, and anyone who stands to lose from the Navy's current success.' He saw Harp's frown. 'The Navy and the arms industries may love you, the black merchants won't.'

'Yes, I see' How many folk would that be? 'So you think someone will try again.'

'I'm afraid that does look likely. A shame you have to come face to face with that side of your new life so soon, but from what we hear we suspect you'll cope, eh? As I said Security will keep you updated, and they're very keen to make amends so I feel confident they'll have your back now.' Feldin settled back a little. Signal of a change of topic?

'On the plus side, we've done a pre-emptive strike on the cover story.'

'Si – ser?'

'Sorry, we got our version of your collapse out first. We've let it be known you returned to duty too early and had a minor, not-life-threatening relapse after the award ceremony. So it'll give you an excuse to duck out of the public eye for a few more days. Plus.' That grin resurfaced. 'My tailor won't hate us quite so much – oh, I didn't mean. *He* doesn't want to kill you, more likely me. *You're* about to make him a lot of credit, not to mention excellent publicity, but even the best workers baulk at producing a basic wardrobe in two days; now he'll have at least five.' The grin became the milder Harpan smile, but just a trifle roguish. 'When he sees you, rather than just your measurements, I'm sure he'll be even happier; he'll have no trouble making you presentable. But remember, you'll do a lot more for him so don't let him bully you?'

Now he was supposed to tell some fancy tailor how to do his job?

Feldin still hadn't done. 'That's the worst over with. Let's change the subject, shall we?'

Gladly. Maybe.

'How d'you like the apartment?'

'Oh, it's very nice, ser, thankyou.'

'Hmm.' Feldin looked around him. 'They haven't changed much, have they? I'd almost forgotten what it looked like, it's been closed up so long. I used to…' He trailed off. 'Sorry, memories. Where was I?'

'You were saying it hadn't changed much, ser.' Though that "closed up" puzzled Harp most.

'Yes. This was your father's apartment here in the Mansion. Part of your inheritance, you might say.' The other man's expression softened. 'You'll have lots of questions.'

Questions? He was speechless. Somehow in all the chaos he'd never thought about – he'd had a father, and a mother.

'I.' Feldin had said "was". 'My… parents. No one said.'

'No.' Feldin let out a breath. 'You know you were abducted.'

'Yes.'

'Your parents were targeted too, you were together.'

Harp frowned. 'But they'd have had security?' Even he knew that much.

'Unfortunately the detail weren't close enough that day. Your parents had taken you out in a small boat on the lake in your family's estate. They wanted some time to themselves and it probably seemed perfectly safe on their own land but alas it proved far from it. We always suspected treachery but we could never prove it.'

'So they, we, were on a boat, on water.' Harp tried to imagine, couldn't.

'Yes. The attack was swift, from the air. Not to mince words brutal. Several Security were killed or injured trying to reach you.' Feldin watched him. 'So were your parents, trying to protect you.'

Harp wished he hadn't just eaten.

Feldin's voice lowered. 'Your father was killed at the scene. Your mother, sorry boy, died later; injuries to her head.' He sat up straighter. 'And till recently we all thought we'd lost you too.'

Harp tried to fit the pieces together. 'Emika said you searched.'

'Oh yes, for several years. There was a ransom demand at first. We made preparations to pay, as well as to track the perpetrators, whether they released you or not. But they never came back with the final instructions and eventually we concluded you were dead, that without you to trade they'd abandoned the plot. What we never considered was that they'd left World for Moon.'

'Why not?' Because his whole life kind of hinged on that omission, didn't it?

'Because the first thing we did was close all the ports. We downed shuttles, searched cargoes, even ransacked the Orbital. We thought we had time to find you. Even now we can't work out how they got you offworld so fast or so well hidden. We only know they must have. And what happened to them after.'

'The crash.' Harp licked dry lips. 'I was on board.'

'And the sole survivor; miraculous really. But the settlers also had a child, hence the mixup. And the records had him down as a four year old survivor so he never came up on our com-search. We didn't take into account that physical development on Moon might lag behind our own. I'm so sorry, Max. We failed you badly.'

'No, I lived.' Oddly, right now thinking about being near two years younger than he'd always thought seemed the strangest part. But maybe he'd feel different later.

Feldin smiled again at last. 'You certainly did young man, and we're all very proud of what you've achieved on your own.' He must have picked up Harp's reaction.

'But enough of that. We had your parents' records copied to your desk here. I imagine you'd rather review those in private, when you're ready?'

'Mmm.' Harp saw his hands were shaking, hid them in his pockets.

'There are some personal items too. I believe your grandfather had them sent to your safe. Ah, I think you'll find it's in your wardrobe? He said the code is your Navy locker code. I expect you'll want to change that to something no one else knows.'

Pretty broad hint. 'Yes.'

'Well.' Feldin rose, hesitated. 'It's a lot, I know, but welcome, Max, and please believe we're all keen to help you find your way. I'm always available if you have questions or concerns, or need to talk?'

'Yessir. Thanks.' Belatedly Harp thought to stand.

'You have nothing to thank us for, boy, in fact it's the other way round. I'll let you rest now.'

'Yes.' Harp gestured vaguely to the exit.

'Don't trouble yourself, Daichi will see me out, and be on call if you want anything. We'll pick it up again tomorrow if that's all right?'

'Yes.' Seemed the only word he had left.

+++

His new desk – his *father's* desk, though it looked like they'd updated the tec – activated for his Navy code, then warned him that was a one-time temp and would autoblock in two hours if not revised. Multiple folders appeared but his gaze tracked straight to one tagged "Family". That produced another endless list but the first file said 'Parents'. It had a personal note attached, from Maxil Snr no less. Back on Moon he'd have got serious respect for a little thing like that. Now… it didn't mean much, but he read it.

"Dear boy, this file contains both public and private records, vid, audio and data packs from before and after your parents' marriage. It won't give you them back but at least you might get to know them a little. It will take you some time to go through it all so I selected a summary subfile you may wish to start from. Maiso, your father, was your Uncle Feldin's elder brother and they have a younger sister who is now once more your Aunt Macilla. When you're ready there's a genealogy included for the whole family. Kai-Chi, your mother, was a lovely person, inside and out. Please be assured they loved you. I think you will see that for yourself.

My sincere condolences, my grandson."

The subfile opened with a holo image of a couple. Maiso Harpan smiled at a woman. Kai-Chi was smaller, generally darker rather than the more exotic later-Harpan version. Harp might have got his skin from her but all the rest, the height, the striking paler hair and eyes, he'd obviously got from Maiso.

Underneath the image was a caption tag. Harp tapped it and a breathless voice recited, "Ser Maiso Harpan and the newest Medam Harpan, looking radiant, are seen here back in Foundation City. The wedding ceremony was held on Ser Maiso's private estate north of the city but in this 'cast the happy couple extend their warmest thanks to all their wellwishers across our twin planets."

Just after their wedding. Harp sent the image to the biggest wall screen, racing through the data that went with it. They'd married three years before he was born when Maiso was thirty and Kai-Chi twenty-five. They'd had four years together, two of them with him.

Maxil was right, Kai-Chi had been a beauty. Harp wondered if it had been a love match as the caster claimed or a political merger; he wasn't the fool he'd once been. But they did look happy and the note said he would see they'd loved him.

An hour later he sat back feeling… empty. They'd loved, loved him as well; a life he should have known, all stolen. He felt emptiness instead. And panic. Maxil Snr had ended the subfile with Maiso's will. Everything his parents owned in life, less small bequests, was his now. This apartment was the least of it. There were two World estates not one, the other somewhere west, both of which came with land, staff and stars knew what. There was a swathe of land on Moon too. Crip, he owned *Riverbend*. There was a word for that – ironic? He'd been a pauper on his own land for a chunk of his life.

There were lists of possessions: artwork, some tagged as "priceless", all on vid, some of it ancient. Cred-stocks, investments that had grown untapped for twenty years. There were several "accounts" labelled things like "Contingencies", "Charities", even "Petty Cash". There was a vid record of all their jewellery. A note added re the absence of four pieces stolen from their bodies during *his* abduction.

Harp discovered he was crying, silent tears. Maybe he should do as Maxil Snr suggested; stretch it out, small doses. So he blanked the screens, except the one that showed his parents – stars, his parents – holding up a toddler. Baby Maxil, barely two years old, was laughing at them, perched upon a mini version of a ranger. According to the notes that western estate had had a "model farm", for him to play with; rangers, steers, lams and some assorted poultry, veggie houses, fruits. A different world indeed, a paradise to any Mooner. And according to the file it still existed, any time he wanted he could visit, stay there even.

He needed caffee. Hell, he had a galley somewhere; couldn't be that hard to find it.

+++

What he'd naively assumed was the exit to the rest of the Harpan Mansion turned out to be another internal panel, with a whole corridor attached. He blinked his way along discovering he had a storage room, more empty shelves and cubbies, two *more* bedrooms – near as fancy as his own – and at the end a second less outrageous office, with two smaller desks, next to the real exit, opposite the galley. Kitchen, kitchen. There, he'd found it.

The... kitchen was dark blue and silver. Galley didn't

really describe it but then he wasn't sure kitchen did either. Food palace? His snort of laughter was unsteady but it made him feel a little better. His parents had left him all this, he guessed he ought to make use of it. Trouble was, he wasn't sure how.

He started by walking round the central island, trying to ID what he saw. Glassite doors revealed racks of bottles and glasses. Had all that wine been sitting here since his parents' time or had someone restocked for him, like they'd upgraded the desk? He tried to ditch the morbid thought and focus on something easier, like caffee, tapping panels, peering into drawers and cubbies. Whereupon that washroom voice spoke up again. 'Can I assist you, Ser Maxil?'

Harp got his breath back. 'Don't do that.'

'I do not compute, ser.'

'Ah, OK. Can you, er, give me some warning before you talk?'

'Certainly ser. Would a musical chord be acceptable?' A gentle trilling sound emerged from somewhere.

'Yes, much better, thanks. How do I make coffee in here?'

'Ser may request the Family's restaurant staff to deliver, as Ser Daichi has done, or ser may choose to make a personal brew on the premises.'

'Yes, that. Is there an autochef or something?'

'Of course, ser.' A yellow light obligingly lit one panel.

When it lifted Harp saw an inner counter area complete with cups, glasses, unknown extras, and a squat mech. 'Is that the autochef?'

'That is your caffee maker, ser. Shall I demonstrate?'

'I think you'd better. Er, what do I call you?'

'I am an Executive Domeciliary Assistant, ser.'

Harp repeated it. 'OK, I'll call you... Eda?'

'Excellent choice, ser.'

Great, now he had an ass-licking comp to add to everything else. But a comp that could show him stuff, make suggestions, even send a tray – Harpans obviously shouldn't deign to carrying the glass – through the walls to a niche that opened in that larger room she called a lounge. What with the caffee, just how he liked it, and a dish of snacks alongside it Eda said was from her "restaurant transfer unit" Harp started to feel his feet at last. Even if he didn't know where they'd take him next.

Thinking of which, he hadn't seen Daichi, not even in that other office. He'd rather expected the man would return, was relieved when he hadn't. He didn't want anyone around right now, just time to think. Or not think. 'Eda, do you know where Ser Daichi is?'

'Ser Daichi is currently in the Security suite, ser. Do you wish to call him?'

'Yes. No.' Never mind. 'Can you tell him he's off duty?'

'Certainly, ser.' A pause. 'Ser Daichi wishes to remind you, you have not eaten, ser.'

'Don't need it.'

'He also informs me you have appointments tomorrow from 0800. Do you wish me to schedule a wake-call for 0700?'

And so it begins? 'Yeah, OK, but make it 0600?'

'Very well, ser. Ser Daichi remains on call should you require his services.' Was there a tiny hint of umbrage at the thought he needed Daichi, when 'she' was here? 'Will there be anything further, ser?'

'No thanks, Eda. You can shut down.'

'I do not completely shut down, ser, merely go into sleep mode till called, while operating a basic subset to maintain essential services.'

'Oh, sleep then.' Hopefully they both would. He suspected he'd have more trouble doing so than the computer.

3

The next day was fun.

Not.

Eda woke him as arranged with the trill and a polite greeting. Harp got up, slower than he liked – the gravity no doubt – but happy in the knowledge he had won a planet-hour of freedom. It reminded him of his orphan days except back then he'd had to rouse even earlier to find some rare alone time.

Washroom. Another set of Navy pants and tee. 'Eda, where can I get breakfast?' Cos he didn't want to face this on a stomach that was now a yawning chasm. They had really cleared his system out to deal with that poison.

'I can order in, Ser Maxil, or the Executive restaurant is on the seventh floor, below you. All levels below are open to Family clearance.'

'Order in please.'

Eda offered menu options, Harp supposed he should experiment while nobody was watching. 'Er, pick something my uncle likes?'

'My pleasure, ser.' In almost no time covered dishes filled the service niche. 'Breakfast, ser. Since your energy levels are depleted I have selected three of the heartier dishes Ser Feldin frequently requests.'

'Um, thanks.' He guessed. But he recognised some of the food and learned a bit about the rest, and he did feel better. Heavier, blame that on World's gravity; he'd better work at getting fit again – especially since he still had people trying to kill him. Sigh. How many times was it now?

When he tried push-ups Eda said the Mansion had its own gym, well, two; one on five for staff and seven for Harpans. 'Yeah? Tomorrow maybe.' Thirty seven, thirty eight... This added gravity was tough, he'd try for fifty but he wasn't sure he'd make it. After that of course a second shower, another set of pants and tee, and info that a cubby in the washroom sent his laundry... somewhere.

Almost time. He felt himself tense up. Then Eda trilled. 'Security inform me your approved visitors have been admitted to the Mansion, ser.'

OK. Fake it till you make it.

Daichi arrived, escorting Feldin's fancy tailor, plus minions. Harp hadn't expected those but Daichi didn't seemed fazed. Harp recalled Feldin mentioning civ clothes. Like the ones Hissack bought he still owed her for? Crip, he had a fortune in his so-called everyday account; he'd better see about transferring some of it.

Apparently Feldin's notion of a civ starter wardrobe was six complete outfits; two "daytime formal", two "informal" and two "evening formal". *And* the tailor assured Harp he'd start on *the rest* as soon these were completed! Which required Harp stripping down to his shorts so they could 'fit' the partially made stuff they'd prepped from his Navy measure. Which point the female minion sighed, audibly, which was actually less embarrassing than the fact the three males did too. Daichi started to feel like protection, especially when he shooed them out, still chattering, an hour later.

The rest of the day was as busy. The morning became a tour of the Mansion. Turned out his apartment was on the eighth level, but the tour began below ground, at a private spur off the City trans system; a Family train, no less. Floors one to five housed Main Security, a visible, ground level entrance leading to lots of offices and admin, and staff facilities, like the restaurant on two. And his 'official' office, on three. Floor five was a mix, some Family quarters, some guestrooms; six an upper Security station and slightly larger Family residences.

Seven was apparently home to an actual water pool, a real shock to any Mooner, that Family restaurant Eda mentioned, plus some other fitness areas, while eight was Feldin's base, including the son's, Felli, in an "annexe", whatever that meant, and those were flanked by Harp's apartment and some "VIP suites". That left nine, the entire floor security, a barrier for ten, the Founder owning all of that – an area *he* didn't get to see – with, he was informed, a final garden level, on the roof no less, that also housed a landing pad could launch a private shuttle. It was more a minicity than a building.

Heads nodding all the time, like they were nervous of him, made it hard to focus. He was allowed a break for lunch. In the private restaurant on the seventh; no chance to relax there though with cooks – chefs – and waitstaff hovering, rows of cutlery, some of which looked like works of art, and several unfamiliar dishes. He reminded himself he probably needed the calories, swallowed some of each offering and thanked everyone for their time.

An afternoon in the inner realms of the 'Upper Security Station' was in some ways easier. Well, more Navy-like. As was knowing the briefing he was getting on other Family, current threats, to whom, and important not-Family he should expect to cross paths with, would all be copied to his desk on eight and his 'official' office down on three for him to study later.

The Security he met were a little stiff. He figured that was fair. For one, they didn't know him; probably laid bets on whether all the hero talk meant he was stupid-reckless and would cause them problems. For another, they'd be feeling mad he'd got poisoned on their watch and even look for him to blame them. Which he didn't; it was their bad luck he was a target. So he tried to show that, smiling when it seemed appropriate, and thought the blank expressions eased a little.

Mz Chan's expression didn't alter much, except maybe she mellowed when she saw the way he soaked up info. Not the idiot she'd expected after all? At least in here. By then he'd worked it out; they'd figured on him playing farmboy-fool, in public. And on using that to *their* advantage. Sad, but not surprising, he was fresh bait, wasn't he? To them the long-lost heir had likely looked a handy pawn to snare House Regis. Still could, if he obliged? He left knowing he'd got four more days of 'recovery', to learn as much as they could cram into him, then they were going to sic him on the planet. Cos he was a Harpan now, and being Family looked much like being

Navy; he would always be on duty, just the orders might be subtler.

+++

Back here wasn't too bad, dark enough he figured nobody out there could even see him. Shame he couldn't join them but nobody would let him off now, would they. Especially new-cousin.

'OK, now it'll be just as we rehearsed. Remember to smile.' Emika patted his arm. 'Call her Dalla, maybe ma'am like she's an officer. She'll love that. And she'll ask only the questions we discussed.' Emika's face said or else. 'Now go out there and let them meet you!'

Crip.

'My surprise guest tonight hardly needs an introduction, but I know all those lucky enough to be in the studio will be thrilled to meet him. So let's welcome the lost heir himself, Flight Captain Maxil Xen Harpan the eighth!'

Emika patted his back, firmly. Nowhere to run so he took a first step from the "wings". Very bright, as Emika had said. He had to remember not to squint, and to use this cane, though the stiff strapping on his knee was reminding him at every step.

She hadn't warned him it'd be blazing hot. He could feel sweat already trickling down his spine; told himself it was the lights then had the sudden thought that might be why she'd wanted him in uniform; it didn't stain so easy as the thin civ tunics lined up in his cavern of a wardrobe. Then a roar went up, then clapping, and he almost tripped, cane or not. The "small live audience" he couldn't see for all the glare was a lot bigger than Emika had let him think.

A stab of annoyance stiffened his resolve. When were they going to stop hiding stuff from him? Mz Chan was OK but Emika especially still seemed to think he couldn't deal with the full picture. If they'd told him everything he wouldn't have touched the sodding wine on the Orbital, would he. Instead she kept feeding him small data bites and it was starting to get old. But. He'd made it through the first vid-interview fine, she'd said. So what if this time it was civs not navy, and had real people out there.

The caster, Medam… Dalla, Dalla… was smiling and beckoning. OK. Tap the fancy cane, proof he was still convalescent. Exchange formal nods, sit, leg out, and try to settle. Emika said there was some invisible tec between this platform and the shadowy mass making all the noise; swore nothing could get through that and their own Security had pretty much invaded round the back, so all he had to do was play the part. And try to do some good while he was at it. OK, Operation Harp, commence. Weapons live, or as Del had put it, "Knock 'em dead." The phrase was so inappropriate his lips twitched in a real smile; did this Dalla look relieved? Harp's chair was the only one facing her; no other guests tonight to help her deal with the novice.

'Captain Harpan, it's an honour to welcome you to my show.'

'Thanks, ma'am. Pleased to be here.' Murmurs from the dark, he figured at the remnants of his Mooner drawl. Emika reckoned folk here found it attractive. Or as she put it "quaintly old fashioned". True or false, while he could tone it down he couldn't lose all of it, nor wanted to. He *was* essentially a Mooner. Which was probably ironic or something.

Dalla was good, leading him pretty smoothly through the story; how he'd been mistaken for the last survivor of a flattened homestead. Then his years in the Orphan Houses, fostered then "transferred" to Moon Militia. Politics there; seemed the tithe system wasn't entirely according to World's rule book so he'd been warned not to mention that. Its "legality was being investigated."

'And our sources tell us your marksmanship saved the lives of several of your Militia comrades.' Dalla paused.

Off camra, Emika looked at him and nodded, everything was ready. They'd rehearsed this. Crip, just do it. 'Duty ma'am, is all.'

'But lives were sometimes in danger, yours and your crew's?'

'Militia's job, ma'am, to keep order, keep folk safe. Sometimes it's delivering emergency supplies, or fighting the prairie fires. Others it's calming folk down.'

Dalla jumped on her cue. 'Prairie fires, oh my.' She looked toward the darkness. 'I believe we have some startling vid for you all, taken recently on Moon.' Images flared across the previously blank wall behind them. Pictures of Moon: a township street coated in dust that rippled in the heat haze. Livestock on cracked ground tufted with too-sparse grasses. Then a distant thundercloud. The camra zoomed till smoke filled half the sky ahead, red glare beneath it. Fire, sending angry sparks into the air, raced at the camra, a stampede. Then pictures of a real stampede that fled before the fire, lam in this one, poor beasts terror-stricken, trying to outrun the roaring giant. Obviously going to lose the contest.

Screams from some folk in the dark. The image faded. Dalla took a visible breath. 'You had to deal with that?'

'Still do, ma'am.'

'Stars.' She led him through the salient facts: Moon was getting hotter, fires increasing. Water shortages; one reason the Militia dowsed the fires with dirt not foam, no drop of moisture wasted. He'd got this chance to talk, to tell. He'd asked for this.

'They tell me Moon used to be like it is here, ma'am, but it's getting real hard for folks to survive there. World did ship supplies, on record, but we didn't always get what it sent, so folk on Moon started to think you'd left them to rot.'

More murmurs in the dark, not happy this time, maybe folk here felt insulted. He would take that if it meant they listened. Dalla interrupted quickly. 'You're saying we sent help, but it didn't reach those who needed it?'

'No ma'am, seems a fair amount got hijacked. They say maybe some of the cargoes never even left World, and it looks like a lot that did only got as far as Moon Orbital.'

'Stolen?'

'Yes, ma'am, pirates. And black merchants. But on record it all got there so folk here didn't know otherwise. I hear they're trying to put all the pieces together now to find who was behind it.' Deep breath. 'In the meantime there's a lot of folk on Moon need help desperately. Moon is half of who we are, our neighbour.' Emika's words. 'We need to make it liveable, even if it's never what it used to be.' On cue, the wall showed people, families, the aftermath of the pirate attack, a downed Militia cruiser, a burned-out homestead. A funeral. Harp turned to watch it with the people in the dark, reliving all the devastation he had witnessed from *Defiant;* all those floating bodies, the repairs he'd helped with. And the pirate leader, Zorr, he'd tried and failed to capture. And to end, the images of all the missing Mooner children.

This time when the images dissolved the studio was silent. Dalla stirred, a hint of tears in her eyes? 'For once I don't know what to say, Captain.'

So he turned her way. 'Say you'll help. We may live on two planets but we're all Harpans, all family. You have so much. What they've lost is no fault of theirs, but you can help.'

She nodded. 'I understand a relief programme is already underway.'

'Yes. My... grandfather... has issued executive orders.' More Emika words. 'But on Moon we share what we can with those who're short. I'd like to think here is the same.'

Dalla's smile resurfaced. 'So would I, Captain. I'll be in line to contribute. But I don't think I'll be the last. What do you say, everyone?'

The darkness roared, a different roar this time. Dalla beamed at the dark then to the camra now floating in her face. 'There you have it. There are public messages posting explaining how we can help. Not just by sending credits, even you children can help right these wrongs. As the captain said, World or Moon, we're all the same family.' The camra backed off. 'Thank you again,

Captain. I'm sure I speak for everyone here when I say a very warm welcome to your World.'

If she'd meant to say more the applause stopped her there.

+++

'Here.' Emika handed him a large glass of water, with ice. A vivid reminder World was so different from Moon. He was so shaky he still downed it in one. 'Well done, Max, really well done. The feeds are being flooded with promises to contribute; clothes, household goods, toys from children and a heap of credits. You did it.'

She meant he'd "harnessed public opinion", made helping Mooners "the thing". It galled, but it would do good. In another push for publicity, Uncle or Grandfather had actually arranged for *Defiant* to deploy for the first aid programme delivery. The ship that had faced the pirates, where Harp and *Raptor* had made their stand, would be on camra, taking Worlder contributions to Moon. The way Emika was talking these Worlders might fill even her holds. OK, the fervour might not last, but he'd take what he could get.

Dalla walked into the room he'd collapsed in. 'Thank you, Captain, that was great. My team will be reporting as the story develops but you've made a significant impact.'

'Thanks.' He thought, hoped. He stood, Emika nodded. Time to get away, but it was all about impressions. Emika said so. 'Thank you, ma'am, for making all this easy for the rookie.'

'Dalla please, and you're no rookie, you're a natural. Any time you want to come back just say the word. I mean it.'

'Well, thanks again, Dalla.' He saw Emika hovering polite version of a loom. 'I guess I have to go.'

'Of course, Captain.' Dalla touched his arm. 'World stands with you. And welcome home.'

Home? Nowhere near, not yet anyway. Six days of

finding his way around an apartment that would have housed three families on Moon; of being fancied up, new haircut, civ clothes, new tec, new foods. Hours with Security, and Emika and Daichi – not a bad guy after all just quiet – memorising reams of data; who was who and where was where, emergency procedures (which basically meant how to do what he was told; they seemed to doubt that) and worst, company manners, which as he'd feared were far too complicated for a farmboy.

And today, two interviews which – gulp – had just aired across both planets. He'd been relieved the first had been a Navy affair, from a "studio" inside the Mansion, but the civ face-off with Dalla hadn't been too bad, had it? Emika said Dalla had "a huge following". A kind of start at the top approach then.

And tonight would see him at another "reception", this one a much more public shindig, his welcome to what Emika had called "Society". He wasn't looking forward.

4

No uniform to hide behind tonight, and he still had to use the cane, but they had let him wear something blueish. Probably thought it'd make him feel better. Probably right. Daichi and Emika were getting the hang of handling the farmboy they'd been dumped with. So the close fitting pants and soft boots felt Navy-ish enough but the high collar and hip length tunic, with gold clips here and there, and sleeves so long they ended in loops hooked over his middle fingers… good thing those were stretchy so they flexed when he did. Otherwise the way he was clenching his fists he'd have ripped them by now, and they hadn't even left his apartment yet.

Daichi, who'd he'd begun to think of as a younger Yentl – quiet, solid – called for brandy, and when Eda sent it out Daichi offered him the glass, and crackers. 'One for the road, ser?' Looked like drinking one had made them think it was his choice of spirit.

'Thanks.' Well, he supposed new-grandfather had given him a taste of the stuff. He felt guilty now he knew the price tag but right now the warmth in his gut was worth the burn in his throat. Looked like it might have to be a habit anyway, a shot of fiery courage when he had to face another challenge. 'OK, good to go, Daichi.' Keep telling yourself that.

+++

This was a far cry from the Orbital "reception". The place was huge. But he'd known it would be; this time they'd finally listened, even driven him across the park to this Assembly Building to inspect this "ballroom". Which wasn't anything to do with games, not the sort with balls anyway. Now he was peeking downward at a transformation, the round tables below this upper tier no longer bare but purple and white and gold, all in his honour, live musicians playing softly in a distant corner.

Stewards, no, civ waitstaff, in white jackets and purple pants lurked round the edges of the chamber, and a mob of the invited drifted in and out each other and the tables. Never mind Emika said not everyone was here yet, it was still too many. Even more intimidating, his grandfather stood beside him up here, and through this doorway was the stair they had to go down. He'd probably trip over the damn cane and go apex over ass to start proceedings.

'Ready Max,?'

'Yessir.' Think of it as a repeat medal ceremony; head up, shoulders back. As Yentl said, the downside.

'Mm, here we go then?' Maxil Snr dropped his left hand on Harp's right shoulder, waved the woman at the door aside and urged him forward. Heads turned, then bodies. The cavern below stilled. Those in uniform came to attention, nods very stiff. Harp concentrated on a game face. Maxil Snr smiled downward. 'Greetings all. Let's make this a night to remember, shall we? Allow me to present Flight Captain Maxil Xen Harpan the eighth. My rather famous grandson!'

Well, the applause sounded enthusiastic.

Harp made it down the stairs at Maxil's side, the strapping giving him a genuine limp. Emika walked behind them, backing him up in a long purple skirt. That Jontig was here too, at Feldin's elbow where he apparently belonged, and he knew Feldin now so the first so-formal nod wasn't too bad. After that there was a lot more of the same, not really so different from that Orbital meet 'n greet so 'pleasure' and 'thanks' about covered it, especially when Emika kept people moving along to make room for more.

Feeling calmer, he could put his mind to facial recognition, comparing the real thing to the hundreds of images he'd spent his evenings so far poring over. Another uncle, Feldin's younger brother Aki who, according to his intel, was considered less important to his safety, mainly cos he seldom visited Foundation. Then came a very thin great aunt, a fat great-uncle, "who exist quite happily upon their Mansion-funded pensions and have no political ambitions" – courtesy of Emika that time – oh, and after them a loose parade of other Harpans loosely tagged as "cousins", plus some navy brass, some top-drawer politicians and the most important merchants. So was Maxil Snr the eldest of his generation, to become the Founder? Harp belatedly recalled that Feldin wasn't, not until his father's murder.

Once that part was over he still had to stay put below the stair with Maxil Snr to welcome late arrivals, those – Emika's words – who "liked making an entrance more than the free drinks". Recognition was easier now cos the woman above was shouting out names. These knew the drill, paused at the top then paraded down, making their nods to Maxil then him then Em, then melting into the crush, where waitstaff could pounce on them with trays. Harp wouldn't have said no to the drinks either. He knew anything he ate or drank tonight would be checked, and he didn't mind admitting he was glad Em said Komar Regis's parents weren't on the guest list. But a drink would have to wait a while. Still, being in this lineup did mean he didn't have to talk much.

Emika brushed his arm, one of their agreed signals. 'Max, keep it cool, OK?'

What?

The woman on the stairs announced, 'Medam Eleanora Regis and Ser Stollic Regis.'

On Harp's left Maxil Snr continued to smile at the man before him. To the right Emika's gloved hand settled on his arm. Regis kinfolk, Komar's grandma. Footfall on the stairs. Harp nodded to the face in front of him, murmured thanks and turned toward these new arrivals, mildly curious perhaps. Unclenched his fingers.

The old woman flowed down ahead of the middle-age man. Eleanora, the matriarch, was taller and thinner than the man who'd stolen from him and betrayed their people. A skeleton in fancy-wear, her long purplish "gown" almost black. Em had explained "dress" wasn't classy enough for evening wear. A lot of folk tonight wore blues and purples, as a sort of compliment to him.

Harp had assumed it was because he was navy but apparently this was his father's colour too, hence his apartment. Different Harpan kin had different, hereditary colour-labels, yet another thing to fathom.

Mz Chan had said House Regis colours were reds and silvers. He figured Eleanora wearing his colour was meant to make a statement: welcome to the farmboy and an underlying loyalty to Harpans. But she wore silver at neck and wrists, and in the steel grey hair ruthlessly styled on top of her head like a crown.

And a nose that bent made it easier for her to look down on the crowd as she descended, and those Regis eyes were dark and icy. She had those in common with her grandson.

The man in her wake was a shadow in comparison, dressed in purple too but darker haired, more florid. A yes-man? Don't take anything for granted here, fool, you've learned that lesson.

'Medam Eleanora, Ser Stollic.' Maxil Snr's smile dimmed but he nodded back, no doubt as aware of watching eyes as Harp. 'Max, may I present Medam Eleanora, head of one of our merch Houses.'

'Medam.' Widen the eyes a little, look impressed? Uncertain, or uncomfortable maybe with the history they had in common, Eleanora's grandson. Or a touch overawed by the grand dame facing him, eyebrows elevated, mouth pursed.

'Captain. I understand we owe you a debt for your bravery in action.' She nodded a jewelled head.

Harp nodded back, maybe too quickly. 'Just doing my job, medam.' Lower the gaze, maybe not comfortable with praise either. Orphans knew all the right signals.

'My House also owes you an apology for the most unfortunate actions of one of my bloodline.'

'Not your fault, medam.'

'I'm glad to hear you feel so. My son, Stollic.'

'Captain.'

'Ser.' The nod slower, somehow, damper, Stollic keen to get this over. Eleanora captured his arm and moved off, stately, serene. Heads dipped and voices muttered. Harp turned to the new arrivals, smiling shyly. So that was the enemy.

+++

'Our boy shows promise. If I didn't know better I'd really think he was that naïve.' Maxil Snr lifted his glass to mask his lips. 'Advanced bloodwork came back.'

Feldin turned his back on the ballroom, a private moment. No one would be crass enough to interrupt them. 'And?'

Maxil sipped. 'More than any before.'

'You really think?'

'Don't you? When every generation escalates the change? Whatever it is, it's happening.'

Feldin smiled, sipped. 'We have to tell him.'

'First, we need to give him time to trust us, Feldin. You did make sure…?'

Feldin turned and surveyed the room, spotting Emika at Max's elbow, Max listening gravely to a lesser cousin very pleased to stand by them in public. 'Emika has her orders, Father. I told her family history could wait till the poor man caught up with the present. She's smart, she won't babble. But the boy's smart too. And I do like him.'

'We're agreed on that. Soon then, but not yet.'

'Father.'

Maxil's focus shifted. 'I see your two have finally arrived.'

Feldin glanced across to the stairs where his son and daughter were waving the major domo away, descending without introduction. Not that they needed one except for Max's sake. And not that trying to slide in late had escaped their grandfather's notice. A sigh escaped before Feldin quashed it. If only… 'I'll go introduce them.'

'Yes.' Maxil Snr didn't trouble to look pleased but smiled genially again when a merchant tried to catch his eye a moment later. Feldin left his father to his socialising, after noting the positions of tonight's protectors. By the time he reached his offspring, circling casually to intercept them, Ho-san and Felli had glasses in their hands and stood together, in the crowd but choosing not to mingle. Feldin felt a flash of anger. Felli at least wore black with accents of mauve but Ho-San...

'What's all this?' He nodded at his daughter's gown, a slender tube in red and orange. A very public snub aimed squarely at their guest of honour?

'Hello, Father. Oh this?' Ho-San looked down. Didn't bother to nod. 'Sorry, the gown I wanted wasn't ready.' Almost believable, if Felli hadn't looked away; his son had never had his sister's skill at lying.

Feldin supposed it was some comfort his son wasn't happy about it either. 'You're late. Come on, I'll take you over to meet your cousin.' People made way for the three to navigate the crush around the corner where young Max leaned on that cane and held court, though Feldin was sure the boy didn't see it that way. Probably thought he was hiding. Hah. 'Max, let me introduce the last two arrivals, my reprobate daughter Ho-San and my son Felli.' His children stepped out from behind him.

+++

Feldin's daughter, and the minor son. Hmm. According to Harp's info the daughter was twentyfive, the son sixteen, but neither Emika nor Daichi had mentioned more than bare details. Harp had wondered why not, now he began to suspect why. The boy gave him a weak smile, the woman didn't even do that, and neither offered a nod, which made Harp grateful for Emika's advice not to nod first, cos this was sort of his party. "They come to you, not the other way round".

So. These two were the last, and not wearing much bluish, when even Medam Eleanora... So Harp smiled. 'Mz Ho-san. Ser Felli.' Assuming you said 'ser' to youngsters here.

'Ser Maxil.' Ho-san sniffed. 'Is that what you call yourself now?'

'Nah, that don't seem right.' He couldn't stop himself, even when Feldin's eyes widened. 'I'm thinking folk here'll sit easier with Max, less confusing for 'em, don't you think?'

If his drawl had startled Felli it clearly disgusted Ho-san; her lip curled. Feldin... looked thoughtful, something Harp was starting to take seriously.

Emika tapped his arm, grinning. 'Stop it, Max. Just because these two lack manners doesn't mean you're allowed to tease.'

'Ah, sorry.' Harp allowed a matching grin to surface. No doubt to observers the exchange looked friendly. 'Sorry, cousins, did I shock you? Couldn't resist.' Yes see, the drawl's much less now. Time for you to rethink?

Felli choked. Emika laughed, sliding her hand through his arm. 'He's been having fun with that accent as long as I've known him, probably a lot longer. I think he does it to test people. The stupid ones so often only see what they want to, don't they?' Aimed at Ho-san? Warning? Challenge? There was more here than Harp could decipher, maybe the lack of info was cos Emika – and Daichi? – weren't too fond. A snooty gossip and a child? He was inclined to agree. These two might be related to Feldin but the vibe Ho-San sent out felt more like Eleanora. Normal, or just for him? He needed to know more.

'Well you two, I'll let you find your friends. Max, if you have a moment, there's someone I'd like –'

Feldin's timely change of subject was abruptly interrupted by raised voices at the top of the stairs. More rudely-late arrivals? Harp turned to see an older couple above, the woman in dark red, dripping with jewels, the man behind her in dusty black. If the wrong colours didn't signal trouble by now the woman was arguing with that announcer lady, though the man looked like he was regretting coming.

When Harp glanced round again Ho-San and Felli had vanished; Feldin, Emika, and him were now the focus of a sea of murmurs. 'What's all that about?'

Emika's hand tightened. 'Security will deal with them. Let's try the buffet. Looks like uninvited guests, and your grandfather won't want you bothered by it.' But if uninvited, how had they got that far? Harp let Emika guide him but scanned the room. His newest cousins were off to one side now. Ho-san still had her haughty expression. Felli was biting his lip.

The woman above was still arguing, hands waving, then she pushed past and stormed down the stairs. Two Security above, who had been trying for discreet, scrambled to catch up while others blocked her escort. 'Emika, what is going on?'

Ahead, Maxil Snr's own Security converged on the Founder, who didn't budge. Emika's hand relaxed, a little. 'It's Komar's parents. Don't look.'

Too late, cos being near Maxil Snr meant Komar's mother had spotted him too.

'You! How dare you slander my son. What are you anyway, except some Mooner brat Maxil paid to tell these awful lies? The courts will award me every credit he paid you!'

Assembly Security finally caught her before she was close enough to touch them, though by now Harp's Security was closing in too. Response came from another direction. 'Enough.' Eleanora cut a path through the crowd; if looks could kill… 'You embarrass the House.' She glared at the Security. 'My daughter is clearly not well. Would someone be so kind as to escort my relatives to my personal transport. I have already notified my staff.'

Komar's mother shrieked with laughter. 'Not well? You come here and pretend –'

'Enough, I said, now hold your tongue.' Eleanora had good lungs, you could have heard a pin drop after. The Harpan Security didn't move but the Assembly's minders jumped, practically carried the woman away, the husband following without a struggle. The woman's voice echoed from above then faded, leaving avid quiet in the ballroom. Nobody was talking, moving even, but eyes fixed first on Harp then Maxil, then on Eleanora.

'Well, crip. I'm so sorry, Max.' Emika squeezed Harp's arm. 'This isn't quite the dull evening I promised, is it?'

Harp's laugh might be more like a snort but it broke the spell; bodies moved, the voices rose. And Eleanora swept in his direction.

'Double crip.' Emika showed an inclination to step in front of him but Harp figured she couldn't defend him forever. He stepped forward.

'Medam.' Might as well find out what the woman wanted.

'Captain.' Eleanora's thin cheeks had spots of red her makeup couldn't cover. 'This time you have my apologies for the poor behaviour of my daughter. Once she calms I'm sure she will tender her own but I fear she has been more affected by her son's fall from grace than anyone realised. I will seek professional help. I hope you can enjoy the rest of the evening.'

'Understood, Medam.' Navy-speak felt appropriate. 'I hope your daughter will come to see this wasn't my choice either.'

Eleanora twitched a smile. 'I'm sure she will, eventually, as do I, ser.' Then she stiffened; Maxil Snr turned up, with Feldin at his elbow. 'Founder, I was just apologising.'

'Yes.' This was the Founder, not the urbane host. 'I'd appreciate it if my grandson isn't accosted again.'

'I'll ensure it, and to that end I'll take my leave.'

'Certainly.' All Eleanora could do was exit with what dignity she had left, every step watched by the Security and all the slavering guests. Noise levels surged.

'All right, boy?' Maxil still looked stern.

'Yessir. I'm fine. Really.' He was used to being stared at, only the reasons had changed.

'We should stay a bit longer then.'

Harp nodded. The Regis faction had retreated, lost face; Harpans didn't. He understood the need, steeled himself to deal with the "sympathetic" words he could expect once these folk plucked up courage.

+++

How much longer was he supposed to stick this sideshow? Maybe if he talked to Feldin. But before he moved his uncle had fetched up beside him. 'How's the leg, Max?'

He was sure he'd jumped. 'Oh, bearing up.' For those in earshot. Harp did that social-smile thing at Feldin. His leg was fine, it was faking injury was a pain. Not least cos he'd strapped his knee again to keep it stiffer and he kept wanting to scratch. And his face ached, from this smiling. Looking blank, he'd mastered that for Moon and navy, but so much smiling was a skill he'd never needed. The rest made it look a lot easier than it was.

Feldin's voice lowered. 'Favour it a bit then I can notice, and we'll swap these bubbles for a glass of something stronger?' Feldin's smile widened, demonstrating that he found their brief exchange amusing.

'Great.' Harp grinned back. He was starting to feel more relaxed around Feldin, maybe even his new grandfather. Maybe. Not that they weren't watching him, of course, as were the Security, including those protecting him tonight. That didn't surprise him; he might be blood-related but they didn't know him any more than he did them yet. Still, Maxil and Feldin did seem pleased he existed. More than he'd have figured. And they'd also said they were "moving to address the Mooner issues", Feldin's words for all the mess they had to deal with over and above the pirates. He thought he might get to like these two, and Emika, and maybe Jontig. Even grim Daichi. For the rest of his new House, as they called it – *not* like Orphan Houses – there were too many to count, let alone count on. Wait and see then.

Feldin's quiet moment hadn't finished. 'We'll leave soon then. Better warn your Security, they're a little stressed. Well done facing Eleanora by the way, Emika said you were good but that display was more than I expected.'

'Practice,' Harp said briefly.

'Hm.' Feldin surveyed the chattering elite. 'Often hid what you thought, did you?'

And what he felt. 'Yessir.' A blank face was normal, showing reactions was harder work.

'Call me uncle?'

'Uncle, sorry.'

'You'll get used to it. You're one of us, don't doubt it.'

'Mm.'

Feldin clapped him on the back and strolled off; job done Harp supposed. Public approval and this 'Inner Family' label applied. He figured the 'Inner' part had a lot of face, socially anyway. Inner, outer, whatever, there was bound to be a pecking order. He'd yet to work out exactly where he fit but he knew enough to realise it wouldn't be that cut and dried. Well, there were so many signals here; the clothes, the way you wore them, the order folk spoke to you, especially who spoke first, the number of Security…

They'd assigned him Daichi and two others this evening. Apparently that was a lot in such a prime, restricted venue, its own already in place too. The same number as Maxil and Feldin. Nah, they probably had others lurking somewhere.

He thought he knew all the Harpan Security faces now, at least those here in Foundation. After all, he'd been drilled to recognise them. In case. He figured "in case" was just something else he had to get used to now. He also had a shipload of smiling faces mouthing compliments, none of which he could afford to believe. At best the smiles masked curiosity, at worst… too complicated.

Life had got more interesting though, as Bayes would have said. Crip, he missed Bayes' simple view of life, even missed being a lowly Militia grunt, when Regis's mistreatment was all he had to cope with.

Eleanora reminded him of Komar Regis, maybe that was why she raised his hackles. She wanted him to see her as an innocent, but no, he couldn't trust her either.

Then there were Feldin's kids. Turning up late had annoyed their father, however much he'd tried to hide it, and Ho-San had made it pretty plain *she* wasn't part of the Harpan welcome wagon. Harp wondered why, figured he probably needed to know. The son, he wasn't so clear about. In a way that was more worrying, that old know-your-enemy thing. Felli felt like one of those pesky grey areas.

Komar's parents now, another nasty moment. He could understand the resentment there, even sympathise, a bit, but it had looked a lot stronger than that. Eleanora had apologised for them. No, for her daughter, not the husband. As if he didn't exist. Or didn't count? Crip, he'd thought his life was complicated before; he'd earned that promised drink.

As if on cue Feldin came back. 'Max, dear boy, you look all in.' He probably did, with thoughts like these. 'More pain?'

'A bit, Uncle.' There, as per instructions.

'Time to go, I think, you mustn't overdo it.'

Emika turned up to blame herself for not noticing sooner. Feldin urged them both toward the stairs; Harp saw Daichi waiting, cos of course in his weakened state he might need help to climb the blasted– hang on, he'd missed something. A nearby guest was backing off, what was the panic this time? 'What just happened?'

Emika laughed then shook her head. 'You still have no idea, do you?'

'About?' He shouldn't have snapped at her, but what the crip had he done now?

'About how intimidating you can look?'

'What?'

'It's partly the likeness to Grandfather, of course. You even smile like he does. Your mouth curves but your eyes don't change. They can't read you at all.'

Intimidating, him? When he laughed Emika grinned. 'And you've just made me everyone's new best friend.'

That sobered him. 'Because they think you're in favour.'

'You've got it, cousin.' They'd reached the top of the stairs, local Security and his making a loose cordon that gave them some privacy. 'Welcome to Worlder Society, the survival of the most ambitious.'

'Are you, Emika? Ambitious?' The thought was unsettling.

'I suppose, as far as any of us can be.'

'So you joined the navy.'

'Yes.' She shrugged, even that was elegant. 'Officer training, of course, couldn't escape that, and I'm always posted on-World, but at least I got some freedom.'

'Except you got dragged back cos of me.'

'I think the Family thought we might relate.'

'Not your choice though.'

'No, but don't go feeling guilty. I was curious and you turned out to be one of the good guys.' Emika slid an arm through his. 'I know being one of us is complicated. I'd like us to be friends, when you decide who is and who isn't, but there's no rush, OK?'

'I think I'd like that too.' Nothing she'd done so far had felt cold or calculated and he knew the feeling; grown up watching for the sliders in the grass. Thinking about sliders... 'Eleanora and Stollic were the only Regis kin invited tonight, yes?'

'Yes.' Pause for thought, something he liked about her. 'They're not a big House compared to most but they are influential, mainly due to trade connections; contracts and investors more than blood.' She meant of course relationship to Harpans.

'So how have these connections reacted to the treason charges against Komar?'

'Some offloaded their stock the same day, but most are holding off, waiting to see what happens next. You being polite to her tonight could persuade them Eleanora's going to float through without too much mud sticking. They probably hope so cos we can ruin her if we choose. We just don't know yet if we will.'

'Mm.' He supposed it said a lot about him that he understood all that. So the Founder, and his Security, didn't want House Regis to feel *too* threatened. Socially embarrassed, sure. Alliances and maybe profit damaged by the scandal, that as well, but not real danger. Softening extreme reaction? So now he'd played a part again, the clueless farmboy, and he figured Eleanora had believed it; her mouth had apologised but her eyes hadn't quite concealed the doubt, and dislike? Entitlement, they called it. Way he saw it, Eleanora was a greedy old steer, maybe not much better than the pirates, didn't like the fact the Harpan herd had grazing land she couldn't get her hooves on.

Was she where Komar learned his morals, did she steal and cheat as well or was she honest in as much a merchant measured. Maybe only guilty of helping her kin escape justice?

Emika was looking at her wristcom. 'Max, your transport's at the doors.'

'Just to circle the park?'

'All part of the service, captain. And your poor leg hurts, doesn't it? Now smile bravely for the newscasts.'

'Of course, why wouldn't I? I'm Maxil Harpan, all-time lucky orphan.' Emika laughed. He didn't.

5

Harp sat and stewed. Medam Eleanora Regis remained unaware of his thoughts. Medam Eleanora Regis should be branded, for the mean heel-biter she was under all the fancy "gowns" and crusted jewels.

In recent weeks he'd had time to learn more about her as the Harpan Security mech dug deeper. Harp honestly didn't understand why they hadn't done more sooner. Surely someone had known what was going on? It gave him some misgivings over Harpan values. When it came down to it, hadn't House Harpan started out as merch-adventurers too? Imagine a different twist of fate, it could have been House Regis went from merch to owning planets.

Only then one long-gone Head of House did all he could to throw away their credits, and their reputation. Out of that debacle Medam Eleanora rose triumphant, and the family fought back to profit; Regis Merch began to grow again, and put out tentacles, including key alliances by marriage. There were even ties to lesser Harpans for a while which had further raised their status. Early sign of her ambitions? Thwarted by House Harpan?

But alliances weren't friendships, and Harp figured Eleanora was the reason the important ties remained standoffish. Eleanora set the tone, a cold one. Outwardly her kinfolk seemed OK with that.

Hmm. Harp supposed it looked like he'd fallen in line with his House too. He had the lux apartment in the Harpan Mansion now. He had a chef on call, he'd been assigned a houseman who looked after anything that Eda couldn't. He still apparently lacked one essential, a "personal assistant", like an aide, once Emika went back to duty, but face it, outwardly he had accepted all of this, including living here for free. His only job right now was being "the lost yokel". No more riding herd, or cleaning ship, even if he did hope to get back to the navy once the dust settled and he'd done what he could for Moon.

Naively, he'd also thought all Worlders would have it easier than Mooners. The cleaning and such still had to be done, but they seemed to have so much more here, which should have meant less roughing it, right?

But the covert vid Security had just obtained showed the Regis family owned several manufactories and warehouses weren't publicly listed, where conditions were rougher than anything he'd ever suffered.

Few who worked there quit though, cos most of those Regis workers were "indentured". Thanks to loans the management so kindly offered new employees that they found, too late, meant all they could repay was interest. Then, of course, they fell behind because some foreman docked their wages for "infringements", breakages, whatever. And they found themselves indentured for a generation.

Was that where Komar Regis learned to cheat his crew on *Mercy*? Regis workers in these hidden places looked worse off than he had ever felt when he was fostered, or on *Mercy*.

While the Regis family grew fat. And no one noticed?

He was finding it increasingly hard to play the game Maxil Snr wanted.

Emika brushed his arm. 'You're staring.'

'Crip.' Harp dragged his attention back to the folk on the stage, the so-called music. Him, he called it droning, but apparently it was "in fashion" which obliged Society to love it. Leastways till some other silliness surpassed it.

The "theatre" was huge, a streamlined flash of black and gold, all fluid lines, supposed to make the sounds go farther. Made a change from blue and gold at least. The floor was tilted, like they'd bolted seats onto a staircase so they didn't topple to the bottom. Same went for this upper shelf he sat on. He was trying not to think about the folk below it might collapse on. Not least cos he'd feel so guilty; most of them were likely only suffering all this cos he was.

His interview with Mz Dalla had borne unexpected

results – at least *he* hadn't expected them. Apparently his talk about Moon needing all the help it could get had hit a whole lot of nerves. Or – cynic version – had become the latest "fashion" folk here wanted in on. Either way, what Mz Dalla had tagged "Moon Aid" had taken off, witness this fancy concert, performers here for free and audience paying over the odds. A big chunk of the credits would buy more supplies for Moon though.

All of which required him on show, to make folk feel good. So he and Emika sat here in the centre of the raised front row, so those below could stare at them too. And Eleanora and a bunch of her kin had scored seats up here too, second row, around the curve to his left. Hence his distraction. He had a good profile view of them. And vice versa of course – more new words. But he doubted his thoughts had shown on his face. He'd learned that lesson long ago.

One Eleanora had never bothered to learn? Her disinterest in the concert was written all over her paler features; narrowed eyes, pursed lips, rigid back. No, she wasn't here for the music either, more likely to show everyone House Regis'd paid for these prime seats and were upright citizens. Yes, the Regis presence would be largely for the "intermission", surely not far off now. What would it be this time?

If Eleanora had been behind the poison she'd changed tactics since. Mz Chan had reported Komar's parents had left town right after gate-crashing his reception; thought Eleanora had got them out of the City that same night. Which would have been more of a relief if various Regis minions hadn't been trying so hard to grease Harp's wheels since. A compliment here. Admiring simpers there. Or invitations, like the exhibition Regis Merch had sponsored, other stuff for Moon as well so World Society had eaten fancy food while trying to out-bling each other, all to help poor starving Mooners. He had had to go, with Emika, to let himself be stared at, drink the fizzy wine – though not without some qualms – and let a Regis woman teach him how to look at Tensile Art. Another "fashion". Play the Mooner farmboy struggling to turn into a real-Harpan.

Looked, and listened, and pretended. Wondering what did they really want. For him to sympathise with all their current loss of face? Certainly they wanted everyone to believe Komar was the impulsive black lam, easily led but not half as bad as the nasty navy and the media called him. Despite the man was years older?

'More youthful indiscretion than criminal'. Those were the words one Regis matron had used, in his hearing. Some other Regis hurried her away when she had added that, 'The poor boy's misdemeanours hardly count, since all they harmed, if anyone, were only Mooners'. He had had to bite his tongue. Still did.

Now everyone applauded and he faced the intermission. Harp breathed in, then out, then followed Emika into the bar beneath their upper hillside. If the thing fell now they'd both be Harpan rollups!

A brunette this time, so they'd given up on blondes. This one wasn't in his Regis file yet, only he was getting good at smelling the connection – often long before Daichi sent the warning to his wristcom. She was good though. She pretended not to see him then stepped back to let an older woman pass. His wine glass, hand delivered seconds earlier, lost half its contents. Some of it splashed down his pants. At least they were dark red to start with, he was learning Harpan tactics.

'Oh stars, it's you. I mean, I do apologise, Captain.' She looked round wildly. 'You, girl, fetch a cloth, or wipes. Be quick.' The waitress bolted, Harp took time to wonder if the poor girl ran because the woman snapped at her or cos he was a Harpan. Either way the girl was back in moments.

Naturally the woman didn't leave it there, she grabbed the wipes and practically shoved the girl aside. 'Oh dear, let me.' She patted at his trouser leg, then the hem of his tunic, edging higher. He'd have been embarrassed as hell except he was sure the wine hadn't landed that far up, which just confirmed his diagnosis. Though he could have done without seeing Emika smirk before returning to whatever conversation she was part of. Emika found these 'overtures' as she called them a lot more amusing than he did. Yesterday, she'd called them 'one of the perks of my current role'. Huh.

He forced himself to smile. 'Ma'am, no harm done.'

'But your clothes.' Dab. 'Oh, they could be ruined.' Dab. Dab. Ever higher.

'They'll wash. No, really.' Knowing people would be watching, Harp reached down and tugged her upright, looking suitably embarrassed, awkward at so much attention. 'These things happen.'

'Oh.' She gazed at him, wide-eyed. 'But you must let me pay for cleaning. I insist.' A hand on his sleeve now, a look said she'd be happy to strip them off him as part of the deal.

Harp smothered a sigh. Considering the number of women who'd come onto him, House Regis and others since he'd been "reclaimed", it was probably a good thing he hadn't felt a lick of attraction to any of them. The warmest he'd felt was with Emika, and there was nothing at all sexual there. Cousin-ish feelings, increasingly, but that was all.

Right now he counted the disinterest he felt, in any of these bodies, as a bonus. Sex would be one complication too many. Who knew, maybe turning more cold-blooded was another weirdness he'd acquired from *Raptor*. And maybe admitting he was weird wasn't the best thought to help him deal with this latest skirmish?

Emika must have seen him lose focus, she appeared at his elbow. A smile, her arm through his and he was rescued. It probably looked like jealousy. They'd begun to foster the notion Harp relied on her – simple truth after all – and that maybe Em had seen his need for her support as advantageous; newscasts even speculated on a budding Harpan romance. But it was only another part of the game, making Harp look "pretty but naïve" as Maxil Snr himself had put it. "Don't want them thinking you're an intelligent hero, boy, do we? Not yet." Ah well, at least the Founder made no bones about his motives these days.

Harp'd be so happy when Maxil Snr knew exactly who the older man intended to rain fire on. He'd lay odds it would be Eleanora but Feldin said they needed clear proof before they could make a move. So, since what Maxil Snr said was pretty much law, the rest waited, and continued to act the fool.

Meantime, Eleanora did what she could to put herself back on that pedestal she valued so much, and the only thing made it bearable was the thought of shoving her off it. Crip, smiling enemies and awful music. Tonight was almost enough to make him look forward to his blasted swim-lessons.

Those hadn't started out well either; deep water was a scary wonder for a Mooner. He still had the occasional panic when he couldn't reach the bottom, a fact everyone round him was trying to keep quiet cos they saw it as a security risk. And probably cos it embarrassed them as much as him.

But he was improving, and determined to acquire a skill these Worlders seemed to take for granted...

+++

Noise, that echoed. Bodies all around him as he hesitated at the water's edge. Too much bare skin in public. His instructors said he'd be fine, he still wasn't convinced. Nor, he figured, were his ever-present minders. Daichi's minions hovered in the background, not impressed with his instructions to hold back. They probably thought he'd drown, or someone in this public pool would hug him to death!

He did sympathise. There *had* been another "lucky escape", falling cargo when he inspected a Moon Aid shipment. No proof it wasn't a genuine accident, but Security didn't like it.

Still, today would be a different sort of challenge.

Harp "strolled", marking exits as Daichi insisted, comparing this pool with the Mansion's. Not much bigger actually, just set up for more people; more loungers and benches, more tables, more wait staff. Security probably hated it but he rather liked the bustle. Staying in the Mansion got too quiet.

Swimshorts weren't as bad as wearing skinsuits either, even if there was less fabric. He'd keep telling himself that. And stares were stares whatever he wore. He was Captain Maxil Xen Harpan VIII, lost heir, destroyer of pirate ships. Quite possibly the stares would never stop. One day he might not notice.

Emika had promised there were pool staff here to help if someone got in trouble. Probably she'd meant to reassure him since she wasn't with him this time. She was still inclined to mother hen him. She'd found him what he wanted though, a public pool, one he could even walk into; no steps at this shallow end just a gentle slope where he could see the bottom. She'd said it was a wave pool, which meant the water could move, but there weren't any waves right now cos his Security had told someone to shut them down for a while. He was getting better at this but sadly not sure he could take water attacking him yet.

But today was about achieving something for himself, about proving he could finally control his Mooner nerves about a mass of water.

He wasn't scared of it as such. It was after all one of the things he'd learned to value most. But he hadn't grown up around it, or with the notion it could be deep enough he could vanish and never come up again. And his parents had died on water, so learning to swim had felt urgent, literally life and death, vital to his peace of mind. And a thing, however minor, he could take control of in his new existence. In the end he'd known being able to swim across the private Harpan pool wasn't enough. If he ever had to do this for real there might not be Security on hand to fish him out. To feel safe, he had to do this without backup.

OK, make it casual. The water was cool on his skin, faintly turquoise – a colour he'd only met here on World

– and clear enough he could see his feet, distorted by the ripples he was causing as he waded deeper. To his waist now, things below had tightened. Oddly, after that it always got easier.

People were giving him space. One or two nodded or smiled, he was a public figure now but Worlder manners dictated they pretend he wasn't. Or they'd seen his Security detail on the rim, one in shorts the other still dressed; covering the bases as Em called it. Still he was as alone as it got outside the Mansion. His lips twitched. It was almost worth the nerves for this illusion of independence, so he'd damn well enjoy it. Or die trying?

Chest deep, he pushed forward. Em had warned him to watch for other bodies but he didn't meet any cos he'd done his homework beforehand and been careful to enter one of the areas with marked "lanes" for more serious swimming. The clamour, the colourful surroundings narrowed to the strip of water in front of him, and in a surprisingly short time the wall at the deeper end stopped him. He'd thought it would take longer.

Feeling pleased with himself, he chose to return on his back, arms lax at his sides. This was the stroke his instructor didn't favour, where only his feet propelled him. On the third lap he gave in to temptation and turned onto his stomach, hands still at his sides, feet moving together rather than in opposition. For him it was smoother and faster, never mind what the instructor thought, and when he came up for air it was cos the end wall rose ahead. Not cos he was panicking, or sinking. He'd done it. Maybe using the public pool had helped?

OK, one last test? He ducked past the lane markers, into an open, less disciplined area. Folk here were still Worlder elite; Em wouldn't have chosen any old pool, but they bobbed and splashed, laughed and shouted, and they weren't nervous. They were enjoying themselves, playing with the water, even bringing toys. The smallest children wore suits that kept them near the surface; he'd started with an adult version. They weren't embarrassed by that though. Some older kids had adults supervising –

been there too – but others didn't. Everyone looked pleased to be here. Where he'd seen an obstacle, they saw a playground.

He floated idly on his back, hopefully without being too obvious. One man swam past slowly, curving in and out between bodies. Another jumped then vanished underwater, coming up behind a pretty woman. Kids were pushing water at each other, shrieking not in fear but pleasure.

He realised he'd used his feet to send himself through the crowd too, like sightseeing in water. Who knew. But his Security were moving now he was surrounded, so he twisted and swam for the nearest edge, using arms and legs like others, with his head up to avoid them; swimming manners.

Reaching the wall he hooked his arms onto the tile, let grav lower his feet and allowed himself to feel smug. Mission accomplished; he felt *good* about this water. If he had to he'd survive it.

'Want a hand?'

The hand was darker than his, more olive toned. And wasn't one of his minders. A stranger, in orange shorts that showed off muscular thighs and a flat stomach. When Harp shifted his gaze higher, dark eyes shadowed by almost-black brows looked back at him, with a hint of amusement? Was this normal here? Safe enough though, surely. 'Thanks, friend.' Harp grasped the hand, pushed with his free one and felt himself spring up. This guy was strong, he knew he was no lightweight. 'Was getting my breath back.'

The stranger let his eyes roam downward. 'So am I, Captain.'

'Have we met, Ser?' See, the farmboy has finally learned not to sound it 'sir' although he thought a little drawl would last forever.

'No, Captain but we all know who you are. How could we not?' The stranger smiled. 'Do you get tired of us thanking you for your service?'

Time for a bashful shrug. 'Sometimes, Ser, yes.'

'Then perhaps I might sugar the pill by offering to buy you a drink? It always feels cold once you get out, doesn't it?' The hand waved toward the pool's bar, unaware Harp's Security were moving faster.

Harp smiled, acknowledging the nerve of the guy, discreetly signalling them off. Security retreated. They didn't look happy, but then did they ever, and they weren't signalling any immediate threat.

A waiter cleared an unoccupied table off as they approached, wiped it down, set out simple, non-tec plas menus, generally hovered. Maybe the Mansion's tec menus didn't like water either. The stranger waved Harp ahead then sat across from him. 'I'm Stannisco. People call me Stannis.' He picked up a menu. 'Stannis Mella.' Studying the choices. 'But my mama was a Regis.'

Ah. 'Really.' Harp glanced at the menu too.

'If I promise not to poison the drink will you still accept it?' Dark eyes lifted, waited. Not so casual.

Wow. 'Why not.'

Stannis waved the waiter in and both men asked for caffee. The waiter left. Harp figured he could be blunt too. 'So what relation are you, to…?'

'To the infamous Komar? Distant sort of cousin. We don't have much to do with that side of the family. They consider mama married beneath her.'

Poor relation? The man's shorts bore an expensive logo. The confidence didn't fit either. Harp could admit he was curious. 'So why go out of your way to introduce yourself?'

'Hero worship?' Stannis grinned. 'OK, I was curious, isn't everyone? And seeing you in the flesh.' A hand waved at Harp. 'Hard to resist, wasn't it?'

More flirting? Or not. The arrival of caffee and a tray of snacks "compliments of the management" gave Harp time to consider. He added sweet, a new indulgence, stirred, tasted, pursed his lips. Knew Stannis watched every move, probably understood the delay. He didn't think Stannis was half as brash as he'd chosen to appear. 'I don't mean to offend, Ser Mella, but.'

'Not interested?' A graceful shrug. 'Ah well, I tried.' The man downed his caffee and rose. 'And now I'm off the hook, and so is mama.' The smile faded. 'Do watch out for Eleanora, Captain. She's never been a gracious loser.'

Harp hoped he looked suitably startled. In truth he was. 'I, um, thank you?'

'Thank *you*. I don't like being pressured, Captain, even when the mark is as attractive as you. Dare I hope you won't hold this against me?'

'I think not, Ser.'

'Then thank you again. And now I'll retreat, suitably vanquished, and tell my betters if you turn *me* down you must indeed be celibate as they're suspecting.' Stannis gave an exaggerated pout, backed away, waited a moment – as if hoping Harp changed his mind? – then threaded his way between the poolside tables, heading for the cabins people here hired to change in.

Harp sipped his caffee, not as good as Eda's. If Stannis Mella had meant to poison him he hadn't had much chance, and Harp assumed Security had checked the waiter. So, Eleanora had pushed Stannis on him, against his will? Stannis being, face it, a pretty hot property, and if ignoring the women meant he was into men… a last ditch effort to seduce the farmboy?

Did he believe any of that? He was inclined to. Not that he thought Ser Mella was an innocent. An upstanding citizen was unlikely to call someone a 'mark'.

So, was his *warning* genuine, or merely a more subtle attempt to lure him in?

Ser Stannis bore looking into. Harp almost smiled. No doubt his Security already were.

6

Days later, Harp was 'invited' to lunch in the City. His uncle called this place "a little caffee". Huh. Lots of space, artwork, tables with snowy covers. Not a quick rollup then, more a sit-down meal, waitstaff and several thankfully-meagre courses. At least the place had privacy screens. The other diners might gawk at the Harpan First Son with the lost heir, but what they said stayed private. Just as well, considering.

'Have you thought any more about some discreet help?' Uncle Feldin eyed Harp's Security detail, currently two large men and one large woman in the ubiquitous plain pantsuits Mz Chan favoured. 'Though they do a good job of letting people forget you could defend yourself.' Feldin obviously knew his background, probably knew he'd been working out too, so this grav was no longer a hindrance. Though Harp feared his combat skills were getting rusty.

Feldin wasn't finished. 'There are times it's useful to have someone who isn't so blatant though, and you should have someone you feel more comfortable with. Before Emika leaves?'

The thought of being without Em's support didn't sit well but he knew she needed back into the navy. Harp only wished he could go too, but he had another job right now, as talking head for all the Moon Aid programmes. Course they wouldn't let him do anything useful, like load cargo. His part was shaking hands and such, but the programme was doing a lot of good. The daily reports confirmed they were making a difference, so he sucked it up and got on with encouraging others to join and feel good about it.

Eda was great, giving him updates and reminders, sending everything onto his wristcom, but Emika had been along to most of his public appearances and his "office hours" on the ground floor of the Mansion. Not to mention she had the whole social/political thing at her fingertips, advising him on who got straight through Mansion Security, who was kept waiting, and who didn't get in at all. So yes, he needed someone to fill that hole, or he'd drown as surely as he would have once in Worlders' water. But his betters had clearly run out of patience.

He nodded, albeit reluctantly. 'I do see that, Uncle.'

Trouble was, he hadn't yet felt "comfortable" with anyone they'd suggested. He was aware Feldin, maybe Maxil Snr too, had been getting squirmy, hence this new reminder. Aware they were keeping a pretty close eye on him too. In fact, he'd begun to wonder if their reasons were as straightforward as he'd been assuming. Was that his problem, not theirs, his own reluctance to let someone new get too close? It still felt like World had different ideas of normal. Cos face it, he wasn't Harpan-normal; wasn't even Worlder-normal.

Would probably never be either.

Was that why they watched so closely?

Plus, he wasn't always clear where their normal and his might clash. He knew that often made him tense with strangers.

But the people he felt safest with wouldn't want to be temp-civs, let alone glorified servants. So maybe he should just say yes to whoever Feldin liked for the job. What did it take really, to get him to appointments looking like he knew what he was doing so he didn't let the programmes down?

Only, it would be good to have someone else to laugh with as he could with Em, not one of the stiff-necked "cousins" they'd paraded for discreet inspection. If only there was someone who wasn't quite so Worlder-perfect either.

Oh. 'Erm, actually, Uncle, I've just had a thought.'

+++

Looked like his info-request had caused a stir. Mz Chan chose to deliver the findings in person, face to face as well, in Feldin's office. Possibly one of the most secure places World had.

Mz Chan wore the same pant suit and bland face as the rest of Security. It should make it hard to tell them apart, but Harp had never doubted she was in charge. He deduced a Navy background too; the close-cropped hair, the way she walked, the way she held her shoulders. It reminded him of *Raptor* training, when he'd picked out civs from navy.

She arrived, sat down quietly, the way she'd walked in, glanced at Feldin, nodded at Harp then tapped her wristcom. 'Ser Stanniso Mella.' Straight to business.

Feldin nodded her to go on.

'Mother: Medam Marisca Regis. Father: Ser Standan Mella.' She rattled off dates and such – Stannis was thirty-one, ten years Harp's senior – then got to the interesting bits. 'The father, third son, trained as an accountant in the Mella family, most of whom are in finance or law. The House has a good reputation, but no longer name Ser Standan, or Stannisco, among its numbers. Standan was removed from his first position for falsifying accounts and bleeding off funds. By the age of twenty when he met Marisca, he was already living mainly on his wits. He may have seen her as easy prey. Whatever the reason, Medam Marisca ran off with Standan when she was seventeen, breaking another engagement, and had Stannisco eight months later. House Regis cut all ties and cancelled her allowance. We believe this decision came from the top rather than her parents.' Read Eleanora. 'Marisca had never contributed to society. Other than shopping,' Mz Chan said drily, 'so she was not entitled to Citizen's Aid. She probably assumed her new husband could support her, but two months after the child was born Standan left them. We have not yet ascertained why, or where, but we know he returned when the child was eight and remained till he was fifteen, when he was killed in a street attack in one of the less reputable areas of the City. In life he showed talent as a conman, enough it appears he did more or less support his family, even when absent. At least there's no record of Marisca applying for City aid for Stannisco. But it appears that after Standan's death mother and son slowly ran out of credit and Stannisco realised he could use his own talents to support them. His first mistress was probably Suniya Regis.'

Feldin blinked. 'Eleanora's daughter?'

Harp raised his hand. 'But not Komar Regis's mother?'

'No, Ser, Suniya is the younger daughter, considered prettier and only ten years older than Stannisco. That lasted several months until, we surmise, Eleanora found out.'

'Ouch.'

'Perhaps, Ser, but word is Ser Stannisco hasn't been broke since. We understand he actually prefers males but doesn't discriminate.' Mz Chan almost smirked. 'Though he doesn't trawl for the ugly ones, and so far hasn't needed to.'

'I see.' Feldin glanced at Harp. 'Max...'

He hadn't blushed. Had he? 'I'm not attracted.' He almost wished he was cos this weird non-interest was starting to bother him.

'Very well, but.'

'If I lose Emika, I'm going to need someone else to keep the paws off.'

Feldin choked, then considered. 'Not such a bad idea, in that sense. But he might expect more than a front. Plus he is a Regis.'

'I don't think he is, ser. My impression is he dislikes that side of his family a lot more than he does the Mellas. House Mella ignored his father, and by extension him and his mother, but with good cause, and before Standan met Marisca, yes?'

Mz Chan nodded.

'The way I see it, Stannis doesn't take that personally, but he does with House Regis.'

'Hmm.' Feldin looked interested. 'Suniya?'

'Yes. I think that could have been a younger Stannis thumbing his nose at all of them, maybe in payback for his mother. I'd guess he took Suniya for as much as he could get?'

Again Mz Chan almost smiled. 'We estimate in the region of two hundred thousand, in credits, jewellery and some company stocks.'

'Mm. So not on their side, and the feeling's probably mutual? I'd like to make an approach. Call it a hunch, but he's clever, socially adept, and I rather liked him. You'll watch him anyway, of course.'

'Of course,' Mz Chan did not smile. Not quite. Maybe he'd made her life more interesting though.

7

Emika laughed. 'They've agreed?'

'Yes, with conditions.' Harp smiled at a passing acquaintance, gesturing Em to precede him. The bar he'd picked wasn't one of Daichi's approved elite but it boasted a rare, real-outside terrace, air that moved and wasn't perfumed. He'd been here several times recently. Em chose an outside table in the last of the sunshine. It struck Harp he was almost as comfortable now sitting in the sun as once he'd hidden from it.

Caffee and cake for Em, a brandy for him; they remembered his preferred label. Em slid him a look. 'Just how long have you been setting this up?'

'Maybe a little longer than my uncle thinks.' Harp grinned. 'It's one of Mella's regular haunts. He might have caught sight of me leaving a few times recently as he arrived. Always alone.' Harp tossed back the expensive liquid, signalled for another.

'Subtle.' Em sipped daintily. 'But what if he's...?'

'Spare my blushes, Em. He parted company with the latest eight days back. He might be circling a replacement but it's early days, and Mz Chan says he doesn't usually rush.' Harp broke the bun that arrived with his second drink – they were very good at appearances here – spread the sweet paste that came with it, didn't taste. 'According to Mz Chan he has a talent for staying friends with his, what's the word, benefactors? Two still give him advice on his investments and several invite him to parties, where he sometimes scouts for future income.'

Emika gurgled laughter, hid it with her caffee. 'Really? And investments?'

'I'm not sure how much he needs the marks any more, not for income.'

'For *fun*?'

'Maybe. Or intel.' Harp's eyes settled on the man they were discussing, right on schedule. 'Time to find out. Would you mind?'

'Oh sure, get me all excited then send me off so I miss the best part?' Emika banged her cup down, rose and stalked off, nose elevated. She might say she didn't like the Family Game, but she could sure play it.

Harp scowled then waved a waiter over, ordering another brandy. Between that and Em's abandonment Ser Stannis couldn't miss him, could he?

'Deserted, Captain?' If Stannis doubted his welcome he didn't let it show, only paused as if he wasn't really stopping. Harp figured the man had it down, how to test the waters as they said here, yet avoid being snubbed. Not that Harp intended a snub.

'Ser.' He scowled again, at Emika's untouched cake. 'Care for a free snack? My cousin lost her appetite.'

A bright smile almost hid the wariness in the eyes. 'Never turn down free food, Ser. Thanks.' He sat. The waiter saw Harp's signals and brought over two caffees, two brandies and more buns. Stannis sipped, the caffee. 'I didn't intend to snoop.'

'No, it's all right. Emika wants back on duty. She's chafing at the delay, makes her a bit abrupt.'

'Oh? I thought ... I *heard* you and she...'

Harp laughed. 'That nonsense? We're friends.' Harp leaned in. 'Truth is, between you and me, it's kept folk off both of us, y'know? But when she leaves.' He shook his head. 'Security's all very well but it doesn't keep Society away.'

Stannis eyed Harp's empty glasses. The waiter thought he liked to keep count. 'Seemed to me *you* were keeping them off, Captain.'

So he had been watching. 'No, Em always rescued me, made it look, look natural, hm?' Harp shook his head, swallowed Stannis's liquor, stared into the glass. 'I'm not much good at that without her.'

'You mean you need a beard? You?' Stannis burst out laughing.

'A what?'

'Sorry, it means a fake "friend".' The intonation added extra meaning.

Harp frowned then nodded, kept nodding. Then studied his companion. 'You ever thought of growing one?'

For a second Stannis froze, then smiled. 'Tell you what, Captain. Ask me again when you're sober and I'll consider it, but in the meantime I'll forget I heard any of this, OK?'

'OK.' For a moment Harp continued to stare, then waved to the waiter.

+++

'I didn't think you'd call.' Stannis accepted a seat, glancing round the expanse that was the Captain's office on the third floor of the Founder's Mansion, somewhere he'd never expected to see. No question, the Family were treating Maxil Jnr precisely as his bloodlines dictated. Which meant answering this call was a big, irresistible gamble. He hadn't expected the active screens either, evidence this Moon Aid business flourished and the 'casts' beloved "Captain Max" was more involved than Stannis had assumed.

His host crossed to a wall panel. 'I wanted to give you some time to think about it. Caffee?' It opened to reveal a tray set up and waiting.

'Thank you, ser.' A semi-friendly approach then.

Both sat and sipped, and studied one another. Stannis waited. Was this a 'keep quiet or else' meeting, or more?

Harp lowered his glass. 'You mentioned a beard.'

'Ah. Yes.'

'I also happen to need an aide. Could you do both?'

The man was offering him an actual job? Careful. 'I'd imagine, but I'm not sure your family –'

'The Family already know.' Again with the smile but this time Stannis saw teeth. Maxil Harpan VIII wasn't the pretty face he'd let people think, was he? Letting Stannis see this office in full work mode was deliberate, demonstrating that. As deliberate as downing too many brandies? To sound him out? The younger man was stone cold sober today.

'I can offer a suitable salary. You'd keep your apartment, of course.'

Of course. Harpan Security would have fits if he suggested moving in.

'There'll no doubt be other perks.'

Like a meteoric rise in social standing, employee or not.

The Captain sipped. For once Stannis hesitated. The gamble had become a lot bigger. The Captain watched him. 'I have read your file, Ser Mella. I'm not likely to be shocked. Gossip might speculate we could be more than colleagues, but you'd do the day job, nothing else, and keep your mouth shut. Still interested?'

'Crip.' Could he do it? Should he? Dare he? Stannis breathed out. 'You really mean it, don't you?'

'Sure as death.' The younger man smiled coldly. 'Which I suspect is what you'd get if you tried to double cross House Harpan.'

'Believe me, Ser, I know that.' Another breath. 'OK, I'm in.' Stannis laughed. 'Where do I sign?'

+++

There *was* signing. This time Harp kept half an eye on proceedings, onscreen from his official office suite. Plus palmprints, retinal scans, genetic markers, all carried out in the bowels of the Lower Security Station by the Mansion's main entrance, and all personally supervised by the infamous Mz Chan. Right now there were two floors of Admin and other 'Executive Suites' between Harp and Stannis, but that didn't mean the man would have access to all of even these levels of the Mansion. The passes being added to his wristcom would admit him to the staff portion of the train, the general admin pods, two of the entrances and up as far as third and Harp's official workspace. Mz Chan was explaining all that as she checked Stannis into Security's systems and confirmed his numbers. Harp watched Stannis reclaim his wristcom, glance down and blink. At the list of permissions? The salary he'd just agreed to? Or the realisation Mz Chan was looking almost smug because she'd just cloned *all* its data? Harp hoped nothing too illegal showed up.

He also saw, cos he knew more these days, that even Stannis's gait had been recorded as he passed the outer checkpoint. Stannis was on record, big time now. The price of his new respectability.

Next, Mz Chan escorted him up to Harp's suite, sat him at a desk Em still used in the outer room near the entry, and started taking him through its tec. So Harp stopped work nearby and watched them, feeling sympathetic. This might be where Stannis changed his mind and ran for the hills.

Mz Chan pointed at the wall screens she'd woken. 'Incoming logged here, subsectioned. The Captain's personals, Family – those should be regarded as priority – Security updates, Moon Aid requests and messages, known contacts with call history, unknowns, and risk files. If in doubt alert us immediately.'

In case – small chance – Security missed something.

'Schedules here. You'll be responsible for organising the Captain's public appearances and engagements. You'll update as he approves them, the desk will auto-update to Security and other relevant bodies.' She didn't elaborate. 'You shouldn't need to follow up there except in the event Security don't confirm receipt of such updates. Understood?'

'Yes, Medam.' The man did look a trifle pale though. Had he still thought Harp did more drinking than working?

Mz Chan still wasn't finished. 'Moon Aid *files* here, historic and active, crossed with scheduling. Draft and final notes for speeches, interviews etc. Selected images for PR – I've alerted our PR department to present an overview and run through guidelines. You'll need to memorise Security protocols, idents for the senior staff in each department you're cleared for, and those assigned to accompany the Captain, as well as staying aware of current trends and influences.'

'Then there are the accounts.' Mz Chan's head turned to Stannis. 'Some files you won't control, but you will be expected to balance the office cash accounts and maintain an oversight of the Aid programme's numbers. Any discrepancies must be reported. The Captain informs me you have some skill in that area.'

'So kind,' Stannis murmured. Did his mouth twitch?

'Need I say House Security also has oversight, and supervises regular audits?'

'Naturally, Medam.' If Stannis had had any ideas about helping himself to petty cash Harp figured he'd abandoned them. Stannis – marginally honest – might be a gamble Mz Chan hadn't wanted, but Harp had always gone with his gut and really, in the end he still trusted himself more than any outside opinion. So Stannis was in – on probation, anyway – and they'd all wait and see, wouldn't they?

When Mz Chan finally left – yes there was more – Harp walked down the corridor. Stannis stood by what was now his desk, staring rather blankly at the menu Mz Chan had left on the lefthand screen for him to "become familiar with".

'Caffee, Stannis?'

Stannis straightened. 'Please!'

'We have a kitchen, across the way.' The other man followed him across the passage, watched as Harp touched the panel for the cubby that housed the mech for hot and cold drinks, including costly wines and spirits. 'Drinks here. Food, you can order from Catering.' Harp smiled ruefully. 'That's Family Catering here, not to be confused with Office Catering elsewhere. You'll get used to it. The washroom's through that panel next door. There's a smaller Security Station between us and the outer entry, but it's not manned unless there's an escalated threat situation, so you're generally the welcome mat – the control on your desk can check the view – and you saw my office last time you were here.' He thought that covered everything re layout. Harp tapped for his usual, strong and black, then raised an eyebrow.

'Oh, white please.' The machine whirred. 'I guess doing that is part of my job too.'

'Whoever's nearest if we decide to help ourselves.' His new aide's disbelief was written on his features. Better demonstrate he meant it? 'Otherwise Eda obliges.'

'Eda?'

'Eda, say hello to Stannis.'

'Hello, Ser Stannisco.' Stannis's head jerked.

'Eda can deliver to each room if you don't want to stop what you're doing. Just ask.'

'Right.' The man recovered quickly, took the tall glass – Emika had denied Harp navy style mugs down here – followed Harp to his office and its generous seating area and chose to sit facing him, leaning back.

'A bit much, I guess.'

The 'mm' was suitably noncommittal, but seeing Stannis glancing round made Harp realise he was actually starting to take all this lux for granted. Calling it an office was almost ridiculous, in Mooner-Harp terms. Add a cot and he could live in the damn place, room service thrown in. Fancy desks, plush seats, big wall screens. This lounge area, the amazing washroom Stannis hadn't even seen yet. Artwork. Vids or music if he wanted. He supposed Stannis was in some degree of shock; he should probably try to reassure the guy. 'My cousin Emika's been helping out. I've asked her to go over things from her side too, before she leaves, OK?'

'Sounds good, ser. When is that?'

'In five days, so I'm afraid you'll be busy.' So much for reassurance. 'Do you have any previous engagements?'

'Nothing I can't cancel if I need to.' Stannis leaned forward, losing the nonchalance. 'I have to say, this doesn't look like any sort of standard workday.'

'I wish. I guess I did ambush you there. I know Emika's hours have often been erratic. But then she is family so she can always sleep here. If time becomes a problem we can discuss it. I understand your mother –'

Both their wristcoms shivered, silent signals. Stannis

jumped, Harp didn't. 'That'll be my schedule alert. You get used to that too.'

Stannis checked his screen. 'Transport on call. Senior Ed Centre Three?'

'Moon Aid. Eda, disposal please?' Harp set his half full glass on the table's receptor plate. 'Eda will transfer it back to the kitchen.' And wash it and put it away without being told. He'd find out.

Stannis hesitated then copied, watched the little hatch slide shut again, almost invisible, but didn't comment.

Harp shrugged and rose. 'I do talks for kids. You can come along and watch or stay here and study.'

Stannis frowned, then followed him out. 'Are you supposed to go alone? I mean...'

'Emika's meeting me, and there'll be Security, to protect me from a crowd of teens and run the tec.' Harp arrived at the washroom and touched the panel. 'You could check I'm presentable when I come out. I swear Emika still doesn't trust me to dress myself.' He shut the panel on the bemused expression, trying not to smile. It made a change not to be the one bewildered.

Civs off, uniform on as per Emika-orders; she really was a House mother. He wondered if Stannis would consider clothing "suggestions" part of *his* job description. The short hair saved work at least. Back out, to find Stannis had diverted to his outer office, door left open, frowning at his new desk. 'This says you have three Security assigned plus a driver, Captain, and you're scheduled to be there one hour, then move on to a Senior Centre?'

'You're obviously getting the hang of it. If you're staying, maybe you could check tomorrow's appointments for any changes?'

'Very well, ser.'

'Mm. Ser or captain's what they'll want in public. Otherwise.' Again Harp went on instinct. 'Let's try Max, OK?'

Did Stannis relax a fraction? 'OK. Max. What do I do if there *are* changes?'

'Send them to my desk. As Mz Chan said, they'll autocopy elsewhere. Now I'd better go before Security panic.' Harp headed for the entry. 'Don't overdo it on your first day, just get a feel. The place will autolock when you leave.' Hand on the panel he looked back. 'I'll see you tomorrow, if you don't change your mind by then.'

Stannis fiddled with a stylus. 'What time?'

'Emika usually reports in about oh seven hundred, if you want to shadow her.'

'Seven hundred it is then.'

Harp felt the man's gaze on his back till the panel slid behind him.

+++

Walking in again almost four hours later the Captain was obviously startled to find Stannis still around. So was Stannis, truth be told, he'd never imagined himself in an office. But this stuff was interesting. And complex, and he did like complex. So when the younger man came back he had a cold caffee on his desk (courtesy of the "Eda" programme that seemed devoted to the Captain – at least "she" wouldn't answer any of the more intriguing questions he'd tried) and his elbows splayed across its surface as he frowned at the gruelling workout that called itself the Captain's next ten-day schedule.

Right now the guy already looked beat. Yet his concern seemed to be aimed at Stannis. 'Hey. You should have given up by now. It really is too much to take in one go.'

Stannis shrugged. 'I've made a start. Are *you* OK?' Where the hell did that come from?

The younger man hadn't noticed he'd gone still. 'Yeah. The kids were great. Emika reckons reaching out to them reaches parents and teachers too, so it's a win-win.' The Captain – Max – backed out of Stannis's space and turned inward.

'But?'

No answer. Stannis stretched out the kinks in his back,

hesitated then followed Max into his inner office in time to see the guy fall into one of the form-hugging chairs and undo his uniform jacket. 'But?' Might as well push a little, if only to see how far he could.

Max sighed. 'Oh, camras, and casters. Everyone wants a moment, you know? Not just the kids. And I forgot to take a change of shirt for the second appearance so I probably stank. Em will say that proves how useless I am without her.'

Stannis wasn't sure if the guy was serious or joking but he did look worn out. 'Caffee?'

'Oh please.' Another sigh. 'I can't, round the kids, it's not "done".' Stannis heard the quote marks, had to hide a grin. 'I take it –'

'Extra black. I noticed.' Plus it was practically the only thing Eda *wanted* to tell him. He was being programmed by a blasted robot! Still, she had her uses. 'Eda?'

'Coming up, Sers.'

The server-niche in here was twin to the one Stannis had found in his smaller office, and just as efficient. The panel opened and a tray slid forward, all Stannis had to do was walk a few steps. He could get used to this, risk or not. 'Here you go.'

'Thanks. None for you?'

'I'll be awake half the night as it is.' And not just from this high-lux caffee. Stannis took the opposite couch. If he ever tried seduction it wouldn't be when the guy was dead on his feet. Besides... 'You really work at this, don't you?'

'I believe in it.' The Harpan – Max – took a healthy gulp then leaned back, glass in hand. 'Moon needs all the help it can get. If me being its mascot works, so be it.'

'But you don't enjoy it.' Stannis didn't bother making that a question.

'Some of it's good, like the kids. Some, not so much. But it's not hard labour. Don't know why I get so tired.' Another gulp. 'Guess I still need to get fitter.' A sigh. 'And not rely too much on Em. I have spare outfits right here in the washroom.'

'Yeah, I noticed.' Understatement of the year. The walk-in closet in there was fully loaded, even had an inventory. He had found it in his files, itemised and numbered; dates worn, dates sent out for cleaning… 'It looks like I'm down for checking there along with office supplies.'

'I guess. Honestly, ask Emika. I'm a little ignorant about all that.'

'I'm beginning to see how you could be.' Stannis hesitated. 'You offering me this job, it's a risk, isn't it?'

Max found a weary smile. 'For who?'

'Everyone, the way I see it. The Family can't be thrilled. Your Security Chief's sniffy. That means it was your decision. So you'll feel a fool if I mess up.'

'And you?'

'Oh, if you fire me now I'm pretty much ruined, aren't I? The doors will slam so hard they'll hear the echoes all around the City.' Which, oddly, didn't worry him now as much as the thought of *not* meeting this challenge. He wasn't going to be babysitting a drunk junior Harpan. Crip, he was going to be supporting a high-profile business-style operation with offworld connections. There were a lot more opportunities here than he'd thought, for him and Mama.

Maybe Mama was right, maybe you could be respectable without dying of boredom? 'But let's not count on that yet.'

'Sorry?'

He'd said that out loud? Amateur slip. 'Just thinking out loud, ser. So, oh seven tomorrow? Anything else tonight?'

'No, I'm done here too, once I transfer tomorrow's who's-who list upstairs to read before I turn in.' A grin, of sorts. 'You'll see, Emika will quiz me on them first thing.'

'Harsh.' What the guy should do was sleep.

But the young man pushed out of the chair and headed for his high-spec desk. 'It works though. I still don't recognise everyone I should. Unlike you, I suspect.' He tapped, presumably sending the data to his private quarters, then straightened. 'I'm afraid you'll find me a lot of work.' The guy meant it, didn't he. 'Do you think you can handle the job now you've seen what it really is? You could back out now. I'd make sure it stayed quiet.'

Could he? Stannis found himself unsettled, not a sensation he often allowed. 'Maybe you should ask me that again in a ten-day.' He followed the Captain out, thinking the younger man might be as much a challenge as the job. 'Goodnight, Captain.'

'Night.' They parted ways, Stannis heading for the outer checkpoint – automatically confirming the location of the camras that recorded his every move. Finding one he'd missed. The Captain – Max – retreated the other way to whatever refuge they'd provided him. Would there be camras there as well? He hadn't spotted any inside the office suite; he'd look again tomorrow. He understood they'd keep an eye on him – even sympathised. Not that they'd see anything to worry them. But, eyes on the Captain, that felt different. The guy was so damned honest it hurt. Stannis could smell a con the way others smelled dinner, which meant he knew the real deal when he found it, and *this* Harpan was about as real as it got. Not a rich-kid drunk. Nor – importantly – a fool, however naïve. And damned attractive with it.

Yes, this job could be a *much* bigger challenge than he'd planned for.

And tomorrow he would face another, probably less trusting Harpan.

+++

Em was wary with Stannis, but polite. Max appreciated it, and said so three days in when they had a moment alone, walking to his office. 'You're helping him a lot.'

'Well, he's trying hard, I'll give you that.' Em decided to be fair. 'And he's brighter than some of Uncle's candidates, picks up what I don't spell out as well. I wasn't sure, but he does seem what you wanted; knows when to talk and when to leave you in peace anyway. I hope he works out, Max.' Even if she still wasn't convinced, and considering staying a while longer.

'So do I.' Max didn't show any worry at all. 'I think he's starting to enjoy it. I hope so.'

Which wasn't exactly what *she'd* meant. Em gave into curiosity. 'Why pick him, really?'

'A gut reaction I guess.' Max glanced her way. 'Maybe two outsiders together.'

That… took her breath a moment. And hurt, for him. So he still saw himself like that? Impulsively she hugged him, hang the camras. 'I wish we could make you see you're not. You're about as "in" as it gets.'

A twisted smile. 'One day, maybe. When people finally come clean.'

'What?' Emika searched for words that didn't sound as false as he'd just made her feel.

Max shrugged. 'Maxil Snr, and Feldin, they're hiding *something*, aren't they? I think this Inner Family thing means more than anyone's explained.'

'Max…'

'S'OK. I figured you'd got orders, but I'm not a complete fool, Em, even if I act like one. I guess being a Harpan makes everything more complicated. Let's forget I said anything.' The office entry slid aside and Stannis looked up from his open doorway, shutting down the awkward moment.

+++

'Uncle, I really think it's time to explain.' Emika looked at Feldin anxiously, hands clasped in her lap. Feldin got the feeling she'd rather be standing to attention.

He patted her hand. 'It was only a matter of time before he started to get suspicious, he's every bit as bright as we hoped. Very well, I'll discuss it with the Founder. But for now, we follow orders.'

'Yes, Ser.' Emika rose and left, head down. Feldin stared after her. It was probably as well his niece was more interested in naval service than Family politics. She didn't enjoy lying, even by omission, and unfortunately it was so often part of the job.

All the more impressive, then, that young Max was proving so astute, and so capable. And disciplined, probably a benefit of navy training. Maybe it *was* time to bring him into the fold, not least because the boy was looking more and more a possible successor for Feldin himself, even if he hadn't voiced that opinion yet.

Amusing, if it wasn't so serious. All these carefully raised cousins and the pick of the bunch might be the farmboy, as he'd been heard to call himself, one dragged up on another planet.

What were the odds?

8

Mz Emika was gone, not even in Foundation any longer. Stannis savoured that fact as he checked into the Mansion, wearing what the captain called "office uniform"; looser dress pants, button down shirt, soft-soled boots. He'd noticed the Captain still wore a lot of bluish colours but after some thought he'd shopped more for blacks, maybe purples, though with the odd splash of bright; he did have a rep to consider after all. So, semiformal but with a nod to his new boss, and more discreet than his usual style.

It still felt slightly wrong. He was a man more used to showing off the goods – however tastefully – than aiming to be self-effacing, but Mz Emika had looked approving. Though he'd bet serious credits the Captain wouldn't object if people stared at Stannis instead of their hero!

Who he was essentially left alone with now. If he didn't count Security, camras, media attention and the Founding Family, from distant cousins right up to the Founder himself. Oh yes, House Harpan still had its collective gaze incessantly directed at the Captain.

Stannis was still mulling that over. At first he'd assumed it was concern the "lost heir" would embarrass them, being so new to all this. But while Max might not be as sophisticated as some he wasn't dumb, he *was* attractive, and he could charm the pants off almost anyone he chose to, often without even meaning to. Yes, the Captain was intriguing, and a challenge. And a danger, Stannis reminded himself. Never forget that part.

The office entry slid open for him; looked like he was the first one here. 'Morning Eda.'

'Good morning, Stannis.' Friendly terms were building nicely there, thanks to Max's attitude.

Stannis woke his desk. The day's schedule appeared front and centre, subscreens displayed details of people tagged for access to the Captain. Everything up and running.

Except for a red-flagged Security alert. He'd been briefed there were possible threats, plural, another revelation he hadn't foreseen. According to this alert, someone was tailing Komar Regis's parents, suspected of trying to poison the Captain. Seriously? This latest report confirmed their current movements were mostly business related, inspecting sites House Regis owned or operated. Only…

Stannis read with growing interest. Dirt, on House Regis, what fun. House Regis had buried ownership of some shell companies, very sneaky? He copied the data, under 'Social Study', to his own apartment – if his own less-than-legal system wasn't still blocking the Mansion security he was dead anyway – but he'd point the report out when the captain arrived, if only to watch his reaction.

Meanwhile, it was still his first day solo; had he forgotten anything? No point calling for caffee before the Captain arrived when Eda could brew it in seconds. And he couldn't wake the Captain's desk, didn't have access. That was mildly annoying, but he couldn't argue. Even Mz Emika hadn't had clearance there. He'd wondered if that had been her decision, choosing to respect Max's privacy, or Mz Chan trying to train the lost heir to keep Family secrets.

Either way, when the Captain arrived Stannis was in the so-called washroom, adding the Captain's medal of honour to the uniform he'd pulled for later. His own more formal change hung in his end of the closet with a few other items Mz Emika – he supposed he should start calling her Captain now too – had "suggested" he installed. She'd called it being prepared, he called it a taste of lux living; assumed she'd known the facilities here were a step up from where he lived.

He'd read the small print in his contract. While he was in the Mansion he was free to wash, dress, eat, drink and even get a shave and haircut, all on the Family's tab, albeit on the office levels. As for the reaction when he "let slip" to his tailor *why* he required several new outfits… perks like that had probably added another, what, twelve percent to the honest salary he'd vowed he'd never sink to. And without whoring for any of it.

He'd wondered about that. Well, naturally. But the Captain seemed to have meant what he'd said; that any relationship people suspected was going to be fake. Getting "involved" might have been amusing, but then again the guy was a Harpan, and things were going well so far without. Besides, it wouldn't do to risk getting attached, would it, not when the guy's life expectancy no longer looked that hot.

Which reminded Stannis to offer the boss caffee like a good little PA, and tell him about that alert.

Surprisingly, the captain seemed more upset by the vids the agent had sent with her report than relieved about the parents' continued absence. Upset enough he spent some time on com with Mz Chan, talking about following it up. If they weren't careful they'd all get pulled into helping needy Worlders as well as Mooners. How soft a touch was the guy?

He was easy enough to handle on Stannis's first day solo. Everything went as smooth as simsilk; every appointment on time, both Captain and visitors amenable to being edged out when their time slot was up. Stannis was also starting to read his new boss, enough to distinguish who he enjoyed meeting from who he saw on sufferance to help his Aid programmes. There was no sign any of them recognised it though, any slight stiffness probably came across as shyness, which it partly was, and the half smile was enough to charm them. He was curious how well the guy would pull that off with a larger audience. The casts made him look good, but casts could be manipulated. Today he'd see for himself, his first foray in public as the Captain's aide.

Ah, well; disillusionment was good for you.

+++

Changing into uniform, Harp thought this day's

appearances looked relatively mild, a Junior Ed Centre followed by a Senior Ed. The only downside was they were some distance apart for once, which explained why they were the only destinations that day. Maybe that had been in Emika's mind when she arranged it? So far they'd been more fun than the adult appearances. The lighter schedule would be good for Stannis's first time too, though so far Stannis had proved more than capable in the Mansion.

OK, ready to go. He'd done this particular presentation four times now and one of Daichi's people – not Daichi today – would handle the vid. All Stannis really needed to do was keep a watching brief.

An hour in, Harp noticed the other man looked slightly less shellshocked; not used to kids then. The kids had listened politely while Harp showed them the vids of Moon, including clips of kids their age. They'd oohed and aahed at steers and rangers, and a milder one relating drought and prairie fire. He figured many of them now saw Moon as an adventure; fine, if helping Mooners let them feel like heroes. That was what these visits could accomplish, motivating kids, who innocently motivated adults.

Stannis sat up straighter when they got to questions, things like had he really herded steers. On a ranger? Did the rangers bite him? Did the steers?

'No.' He grinned. 'The steers have blunt teeth. But with so many legs they do kick. And spit.' The "ews" at that included Stannis, getting with the programme.

Then a small girl stood. 'Ser, do lots of children on Moon not have parents?'

He expected it now, it was possibly one of the strangest things they were learning about Mooners. They had no concept of what being orphaned meant, none at all. Oh, one kid said he had two fathers, another kindly explained she had three mothers. A third was part of some group arrangement – he always learned something on these visits. But they all had at least one officially recognised parent because, as Hendriks had guessed, if they didn't then Worlders shipped them off to Moon, a sort of human surplus.

No wonder none of the recruits he'd trained with here had despised him as much as he'd expected. Neither being orphan nor bastard would have been as real to them as it was to him.

So questions about being raised so differently took up a chunk of the allotted time, and had Stannis's eyes widening along with the kids'. It wasn't Harp's favourite part, but he wasn't going to lie, and it was plain most of the kids took it to heart. Maybe they'd appreciate having parents more as a result?

Anyway, there he was again. Stannis looked interested. Security were relaxed, as much as they ever were. Teachers and a smattering of parents – always some who managed to get in – looked impressed. And the kids were one of the best things about his new existence, even if they did ask questions brought bad memories with good. And he was tiring now, but Stannis was rising, right on cue, to remind him they had somewhere else to get to.

Smiles. Handshakes. Effusive thanks. Stannis moving him forward without needing Security. Water and a clean shirt waiting in the transport, the windows already opaqued so no one would see him strip, wipe down and change. Rinse and repeat as Em had called it. He'd miss Emika, no lie, but Stannis was proving someone else he could relax with.

They completed the second visit without a hitch, returned to the Mansion, ditched the Security, who probably went off to report to Daichi, and changed back into normal clothes. Em had never scheduled office appointments after these appearances, she'd known Harp wasn't on top of his game then, but they'd habitually discussed the next day's arrangements before they called a halt. Stannis had sat in on those before Emika left, now it was just the two of them, sipping caffee and staring at the screens in Stannis's office, nearest from the washroom.

Harp pulled a face at two of the entries. 'Them again?'

'Fraid so. I can put them off if –'

'No, I guess they're necessary evils.' Harp remembered his manners. 'You did well today. How did it feel?'

Stannis looked up. 'Honestly? It was more interesting than I expected. Your life, before all this, it was tougher than we think, wasn't it?'

Suck it up, you knew Stannis was sharp, now you have to live with the fact. 'No one on Moon has it easy,' Harp said mildly.

'No. I saw that.' Thankfully before Stannis said any more his desk alerted, Mz Chan no less.

Harp leaned in. 'Accept visual.'

They got Mz Chan's head and shoulders. No smile. When was there? Almost a frown? 'Ser – ah, Captain, my apologies. There's no immediate cause for alarm.' That couldn't be good. 'Merely a heads-up that we've temporarily lost contact with Medam Sirena.'

Crip. Was that why Daichi had stayed behind? 'Just the mother?' The least stable. Not that he was going to blame Security. He figured Mz Chan was doing that for him. 'Do you think she's back?'

'There's no sign of that, but we have picked up some encrypted chatter between House Regis and Moon.' Mz Chan looked bland. 'As far as we're aware House Regis has no business involvement on Moon.'

'You think that's where she's gone? Harp caught up. 'To meet *Komar*?' He was vaguely aware Stannis's jaw had dropped but all he got from Chan was the hint of a frown.

'A risk, obviously, especially on Moon. But it is a possible scenario.'

'Or Moon Orbital maybe?'

'Or a point between World and Moon. Komar wouldn't want to risk being recognised and Medam Sirena might not want to anger Eleanora more than she already has.' Harp considered. 'By leaving her husband behind she may think Eleanora wouldn't realise.'

Mz Chan sniffed. 'She's not known for her computing power.'

'I see.' Like if Sirena wanted to see her darling son she was the type to go with the impulse, and arrogant enough to think she could, a trait she obviously inherited. Hmm. Eleanora would be royally pissed if this was true. Or would she? More importantly, 'Is there any chance we can track the woman to Komar?'

'We are trying.' Mz Chan's face said no luck so far.

He sympathised with her frustration. 'I'm sure you're doing everything possible. You'll update me?'

'Of course, Captain. Good evening.' That screen went black.

Stannis had finally closed his mouth. 'How much danger are you in?'

Harp sighed. 'No more than I was before, and Mz Chan will warn me if she thinks it's unsafe for me to leave the Mansion.' Which made him think. 'Would you prefer to stay here overnight, till we know more?' He had to smile. 'I'm sure we can find you a corner somewhere.'

At least Stannis laughed, which lightened the mood for both of them. 'Staying here does sound attractive but I think I'll head home. I'll see you in the morning, Captain.'

'Max in here, remember? And thanks again for making my day go smoothly.'

'All part of the service.' Stannis shut his desk down, dumped his glass, called 'Goodnight Eda,' and departed. Harp figured he might as well do the same. He *was* as safe here as anyone could be, and the thought of Komar being caught might even send him to sleep smiling.

9

No change next morning, but Stannis was still rivetted. It was… fascinating being, as it were, a fly on the Mansion's wall. Mz Chan was in a snit cos she was charged with Max's safety and Moon Orbital's new surveillance system wasn't up and running – priority shifted to Moon's surface after the pirate incursion – though she still believed a rendezvous in space more likely. As she'd said, if Komar was spotted on Moon he'd be lucky to live, let alone escape again. In the void, Sirena could assure herself her darling was OK and pass over open credits so there'd be no evidence.

If that assessment was right the mother would probably return to World shortly where House Security could resume surveillance. Maybe reverse track her route to apprehend the traitor? The Captain obviously hoped so.

This time Stannis interrupted. 'You're sure she's not already back, Medam?' He didn't want Security feeling too secure about it.

Mz Chan's lips tightened. 'We have alerts out on all docks, Ser Mella, including private and public shuttles.'

'I see.' Stannis let it go. When the call ended there was just enough time for him and the Captain to change, for Ed Centres Seven and Ten this time. It was starting to feel normal. The visits were supposed to be unannounced but there was almost always a leak so the crowd outside when they arrived at Seven wasn't a shock. Somehow there were always media wanting inside too but Max's Security would keep things semi-private. Though Stannis knew some of the kids, teachers and parents would ensure they didn't, sneaking personal recordings onto pubnets.

Still, the Captain liked kids, it showed. Maybe he found them more trustworthy than adults. And kids, as far as Stannis had observed, liked the Captain, and developed sympathy for Mooners. So, mission accomplished and onto the next. Hark at him, he was starting to sound like Max.

+++

Max was in the groundcar stripping off behind the shaded windows when Stannis's wristcom buzzed softly.

'Problem?' Harp reached for the wipes.

'Not really.' Stannis frowned, diverted from the view. 'Centre Eight say the crowd outside is so thick they're worried about you being mobbed. They suggest we use a delivery entrance that's out of sight.'

Harp pulled the fresh shirt over his head. 'Not unknown. You got that, Tima?'

'Ser.' The woman in front tapped the controls. 'Logging a new route, ETA now plus six minutes. Should I confirm that with the Centre?'

'Please.' Harp tucked the shirt in. 'Wonder why they called you instead of Security'.

Stannis offered the jacket. 'I checked in when we finished the first session. Maybe they just hit reply?'

'That would do it.' Jacket on, fastened, fingers through hair; no cosmetists required for a live appearance; take a deep breath. Another. The car's windows were one way right now so he'd just see the light brighten when they got near. Tima was muttering, probably to the escort behind, then spoke louder. 'Almost there, ser. I'll get out first as usual.'

'Mm.' The basement access had swallowed them, it felt gloomier. Harp had never used a delivery entrance before; Harpans used the front, and didn't always see much of that in his experience, not past Security and gawkers. Curious, he peered forward. This one was basement-level, with bays either side, some closed. Presumably storage. Their entry lay straight ahead, a raised platform with a wide door, not unlike an Orbital warehouse. Yes, a small door in the big one was opening and a man, then a woman, were emerging.

Tima stopped the car, checked the surroundings then stepped out. The woman above stepped to the edge of the platform. Harp hit his door release, aware Stannis was exiting the other side and other bodies exiting behind them, moving up to flank him, same as always. Stannis rounded the car, then stopped.

Harp looked back. 'Forgot something, Stannis?'

'No.' The man lunged forward.

Weapons fire crackled. Harp saw Tima falling, vaguely registered the male dropping to the platform. His Security, behind him, were returning fire, pulses flaring. Something burned his shoulder. Stannis barrelled into him and knocked him sideways and he felt a second impact lower down as Stannis floored him. Winded. Move, fool. Damn World gravity, it wasn't helping.

'Damn it, Max, stay down.'

Who said that? Medics always seemed to say that when he woke. Had he been hurt again? His side hurt. And his shoulder. Somebody was pushing at him, that hurt too. Then it got darker, then the dark took over.

+++

A jolt woke him up. 'Stay still, ser.'

See, they *always* said that. He wasn't still though, he was moving. On his stomach? 'Wha?'

'Easy, Captain.' This time he recognised Daichi's voice; he always sounded patient. 'You're en route to the Mansion.'

Medical. 'Tima?'

'She's behind us, ser. Not fatal.'

'Oh.' Good, good. He tried to think. 'Stannis.'

'Ser Mella is also unhurt, ser. We can discuss the rest when you're fitter.'

Seemed like a plan. Harp felt his eyelids droop, had Daichi given him something? 'Bett'r let…' Crip, he'd forgot what he was going to say…

+++

Harp got back to his apartment four days later. Four days stuck in regen. The Mansion's Chief Medic, a man called Akio Harpan – naturally – had remarked 'Maybe they'd best keep a tank reserved for him'; seemed to think Harp got shot at purely to inconvenience his profession. But Harp much preferred gruff sarcasm to the gush of sympathy he was getting now, from other cousins and the public. Inevitably word had got out. Apparently his office was deluged with messages he "wasn't to worry about". And gifts. Feeling grumpy, he'd told Daichi to send those to Moon Aid. Result: Daichi said the gifts *increased*, the only good in all this uproar.

Maxil Snr had "dropped by" to confirm Harp was still alive. Emika had sent orders to "be more vaccing careful". He'd even had a brief visit from Feldin's kids. The boy had been wide eyed at the sling he'd been bullied into. The woman had raised sculpted eyebrows, like she figured he was faking! Awkward, but they hadn't stayed long. Maybe Feldin made them put in an appearance.

Uncle Feldin and Mz Chan had scheduled an hour to update him, and he now appreciated how much the Mansion was shielded from outside eyes and ears, human and tec.

When he hadn't heard from Stannis, no update, nothing, he'd worried Stannis had been hurt after all. Right now, he almost wished he had been. That message – false of course, they knew that now – had gone to Stannis not Security. A fact Mz Chan considered damning.

'But he was in touch shortly before.'

Mz Chan didn't waver. 'The attackers knew Mella's code. And he didn't alert Security.'

'Because *Tima* made contact.' Neither Mz Chan nor his uncle looked convinced but they were wrong. Weren't they? 'I want to see him.'

Mz Chan looked stubborn. 'He has been informed he is not required till you feel well enough to resume your schedule. I have people on him but so far he hasn't spent much time in public, and his only calls appear to have been social, or to his broker. We are still investigating his other accounts.'

'Well, now I'm fit.' Harp stared back. 'Eda, please invite Stannis here at his earliest convenience.'

'Invitation issued, Captain.' A pause. 'Confirmed received.' Another pause. 'Ser Stannis is on his way, Captain.'

'Thank you.'

Mz Chan looked stiffer, Feldin startled. 'Max, for you own safety…'

'I'm sure Mz Chan and Daichi have done their jobs, Uncle, but I'd prefer to handle it now. Have Stannis shown up here when he arrives, will you, Mz Chan?' It was a struggle to sound so calm. He didn't want to believe their expressions. Didn't want to believe… but damn it, how was he supposed to cope in this maze he was in now, if he couldn't trust his instincts? When sometimes it felt like they were the only things left he *could* trust?

+++

Feldin and Mz Chan were gone at his request but only after he'd agreed to Daichi's presence. Not being a complete fool, he'd told Eda to record the meeting. And to put a block on any other surveillance, including Mansion Security. Let them bitch all they wanted, for once he wanted to *know* his life was his own. Daichi would report back what he could. Later though. Eda had just confirmed she'd shut down Daichi's wristcom too.

Childish? Maybe, but he was no longer sure anyone here on World was being completely honest with him, so why not? He'd been patient. He'd ascribed his growing doubts to Maxil being cautious, to Feldin's concern for his welfare. But no longer. If his gut was all he had he'd damn well go with that.

Daichi preceded Stannis into Harp's lounge. If he knew his com had gone down it didn't show on his face. Yet.

Stannis's eyes flashed to the sling, but his face stayed equally blank. Harp told himself that was natural; the man must realise this meeting was decisive.

'Stannis, come in.' He'd promised not to get up, to take it easy. 'Caffee, yes? Eda?'

'Yes, Captain.' The server hatch in here slid open seconds later. Eda was second guessing him again, something she was getting increasingly skilled at. Presumably from accumulated data. Harp wondered suddenly how much data Security had accumulated on him, and how much of it might be from Eda; something to look into later?

When Daichi didn't move Stannis collected the tray, and maybe relaxed a fraction as he poured and served. Daichi on the other hand stood stiffer. Oh enough.

Harp took the glass, still awkward using the wrong hand. 'Thanks. Any poison in it?' Stannis choked, head jerking round to face him. The fellow was a player, probably a consummate liar, but... Harp grinned. 'No point edging round it, is there?'

'No.' Stannis's whole body sagged, not much but the change was discernible. 'And no, I didn't set you up, even if no one believes me.' He faced Harp, and waited.

'So why did you push me?'

Stannis huffed. 'I told –'

'Please.'

'All right. Again. It was the people. The woman was dressed down, like low level admin, and the man moved wrong. And we'd checked the head teacher's file and it didn't look like him either. It struck me it was his moment in the spotlight, y'know? But the guy didn't rush to greet you, and no one does that. I just knew something was wrong.' Stannis looked defeated. 'I know how it looks, I know I was too late, but –'

'You jumped at me.'

'To pull you back till they checked things out. Only then the woman started shooting and you were hit, and hit again before I got you on the floor. And I wasn't touched, was I?'

'I'm glad.' Harp remembered to drink.

'You are?' The look this time was pure cynic.

'Of course. Drink your caffee, we have a lot of rescheduling to do.'

If possible, Daichi's face got even blanker, but Stannis's hand shook caffee down his fingers. 'You believe me?'

Harp looked him in the eyes. 'Yes.'

'I.' Stannis put the glass down, wiping at his fingers. 'I don't see why.'

'Well, there's been no poison in the caffee so far.' When Stannis stared Harp went on gently, 'But there could have been, any day you chose. So are you OK with coming back to work, or would you prefer a less dangerous occupation? I could arrange it.'

Stannis laughed, more snort than laugh; it startled Daichi. 'Leave, now? When it's getting interesting?'

Harp smiled back. 'Eda, screens please.' One entire wall refigured. 'Have you eaten?'

Stannis seemed to find the question more important than it sounded. 'I could eat.'

'Eda, some rollups or something we can eat while we work? Daichi? You too?'

'Not for me, ser, thank you.'

'Eda?'

'I am placing the order, Captain.'

'OK. Bring up all the cancelled appointments, plus the next ten-day's schedule.' Harp leaned back to ease his aching shoulder, feeling better. 'Let's see what we can rearrange.'

+++

Stannis left with the spring back in his steps, Daichi showing him as far as the door, where another Security would escort him down to the ground floor. Daichi returned, looking particularly patient. 'My wristcom has just reactivated, Captain.'

'Mm.' Harp's attention stayed on the screens; the new schedule was going to cause some protests.

'Captain, is this wise?' Daichi glanced at his wrist. Harp guessed his wristcom was back. 'Excuse me, Mz Chan is calling.'

'Of course, go report, I'm fine.'

'Ser.' Daichi hesitated. 'That appearance was almost the first chance Ser Mella got to intervene, outside the Mansion.'

'True.' Harp shifted to study Daichi. 'Point out to Mz Chan that Stannis knew he took a risk working for me. Knew he'd be investigated more than ever before. That, as he'd described it, doors would slam if he was ever fired. Apart from all that, I don't believe Stannis so stupid he wouldn't make darn sure he wasn't the obvious suspect if I was attacked again. If he felt he needed to be involved, he'd have made sure he *did* get injured.'

10

The call from Maxil Snr came that same evening, at a time Harp was aware the older man was scheduled to attend some public performance. Looked like Harp's activities, no doubt faithfully reported to Mz Chan, had put Maxil off being sociable. But when Security passed Harp into the Founder's apartment he didn't look it.

'Max, come in boy. How are you? No, a real answer?'

'I'm tired but OK, ser.'

'First day back to work is always the worst, eh?' Han, who looked more clerk than Maxil's Personal Head of Security – as opposed to Mz Chan's House-Head-of, which he guessed made her the overall boss – placed a tray on the table before them then left. 'A snack to tide you over till dinner?'

'Thank you, Ser.' Substantial snack; looked like dinner might be a while.

'Now, about Mella.'

'Ser, Mz Chan is playing safe, nothing wrong with that, but she's choosing suspicion over facts. Ser Mella would need a very substantial reason to support House Regis in anything. In fact, he has more reason to keep me alive than see me dead, now more than ever. He knows if there's any real cause to suspect him, he's ruined. His best case scenario would be to flee World, almost certainly leaving behind the mother he's supported all these years. It does not compute, ser.'

'So you're basing your decisions on logic.'

'No, I'm demonstrating the logic for you, and Security. I'm sticking with my original assessment.'

Maxil sighed. 'Very well, your decision.' The "for now" didn't need saying. 'But it's clear these attempts on your life aren't over. Your uncle and I have been talking over our options.'

'Ser?'

'Security is active, but the digging takes time. So, when an opportunity presented itself we thought why not.'

Maxil pushed the tray at Harp. 'Eat. That's better. You've lost weight in regen. The Kraic have sent an invitation. They'd like you to visit.'

'The nearest aliens?' Harp didn't choke, not quite, but on the upside chewing gave him time to recover. 'Er, why, ser?'

'I gather they want to thank you for coming to their aid. Some medal or the like. Yes, I know. The navy. Duty. But you *were* the spearhead, that's public knowledge. And you are a Harpan. So from their point of view you embody both our military aid and a new political climate.'

Hungry or not, Harp's appetite died.

'More, it gives us a valid reason to remove you from the public eye for a while, and give Security more time to uncover the threat.' Maxil rubbed his hands together. 'It couldn't have come at a better moment.'

Harp's opinion wasn't repeatable. Not to mention, 'But would I be any safer there, ser?'

'Frankly, yes. The Kraic have a reputation for honest dealing that makes them a rarity.' The famous smile. 'You should get on well there.'

Harp hesitated, then went for being equally blunt. 'You mean you figure I'll cope with aliens no worse than I do with Worlders.'

Maxil's lips twitched, but Harp, crazy thought, was getting used to his grandfather's "tells" – in approval. 'Quite the opposite, boy. You're a sight less insular than most of us, plus they're very keen to meet you, and right now it's useful.'

'Politics.' He knew his mouth had twisted. Politics seemed to be where he and his new grandfather parted company. Maybe trust as well?

Maxil Snr didn't seem affected. 'Love it or hate it, boy, it's always with us. It's survival. And you'll be better off there than here.'

He'd said you'll. Not you'd.

'When, ser?'

'The *Defiant* docks in four days, ready to leave in eight.'

Defiant? He supposed that was some consolation; at least he might be with folk he could actually trust.

+++

Or not.

Maxil Snr had vetoed Stannis going with him. Instead he had another cousin, out of Diplomatic, Alin Harpan-Lee, an aide to somebody in the Assembly. More politics. Harp hadn't met the man before because, as he informed Harp on arrival, "his normal role prevented mere casual socialising".

The Harpan connection went back five generations, a pretty distant relationship. The man was in his middle forties, slightly overweight, his not-so-Harpan mid-brown hair thinning. He was 'versed in etiquette and good at kissing ass, according to his Senator' as Feldin chose to put it in a private briefing. Feldin was starting to feel more related than Maxil. 'He's Family of sorts, experienced and organised, I'm told', which Harp reflected, at the time, was what he likely needed. He'd rather have Stannis, but beggars couldn't be choosers, and he couldn't blame the new guy.

After one day of Lee in his office, he'd already reversed that opinion. For Family, read pompous. For experienced, read lecturing. For organised... the guy wore two wristcoms, on different coloured bracelets, consulted both before answering the simplest question, and phrased his "suggestions" as if anything else would just *prove* the farmboy a fool. A complaint that Lee couldn't access Harp's private files was the last straw.

'My private files are just that, Ser Lee. I will thank you to remember it.' And no, leaving off the double House name wasn't accidental; it was clearly time he mastered what Emika called The Art of the Snub. 'I see no reason for you to access anything outside my rescheduling issues. Which reminds me, I notice you have removed Sergeant Hissack from tomorrow's appointments list and substituted a Senator Kloss. Please reverse that.'

'Surely not, Captain.' Lee even managed to make his rank an insult. 'A Senator's request obviously takes precedence over some enlisted person's.'

'To the Senator, perhaps, but not to me. If you've already contacted either party please do so again, immediately. We wouldn't want to embarrass the Senator by turning him away at the Mansion door, would we?' There, manipulative *and* high-faluting, not bad if he did say so himself. All the hours with real-Harpans, not to mention Mz Chan and Daichi, were finally paying off!

Hissack's arrival next day, trying to hide her nerves behind her well-tailored uniform, was such a relief he probably beamed at her. Though she hesitated again when Lee escorted her through to Harp's office.

'Hiss, it's good to see you. How's Navy Legal suiting you? Thank you, Lee. No calls, please.' Hissack glanced at Lee's stiff back as he departed, then at Harp, eyes narrowed. 'Sit down anywhere. No, I don't like him. Caffee?' Harp made for the server panel. 'Eda?'

'Coming, Captain.' The panel opened as he reached it. Caffee and some snacks appeared. By the time he set the tray down Hissak had recovered.

'Well, you always did speak your mind.' Her mouth curved upward. 'When you said anything at all.'

Harp sighed. 'You have no idea how nice it is to do that.' An eyebrow rose. He grinned. 'I'm trusting your legal training will regard anything I say as privileged information. Do you have what I asked for?'

'Yes. I had to tell my CO why I wanted it.'

'Your CO being your mother.'

'Mm.' Perhaps she twitched a little.

'Oh, I'm not complaining, I'm the poster child for nepotism, and I'm sure your mother values any Family connection.'

'Wow.' Hissack's glass stopped halfway to her mouth. 'Are you turning devious on me?'

'I'm turning Harpan.' Harp set down his glass, leaned forward. 'Sometimes I don't like it much, but... So what can you tell me?'

An hour later they gripped hands like the friends he found they still were. Hiss said she would show herself out before his next appointment arrived. Then looked back. 'This Lee fellow, he's Diplomatic you said.'

'Yeah.'

'Why didn't you get all this from him?'

Harp stayed honest. 'Because I don't trust him not to pick and choose what he passes on. The brass want him along, and he thinks I'm an idiot.'

'Ah.' Hiss smiled. 'How long has he been here?'

'Two days.' And the thought of being stuck with him a lot longer was already darkening his mood.

'Well, at least you haven't flattened him.'

'Yet.' Harp laughed. 'Will you defend me if I do?'

'Defend a Harpan? Who'd say no?' She left still smiling.

It was a push to clear his desk before departure; Stannis worked a lot faster than Lee. But Stannis was still under what Mz Chan called "discreet surveillance", and informed Harp's absence was a naval mission. Harp figured the man could read between those lines fine, but that meant Moon Aid would be treading water, a phrase he understood now as marching in place. Stannis'd been in the middle of researching home-grown science types, said he'd almost built a shortlist of candidates who could search for the cause of Moon's troubles, or at least ways to improve conditions. That would have to wait now. Feldin had agreed to oversee the everyday operations though, so any minor problems would be dealt with. He hoped. Cos worrying sure wouldn't change anything.

All too soon he was packed and heading out. Hadn't done his own packing of course, or made his own travel arrangements, but thankfully he and Mz Chan *had* managed to stop the media parade Lee had intended, so at least his departure was discreet. The Navy's dockside checks weren't casual, even for Captain Harpan and party, but where Lee chose to complain at the holdups Harp felt reassured. The Family weren't advertising where he was going so the 'casts only chattered about another tour of duty on *Defiant*. If only.

There was still speculation of course, but for now it didn't look like anyone was expecting miracles from the barely House-trained Harpan who, as Hiss had said, was no way diplomatic. He still thought he'd have been better with the smooth-talking Stannis than this clinging, irritating cousin.

A final glance round the dock, habit nowadays to keep an eye on his surroundings. Damn, that looked like Stannis for a moment, only then the distant figure slouched away, the clumsy movement totally unlike him. Wishful thinking, that was all. Imagination. Suddenly the dockside felt much darker, lonelier, for all he was surrounded. He tried to shake the feeling off. Stannis knew they were still good.

Or did he? Crip, he should have contacted Stannis again before he left, not followed orders, even Maxil's. Stannis deserved to know he still had the job, and Harp's trust, whatever Security thought. Yes, he'd send some reassurance from *Defiant*.

Navy shuttle, so no obvious frills. Harp's mood, lightened when Daichi manoeuvred Lee into a forward seat with the crowd, felt almost mellow by the time they neared *Defiant*, her matte-grey, corrugated hull impervious to sunshine. He'd worn the pants-tee-jacket combo that declared him navy, one of them; not civ. Not brass. He doubted they'd accept it but he'd made the statement. And enjoyed the contrast when Ser Lee turned up on dockside in a fancy suit that screamed civilian-and-entitled. And OK, enjoyed the disbelieving looks some navy ratings gave it.

Daichi was unmistakeable of course, as were his team of six. The ratings' faces showed that too.

Now *Defiant* filled his porthole. Red light; docking. What would it be like, returning?

Green light; the umbilical connected. Harp stood up and tugged his jacket straight. About to find out.

Navy guard at the inner hatch. He chose to regard it as being there cos *Defiant's* captain and XO were in attendance. And Ngow, that was worth an inner smile. He gave them the appropriate brisk, navy nod. They returned it. Harp introduced Daichi, then Lee. Daichi handed off the files on himself, Lee and the Security team; navy liked to know their passengers. Harp wondered how much Daichi's was watered down; he hadn't managed to dig very deep himself.

Harp was back on G deck in the fancy cabin, Daichi and two of his people next door. Lee had been given an apparently empty two-berth junior-officer cupboard not far aft and the rest of the team had one of the officer wardrooms, turned into a dorm come armoury. No one objected to the ordnance cases they shipped in.

Now the welcome dinner – dress uniform – was over too. The captain and XO were still inclined to be formal but Ngow had got more relaxed, almost paternal. If Harp was clever he could surely find an hour for himself now. First send Lee off duty for the night, which meant assuring the idiot he could undress himself and put his uniform down the right chute. Inspired, he told Lee it was vital the man updated himself on ship's regs, especially the safety procedures, attack protocols, evac manoeuvres and such. Oh yeah, that did the trick.

So finally, alone time. Harp exchanged the pants for a one-piece and yes, put the worn clothes down the laundry chute. Then ventured out of corridors reserved for brass and VIPs into *Defiant's* forward bowels. Ngow's presence should mean he could catch three steers with one net; Yentl, Del – and Hamud?

One wish fulfilled; mission Flashback was in the J deck mess, and Hamud was still in its Marine detachment. All three comrades gaped at him when he appeared in the doorway. Naturally Del recovered first. 'Well, if it isn't our very own hero! Slumming, are we?' Yentl followed, meeting Harp halfway. At the Marine's table, Hamud hesitated until Harp locked eyes then joined them. The four of them ended up in a quiet corner with caffees they'd fetched for themselves, like normal people. By then the others had relaxed; maybe he was getting the hang of putting folk at ease. Relaxed enough to pump him.

'So, a stopover at Kraic IV.' Del waited.

'Yeah, cos of our help. You're going as well.' If he had to pull Family-rank to make it so. They'd been on *Raptor* as well, and if he could co-opt Ham too he damn well would. He'd had enough of being surrounded by new faces. Seeing Hissack again had reminded him how good it was to *know* the folk who had his back, and be able to say what he really thought. He wanted that again, even for a few weeks. Even, Hamud willing, to get combat-fitter now he was recovered, before someone attacked him again. Kraic IV might be duty, but maybe his *Defiant*-time could still be furlough?

11

'Ow.' Harp picked himself up, again. 'I know I said not to go easy, but…'

By the wall, Hendriks winced, that new stripe still shiny on his shipsuit; turn your back a second and he'd made corporal. Hamud – not promoted early – grinned, but either he'd bulked up or Harp was more out of shape than he'd thought. He was going with bulked up; he'd spent an hour in the Mansion's gym almost every morning since he'd got there. Plus Ham was taking his request very seriously. Two, two-hour sessions a day seriously. With permission from his own CO and *Defiant's* commander. The newscasts had aired some of those attempts on Harp's life; the navy didn't like their toys broken. The fact he was sparring with Ham and not a Marine sergeant only proved Family clout had got Harp what *he* wanted. Not that a Marine instructor hadn't supervised the early sessions.

Ham circled again. 'Too many fancy dinners, that's your problem. Or too much dancing instead of fighting?'

Harp sighed; he'd concede the dinners, they were part of the job, but, 'I don't dance.'

'What, with all those eager women?' Ham feinted left. Harp wasn't fooled. Ham backed off. 'We see the vids, y'know.'

Hendriks laughed. Ouch. Some of those had looked even more embarrassing than he'd thought, especially the one where some fool woman bared her breasts. In real life Security had got there so fast he hadn't actually noticed, but a camra got it. Daichi thought a newscast had arranged it.

Still, dancing was a charge he could refute. Dance and talk at the same time? Not going there, ever. 'I'm no good at it, and I'm always working the programme at affairs like that.'

'Moon Aid?' Hendriks stopped whatever he was up to on his wristcom. 'The holds were full for our donation run. But we haven't done another, so I thought...'

'Using *Defiant* the first time was my uncle's idea, for the camras, but she's hardly a cargo hauler. Since then we've found a mix of volunteers and surplus space on smaller ships.' Harp's lips lifted. 'Civ ships soon sussed out both Orbitals give Moon Aid cargoes preference, which means *theirs* moves faster with it.'

'Clever. Your idea?

'Partly.' Automatic answer. Habit now. To own it publicly belied the farmboy image. 'Once they realised the benefits most started offering us hold-space.'

Ham abandoned training, tossed him water. 'We spent a few days on Moon Orbital, it looks a sight better now than last time.'

'Mm.' Harp drank, uncomfortably aware he probably knew more about that than they did. Though in Hendriks' case one could never be sure. 'I'd like to go back if I can. Maybe after we're done on Kraic IV.' Except it wasn't on his schedule. He figured he could override Lee's objections, but that still left *Defiant* command. He doubted he had enough clout to divert the navy from some other mission.

Hendriks seemed to be thinking along similar lines. 'Well, it's on the way back, as much as anywhere is out here. And you do have influence, so why *not* use it?'

But that remark reminded Harp of something else entirely, and he figured asking them would be less embarrassing than anybody else here. After all they knew he hadn't had much real education. 'Yeah, all right, you say it's on the way, but I'm not too clear how far we're talking.'

'Huh?' Ham raised an eyebrow, an impressive trick that Harp had always meant to copy.

'Well, see, *Defiant* – *Raptor* – was my first real look at vacuum. So I didn't know much.'

'Ours too,' Ham pointed out.

'But you both had years of file learning. Me, I sort of muddled through the navigation stuff in Basic, picked up just enough to scrape a pass.' And most of that from listening to Hendriks. 'But I pretty much gave up on the rest. I mean I was never going to be bridge material like Hendriks, was I?'

Ham snorted but he nodded understanding; Harp-that-was had infinitely lower expectations. 'OK, so what aren't you clear about?'

'Getting from World to Kraic IV. Well, getting anywhere really. Basic was all about how to be *on* a ship. Then when I got here it was all about *Raptor*. I get the feeling I missed out on a huge amount of other stuff.' He saw that Hendriks' mouth was open. 'So I'm right?'

'Yeah.' Hendriks winced. 'A lot, right Ham?'

Ham frowned. 'You might have got more nav than I did. Marine grunts get other stuff. But yeah, we got the basics.'

'Right.' Harp cut to the chase. 'I never had time to even think about how *Defiant* got us from A to B. I never even knew how long it took us to get to Kraic space. But I'm pretty sure it wasn't as long as I'd expect. So how?'

They ended up sat on the training mat in a corner of the gym, about as private as it got short of going up to Harp's fancy cabin – not something he wanted to shove in their faces. Hendriks subbed as teacher this time. 'OK, so you know about FTL, right?'

Ah, starting at the bottom. Well, the guy had that right. 'I know ships in space sometimes go faster than light, yes, but that doesn't mean I understand how.'

'All right. My teacher explained it as skipping over gravity.' Hendriks considered. 'We know planets have gravity.'

'Yeah.'

'And you've heard of dark matter?' When Harp nodded, doubtfully, the smaller man continued, 'Well, the theory is there's gravity out here too, between planets. Just not so obvious. So a ship can skate along gravity waves, like on air currents.'

'OK, but.'

'Yeah, but that would still take years, centuries even. Except the waves aren't flat like a road, they're sort of folded up. Here, pass me your towel.' Hendriks laid the towel flat between them. 'So here's what you probably think of as the space we're travelling, right? Maybe old ships still might, only it's not like that now, it's more like… this.' He ruffled the cloth, so it made irregular humps and hollows, like hills and valleys. 'Now, if we were on a road we'd have to follow all these ups and downs, yeah?'

His audience nodded, Ham too.

'But we can hop over the dips. They discovered that even before World was settled, so everyone takes it for granted now. And that.' Hendriks grinned triumphantly. 'Makes a trip a lot shorter, and a lot quicker. Add in pulsetec, which the navy has now, and there we are; no more generation-ships like OldEarth stories, not even cryo chambers any longer other than emergencies or really long-range exploration.' Hendriks saw their faces. 'Hey, World may have a stay-at-home mentality, but some might want expansion. Odds are NewEarth always did. I never have worked out how they never found us.'

Ham shook his head. 'Where d'you get all that "NewEarth" stuff? I'm sure it wasn't in our history files.'

'I like to know things.' Hendriks tried to look modest, as usual failed. 'It's not hard, even to track some old NewEarth stuff, once you figure where to look. But does that help, Harp? I can send you a couple text files if you like.'

'As long as it's for dunces.' Harp grinned, despite some qualms. What exactly had Henriks been digging up? Though he didn't seem so dumb if others didn't know stuff either. He was still ignorant, but maybe not alone? 'Yeah, please. People forget I don't understand stuff, y'know?'

Hendriks still looked solemn but at least Ham smiled. 'Did you have to give him a chance to show off? I spend half my downtime trying to take him down a peg now he's been promoted ahead of me.'

'As if that'll last.' Hendriks rolled his eyes. 'Like to hear your last evaluation?'

'You…? Didn't we talk about stuff like that?' Ham

tried for outraged but the result looked more like, well, constipated. Harp fought off laughter, knowing Ham was right. Talented or not, Hendriks was playing with a universe of trouble, uncovering things maybe not meant to be found?

Ham threw up his hands. 'See what I have to deal with?' A glare that promised dire warnings later. Hendriks' smile didn't promise he would heed them.

Ham, who knew enough to choose his battles, maybe trusted fortune more than Harp did, shook his head and changed the subject. 'So the old Harp's still playing catchup, figures. What's it like being the new one?'

'Complicated,' Harp said grimly, picking up his towel.

This time Hamud chuckled. 'I'll bet.' He too headed for the showers.

+++

Feldin leaned in closer to his screens. In his own office, Maxil Snr settled back but the third screen showed Mz Chan stayed militantly upright while they studied what she'd sent them. 'The images from the dock weren't perfect, but Ser Mella seems worryingly familiar with the location of the security camras. Still, the operator was awake, noticed the Captain stopped and looked, and zeroed in on the direction, otherwise we might have missed him. You'll notice the slouch is only evident while he's on Navy territory; he straightens up two blocks into civilian areas.'

Feldin watched as a clearer shot from later camras appeared. 'But he didn't go near Max, or the shuttle?'

'No, ser. It doesn't look like he made any attempt, just watched the Captain leave. But it's suspicious.'

'Agreed.' Maxil Snr finally joined in. 'We obviously need to keep Mella away from Max.'

Feldin shifted. 'I doubt Max will agree. He still likes the man.'

'Humph. Then you'll have to explain why it's the only safe solution.'

'Yes, Ser.' Feldin pursed his lips. 'But not while Max is away, he's got enough to deal with at the moment. And he won't react well to us acting behind his back.'

'Very well, but make it as soon as Max is back? Mz Chan, make discreet arrangements so we can terminate Mella's contract whenever we're ready. Nothing that could be used against us, any separation payments made in full, no black marks on his record.' He glanced to Feldin. 'That would sit better with Max, yes? Who knows, by the time the boy gets back maybe he'll see Ser Lee is the better candidate anyway.'

'Ser.' Mz Chan's expression didn't alter. 'With that in mind I'd suggest we run a deeper check on Ser Lee too. His Senate file is thinner than I like.'

Max Snr nodded. 'Good. Let us know what you find but don't end Mella's contract till you hear more. I don't want Mella trying to reach out to Max for help. The captain needs his mind on the Kraic.'

'Ser.'

When Maxil nodded all three closed the link, discussion ended.

Feldin wondered if he was the only one wasn't sure they were right.

+++

Back on *Defiant*, Harp declared he needed 'a snack'. Ham laughed. They ended up in familiar territory. J20 was Hamud's mess, Harp still had clearance and they pretty much smuggled Hendriks in as Harp's guest, Harp being Ngow's golden boy, as Hamud put it. Hendriks went from pleased to disappointed once they got there. Naturally Hamud noticed. 'What did you expect, flashing lasers and armed guards on the caffee? Don't tell me you haven't hooked into our surveillance systems.'

Hendriks morphed to peeved. 'I haven't broken it. Yet.'

'Hallelujah, there's actually one reg you haven't broken.'

Was Hamud serious? Harp would have dug deeper, but

Del and Yentl sauntered in and saw him so they ended up together, Del and Yentl eating with him, Ham and Hendriks settling for caffee.

Del looked at Harp's full plate and whistled. 'Aren't you eating with the Execs?'

'Yes, but I've been sparring, need replacement carbs to tide me over.' Harp picked up his fork and dug in.

'No change there then. I think almost the first words we heard from you was "I'm starving".'

Harp shrugged, it was easier than admitting he ate even more lately; that the formal meals in the officer's mess – three fancy courses – wouldn't cut it for him even if he wasn't training. He suspected he wasn't the only Harpan with an outsize appetite, but that was another thing nobody was talking about.

'Seriously though.' Del threw himself back in his chair. 'Are you likely to be in any danger on Kraic IV?'

'The consensus is I was more at risk on World,' Harp said between bites, 'and Kraic IV will be a safer distance.'

Hendriks nodded. 'It'll be easier to spot other humans, that's for sure.'

A subject Harp had been wondering about but Lee hadn't so far considered important enough to impart wisdom on. 'How much human traffic does Kraic's orbital see, d'you know?'

'Not much. I checked.' Hendriks looked smug. 'Their Orbital gets maybe thirty or so human ships a year, all ours or alien, bar a couple of interesting strays that have stumbled our way I *think* were human. Their year's about a third longer than ours too, and I don't think they import much from any other non-Kraic sources anyway. Most of their recorded traffic is with Kraic Prime.' This time no one enquired how he'd found out.

'You found out that much.' Harp kept his voice down. 'What, exactly?

Hendriks failed casual. 'Oh, that NewEarth's almost certainly still out there. Though there's no record of contact.'

Ham's brows lowered. 'You think they're Isolationists?'

'Maybe, perhaps we just don't have anything in common, like the Kraic didn't, till the pirates. Or *we* didn't, till the pirates. Hence this Kraic visit, as their planet's nearer? I mean, NewEarth's probably so far it might as well not exist, and even if we can now find the Kraic we can't talk to them.'

'No talk, at all, ever?'

'Sounds like it.' Hendriks missed his own joke. 'Far as I can tell they only make clicking noises.' Which matched the extremely short vid Lee *had* shown him. 'But those seem to signal emotional response, not information, and Navy Intel hasn't managed to get much of a read on those anyway.'

'Lee says they barely pass the bar as sentient.' Harp frowned. 'But Hissack –'

'You've seen Hissack?' Ham's cup hovered. 'How is our Legal brat, still on World?'

'She's fine, likes it in Legal except she was bitching it's keeping her grounded. I asked her to give me what she could on the Kraic, it seemed sensible.'

Ham grunted. 'After you met Lee, you mean.'

Hendriks grinned. 'You figured Hiss would ask her mother and come up with the real deal.'

'Both.' Harp swallowed. 'Some of it agrees with Lee's intel.'

'But not all?' Del's eyes brightened too. 'Tell all, Captain Harpan.'

Harp figured if he wanted them with him on Kraic IV they deserved to know as much as he did, so he set his fork down. 'We all know what the Kraic look like, yeah? As Hendriks said, they make clicking noises but don't talk so we'll communicate via their translation units; flat, lozenge shaped screenpads wrapped round where our necks would be.'

Hendriks cut in. 'Kraic Prime manufact them, don't they?'

'Yeah, and Hiss said they've indicated they'd be willing to sell now, to anyone interested in talking to them or humans. Hiss's data said they're simple but effective, and cheap enough several other species are latching onto them.' Farmboy Harp was still getting his head round the "several other species" part she'd tossed so lightly, yet another "fact" all Worlders seemed aware of he was slowly learning, and another gap he'd have to study up on, later. 'Humans talk, the units translate, then – we don't seem to know how – convert the Kraic response back to human Standard on the screens. Hiss said it sounds complicated but all the reports say it works like a charm.'

'Huh.' Del studied Harp. 'So you won't have any trouble communicating.'

'I don't think so, no. I'm just not so clear about their customs,' Harp admitted. 'Lee's drowning himself in big words, but I don't think he knows much, and Legal rate them a sight more intelligent than he does – think the trade contracts they've studied are everything we could wish for. I got the impression they'd expect any loopholes to be human error not Kraic.'

Ham pulled a face. 'So the Kraic are, like, alien lawyers? I'm starting to see why you're worried.'

'Nah.' Del waved away concern. 'You're the honoured guest, you can be twice as stupid as any merch or rating can and still get away with it.'

'Except I'm supposed to rely on Lee to guide me through it all, and according to Lee we've only ever met the brightest and best.'

Ham looked unimpressed but Del and Yentl straightened and for once the quiet Yentl voiced their obvious reaction. 'I'm not sure you should rely on Ser Lee's opinions. By all accounts the Kraic are very private, but if we only see the small contingent who man their Orbital, that doesn't mean the rest are primitive.'

'Agreed.' Harp sighed. 'But they reckon some of the Kraic brass will come up to the Orbital to meet me. Brass who've maybe never met another human?'

'Wow.' Hendriks's turn to comment. 'So you have no real idea what you're walking into?'

'No. I'm worried I'll insult someone important without knowing.'

Hendriks huffed. 'We must know something about their world, even if it's hearsay.'

'It's got a lot of cloud cover, and trees,' Harp said glumly, 'which means what scans the Navy have managed generally only show...'

'A lot of trees,' the others chorused.

Except Hendriks. 'I could –'

'No!' Both Harp and Hamud cut him off. Harp adding, 'I do not, repeat not, want you creating an interplanetary incident while I'm in the middle of it. Are we clear?'

'Wow, you really are a Harpan, aren't you.' Hendriks sighed. 'All right. Ser. Message received and understood.'

Harp prayed he meant it.

+++

Defiant journeyed on. Harp took to avoiding Lee whenever possible, aided by the inestimable Daichi, though nothing was said. Helping the *Raptor* tecs refine their new sim helped, plus time below with former comrades.

Feeling guilty, he also found time to message Stannis, on Navy com, and probably recorded. He couldn't very well say everyone else distrusted the guy so much they'd kept him away so he said he was sorry they hadn't got together in all his rush to report back to the *Defiant* – cos he had to remember Stannis wasn't allowed to know any more than the newscasts – and he'd send an alert to warn Stannis of his return to normal life. He hoped Stannis would enjoy the break, treat it as a paid holiday, civ word for leave. There; if nothing else his employer felt better.

Alongside all that, *Defiant* skipped across Hendriks' gravity waves or whatever and suddenly they were on final approach to Kraic IV. When *Defiant's* general com announced there were six days to go Lee took to inspecting every item of clothing in Harp's locker, declared them all unsuitable and badgered the ship's tailor – they had an actual human tailor up in officer country to avoid those annoying little imperfections in the processor stock. Lee wanted four new outfits for Harp, and four for himself, all featuring the Harpan red and gold.

By then Harp had had enough. He told Lee he didn't need anything, then found Daichi and told him to make sure the order was cancelled, with his apologies. 'If Lee wants a new wardrobe he's not ordering it on my credit or the Family's. And I'm not meeting the Kraic in fancy-dress!'

Daichi smiled, slightly. 'If I may ask, ser, what do you intend to wear?'

'My uniform. The Kraic invited a Captain and that's what they're getting.' Even if he had to fake it.

'Excellent choice, ser.'

He sounded so like Eda Harp's annoyance melted. Guilt replaced it. 'I'm sorry, Daichi. I've left you to deal with Ser Lee a lot more than I should, haven't I?'

'With respect, ser, ensuring your life is trouble free *is* my job, in whatever form is necessary. And I think Ser Lee now understands his role is that of a member of staff, not a principal.'

'You think?' Harp pulled himself together. 'He's what we've got, Daichi, so I guess we'll have to make the best of him. I just don't get why they picked *him*.'

That was still on his mind when he spoke with Feldin four days later – what he figured was a final briefing – past the time lags. Assurances Feldin considered Harp "entirely capable of a successful meet" fell flat when he remarked "the guidance of a seasoned diplomat would simply make it smoother". Vacc it, time for some plain speaking? 'Forgive me, Uncle, but can you tell me why Ser Lee was chosen for this mission?'

'You have some doubts about the man?' At least Feldin wasn't dismissing the question. 'Diplomatic only has a small staff for xeno-diplomacy; mostly we haven't needed any. But they suggested he would suit, and I figured he'd be well disposed toward you, being Family, and discreet about anything he stumbled upon.'

Ah. Like any social gaffe the farmboy committed on alien territory. Or any more attempts to kill him. 'Can I be frank, ser?'

'Always, Max.'

'He… he's driving me crazy. He's pompous, long winded, supercilious…' He hadn't realised how much his vocab had expanded till the words burst from him. Now he took a breath and tried to act adult to match. 'Daichi's been his usual capable self and kept the man under some control, and frankly off my back, but Ser Lee seems convinced our Kraic hosts are primitives, and I don't trust his briefings on the subject. In fact I'm increasingly convinced someone's landed me with a xenophobe. Ser.'

'You're serious?'

'Yessir. I realise he's your choice but it's me he'll be standing next to, telling me what to say and do, and I'm not looking forward to it.' There. Nothing diplomatic about that but it was said, and in trouble or not he felt better.

Feldin obviously didn't. 'My dear boy, why didn't you say? Of course, we shipped you out so quickly you didn't have a chance to get the measure of the fellow, did you. You really don't trust his advice?'

'No, ser,' Harp said heavily. The magnitude of what he'd said was sinking in. He'd just announced a mission to an alien species was at risk, where simply saying it could ruin Lee's career cos Harp was now a real-Harpan. But he couldn't alter his opinion.

Feldin seemed to see that. 'I'll sic Mz Chan onto it. We'll sort it out before you land, don't worry.'

Like he could stop?

12

Harp reread his altered orders. What Mz Chan did, said, discovered, he still didn't know, but Ser Lee was not taking *Defiant's* shuttle to the Kraic IV Orbital, and Harp was to do whatever he thought best. OK. An embarrassing tantrum after Harp made Lee aware of that only reinforced Harp's relief, not to mention making him grateful yet again for Daichi's support. Who knew a diplomat would know so many swear words. So Lee was currently confined to his quarters, and Ham had assured Harp he'd had 'a word' with his fellows about keeping Lee out of Harp's hair for the rest of their mission.

So Harp was back in pants, tee and dock jacket when they walked into the shuttle. He had Daichi and his team around him, Del and Yentl as his fellow crewmates, Hendriks as his "aide" – and Ham as his personal valet or something. The XO called it "batman". Hendriks was still teasing the guy about that, but it was a solution, cos face it captains didn't rate an aide and a Marine rating wasn't senior enough to represent *Defiant* when *Defiant's* XO and Colonel Ngow more than covered that position. So by the time he added *their* people, a marine honour guard and the medic-in-attendance he could never seem to dodge now, well, it was a mob. But one he trusted. Even more so when he recognised the navy's medic. 'Mac?'

'Captain.' Mac nodded, proper navy. Vacc that.

He hugged her. 'Hi, Mom.' She slapped his chest and blushed!

Harp laughed. He hadn't felt this good, this safe for crip, how long now? Then the XO coughed, reminding him of duty. 'Sorry, Ma'am. Ready when you are of course.' But she was biting back a smile too and merely waved him forward.

OK, here we go then. From what he'd seen during final approach the Kraic had been rebuilding *their* Orbital with a vengeance. What had been a single, badly broken stick last time he'd seen it, out from Raptor's see-all walls, was now three equal spokes joined by a bulbous module at their centre. More storage capacity? An intention to dock more ships? Or more defences? Whatever reason lay behind the change this Orbital was still smaller than Moon's, let alone World's, so there'd be no way he could get himself lost.

One worry removed. That just left the rest then.

Defiant was too big to dock, hence the shuttle, extra-polished for the big occasion. Not that on past experience – not his, of course – the Kraic were remotely likely to enter it, but that was navy for you. The delegation settled in navy fashion, officers at the front end, not the way the Family did it. Funny how such things could seem important.

Hendriks got to sit behind him, so did Mac, while Ham went aft and joined his marine comrades. Del and Yentl settled either side of him. He'd pushed for all the *Raptor's* crew to meet the Kraic and a Harpan evidently got what they "suggested", leastways at the moment. Harp restrained a smile; this reminded him of Moon, of being lured into playing real-Harpan, Del and Yentl as his escort. This time they were doing it for real, weren't they – he really was representing the Family. That in mind again he went over what he should expect.

He'd never met any aliens before, Kraic or otherwise, nor he suspected had many of the party. He figured any previous interactions, if any, were about trade. Ngow had, he said, discussed pirates, and he'd gathered the XO had experience, but not with Kraic. Yentl said he'd talked with aliens a couple times but only navigator-comtalk. So Ngow might be it for Kraic unless the shuttle crew or the marines had been here prior to their posting to *Defiant*. Harp had vaguely thought someone would pick folk who'd done this before. Maybe Lee was meant to fill that hole. Or Harpan's Worlds didn't have any more experience than he did?

And this was meant to mark a new relationship?

No pressure then.

Docking; Kraic Umbilical. Half the marines formed up

at the front, then Ngow and the XO, then Harp, Del and Yentl. The gravity felt lighter – yay – and this umbilical was shades of green not bare grey mepal; definitely unexpected. Ngow didn't look surprised. So what else would be different?

Oh. The dockside air hit him; shockingly warm, slightly moist. Real plant stuff actually growing on the walls above them, sort of hanging; he could swear he spotted something flying. There, again some tiny creature.

Crip, mind your manners, fool. No gawping, there'll be people – alien people – watching, waiting. The human honour guard split, only Ngow and the XO to follow now. He'd thought he was prepped. Hell, Hendriks had been sending every image he could find on top of all the data Hissack's ma and even Lee had input. But his first reaction was: not human.

Of course he'd known that. Likely the Kraic were about as not-human as it got. Hence Lee's animosity? But seeing it for real, only a few paces ahead...

Navy slang – *not* to be used here – called them 'pedes', probably short for centipedes. Though they didn't have a hundred legs, only eight. And they had exoskeletons, so beetles might be more accurate? Only he thought beetles, the ones he knew anyway, looked more armour plated where these guys – gals – his briefings said to call them 'it' – looked less shiny and more... cuddly. If something rearing up on a tripod, two hindmost legs and a stumpy tailend, so a human head was level with what ought to be its shoulders, could be cuddly? But the image stuck. Perhaps it was the droopy whiskers, or the tiny, rounded ears. Or the colours.

There were three Kraic ahead backed up by a semicircle he figured were junior ranks. The leading three were taller, and duller, the middle one shades of pale green, the other two pale pink and pale mauve. The rest? More colours than Harp could name, some brighter than others, all brighter than the front three. Younger? Navy brass wore brighter dress blues, the opposite. Did that confuse the Kraic? Or indeed the fact humans could change their choice of colour? Because apart from those clear translator collars it looked like all the Kraic wore was their own pearly skin.

Well why not, it was sure warm enough up here. Thank the stars he was in his plainer duty gear not the higher-collared dress uniform. And thank the stars all he had to do right now was follow the crowd and look friendly. He reminded himself; that meant smiling *without* showing any teeth.

The XO and Ngow exchanged greetings with Big Three. These trans-collars really did make things straightforward, once you got used to dividing your attention between the screens and the Kraic faces. Not that Kraic faces told him much, staying pretty much round and bland. The big, facetted eyes sorta reminded him of the central bulge of this Orbital. Or his turret on *Raptor*.

His thoughts jumped back to those around him. The XO was introducing Ngow as the officer in charge of *Raptor*. A Kraic neck-screen flashed up [GRATITUDE ADMIRATION]. Ngow said it was all part of the job. The XO turned and nodded, his turn then, don't blow it.

'Embassador, may I present Captain Harpan and his crew.'

Crip, he was only the gunner, but a warning look from Ngow had him swallowing a protest. He'd apologise to Del and Yentl later.

A shiver went through the Kraic rainbow, then stillness. Humans still studied insects, under scopes. He figured he knew now how that felt. The facetted eyes made it feel like there were thousands of them, all on him. He forced himself to take a step and nod. 'An honour, sers.' Meeting giant caterpillars; how much weirder could it get?

[HONOUR OURS YOUNG MALE.]

Did the leader's eyes glow brighter for a moment? Introduce Del and Yentl, quick. Harp did, then tried to fade into the background.

Not about to happen.

[PLEASE COME FOOD.] Big 1 beckoned with its two front arms then flowed down and forward. Even horizontal its head came up to Harp's waist. There was some sort of platform waiting ahead, not noticeable till they moved aside cos it too was greenish. Less built, more grown?

Ngow nodded Harp to follow Big 1. Ngow's shoulders were tensed; maybe he didn't know what to expect either. Was everyone winging it? Still, they were allies, Harp reminded himself, and not a pirate in sight. Nor a Regis, that was worth a smile.

The platform took Bigs 1 through 3 plus all the human delegation, but not the rest of the Kraic. Probably cos when the platform started to slide up the wall, the rest of the Kraic swarmed straight up said wall as if it was horizontal. There were human murmurs, quickly muted. OK, so the Kraic supposedly lived down in their forests, but he hadn't figured –

'Awesome,' Del breathed. It was. Their short legs seemed to flow and their segmented bodies sort of rippled and they just... stayed on.

Except one smaller, brighter blue one nearby was almost skipping upward. Harp got the sense it was from sheer enjoyment, or excitement. *Hey, go for it, wish I could.*

The Blue hopped on the spot, clung in place and turned its face to Harp. <*Can go faster*> The little guy was talking? But the Kraic couldn't. Then Harp realised he was the only one reacting. Hadn't anyone *heard*? They hadn't, had they. What?

<You hear, you hear> More hopping.

Harp swivelled round to keep the little one in sight, opened his mouth then closed it.

<*Mans not hear. You can. Wonderful/special/must continue*> At that point Blue realised the platform was leaving it behind again and demonstrated serious acceleration, catching up in seconds. <*I am –?–*> A pause. <*Not hear that.*>

Harp took a shaky breath, looked round then tried to – well, to *think* an answer. *<No, you lost me. You are, what?>*

More hops. *<Look me.>*

Look? The word meant... what he looked like? *<Blue?>* Harp winced. That probably wasn't polite – like someone calling him yellow.

<Blue. Blue.> The little Kraic kept pace now, practically face to face. *< And you... Harpan.>*

<Harp.> This think-talking was getting easier, and crazy as it felt it *was* like talking. *<But I still don't understand how I can hear you.>* When evidently no one else did.

<Nor Blue.> Hop. <Must tell progenitor.>

The platform halted several levels higher at an open archway. Everyone got off, and somehow Big 1 and Harp ended up in the lead. The mass of Kraic now lined the tunnel ahead, like a pearly guard of honour, all but Blue, who caught them up and trotted –still had too much bounce to flow – beside his leader. Elder? Parent? Suddenly Big 1 stopped dead, head bent toward the smaller Kraic. Crip, the two were talking, in their heads, the way he'd stumbled into. Only now he couldn't hear either. No prize what about though, the way Big 1 looked at Harp a moment later. Nothing happened though. Nothing was said, onscreen or otherwise. Big 1 just moved on again, so Harp did too, not sure if he was glad of it or sorry. Maybe the big guy didn't believe it. Maybe Harp had been hallucinating. Only if so why him? Or were the rest hiding the shock better? Ignore it then and try to act like Harpans should, whatever that was.

The tunnel opened on a large rounded chamber, yet more plant stuff. That meant a lot of pale, greenish stems and leaves – if those weird, plate-like shapes were leaves – and an astounding variety of coloured portions, some like what he might have thought were Worlder flowers, others more like fluffy balls, or even fancy spears. Harp figured several of the human contingent were memorising everything, if not secretly recording. If so he'd definitely ask for copies. He could always say it was for Feldin.

A large greenish table, shaped like a hollow ring, took up much of the room. The marine officer chose to position his men, and himself, around the outer wall. So did Mac, and Ham, and Daichi waved his team aside as well. The Kraic heads stilled a moment then a swarm of Blue-sized Kraic waiting in the table's central hollow scurried out and screen-invited the remaining humans to the table. Each smaller Kraic had a padded stool, carried like a saddle. Somehow everyone still looked a guest now ended up around the outside of the table, humans flanked by Kraic, two to one, except that Harp had Big 1 on his left and Big 2 on his right, and felt surrounded; they'd rearranged the seating to accommodate the altered numbers on the fly, so fast he hadn't even seen it coming. So much for Ser Lee's opinion.

The stools were generous for a human, enough the Kraic could sit or lie on them, but the Kraic's stools stood slightly lower. End result: the different heads were roughly level. By the time they'd settled the smaller Kraic had dropped to all eight legs again and flowed beneath the table, turning back to stand and face the diners. Little whiskers quivered for a moment then they turned– and dived into holes in the floor.

'Whoa.' Hendriks tried to peer after his "attendant", got frowns from Ngow and the XO and shrank back. But he had summed it up. What next?

Next was the littles popped back carrying trays in their front legs, and in seconds there were glasses set, and shallow bowls and oval mats he thought were woven. The mats varied, green to brown to near-white, sometimes all three, maybe plant stuff too. The glasses were the same as people used back home though. Maybe traded?

The dishes were different colours, with a soft sheen. Like the Kraic. Harp glanced from bowl to host. Crip, was he expected to eat from someone's skeleton?

Big 2 provided commentary as the little servers poured... juice? Wine?... into the glasses. And water? Into the bowls. Small Blue had supplanted Big1's server.

Harp thought it looked faintly smug, though why he should he had no notion. According to Big 2's neckscreen the juice was for drinking, made from a local fruit, safe for both species, but so far none of the Kraic were touching it. Ok, he would hold off too, copying Big 1 seemed the best approach. The rest of the humans evidently felt the same.

All the small Kraic dived from sight again then reappeared, this time carting trays of foodstuff. Much like Harp's own first reception; finger food as Emika had called it. He identified the crackers and a tiny rice cake looked familiar, stuffed with something didn't.

Big 2's screen lit. [EAT ALL HUMAN GOOD.]

Big 1 waved at Harp. It took him a second, and a nod from Ngow, to work out they were waiting for him. Oh great. The whole room watched him select a cracker, lift it to his mouth – he heard Daichi take a breath – then bite it. Creamier than he expected, cool and tangy, better than the navy version. 'Excellent,' he murmured. Big 1 clapped its pincers, four of them, and started on its own selection, all four front legs delicately busy. Everyone tucked in with varying degrees of comfort. Ngow and the XO solemnly polite, Yentl with modest bites while Del munched everything with gay abandon and overt enjoyment. Hendriks, being Hendriks, showed a tendency to tap and squeeze before he tasted. Harp decided he would match what Big 1 chose in what might be the proper order, and the stuff was good, assuming nothing here was poisonous to humans as they promised. He relaxed a fraction.

Others not so much. Stilted exchanges circulated, made more complicated by the fact the Kraic could eat and 'talk' at the same time. It was kinda funny watching the XO trying *not* to answer with her mouth full. And, well, impressive how much food you could pack away if you could use two pairs of pincers at once. There'd been times he'd have paid for that ability.

But Harp had Big 1 and Big 2 flanking him, which meant a lot of head turning at first, till he worked out he could see the glow when their screens lit up. They mostly made remarks about the pirate battle in their orbit. They admired what they'd seen of *Raptor*, maybe cos it was also a bit insect-like with all its weapons facets? They were polite about that though, not pestering about its tec. Maybe they realised he wasn't allowed to reveal anything.

The pirates were the next topic. Harp could describe Argon Zorr, and mention his worry the human might still be at large. Turned out the Kraic already had his description and were on the lookout for everyone on the navy's suspect list. Big 1 wanted Harp to know they were keen to help, to repay the debt. Looked like debt was like face, so it was a serious obligation.

Juice was refilled, trays removed down holes, new trays delivered. He recognised fruits and some kind of pastry. Big 1 extended all its eating legs, to the bowl, and dabbled, so those were for washing. Harp dipped fingers, waved them, found his server standing tall to offer him a length of fabric, noted Big 1 flicked its legs and magically dry itself without one. Something else a Kraic could do that humans couldn't. Crip, he had so many questions, but he couldn't ask for fear of offending.

Only it began to look like he was going to get some answers anyway, stemming from the way he was inspecting the towel. Big 1's neck-screen flashed for his attention. [EXPORT THIS ADMIRED.]

'It's very fine, ser.' The swirl of pastel colours looked fragile, felt strong and sucked off moisture. 'I imagine you sell a lot.'

[BIG PRICE.] Big 1 made humming noises and its whiskers lifted. Smiling?

Little Blue did likewise. Harp heard <*Keep best.*>

Crip, they sold the stuff they didn't rate, the rejects. Surely Blue wasn't meant to let that slip.

Big 1 wasn't finished. [CAPTAIN SEE MORE.] An invitation?

'Really? I would love to.' Maybe the Orbital's new, additional arm was the manufactory and they wanted to show it off.

Little Blue hopped up and down. Harp guessed someone else wanted to go. Big 2 turned to Ngow, farther round the table. That meant Harp couldn't read its screen any longer, but he could see Ngow's face. The colonel looked at Harp, then nodded. Not that Harpans needed anyone's permission, Harp reflected, though he should remember he *was* still a lowly captain. Then he wondered, how well could the Kraic read expressions? Crip, could they read humans' thoughts as well, but kept it quiet?

What to do. Warn the XO, or Daichi, or keep quiet too? The navy would see a threat, Daichi a security risk, both would probably react, strongly. Though Daichi might decide it was intel for the Family, something to keep to themselves.

The Kraic...maybe hadn't intended humans to know about mind-talk? But now Harp did they were being very friendly, very cooperative. *Because* he'd "talked" to Blue? They weren't advertising the fact though, were they. They were still using the screens. So maybe they wanted it to stay a secret. Maybe going along with that, for now, would count as making friends and influencing people, which was the reason he was here.

What would Maxil Snr, or Feldin, do?

Events moved on again before he found an answer.

13

Big 1's offer seemed to require further discussion across the table, half of it out of Harp's line of sight. First the XO then Ngow weighed in, then the marine commander. By then Daichi hovered at Harp's shoulder. 'Ser. I gather you've agreed to a tour.'

'Yes.' Cos a) he wanted to, and b) he wasn't going to insult Big 1 by seeming to doubt his safety.

Daichi's brows had lowered, big reaction. 'Ser, I gather the Kraic have only invited you. I realise it's a friendly gesture but...'

Ah, Daichi was having a calf cos he wasn't included. Hang on. 'No one else?'

'No ser, I have to advise –'

Big 1's screen lit. [WISH GUARD INVITE.]

Harp was getting good at recognising questions. 'It would set his mind at rest, ser. The Founder made him responsible for me.'

[FOUNDER WISE INCLUDE.]

'Thank you, ser, I'm sure he'll love it.' If not Harp was sure the man could fake it like the pro he was.

Big 1 rose, well, undulated to the floor. Harp figured he was meant to follow. Ngow acted spokesman, extolling their new 'special relationship', thanking them for such a gracious welcome and – a speaking look at Harp – for issuing a 'signal invitation to the captain, who is very conscious of the honour'. Then, oh boy, the lesser Kraic ushered the rest of his party back the way they came and only Harp and Daichi remained, surrounded by Kraic brass.

Big 1 led off, the other direction. Harp followed with Daichi glued to his shoulder. Big 2 and 3 fell in behind them. Little Blue appeared on Harp's left and skipped beside him, whiskers twitching. Only they didn't seem to be heading for the Orbital's arms, more like the centre. Daichi's hand fell on Harp's arm. 'Ser, this wasn't discussed.'

'Mm. Embassador?'

[CAPTAIN QUESTION.]

'Where are we going, exactly?' But he thought he knew.

[FABRIC LEAF LEAF FOREST FOREST–]

'Planet?' Stars, he'd started talking Kraic.

[EXACTLY] Twitching whiskers.

Damn if he wasn't being kidnapped again. He realised he'd grinned, all teeth as well; not diplomatic no, but honest. As Big 1 was being? Vacc, go for it then. A chance to see a planet nobody except the Kraic, and maybe pirates, had? He wasn't backing out, whatever Daichi said. 'Looking forward to it,' he assured Big 1. 'Don't you agree, Ser Daichi?'

'Of course, ser. Lovely.' Shame Daichi's expression didn't match his answer but we couldn't all be diplomatic. Harp resisted teasing, more intent of following Big 1 onto a real Kraic shuttle. The interior was…green, surprise. Longer and slimmer inside than *Defiant's* but the seats were more like couches and had pretty fabrics. Recessed strapping hinted that the Kraic strapped down to horizontal, but – perhaps in deference to humans – Big 1 stretched along a seat but didn't fasten itself down. Harp was relieved, he didn't fancy being tied down like a captive. So he sat, Daichi too, and engines purred. He heard a hiss as clamps released them from the dock and saw the shuttle fall away and veer toward the planet.

He couldn't see much of that yet but like the images he'd studied most of the surface was hidden by cloud, with occasional glimpses of what lay below. The navy, and therefore the Family, had a composite holo, an attempt to stitch what scattered images they had together, but it wasn't much improvement, just enough to see what they already knew; a lot of Kraic IV was forest. Jungle. Some variety of plant stuff.

Harp realised he'd expected to see damage the pirates must have caused, as he had on Moon, but either the pirates hadn't caused much on the surface or the Kraic had performed miracles since.

Big 1 watched him staring out. [TREES GROW.]

'So fast?' OK, how many words did it really take.

[TREES CURE.] And right there was the downside; fewer words equalled less information. They'd mended the trees? The trees had mended themselves? Did they intend to show him? Even landing might make him the Harpan expert on the Kraic, which led him onto... 'Did many pirates land, ser? How bad was it for your people?' In the next seat Daichi practically stopped breathing; Security loved intel.

[PIRATES LAND STILL HERE.] Whiskers lifted.

That didn't just mean they stayed, it meant, crip, none survived? Not exactly an encouraging thought when he was next to visit, but little Blue was whisker-smiling and he sort of felt Big 1's were... smirking. And the pirates hadn't been invited so OK, he had no cause to panic.

The shuttle dropped through the cloud layer. Harp's thoughts fragmented. He'd thought all the greens on the Orbital a bit excessive, but this...

There wasn't anything to see *but* green; green that was almost black to almost white. No pattern to it, no deliberate gradation, just an ever-changing complex shift of colours.

No buildings? No landing site? Had they picked the most remote spot they could? He supposed that made sense if they were so reclusive, private, shy, whatever. It certainly ensured he wouldn't see more than they chose. Hey, maybe it would be like Foundation City, all the major transport underground with blanked out windows. Well, he wasn't arguing, the chance to see a tiny fraction of this planet would be worth it.

Worth recounting later to the navy, and to Feldin? Maxil too? Suddenly he wasn't sure he wanted to. He'd learned loyalty to comrades, but to World – or even Family – he realised he wasn't sure yet, a disquieting thought that made him conscious, yet again, his so-called Family were holding back, not sharing everything.

He'd told himself be patient, they would need to get to know him too, but for the moment, no, he wasn't sure how much he wanted to reveal about the Kraic. Not even owning to his own impressive sight and hearing, or how fast he healed, without scarring. Or his recent non-existent sex drive? No, he definitely wasn't coming out on that part.

So he'd been holding back as much as his new-found kin, while here, the Kraic were offering an unheard-of level of trust, when all they really knew about him was he'd shot down pirates, at the navy's orders. If there was a Kraic debt to pay then surely it was to the navy, or the Founder, not a simple captain.

Except he'd heard the real "voice" of little Blue, and *that* was when Big 1 began to let its non-existent hair down. All the hints, the humour, had come after. His exchange with Blue was what had changed things, not that telling would be up to him anyway, not with Daichi all eyes and ears.

Meanwhile, they appeared to be hovering above these treetops. If their pilot dipped these stubby wings the merest fraction…

It didn't. He must remember to tell Del he had competition. Little Blue jumped off its couch and skipped toward the aft exit which irised open on a narrow ramp, still sliding from the hull, that looked as if it aimed to be a pathway. To the trees below them?

Big 1 slithered from its couch and headed after Blue; no choice but follow.

Crip, these trees were big, he thought dizzily. What he could see from the ramp was a hell of a drop. Though with the lesser gravity here, surely less than Moon, maybe he'd float?

'It's better not to look down, ser.'

'You think? I reckon we'll need to get used to it.' Because there were an awful lot of Kraic scurrying along these upper branches, like it was a vaccing highway. Not to mention going up, or down, the vaccing treetrunks. Whoever had come up with the theory Kraic were tree dwellers had been more right than they realised.

The shuttle's ramp led onto another, this one actual

tree, shaped into a corkscrewing path down and round the nearest enormous trunk. Blue waited, hopping with impatience. Big 1 started down, with Harp behind him, round and round – good job he was no longer dizzy. 'You OK back there, Daichi?'

'Yes, ser.' Though the other man did sound a trifle breathless.

'Not far now.' At least, Harp figured they'd passed the halfway mark, so it wouldn't be *so* far to fall. If Kraic ever fell. Hang on, a lot weren't even on this path. 'Embassador?'

The round head twisted, and the neck-screen. [CAPTAIN]

'What is this pathway, er, usually for?'

[ANCIENT KRAIC HURT KRAIC.]

Oh, for feeble Kraic who couldn't climb. Nice, another area where humans didn't rate. But they were finally approaching ground level, and feeling smaller than his hosts had morphed into feeling a *lot* smaller than their forest. He'd seen trees before, even on Moon; larger, straighter on World, but these...

Impossibly tall, like... Mansion-tall. Another cautious recon. This trunk was silvery green, its fronds – way too big to call leaves – were every shade of green through purple, the undersides paler. Underneath, so many flowers, blues and mauves and pinks and golds... Harp stopped and stared, it was a fantasy, a wonderland. He'd never dreamed.

It wasn't just the colours. Here at ground level all the trunks were bare, like pillars holding up a living roof, but the branches overhead arched outward and connected with each other. Every tree was linked to several others. Or had several treetrunks?

And everywhere he looked were Kraic, flowing high and low and even upside down, defying human reason.

Blue hopped up to claim attention. <*Follow.*>

Harp stopped himself before he spoke out loud. This at least he could conceal from Daichi, till he chose to share, or knew more. <*Lead on?*>

This time he figured Big 1 had listened in, the way it turned and flowed away as well. Harp waved Daichi onward. Maybe his Security looked nervous, Harp just felt excited; what else would they show him?

The ground between the trees felt cushioned. It took him a while to work out fronds had fallen from above and sort of melded into vari-coloured carpet. One that rustled softly underfoot, a gentle whisper that accompanied their progress. It was peaceful, far removed from what his life was now on World. Ironic that he had to visit aliens to find some sense of calm. That knowing Kraic were everywhere, some visible some surely not, felt less intrusive.

Big 1 turned, flashed [FABRICS] at them then veered left, though how it knew which way was which escaped him. Hidden signs? A homing signal? But he heard the sounds a moment later, shushing noises, then the pillars parted to reveal a fabric-roofed-in sort of space between the trunks, more generous, and being used for...

Weaving fabrics.

Threads so fine he only saw them cos they glinted slightly, strung between the trunks at different lengths so that the Kraic on the ground and in the trees could weave between with nimble pincers, conjuring half-formed designs that made him want to see them finished. The Kraic here came in different sizes too. The longest stood – four legs – or sat, – two legs and tail. The brighter seemed to act as servers, runners. Pupils?

[TREES GIVE] Big 1 waved a pincer upward. Yes, of course, the coloured threads weren't dyed but natural; the leaves and flowers themselves. Who needed dyes when nature made so many colours for them.

[–?– MASTER HERE SEE] Another name that didn't translate, but the Kraic Big 1 signalled to turned round and dipped a greeting so Harp nodded back. The Kraic here hadn't gone with neck-screens, well, why would they? So the master turned and went to work again and Harp stood by and watched it, fascinated by the speed and the dexterity those pincers managed.

[SPECIAL FABRICS HIGHER] Big 1 flashed.

'Oh? Permitted?' He was talking Kraic again. But little Blue skipped to the biggest trunk in sight, swarmed up some way then bent double to look back at him. Another invitation? Challenge? Well, he'd clambered into stranger places back on *Mercy*. Harp took a running jump – this lesser grav was awesome – landed on a branch beside the little Kraic and started climbing; heard Daichi shout but hey, adventure beckoned.

Climbing a tree wasn't as easy as the Kraic made it look, even with the blessing of less grav. Where they swarmed he heaved but eventually Big 1 and Blue lay waiting – looked like even Blue had calmed up here – and a hollow inbetween the trunk and two adjoining branches made a pretty comfortable place to settle in, his back against the trunk, to face them. OK, so where was all this "special fabric" Big 1 wanted him to look at…

+++

'What the?' Harp blinked. The world returned to focus, giant tree once more behind him and beneath, the Kraic laid along the branches, watching. Crip, he couldn't see the ground at all from here. 'Who was I just talking to?' He thought he knew the answer, but he really needed confirmation.

Big 1's whiskers lifted. <Amgoth is the Elder of this gather.>

<And Amgoth is…>

<*Central Growth.*> More whiskers, Big 1 found this funny.

OK, breathe. 'So Amgoth is… the tree I'm sitting on. In.' The tree at the centre, the focus of the other trunks around it. Amgoth… was a sentient tree the Kraic could talk to, in their fashion. But they'd never passed that little fact to humans either. Till *he* came here?

It was a lot to take in, maybe that was why he felt a bit faint. Amgoth's "talk" had been all in Harp's head too, more like a trance than with the Kraic, but he was guessing that while the Kraic understood him speaking with his mouth this Amgoth didn't hear humans that way, only sensed their presence. So talking out loud to Big 1 had been like, like he was ignoring Amgoth? All right, he could do this. *<I had no idea, I mean.>*

<Mans very young animal. Such things take more time.> The tone inside Harp's head spelled understanding, of a lesser species. Ouch. <But offspring is right, you are new beginning. We will watch with interest.> Curiosity. Perhaps excitement?

<Thank you.> I think.

Leaves rustled, Big 1's whiskers twitched. Blue hopped along its branch. All of them could sense that he was overwhelmed but he was still alert enough for urgent questions. *<Why me?>*

Big 1's turn. *<Hear us. Never met a mans could. Stopped listening, but you call 'Blue' is young, and careless, does not follow rules.>* A mix of disapproval, resignation, and warmth? Apparently being a parent created the same responses, human or Kraic. *<So Blue listened.>*

Blue hopped closer. <Mans like dead wood, not Harp-friend. Alive.>

<Alive, like you and the trees.>

<Yes, yes.> Hop, hop.

Harp's head buzzed, because Amgoth cut in, its "voice" vibrating, denser somehow than the Kraics'. *<New mind. We asked to bring you closer.>*

Asked, or told? Harp had the sense of power, age, he hadn't got from any of the Kraic. *<I guess you wanted to weigh me up.>*

<Of course.> Unsaid, but obvious, as ally or threat. Blue just called him friend, but what did Amgoth think? How influential was it?

<I have no wish to harm anyone.> Except pirates.

<See mans can grow. 'Pi-rates' enemy too. Perhaps grow closer. We will help, but we have roots. Mans not.> Images formed in Harp's head, Moon, then World. <We will send a seed to birthworld. It will root, and speak.>

Harp's brain reeled. <You want me to talk to this seed?>

<Your roots do not burrow, so Kraic will tend it and translate between our peoples.>

Stars, they wanted to send a permanent, alien embassy to World? Could he even agree to such a move? Would Maxil want it? The answer ought to be a resounding yes, but Harp wasn't Maxil Snr, or Feldin. He didn't live politics, didn't want to, but this, this felt like an incredible offer. <*I'm truly honoured, but I have to send your offer to my grandfather. It's his decision.*>

There followed an exchange Harp barely kept up with, Big 1 explaining what the Kraic had learned of humans, and specifically of Harpans. Which for a reclusive race World hardly knew was a whole lot more than Harp expected. The Kraic had been collecting data on humans, basically hoarding it, but the tree – trees – hadn't been interested, till now. As Blue had put it, humans had been dead wood, little value. But now the lesser species might have been promoted? He needed help, asap.

<I'd agree, with pleasure, but I need to return to my ship and contact my superiors.>

14

'Hi Daichi, I'm back. You weren't worried were you?' Harp's boots hit the ground and almost bounced; he had to remember the grav. 'I saw the weaving, and climbed a real tree, but our hosts say it's getting late so I guess we should head to the shuttle?'

Harp couldn't stop the smile, he'd never seen a tree big enough to *need* much climbing back on Moon and so far his life on World hadn't included much of anything natural. Boasting a little also helped camouflage the bigger deal, the offer of a permanent alliance, with not one but two alien races? And Kraic IV owed allegiance to Kraic Prime, so he had to think Kraic Prime would be involved at some level too. This was huge, even he could see that.

But he couldn't say anything till he talked to the Family. So hey, more secrets.

That merited a sigh; Daichi noticed. 'Sorry, Daichi, I guess I'm tiring too.' He looked back up. 'Good thing the gravity is friendlier here, huh?' A sudden flare of doubt; would World's heavier gravity cause problems, if this seed got planted? Should he explain that? No, no point borrowing problems as Missus Destra would have told him. Time enough to worry about that if Maxil Snr said yes. 'Daichi, I need to contact the Founder, asap.'

'Ser.' Bless the man, he didn't ask, just reached out on his wristcom. By the time Harp left the Kraic Orbital, *Defiant* had a link set up, and assured him it was scrambled and there'd be no record on *Defiant's* com-log. So Harp chose to trust all that, especially when Hendriks nodded at him in the background. It was really good to have his comrades back again; he'd miss that when –

But even as he sat, behind *Defiant's* senior captain's desk no less, the screen before him shivered and Ser Maxil's head and shoulders faced him. 'Max, I gather we need to talk privately. Is everything all right?'

'I think so, ser. We've been offered a new alliance.'

'That sounds like we should include your uncle.'

Feldin's head appeared, his office in the background, taking half the screen from Maxil. 'Hello, Max, I was already on call. What do you have for us?'

Missus Destra had a word she claimed had been handed down from OldEarth; flabbergasted. Harp figured it pretty well fit their faces by the time he finished.

'The Kraic are telepaths, and their trees are sentient? I think I need a brandy.' Clinking sounds offscreen resulted in a glass by Maxil's hand.

'I think I'll join you, Father.' Feldin's head turned, but he went on talking. 'And you have this seed?'

'Not yet. I didn't want –'

'Of course, stupid question. What exactly do we need to arrange?' Which meant Feldin's vote was yes, but Maxil?

Maxil was already nodding. 'Don't look so worried, boy. You've done well, amazingly so, and we'd have to be fools to turn this down, however complicated it gets. But Feldin's right, we do need to take care of whatever it is, or this alliance will be dead not strengthened.'

'Yes, ser.' Deep breath. 'I think the Kraic want some of their own to take charge of it.'

'Stars.' Maxil Snr took a visible breath too. 'Did you realise? We've never had one alien race visit World, let alone two at once. Some of our more daring ships have made trade exchanges this century, and the navy have had minor contact, since the pirates, but we've always kept a cautious distance.'

'Father, this is going to change that.' Feldin's brow furrowed.

Ser Maxil grinned, practically rubbing his hands! 'We're going to be stronger.'

The grin sank in. Harp realised just how big this could turn out to be; more face, more influence instead of none? More trade. More alliances? More contact?

More interest in, and from, the distant world of origin that Hendriks was convinced of? That he thought their ancestors deserted?

'Ser, are you sure we want to be that noticed?' Aliens apart, everyone seemed to think keeping to themselves was a good thing. Maybe generally hoped anyone else had forgot them?

Feldin eyed him thoughtfully. 'You're not thinking about aliens now, are you?'

Harp sighed. 'I'm first to admit I don't know what I'm talking about here, sers, but there was some talk.'

'About our isolation, huh? About NewEarth.' Feldin paused until Ser Maxil nodded. 'The only answer I can give you is we don't know any more. It's possible some of the very rare, Outworld traders who found the Kraic might become aware of us, but the last-known *Harpan* contact with another human was the first Founder, and we've always believed she came out this far to avoid them, so... and who knows what relations might be like by this time.'

World and Moon began because the Harpan Founder wanted clear of other humans? Something *they* might know about but ordinary people didn't? 'Sers, do you know *why* she wanted to get away?'

'Probably didn't like taking orders, son.' Maxil's smile was too... political. 'We don't, do we? But your new alliance could deflect that ancient problem.' Harp gaped. The smile widened. 'Son, we could be noticed now anyway, the pirates and our nice new weapon saw to that. My worry was if NewEarth did finally notice, someone out there *would* try to butt in. It might take years of course, even decades, but a strong Kraic alliance could be just what we'd need if that happened.'

'To keep others away?' Harp didn't want to argue, but.

'Oh, I don't think we can count on that any longer, but it might keep 'em polite.'

Polite. 'You really think?'

'I've always believed in forward planning. That's my job, don't you think?'

They were asking him? 'Ser, I'm no expert.'

'Oh yes you are, son, you're our new Embassador to all the Kraic. Not just local hero any longer, you're a major asset.' Maxim's lips curled upward. 'With any luck even Eleanora will realise you're too valuable to lose.'

Embassador. Oh crip. 'I can't. I mean, I don't know how. There must be someone better suited.'

Maxil snorted. 'Like Lee, or his senator? You're it, son, at least till you find someone else to mind-talk, as you put it. Can you honestly tell me that *isn't* the reason behind this?'

He couldn't, could he. 'Do I, does that mean I have to stay out here?'

'We'll cross that galaxy when we come to it, eh? For now, make nice with the Kraic leaders, and arrange for this seed they want to give us. If they ask you to stick around after that tell them you need to escort the seed to World and talk to me before anything else can be decided.' Maxil sat back at last. 'I'll leave orders your calls have priority.' Harp's head might be spinning but for Maxil it was clear the talk was over.

It was back into the shuttle, out to the Kraic Orbital again. Talk to Big 1, and Big 2. Then a flurry of activity on board *Defiant*, to evict several senior officers from cabins near Harp's and install Kraic 'nests'. At least those weren't much bigger than human bunks so the XO decided they could just be fixed on top. After the previously grey-on-grey cabins got sprayed in shades of green, and had a lot of plant stuff ferried up and settled round them. The Kraic might be willing to travel through space but they were adamant about taking home with them. Harp wondered what the lucky officers would think when they got green quarters back. Personally, he'd have been delighted, but who knew with Worlders.

Then the Kraic party arrived, ready to board. Sixteen adults. Plus little Blue.

Of course. Big 1 read Harp's surprise. <*Offspring wishes see mans world, mans ways. Problem*> it was so much easier to talk in mental 'sentences' than onscreen fragments.

<*No, ser, of course not.*> It was however challenging for a mere human to hold two conversations at once, one

inside his head, the other in response to neck-screens. Cos it looked like neither side wanted to advertise the fact the Kraic were telepathic. Now he could "receive" which was as far as Harp was going to accept about himself, he also saw more testing in his future.

Maybe he wouldn't be alone though. Maxil and Feldin would be keen to see if there were any more candidates for the job of Embassador, hopefully better qualified.

The seed loaded last, hidden in a large, woven-looking ball; more plant stuff, and large enough the XO issued orders to gut the designated cabin – no way was all that going to sit on a bunk, it would need the entire space. She gave Harp a less than thrilled look about that surprise, but he hadn't known either. He apologised anyway, being responsible and all, and he thought she forgave him, at least till the next time. There was bound to be a next time, wasn't there, cos while the Kraic escort obviously meant well, it was already plain they couldn't help spooking some of the crew.

Not to mention Blue's overt excitement. The hop and skip that characterised the younger alien easily distinguished it from its elders, and it clearly had no thought of hiding. By the time the party reached G deck Blue had hopped at the greyness around it, clicked its first four legs at the grav chute, played dodge-the-ledges and plainly couldn't wait to see what came next. Harp found it only partly reassuring that none of the older Kraic seemed concerned, or at least weren't showing it.

Any hope *they'd* rein Blue in was quickly quashed anyway. It was billeted with one of its elders but it barely glanced inside before it wanted to inspect Harp's quarters, whereupon it clicked and hopped, and Harp acquired several pots of plant stuff, which the Kraic somehow fixed against his cabin walls by nuzzling at the containers. Spit-glue? Hopefully he'd kept his doubts to himself; he was starting to get the hang of mind-talking but he knew his thoughts were still liable to slip.

Once embarked, *Defiant* set up a formal dinner in the Exec mess, where crew watched neck-screens and were carefully polite, deferring to him even more than before. Harp suspected the XO was covertly assessing crew reactions. Did these officers realise their behaviour tonight could influence their whole careers, that humans who could relax around the Kraic had just earned promotion points?

For their part, the Kraic seemed to have come with a supply of stock screen-phrases; mostly short expressions of cooperation and admiration of the navy's victory against the pirates. That last endeared them to any officers willing to engage, and the atmosphere definitely relaxed when the Kraic sampled the juice served at table. Turned out human fruits might be a potential high-cred export. The fermented version, even served in smaller glasses, went down even better. Harp shot the XO a look. She signed discreetly and the stewards didn't come around with refills. Harp had no idea what drunken Kraic were like but figured it best not to find out.

With that in mind, he ducked his head and pushed a thought toward Big Red, their leader. *<Should Blue be drinking this? It's meant for adults.>*

Whiskery amusement, both about the question and the name Big Red had graciously accepted. Actually, Harp thought it liked the fact it was similar to the one he'd given its boss, president, king, whatever. Harp had already sensed some surprise humans were sufficiently evolved they *could* name Kraic that way. Evidently the all-pervading greys and blues Kraic usually saw had given the impression human colour sense was far too limited to register so many colours; humans being dead wood again.

Big Red shrugged off the drink query. *<Will learn, as we will.>* Not entirely reassuring. Hopefully they'd all learn enough by the time they reached World.

Blue certainly "learned" at every opportunity. It explored, sometimes scaring crew to death appearing out of vents or scuttling down walls or ceilings. Its elders stuck to floors, mostly, but they didn't stop it. A deliberate ploy, using the junior to educate the humans?

Deliberate or not, Blue was enjoying itself. Only the Marine Security details he'd requested were containing its intrusion into places like the engine module, or *Raptor,* though Ngow was busy keeping *Raptor's* sections out of sight. Harp understood, even though that meant he was forced to avoid the parts of the ship he felt most at home in.

Happily, the *people* he felt most comfortable with stayed closer, with the XO's blessing. So far what the Harpan Ambassador wanted the Harpan Ambassador got, including keeping Ser Lee away from their guests, and him. When Harp enquired, the XO said they'd given the man a job in HR. Apparently "crew shortages" called for him to be "co-opted" into listening to crew grievances and organising leave schedules, on the grounds being diplomatic made him experienced at people-handling. Oh boy, would she regret that. But it meant Harp could pretty much do what he liked, and a voyage packed with friends, old and new, was the least stress he'd felt for quite a while.

Till the Kraic picked up the fact *Defiant* was only bound for World.

15

[BIG PLANET NOT GOOD] said Big Red's neckscreen. [SEED GOES SMALL PLANET] This wasn't a private conversation between minds, it wanted this public.

Talk around the officers' mess trailed off as those not close enough to read the screens were clued in by their neighbours. The XO froze, her fork mid-air. She looked to Ngow, Ngow looked across to Harp who always got the seat that faced Big Red. Harp... tried to make the words come out a different way, and couldn't. 'You wanted to take the seed to Harpan's Moon, not Harpan's World?' He hadn't seen that coming.

[SMALL PLANET]

OK, confirmation. All he had to do now was either change its mind or break the news to Maxil. A collision course either way.

Big Red stayed certain. One could say fixed, if two words repeated on a small screen could do that. Harp couldn't say no, nor did he think saying 'I can't' would work much better. He opted for discussion. 'So, Moon is better?'

[FOR SEED]

'Ah. Er.' The XO's nod said carry on. 'In what way, ser?'

[GROW BETTER]

Which said everything and nothing. 'Right. Didn't realise there was a difference.' Harp ducked his head and went on eating. This was way above his pay grade, it would have to wait until the meal was over.

+++

Onscreen, Feldin blinked, and Maxil Snr burst out laughing. 'They want to go to Moon? Didn't you know before?'

'No, sers.' Harp sat straighter. Talking to two separate screens was starting to feel commonplace. 'I messed up.'

Maxil shook his head. Stars knew what it was costing. 'You hardly did it on purpose, my boy.' He sighed though. 'They're determined?'

'As far as I can make out they're convinced the seed will grow better on Moon than World.' Harp hesitated. 'Which, er, makes me wonder how they'd know that.' Because as far as Harpan Security and Navy Intel were aware, the Kraic they were dealing with had never left Kraic IV. And no Kraic had ever come to World, or Moon, not even commed except by neckscreens didn't lend themselves to complex conversations.

On his screen, Feldin's eyebrows rose. 'Yes, that is interesting. You think they've been watching us?'

'It would make sense, we are their nearest neighbours, ser. If they feared we were in with the pirates... but I don't see how.'

'Hm.' Neither Feldin nor his father looked shocked, or offended, but then the Family had probably kept tabs on the Kraic too, all in the name of good relations of course. Was that why Lee was such an asshole?

Never mind, back to the real question. 'What do you want me to do, sers?'

'Oh, take them to Moon, dear boy. There's a treaty at stake, what choice do we have? It might be safer housing them on Moon than here.'

+++

On *Defiant*, Max's image blinked out. On World, Maxil's and Feldin's didn't. Maxil Snr spoke first. 'So the Kraic think Moon's a better breeding ground.'

'Mm.' Feldin waited, aware his father's thoughts had shifted during the discussion; Maxil Snr had been a touch too casual in his agreement.

Maxil Snr responded. 'It occurs to me Moon might be better at breeding other things as well. Or people?'

'Ah, you think *Max*...'

'It does seem very possible environmental influences played a part.' Maxil paused.

Feldin filled in the gaps. 'It will take serious persuasion to get any other Inner Family to move to Moon, father, even as a temporary measure. Especially now they're all aware of the conditions.' Feldin froze. 'But you've already considered that.'

'Yes. I fear we must send somebody to blaze a trail, to encourage others.' Maxil might look sympathetic but Feldin knew his father; underneath the sympathy was iron determination, and being his son wasn't all privilege. Sometimes, like now, it could become a less than pleasant duty.

+++

At least that conversation got Harp headed for Moon.

Defiant rerouted, Harp got to bed, though hardly to sleep. He'd assumed he'd be handing the Seed over to someone else, now it was firmly back in his lap. His tired brain flashed problems.
1. The Seed had to be planted, in Moon's arid soil.
2. Mooners were going to be very surprised. Maybe not in a good way.
3. By the time he woke he feared Big Red also expected a much bigger planting area than an ignorant human had assumed. Harp supposed he should have known, he'd seen how the Kraic 'trees' liked to spread out. Spawn? Take over? Crip, what had he started?
4. Cos if he was right wherever they planted it was probably going to be invaded, cos they'd need a Security presence round the seed, and its gardeners as well.

All of which spelled potential for distrust and conflict Harp had figured somebody on World would deal with. Not the clueless farmboy. How the stars was he supposed to produce a site that would suit the Kraic but didn't piss off any human landlords?

Landlords!

'Vacc it, Riverbend!' Harp's head left the pillow.

'Crip.' He fumbled for the shipcom on the wall beside him.

'Bridge here, Captain.'

'Yeah, er, can you open another secure link to the Mansion?' Who though? 'To Mz Chan this time, or failing that to Family Legal?'

'Ser, it might take a while. Shall I alert you when we're through?'

'Yeah, good, thanks.' Mind reeling, Harp dashed into a wakeup shower, and had grabbed a caffee by the time the shipcom warbled. After that it got hectic. Mz Chan agreed to organise checks on his, and his tenants', legal rights, probably – when Harp belatedly did the math – dragging Legal out of their beds too. Meanwhile Harp had a serious talk with Big Red and its team about preferred planting conditions. He gathered Moon as their option could relate to its gravity being closer to Kraic IV's. Turned out the hotter climate was another point in its favour. OK. But what about the blasted drought, and ground as hard as steer-hooves?

+++

Big Red seemed suspiciously unconcerned. [WATER AT FIRST] was the public response, cos by then Harp needed to add Ngow as *Defiant* liaison, and Hendriks had turned up, acting as his aide again, passing stuff around and probably recording "Captain Max's" heartbeat. Under that reply though. <WORLD SENDS WATER ONE PLANET ORBIT BY THEN SEED SETTLED> made it suddenly feel very real.

One year? Why did Harp think even that reply was way too short on detail? As if it heard, Big Red then chose to *bury* them in details, the exact volume of water per shipment, the number of shipments, a list of essential soil nutrients, which might if necessary be obtained from Kraic IV.

Big Red also wished to establish [FRIENDLY RELATIONS MANS VICINITY]. In the hope some might take part in the cultivation? Perhaps the nice navy mans might investigate that?

'OK, OK. Got that. Hendriks?' Harp dragged them all back to his own concerns. 'I've explained Moon's climate, so how hot is too hot, for you as well as the Seed?'

[WORLD NOT GOOD]

Not helping! OK, the biggest question, even if he hadn't had a go-ahead from Chan yet. 'Moon also has two newly active volcanoes. Isn't that a problem?'

A pause, maybe Big Red needed to translate –

[VOLCANO GOOD]. He'd swear Big Red was dodging something.

'I... see. Well, is there *anything* you'd have to say no to?'

[MOON GOOD] flashed up at once, back where they'd started, though what Harp received internally was <*Hots good for seed*>

How the crip... Harp took a gulp of caffee. <Even v*olcanic ash, or the risk of a lava flow?*> He pictured molten lava, like a liquid furnace. Did they realise?

But <*Volcano good*> was apparently all he was going to get.

All right. 'Moon it is then. If you could be patient just a little longer, ser, I'll consult about the best location?'

[EXCELLENT. EVERY TRUST]

He gave in; meeting over.

+++

It felt inevitable now that while the Kraic had rebuilt, even extended *their* damaged Orbital, its counterpart on Moon was still only two thirds put to rights, bodies in evac suits still working outside it when he and his company saw it again from *Defiant's* shuttle.

It was the Militia Rim Sector wasn't done yet. He supposed that made a kind of sense. Most of the Militia cruisers were out of action, and the three small naval ships Maxil had sent to cover that would have docked in their own Sector. The XO reckoned it might be another year before the Station got to anything she'd call normal.

On the plus side, reports *Embassador* Harpan was now privy to said new alarm systems, and some extra outer beacons to alert them sooner. Add to that, selected militia officers had been transferred to World for navy-style training while selected naval personnel had been transferred to Moon to write a brand-new training programme for the others.

The icing on that bun: that fancy VIP Sector he'd never seen was pretty much in mint condition; not a bad welcome for their alien visitors. Though Embassador Harpan had requested additions. The temperature there had been raised, and a superfast from World had arrived only hours before them with a raft of Worlder plants to fancy up that modest arc and make it feel more Kraic. OK, so they were under protective glassite shells but it felt more Kraic. Less primitive? He crossed his fingers.

Actually it looked like the residents approved the changes too, and according to Hendriks plantstuff made sense anyway – something about improving the air quality. Maybe that was why the Kraic did it. So there were plants, some even flowering, and the mepal panels had been resprayed, in the colours of the Kraic party.

[COMPLIMENT APPRECIATE]

'Thank you, ser.' Harp, Big Red and even Blue were being careful to talk "publicly", a tacit agreement not to rock any more diplomatic boats unless they had to. Certainly not near *Defiant* Execs, a Marine honour guard, Daichi's team, Harp's "personal escort" *and* a very nervous looking Orbital welcoming committee.

In the end Harp thought the Mooners ended up the most relaxed. The Kraic hadn't visited before, but some of their unlicenced trader ships might have – cos Harp knew a behind-the-scenes barter system had existed on Moon, as long as he remembered. Maybe on Kraic IV Orbital too – and Bayes had said most spacers *lived* for gossip. Either way it looked like whatever tall tales Mooners shared had painted Kraic as friendly; Mooners were wide-eyed but not overtly hostile.

Harp relaxed a fraction. According to Daichi the rushed arrangements were "in hand", accommodation arranged for the Kraic, on the Orbital, both Daichi and the XO deeming that more secure for the present, and there was nothing else he could do till Riverbend. He only hoped that was the right solution. Right now, he felt like a steer cut off from the herd, left to survive on brute instinct and dumb luck.

+++

'Well, well.' Stannis's hands stilled. Just when he'd begun to think there was nothing useful to find, that despite the captain's nice message odds were one Ser Stannisco Mella would never get near his young employer again... he found this morsel. This could change things, a lot. Or finish what the Founding Family's distrust had started.

Stannis stared unseeing at the screen before him. Clear, delete and back away, or... he'd always opted for discretion in his gambles, but today the stakes felt infinitely higher. Was it, maybe, time to party with the big boys? Eleanora even? Well, he was half Regis after all, backstabbing was in his genes. Why break tradition?

Stannis had a date; he cancelled, foreseeing an all-nighter of a very different flavour. Information equalled power, he needed more. Assuming he could avoid the Harpan Security shadowing him.

Stannis' smile turned wicked. As if he hadn't lost them twice already for a moment, just for practice? Good thing the boss was still away. Young Max did seem to have a knack for seeing through him.

+++

Back on Moon; the smell of hot, dry air confirmed it. From inside the shuttle's ramp Harp surveyed the waiting crowd, took a fortifying breath and stepped into sight. Mz Chan had confirmed it, Riverbend belonged to him, always had, the whole vaccing lot; town, mines, even Collar Mountain. And as owner he could pretty much do what he liked with it, including evicting locals who had lived there generations.

Not that he wanted to do anything as draconian – big word. The way he saw this, he wanted the opposite. If he could talk them into it.

So far it looked like they were smiling and waving, even calling welcomes to their "hero". He guessed it might finally help that Mooners still thought he was something he wasn't.

Daichi joined him, murmuring, 'Looks friendly so far, captain.'

'Well, he's Moon's own Harpan.' Hendriks answered from behind them. Hendriks was getting a sight too blasé around the Kraic situation, and the pirates. 'He grew up here, beat the pirates, then got World behind the cleanup. Everyone here knows who to thank.'

'Hendriks, don't-'

'Don't tell it like it really is, Captain Harpan, ser?' Hendriks grinned. 'This is one place you can't hide. Or do anything wrong!'

It didn't feel like that when Harp thought about what he needed to do in the next few hours. An estimated seven hundred locals had chosen to return after the evacuation, the rest opting to relocate. According to Hendriks most of the returnees were long-time residents and miners gambling the mines would be reopened. Official files, slimmer than Daichi liked, suggested a mix of good and bad. Harp wanted to keep the good; wasn't sure yet what to do about the bad. One of whom might be the current mayor, now stepping from the crush to greet him as he hit Moon soil?

Before landing he'd reminded himself; innocent until. After all the mayor he remembered was the father. But this man looked so like his elder, same cropped hair and beard. Same thick lips.

He'd faltered, hadn't he, and maybe his expression... for a second he'd been an orphan once again. His last trip here, to see those kids, had been OK but this, this sudden jolting memory was unexpected, and unwanted.

Maybe Tayla Junior saw, the man's smile widened. 'Captain, pleasure to see you again.' Again? 'You must have been one of m'father's proteges, eh?'

That word. Harp's heart thumped, his palms felt clammy. Thank the stars not all Mooners shook hands these days. 'Not that I recall, sir. Did he sponsor some of the orphans?'

The condescending smirk faded; not so sure now. 'Oh, several.' Tayla didn't quite back off though. 'You sure he didn't... help you, personally?'

The real answer would be 'Almost'. Harp's hands clenched a moment. He'd been new to that Pre Employment House back then, but he'd already learned to fight, a decent scrapper by the time the older Mayor had seen him, but he knew of others hadn't got away with only bruises; hadn't marked the older Tayla bad enough at first attempt the pervert didn't risk another try, no doubt for fear of awkward questions *why* a scrawny kid had kicked him in the head – thank stars for heavy orphan boots – and scratched that oily face so badly?

So the son had known, about the father. And had maybe thought he could intimidate a Harpan? Well, that was one question settled.

Captain Maxil Harpan smiled. 'Generous of him then. So many couldn't spare much for us. Real shame he's not around to see the payback.' Did the other man look worried? Harp slid past, his entourage – another fancy word new-Harpans were supposed to know – behind him.

Too soon after that he was striding through the crowd of locals finding seats in the township's battered meeting hall, excitement on their faces. That and curiosity of course. And yes, he was a real-Harpan now, no longer nameless; didn't need to wait for Tayla Junior to "oversee things" as it looked, the way the man was pushing up behind him.

Not in the mood to oblige, Harp climbed the four scarred steps onto the little stage and got straight to it. 'Day, folks. You'll have heard there's a Kraic delegation on the Orbital?' Quiet now. A rustle here and there as folk leaned forward. 'I met with their leaders recently, on Kraic IV.' Both sorts, but that was classified. Someone gasped anyway. 'They don't look like us but they're friendly. Both sides want an alliance, and not just to help each other beat off any future pirates.' There, self-interest was involved. 'Our new partnership has already had one important result; a gift from the Kraic that's both a friendly gesture and an asset, to *this* planet. I'm here because the Kraic bringing it are coming to Riverbend. They'll build a neighbour-village, called a Kraic Embassy, a bit of Kraic here on Moon. No doubt you'll get acquainted, probably for years, possibly for ever.'

'Oh now, Captain, just a minute,' Mayor Tayla interjected, rising from the seat behind he'd helped himself to.

Get it out the way then? 'Yes, Mr Mayor?' He'd had to practise saying Mr again.

Tayla strutted forward, side by side with Harp now. 'I'm afraid you don't understand how a township works, Captain. You never really being part of one.' Some faces in the crowd looked shocked. Others smirked. Harp figured both would be recorded, by Daichi and the ever-curious Hendriks. Tayla must have registered he had supporters down there too, his shoulders settled and he smiled. 'Riverbend ain't the navy, you know, Captain.' Not the first time Harp had heard his rank become an insult. 'The town council will need to discuss this proposal at some length. We'll need to arrange a meeting, which according to the town charter I regret to say only the councillors –'

'I'm afraid the town charter doesn't apply in this instance.' Harp returned to the larger audience, now agog. 'Apparently I can make any changes I choose, since the land actually belongs to me.'

Shocked silence. Wait a minute there'd be uproar so

Harp didn't wait. 'Folk, the Kraic leaders have honoured your town by accepting Riverbend as their hosts in this new venture. That means Riverbend residents will represent everyone on Moon, and World.'

'OK, but what does all that mean?' The speaker below had miner's muscle, and the stubborn expression Harp recalled as often going with it. What he'd hoped for; somebody who'd ask straight questions.

'It means a small delegation of Kraic, plus human Security, will be your nearest neighbours.' He overrode a couple outbursts. 'It means regular shipments of goods and materials this way, including larger volumes of water. It means construction work for some time to come and new custom for many local businesses. Probably the town's expansion too, as the Kraic are keen to blend into the human community. It means –'

'It means they're coming, and you're saying we might as well make the best of it,' the miner summed up.

Harp grinned at him. 'Yes, it does, but that could be a whole lot more than you have now.'

A woman rose. 'But we got kids here, Captain. How'd we know it's safe letting 'em come into town like you say?'

'All the Kraic I've met have been trustworthy. My word on that.' Cos when you got in someone's head you damn well knew that. 'And remember, those sent here have been selected to represent their kind too.' Put it out there from the start. 'Frankly, from what I know of them I'm more concerned someone among you will offend them than the other way round, but I figure you'll know your own, and how to make sure they behave.'

Another silence, shocked but thoughtful this time?

'So we behave or else.' The miner glowered. Someone nodded.

'I'm saying, very simply, go with this programme, or leave before it kicks off. I'm willing to expedite transfers. I'll even give folk as much choice where they go as I can, plus crediting them for anything they leave can be reused. But I'm hoping most of you will have the guts to stay and help build something important. Call it an adventure. I visited Kraic IV with one other human. You'll have a whole town at your back, and people in authority to call on if you have concerns. Including me, even if I'm not physically here.' Would they listen?

A voice from the back. 'You'd pay us to leave, if we don't like it?'

Not what he'd wanted to hear, but... 'In effect, yes.'

Another. 'How 'bout payin' us to stay?'

'Oh no.' Harp stood tall and faced the hall. 'To be clear, Riverbend is part of my personal territory. As of today that means any changes to local bylaws will be subject to my approval, and any town resident with a genuine grievance will have my office as their final arbiter if they need to appeal a local ruling. That clear enough for you? Riverbend is going to see changes. I'd like for you to see them as opportunities.'

Harp made himself relax; looking nervous wouldn't help. 'Now, I realise this has hit you out of nowhere. I wasn't expecting it either. But it's ours to deal with, so Sergeant Hendriks here has a magic wristcom. Tell him you intend to stay, he'll enter you on the new town register. Anyone staying will also get what we're tagging a small Embassy Supplement, in recognition of their involvement in a major diplomatic startup. Give him your name as interested in *work*, and a few days from now he'll be sending you job offers you can say yes or no to. Oh, and any existing businesses who want new customers should register an interest in both categories.'

Breathe. 'Plus, all registered adult residents will be entitled to vote in all future township elections.' Harp heard Tayla gasp behind him.

'*Everyone* who stays?' a new voice shouted. He'd been right, that register *had* been too small.

'Everyone who's registered,' Harp said firmly. 'If you live here, and you're law-abiding, you're responsible for what happens – so you get a vote.' He smiled. 'You can even vote on who oversees the ballots.'

Chuckles here and there suggested they were thawing.

Sharper minds, he hoped, were adding and subtracting, weighing, even coming to a quick decision? Heads had dipped, talk buzzing, while behind him, 'Captain?' Hendriks, quietly for once and on his best behaviour.

'Sergeant?' Harp resisted grinning, Hendriks was so very pleased about his "field promotion", even knowing it was more a diplomatic gesture.

'You'll want files on the people who spoke.'

'Leave that to Daichi, he's already started. Focus on the numbers.'

The buzz below them faltered. Time for the next move. 'If any of you folks have questions, feel free to talk it over with the sergeant here, as of now?' Harp sat, and mentally crossed all his fingers, faking checking something on his wristcom. Hendriks took the hint and settled at the table Daichi had installed below the dais.

After a tense pause a family group, two adults two kids, marched up. Hendriks sat the parents down. The kids watched solemnly until he handed over fruit drops. Harp's suggestion; he remembered how such treats were rare here, even for the workers' children.

Smiles pretty soon replaced doubt, the parents' faces lighter as they nodded, stood and walked away, heads up; no handshakes, even if the nods were clumsy. Moon was changing, more attuned to World these days. He'd wondered where the handshakes came from but he thought the custom almost over, nodding more accepted. Would that make it easier for Kraic? But the next group hovered; soon there was a queue. Because they saw what this could be? Only as far as another meal? Or because they were putting their trust, their futures, in Harp's hands?

Daichi leaned in, blocking Tayla's glower. 'Time to leave, I think, ser. I've detailed an escort to stay with the sergeant.'

'Fine, let's move out.' Harp stood. 'Folks, I have to go now.' Startled faces in the line below him. 'The sergeant'll be back tomorrow after you've had time to think, though by the look of things he's going nowhere yet anyway. I'd be grateful if you'd find him some coffee so he doesn't get too grumpy.' Muffled laughter. Some still-doubtful faces and a couple scowls. But hopeful.

'Captain Harpan.' Tayla too had risen. 'This is all very –'

'Mr Tayla, can I be blunt?' Harp didn't lower his voice. 'I haven't yet decided what will happen as regards the council. I do foresee a need to reassess its role, and procedures, but right now that's not at the top of my list so I'll expect the present membership to maintain the status quo until I have a clearer picture. I assure you it won't be too long.' There, real-Harpan was the part to play here.

Tayla's mouth opened then closed. 'You, you really own Riverbend?'

'And about five hundred klicks in all directions.'

'But, that includes the mountain.'

'And the mines, yes, though they're not currently operational, are they? As for the town, you must have been aware the council was responsible for collecting the ground rent.'

'Yes, but it went to the govment, not –'

'World government collected it, yes, because it was Harpan land.' He still wasn't sure why, it hardly seemed likely Maxil Snr was sentimental. 'The funds have mounted up while I was missing, which is how I'll be covering the cost of setting up the Kraic village. Riverbend reinvesting, you might say.' Harp saw the flicker in the mayor's eyes, raw anger quickly hidden. 'Now I really must go. Don't forget to tell the sergeant your own intentions, once you've considered your choice.' It would be nice if the man decided to leave, but gut instinct didn't see that happening; too easy.

Harp quit the dais, Daichi at his shoulder again. 'Ser, I've scheduled the sergeant to return midday tomorrow. We'll post the time. And I've detailed surveillance on the councillors as requested.'

'Nothing too overt.'

'No, ser, a small Security presence tomorrow, primed to answer questions to assist the sergeant. They'll plant more interior taps. The remotes are already in place.'

'Good.'

Of course it took a while to get out. Folk had questions. Old folk reminisced, or talked of pirates. Asked about lost children. Harp had no new info for them there except to say the navy were still searching. The few kids he'd personally helped were locals – that maybe made them kinder than they might have been some other townships, but that didn't stop him feeling guilty. He'd been trying to help, but time ran off with him these days, and now the Kraic had made things yet more complicated.

Right now, all he could do was wait for people here to make their minds up.

16

Hendriks beamed. 'Four hundred forty-three residents confirmed and two hundred sixty-one of them applied for work, mostly ex-miners. And the applications are speeding up.'

Hendriks was right, it was a good haul. Didn't matter the Riverbend he recalled had had over three thousand adults, this was still most what the pirates and the evac had left, and enough for what he wanted.

Hendriks wasn't done. 'They hate the pirates so the promise of alliance with the Kraic won a lot of them over, uneasy or not. And they're trusting you, of course. Your word is golden. That's why we've had results so quickly.'

His word, and his trust in the Kraic. Crip, he hoped. 'Good. Send an update to *Defiant,* copy to Big Red. Tell them I'll be staying here at least until the Kraic move in.'

'Already done.' Hendriks looked smug.

Harp pitied Hendriks' next superior officer trying to rein him back in. 'What else have you "already done"?'

'Navy engineers are incoming, and most of the local construction hires will report to the site oh-six-hundred tomorrow. I gave the go-ahead for fuel cells for their transports.'

And so it began; a small team of navy engineers in charge of a local workforce, mostly good strong miners used to working in Moon's harsh ecosystem. Harp had planned for it, Hendriks had organised it. Hendriks was the only one of his *Defiant* comrades he'd managed to co-opt, that much probably another sop to his new status. Ngow wasn't letting any of the other Raptors down here, and Ham didn't have any excuse, not with Daichi around, but having Hendriks along had already made this mission smoother. Even with Hendriks' growing tendency to anticipate. Crip, just plain take over.

+++

Two weeks later the Kraic "residence" was near complete, and the human parts of the village were taking shape. Canny miners had quickly emptied navy's cargo modules and converted them to shelter, stretching navy-borrowed canvas over gaps between them; shade and rations always Mooners' first priority. They'd also roped overlapping awnings across the open central ground already being called the Circle. Major Valt, the greying navy engineer who'd thought she was in charge, admitted quietly to Harp she'd thought they had been slacking off, before she got to know the climate. But Valt was a good officer, she'd adapted fast and wasn't slow to listen to the miners, even sometimes on construction. She was definitely popular when she issued the sand-coloured pants and tees, looser, thinner fabrics to replace the navy's gear, and the locals'. Harp had taken to them gladly. So had all the locals; tougher than they looked and didn't cost a credit!

As for progress on the perimeter buildings...

Harp, Valt and Hendriks had been doing a tour of inspection. Harp was even more impressed with the woman, and the Riverbend crews. The Kraic domicile at the core wasn't quite finished outside but the interior walls were smoothed and already sprayed in several shades of green, exotic colours these days to a Mooner that had caused a deal of comment.

Harp thought the domed design, result of long discussion with various Kraic, was essentially a pale echo of the Kraic's forests. The entry was a wide, open archway, its roof extending out toward the common area so it met the now-enlarged awnings. Kraic could stay in shade throughout their village.

Past the arch, a shady tunnel-like passage led into the central "rotunda", as he'd learned to call it, that had a tinted glassite roof that filtered light into the central "clearing". A circle of pillars – think trunks – supported entrances to eight more shaded, inner alcoves, then another, outer circle housed the sixteen screened-off living quarters and a couple extras Harp had guessed were guest rooms. Blue presumably was in one. Whenever Harp considered it he saw a forest. Right now, one of the inner alcoves was being set up for food prep, another for communal bathing and a third for meetings or communications. Hendriks had had the bright idea of sending regular images back to *Defiant*, keeping everyone updated, so with any luck there'd be no major problems. Messages coming the other way claimed the Kraic appeared excited, eager to move in. So time to start it?

Harp turned round to Valt. 'Major. I think we're ready to invite our lodgers.'

'Ser, we're not half done yet.' Valt pulled a face, waved at the organised chaos outside the dome. 'But you're right of course, we have to get things underway sometime.' Maybe the woman was nervous about the Kraic, the responsibility – crip, the navy's good name or something. Harp still didn't know her well enough to pick one. But as far as he was concerned Riverbend folk had already had too much time to second guess their choices; he figured the best way to establish amicable coexistence – hark at him – was diving in so deep it had to happen. 'Right. I don't think the Kraic will mind a building site, they're keen to come.' Harp started for the open air again. 'We'll make it an occasion. Invite everyone who's been working on the site, their families as well, and I'd like Mr Sulis in the official welcoming party, maybe even get him to show the Kraic round.' Hendriks was already taking notes. It was almost annoying sometimes the way the man could do that and still keep up, but it was certainly a bonus; Hendriks never missed a detail.

Valt's steps faltered then resumed their measured tread. Valt was in many ways the obvious choice to play guide, being officially in command, but if she wasn't comfortable round the Kraic... besides the woman wasn't dumb. She knew she wouldn't be staying on once the construction phase was over. A moment's thought was all it took her. 'A local welcoming them. One you plan to be in regular contact?'

Hendriks smirked. Harp smiled approval. 'Mr Sulis checked out; several generations here, supports his parents, respected by his peers, supervisor role in the mines. He probably came back cos all that experience wouldn't count for so much somewhere else. I'd guess like others he was praying the mines would be reopened, that maybe we'd drill new shafts farther out from the mountain, or go down more than horizontal.'

Harp found he was frowning. Finding out a lot more about what were now *his* closed mines was yet another thing on his to-do list. Non-employees hadn't been allowed up there, and it had always nagged him he didn't really know what the people he'd lived next to actually did. But back to current business. 'You did say he'd been an asset here.'

'I did, and he is. Yes, ser, a good idea to use him.' Simple words that gave up any thought Valt might have had of being centre stage, of furthering her own career. Yes, a decent officer. If she could work with locals as well as she had, and interact with the Kraic reasonably, well, if a new-Harpan could nudge promotion her way he'd see what he could manage when the engineer was posted. After all, the need for engineering would soon give way to permanent things like security, "xeno-diplomacy" and "acclimatisation". More big words to swallow. Harp, via Hendriks and Daichi, was already vetting the first wave of applicants, a lot more careful about any candidates World Diplomacy were putting forward.

Valt's mind hadn't wandered. 'And, Mr Tayla?' Valt was the only other one in the know there. Harp had kept the details in his current inner circle.

'Will naturally be invited, along with the rest of the council, but since Mr Sulis has much more first-hand knowledge of the site I think he might be a more logical choice as guide on this occasion. Don't you?'

'Quite so, Ser,' Valt said gravely. 'I, er, take it we don't have any further intel?'

'No.' Harp reminded himself Daichi's frustration was

probably enough for both of them. His gut said there *was* more to find on Tayla, but so far neither Daichi's use of the Family network nor Hendriks' use of... whatever Harp wasn't supposed to know about... had found more than the official files told them. Tayla owned the only general store Riverbend still boasted. His prices were stiff but not quite extortionate given the state of everything here. His posted accounts seemed in order, his tithes paid. Council minutes revealed only legitimate and reasonable-looking decision making, even if Harp didn't approve the shift to closed council meetings in recent years. No, so far the only thing raising Harp's hackles was how Tayla had paid every tithe on time. Even after the drought worsened, the mine had to close and his customers all evacced, him included?

Harp thought that bit of cleverness a slip on Tayla's part, and he couldn't ignore what he knew about the father. How often did the calf stray far from the steer?

But the lack of results meant Harp had been delaying the new council elections he'd practically promised folk, and he wasn't sure how much longer he could. Daichi said the locals were becoming restless on the subject, when they didn't realise Daichi's taps could hear them. Well, the Kraic's arrival might divert them for a while, so that was another benefit to getting everyone together?

Formal invitations, fancy printouts, hand delivered to the folk involved here, navy and locals; Hendriks notion. 'They'll be heirlooms, proofs of "I was there" to show the grandkids. It'll make 'em feel special and they'll have another reason to approve of Kraic.'

Harp couldn't argue with the logic. Even a few shifts in attitude were worth the ridiculous cost.

+++

Defiant's shuttle was enroute, bringing the first Kraic to the designated landing area, marked out past the site perimeter. More canvas was pegged outside the nearest outer modules to provide a shaded path inside, and with an hour to go, Harp was laughing; Hendriks was unbelievable. This edge of the Circle had become a party; food and drink, even games for the children. Harp's smile faded, guilt and sorrow banishing amusement. The attacks on him, escorting the Seed, were no excuse; he'd not yet traced the kids still missing.

Problem was, he knew Maxil Snr and Feldin would say this event took priority. And he couldn't quite say they were wrong. Few against many was a telling argument, like it or not. Having so much power – he supposed he did now, even if he still had less than others – was a lot more work than he had once imagined.

So he stood here under all the fancy awnings, trying to appreciate the shade and waiting for the navy to deliver Riverbend's salvation. Because whether the township recognised it or not he *had* potentially done that much. A mining town without a mine was doomed but a town that played host to an alien embassy could grow and flourish even if the mines didn't. The trick was to smooth that path and ensure new wealth got spread around, not hoarded by a selfish council. Harp didn't think he'd ever been that selfish. Needy. Ruthless, maybe. Selfish, greedy, bullying; he didn't understand it, even though he'd learned to spot it, and avoid it.

But there was a speck in the sky hadn't been there before, growing rapidly. The Kraic were arriving. 'Hendriks.'

'Yes, I see it.' Hendriks was already turning. 'Incoming, Major.'

Suddenly Valt was inspecting everything again and Hendriks calling out to townsfolk, shooing children safely back to adults. Harp watched Tayla's chest puff out, and noted who were quick to join him in the forefront. Nearer Harp, Ser Sulis drifted to the front as well. His wife and son, behind him, looked on edge, but Sulis didn't, he was busy watching Tayla. Then the miner looked at Harp, and smiled tightly. No, the mayor didn't know, and yes, mean spirited or not, they'd both enjoy this.

Ten Kraic, and Blue, at the rear for once, flowed down the ramp in pairs, onto the hard-baked ground then shifted upright. The other six were staying on *Defiant* with the precious Seed until the planting site was ready. As Harp stepped out into the open gasps and exclamation trailed into silence. Big Red only looked at Harp but some of its team, crew, family, looked round, or up. Not used to so much open sky of course, or such attacking heat. In some ways they'd have to adapt to Moon as much as the locals would to them. Harp reached Big Red and gave the respectful Harpan nod, slower than a shipboard salute. 'Welcome, Ambassador.'

[THANKS TO HARP FRIEND] Big Red's head swivelled, farther than a human's. [MUCH WORK]

'Not complete as you can see, ser, but I hope enough for you to manage.' By that time Red's people had recovered too and formed their usual semicircle, back to solemn. Or in other words actually still.

Except for one of course, behind Big Red but hopping just a little. <*Hot here*> reached Harp's mind.

<*Yes, Blue*> Harp replied, then tried to focus on his job. Blue was good at forgetting a mere human had trouble holding two conversations at once. Harp waved the Kraic toward the wider shade where everybody else was waiting. 'The people you see, ser, are the current Riverbend councillors, and adults who've been building here, and families. They're here to bid you welcome too.'

Big Red flowed beneath the larger awnings, halfway rose again then faced the watching townsfolk. Its translator morphed to bigger letters. [MANY THANKS TO MANS FOR BUILDING]

Harp's eyes met Sulis's, his cue. 'Aw, none needed, sir, I'm sure.' If Sulis was afraid he didn't look it. 'What's good for you's good for us as well, see.'

'Ah, Mr Sulis.' Harp half-nodded, not as formally as for Big Red but recognition. 'I'm told Mr Sulis has been a great help on the site, ser. In fact he's an excellent choice to show you your new residence, if you'd like a tour?'

[SULIS PLEASE.]

And done. Sulis ambled out of the crowd, nodded amicably to Big Red and waved toward the Kraic's dome. 'Better start over there then, I guess, your place is about done.' The man carried on walking. The Kraic delegation flowed down onto all eight legs again and undulated off around him, heads a trifle lower than his shoulders. Harp heard Sulis saying, 'If there's anything ain't as you want…'

That left the townsfolk buzzing, getting over the first shock of an alien presence they finally saw in the flesh. Shell. Carapace. Valt and her people kept a calming eye on them and Daichi's lot watched councillors, so neatly side-lined. Looked like Tayla was watching the Kraic disappear in disbelief, but then his gaze came back to Harp. The rage showed for a second – Harp pretended not to notice – then the man swung round and headed for the buffet with his closest cronies flanking him in wary silence.

Daichi sidled closer. 'The locals still move aside for him.'

'Yes.' Still too submissive. New-found prosperity hadn't yet altered old habits. Tayla-father and Tayla-son had had authority here since before Harp was born. Intellectually, Harp accepted it'd take more than a few weeks to change the mindset he was seeing, even for those willing. Emotionally, it chewed at him, but he had to be patient. Valt, Daichi and Hendriks were giving his people a shiny new template for what authority *should* look like, and the workers onsite were increasingly looking to Sulis, for opinions as well as work orders. If Big Red approved Sulis too they were halfway home; Sulis oh-so-casually now positioned perfectly for folk to vote him in when Harp set up elections. Hendriks called it "Harpan machination". Harp just thought he had to fight corrupt with sneaky.

Meanwhile the humans were back to eating the free food and sharing first impressions. Harp went back to "circulating", Daichi at his elbow. Somewhat to Harp's surprise Tayla didn't approach him, choosing to fill a plate and settle at a shaded table. No doubt Daichi was as interested as Harp to see which council members joined him. And which drifted off and chose to chat with others? Daichi would be recording, likely Hendriks less officially. Not that a councillor distancing themselves from Tayla meant much. Some might not be willing allies but they could as well be playing neutral party till they found out how the land lay.

Course, they wouldn't know about the tiny drones Daichi had housed beneath each table, like the ones he'd planted in the township. Hah. Harp smiled, agreed with one man yes the Kraic did look like the vids the locals had been shown, assured an older woman he had got on well with them, counted them as friends in fact, agreed with a solemn little boy explaining steers had two less legs so that was probably why steers couldn't sit up like the Kraic. Nor steers couldn't swivel heads right round like that, nor –

His mother rushed in to the rescue. 'So sorry, Captain! Rill's as bad as his da, always wanting to see how stuff works.'

Of course, this was Sulis's family. Harp hadn't met them before except as a note in Sulis's file. 'No problem, Madame Sulis, it's good he's curious.' Harp looked down at a frowning child. 'Rill, is it? Perhaps you'd like to meet one of your new neighbours?'

The little mouth fell open. 'Ma? Can I, Ma?'

Madame Sulis hesitated. Rill was what, eight? And the Kraic had pincers and those beak-like mouths; a mother would be worried. But he was a Harpan, and as Hendriks said *their* Harpan; there was only one possible answer. She drew a breath then held out a hand. 'Let's do that, son. But mind your manners now, these are our new employers.'

'Yes'm.' Rill looked hopefully at Harp, who sent out mind-talk, hoping he could reach across the Circle. <*Blue?*>

<Harp call>

<Want to meet a human young?>

<*Coming Coming*> Harp and company weren't even halfway across to the dome before a familiar shape skipped out through the arched entry, "saw" them and headed over. Blue flowed upward, sitting on its rear two legs and tail. Good call. That put its head about level with Harp's chest, not too much higher than Rill. Blue hopped several times before its neckscreen flashed up [MEET PLEASED HARP MANS NAME BLUE]

'Yes, this is Blue, the youngest of the delegation. Blue, this is Rill, and his mother Madame Sulis.' <*Sulis's family, Blue*>

<*Offspring*> Blue was ducking its head to greet them, something both Kraic and humans had in common.

<Yes>

Blue looked down at Rill. Rill looked up at Blue, then at Harp. 'Is his name really Blue?'

'Probably not, but we can't pronounce Kraic names. Luckily he says he likes having a human name as well.'

Rill continued to frown. 'You called the other one *Big Red*.'

'It's in charge, so I was extra polite.'

'Huh.' Rill turned back to Blue. 'How'd you turn your head so far?'

Harp shook his head at Rill's embarrassed mother, who closed her mouth and looked resigned. By then Blue was demonstrating it could in fact turn its head a whole three sixty. Rill watched then showed Blue how far he could go. Blue's head tilted, looked like it was startled by the difference; almost certainly pretending since it should be used to humans. Nice gesture though. Blue was older than Rill, maybe teenage-equivalent, but it was its parent's offspring, versed in public interactions.

And it knew it had an audience, most of the adults watching now, some openly, some furtive. Other kids were even edging closer. One, a slightly older girl with ribbons in her paler hair, announced, 'I'm Attima. *My* father is the mayor.'

Rill scowled. Blue turned its bulbous eyes her way.

[MAYOR COUNCIL FOR TOWN.]

'Yes.' She flashed a boasting smile at the kids who'd followed.

Blue hopped. [TOWN WORK FOR HELP KRAIC COUNCIL WORK FOR TOWN]

Harp almost choked; it took an alien... The girl blinked. Several adult jaws fell open too. Harp figured none of them had ever thought of the council as working *for* them, but he could almost see the notion taking root. Help it along then? 'Yes, Blue. The townsfolk can choose the best humans to get things done for everyone else.' Hah. Remember *that* when you get to vote.

Blue looked at Harp. [BEST LIKE HARP]

'You flatter me, you know I'm not.' Harp forced himself to laugh that off; a joke. A bad one. No one voted Harpans into power, they'd got there by blood, and wealth, and history, him too now. He wasn't an example for these folk however they stared. Crip. 'Maybe you kids would like to introduce yourselves too?'

A stutter of names, that Blue repeated on its neck-screen. Giggles at some unexpected spellings. Inevitably it was Rill who asked why Blue didn't talk. One kid stumbled back when Blue demonstrated "talking" with its first four pincers. To Harp the clicking was more emotions than words; he read these as a mix of laughing and clapping. Still it satisfied these youngsters. They edged closer, but since only Attima was taller than a seated Blue Harp figured it could cope. Madame Sulis wasn't the only parent keeping watch, and no one here should want to unseat this new ride.

Harp noticed Attima's ma – he had Mz Chan to thank for how he'd learned to memorise so many faces – had moved up next to Madame Sulis and was giving her the gracious sort of smile he'd seen on influential Worlders. Someone quick to see which way the wind blew? Quicker than her husband? Madame Sulis didn't look so comfortable, Harp could only hope he wasn't going to cause the woman too much trouble. But he needed Sulis, so he guessed she'd have to deal.

Talk of the devil, the rest of the Kraic were flowing out of their dome with Sulis in their midst seemingly easy with this new sort of conversing; it looked like he was managing to exchange remarks with three screens at once. When Harp jerked his head his new site super took the hint and led the Kraic across. Harp smiled at Big Red. 'I hope Mr Sulis has shown you everything, ser?'

[SULIS MOST HELP RESIDENCE WELL BUILD] Again with bigger letters folk farther away could also make out. [MANY THANKS RIVERBEND MANS]

'Good. Now there's food, if you would like to join us. Oh, this is Madame Sulis, and offspring, called Rill.'

[OFFSPRING TWO PROGENITOR]

'Yes, ser.' Harp still wasn't sure how Kraic reproduced, and wasn't rash enough to ask.

[MADAM RILL] Big Red bobbed a nod, so did his companions. Medam gulped but managed to nod back when Sulis nudged her.

Rill gazed higher, then at Blue. 'He your da then?'

[PROGENITOR BIG RED LEADER BLUE APPRENTICE] A word that to the best of Harp's knowledge Blue hadn't come across. Just like its elders shouldn't know so much about the human neighbours. But Rill nodded, apparently satisfied, and Sulis and his wide-eyed partner steered Big Red toward the buffet tables, where Hendriks pointed out Kraic-approved options and three of the Kraic bravely opted to sample new local dishes.

Slowly, species mingled. Tayla and his wife engaged two lesser Kraic in conversation, full of smiles. The kids lured Blue to all the sweets on offer, luxuries both species gobbled. No doubt the humans'd be bouncing off the walls by bedtime but right now they watched in awe as Blue's four pincers flashed and foodstuff simply disappeared.

Harp's people were primed, and used to Kraic, so it didn't take too long to get a fair proportion of the locals interacting in some fashion. Not a bad start, Harp considered, not bad at all. Yes, some humans still hung back, and didn't smile, but the number who now looked relieved was larger. Harp reached out. *<Big Red, when you're ready, ser, feel free to retire to your dome? We'll clear out here.>*

<Yes. Hot>

<Yes, ser.> That had been a worry. <Will you be able to adapt?>

<Prepared>

OK, prepared, whatever that meant; he would have to trust the Kraic to say if someone had a problem. Or not. *<You'll remember you only need to ask if–>*

<Kraic prepared, and Harp-friend should not worry>

<Yes, ser, thank you.> And now get back to human talk before these people notice you've been staring into space? Big Red was so much more adept at this than he was.

When the light began to fail the lamps Ser Sulis had strung under the awnings flickered on, giving the scene a yellower glow Harp thought the Kraic enjoyed. Soon after that Big Red flowed down and away through the crowd. His deputy, Big Grey – a name Harp could as easily have chosen for its personality as for its colour – flashed up thanks to all the locals for their welcome, food, hard work, and ended with apologies for leaving but, it said, the Kraic had found the shuttle ride and the excitement of this new beginning tiring. They would now retire to enjoy their most impressive quarters. At least, it said that in a lot less words than it translated into.

The Kraic flowed under their deep archway and down their tunnel. The humans went quiet. Harp figured it was sinking in; their visitors were here to stay and Riverbend would never be the same again, so it was understandable if human faces showed some doubt or people took some deeper breaths.

Blue gone, the kids rejoined their elders, full of *their* experience and sharing it. Like all his talks on World, new info reaching adults via enthusiastic youngsters. Blue would be an asset here as it had been on *Defiant*. And Harp had better talk to Sulis, find out if Big Red had asked for any changes.

17

Twelve days later early morning saw another scheduled shuttle delivery, several Kraic out and about, helping to unload, some of it their own supplies. Flaps on their long packages dropped down to fit them, like a saddle. Nothing fell off Kraic backs, and those eight legs moved cargo twice as fast as humans. Folk were used to that by now, though there'd been shock the first time.

Add some open mouths when Blue, of course, got bored with going to and fro and chose to skip and hop right *up* the outside of the dome and sit on top of it, presumably to see the country all around it. Big Red had promptly gone up too, its head a-swivel, no doubt noting all the sensors that Security had planted, stubby weeds that would give ample warning of arrivals. Later, other Kraic had gone up there to sightsee every now and then as well, when folk took breaks, their climbing skills an entertainment for the humans. By then, breaks saw Kraic and humans often sat together, sharing shade and questions. Humans had got curious. The coexistence Harp had wished for was increasingly more fact than theory here in the village; long might it continue.

This morning, Harp found Valt and Sulis in discussion with Big-Grey, it sounded like something to do with the dome's flooring. He was about to ask more when the first shuttle took off, blocking talk, and a second one replaced it with more cargo. Which included one item he definitely hadn't expected. Felli, Feldin's youngster? What the?

The youth stepped gingerly down the ramp in the midst of the cargo, wearing navy blue, that would show every speck of dust, and carrying a bulging, clearly brand new duffle on one shoulder. Then hit level dirt and halted in his tracks, worst place he could have. Locals detoured round him, showing brusque impatience at the roadblock. It was hot out there and everyone more interested in unloading than some idiot stranger. Kraic practically flowed through him, making less allowance. Kraic, they'd discovered, didn't have much concept of "personal space".

Harp hid a smile. Was Felli shocked cos he was seeing aliens, Moon, or cos no one here was nodding to a Harpan? He didn't think Felli had noticed him, back in the shade, too busy gawking at the Kraic wooshing past him. But Valt had recognised the Harpan heir, Daichi too. Daichi's face remained impassive. 'Ser?'

'No, I wasn't. Were you?'

'No, ser, I would have said.'

'Of course. My apologies for doubting.' Fancy Harpanspeak seemed called for, he'd just insulted his own Chief of Security, hadn't he? 'Well, I guess we'd better say hello then.' Daichi followed him toward the shuttle, Harp debating whether to reach out to warn Big Red. Felli might be underage but he was still a Harpan, and this Inner Family. Maybe Harp should test the water first? 'Ser Felli, good morning.' A local did a double take.

Felli swung his way, and stiffened. 'Captain.' A jerky nod, a sideways look at Daichi. 'I was told I should report to you.' Tiny pause. 'I'm afraid my sister was forced to send her apologies.' The youth's eyes shifted to one side. 'A sudden illness prevented her coming.'

A lie? Ho-San had ducked out and left her little brother to it? More importantly, why the stars was Felli here? Harp retained his public smile, aware Daichi saw it. 'A shame. Nothing serious, I hope?'

'Hopefully not, ser. I believe the medics were being cautious.' Facing Harp once more; a half truth this time.

'Good, hopefully she'll soon send you word she's feeling better so you needn't worry.' Felli's face had blanked, what had he said? Forget it. 'But let's move into some shade, let these folk get on with unloading. So what can we do for you?'

A frown. Maybe a hint of affront? 'You weren't expecting me?'

'Actually, no, but you're welcome of course. Did your father want you to spend time with the Kraic?' It was the only reason came to mind.

'Er.' A cautious glance at busy, eight-legged bodies scurrying across the shaded clearing. 'Grandfather sent us, to see Moon, for ourselves. And see if we could help out.'

If the kid looked reluctant it wasn't so surprising – he probably had zero experience of anything like this, without adding the Kraic into the mix. Probably never been to Moon before, or even into space. Or, very obviously, in the middle of a cargo drop. But he'd been sent, so what was Harp supposed to do with him? What was the kid even good for here? First things first though. 'Daichi, we'll need to find Ser Felli somewhere to sleep.'

'Ser.' Daichi tapped his wristcom, muttered.

'We moved in here now the Kraic have. Our accomodation's not going to be what you're used to, I'm afraid, but we can at least find you a bed. Unless you'd prefer to lodge in the township?' Except the kid didn't seem to have brought any personal Security. If not he guessed he'd have to send some along with, and –

'I'm sure somewhere here will be acceptable if you're staying here, Captain.' Kid looked less than thrilled, but also looked determined, judging by the way the chin had risen. Saw this as a challenge, did he? Or was Harp the challenge? Crip, as if he didn't have enough to deal with?

'Well, come and look then you can decide?' Harp waved to the first of the prefab blocks they had erected, the human curve around three quarters of the central space, inevitably tagged "the barracks". It was the block he was in; wouldn't be polite to house the boy anywhere else. He suspected Daichi might have opted for less polite, but... 'The walls are up and the plumbing's in, such as it is, but we're still waiting for some of the extras. With luck maybe they arrived with you,' Harp prattled as he walked the boy beneath the mass of awnings that had made the central circle of the "village" safe from heatstroke. He'd told Valt, and Sulis, the Kraic would be more comfortable with curves than rigid lines. Result: they'd managed to prefab semicircle frames, like rounded tunnels once they added on the insulated outer panels.

Valt had called it rainbow-shaped but Harp had never seen a rainbow so he'd had to research that one.

'This is A block.' Offering a view of one of Daichi's team removing gear from one of the last cubicles on the left of the central corridor. Figured; Daichi knew Harp was early in on the right, after him. 'And it looks like you have a room.'

'Oh. I didn't intend...' The boy flushed, peeked sideways as the woman passed them.

'There's room enough in the other blocks, but here'll feel more familiar. You'll know Ser Daichi of course.' Since Harp was pretty sure his Security chief had been promoted – or not – out of either Feldin's or Maxil's office. 'Major Valt is quartered here too, she's the engineer in charge, and Sergeant Hendriks, who's seconded as my aide right now, so there'll be people you can go to when you have a question. I'll introduce you to Mr Sulis too, the local foreman. You'll probably see his young son playing with the youngest Kraic.' Which was happening whenever Rill could talk his father into coming.

'*Mr* Sulis?' So the kid was taking notice.

'Yes.' First lesson. 'Mooners don't always use ser, more Mr or Madame. And they might shake hands. It's different but you get used to it.'

'Mm.' Felli hesitated at "his" open doorway. It was a cupboard, and a pretty bare one. A hard navy cot, now stripped of bedding, a very small table, low enough the cot could double as a seat, an overhead light that was either on or off, no shading. Harp supposed he'd better break the rest of the bad news. 'The head, sorry, washrooms, are at the end of the corridor, no air-dry but there's lots of local towels.' He'd deliberately bought from Tayla, on the principle of catching more flies with sweet. Mayor or not, they'd still likely meet. 'Laundry goes into the big carton we passed by the outer door. You'll find a bag by your door, and a new business in town collects each day.' The plan was everyone here patronised local businesses. 'You'll need to check your things are labelled with your name.'

Complete silence from beside him. It wouldn't be polite to laugh but it was funny. The only thing funnier would be if the even snootier Ho-San was standing here too. Hm. Harp decided to be thankful for small mercies. If Felli was shocked to immobility stars knew how his nose-in-the-air sister would have reacted. On that note. 'I'd suggest a change of clothes before you explore. It's a *lot* hotter here than World. We spend more time in the open air too.' That outfit the boy had on must be roasting him by now, especially the fancy jacket. 'Do you have anything lighter with you?'

'I...' Felli lowered the expensive multi-pocket duffle – he'd probably thought it navy-appropriate, or roughing it – onto the unmade cot, frowned and brushed at an already-dusty sleeve.

'Why don't I send over some local things, in case, and leave you to decide what suits? Major Valt organised a consignment of stuff from *Defiant*'s replication and a lot of the locals have taken to them. It's practically uniform around here.' Yes, the locals had loved the free wardrobe upgrade. Harp had spotted a few family members sporting it too, another perk the town was getting. It would be interesting to see whether Felli chose comfort and blending in, or fashion and status? Harp took a step, which put him back in the corridor. 'Come find me when you're ready for the grand tour?'

'Mm.' Felli didn't look up. Or use Harp's rank, or any honorific. Daichi's brows twitched. Harp chose to give the kid a pass, he was probably in shock, but Daichi was tap-tapping on his wristcom, sign of something he didn't want overheard. No doubt Ser Felli was acquiring some discreet surveillance. Walking back down the passageway, Harp wondered whether Daichi was protecting the young Inner Family member, or Harp. Daichi's non-reaction said he didn't see the kid as one of Harp's allies, but he was surely no real threat? Nah, it was Daichi being his usual paranoid-security self.

Daichi didn't speak till they hit the baking air outside.

'Ser, I've informed appropriate parties of Ser Felli's arrival, and requested intel from *Defiant*.'

'Fine. Hopefully they'll know when they're supposed to be taking him home.' And why no one had warned them he was coming.

'Ser.' The non-expression was sufficient comment.

Clearly the news had spread to the rest. Harp saw surprise, some pleasure, some panic. Harp might be a Mooner-Harpan, Felli was from quite another herd. Harp made what Emika called an executive decision. 'We need to find him a job.'

'Ser.' Daichi scanned the mayhem that was currently the village-in-construction plus unloading, Kraic and humans intermingled in what often looked like chaos though the two were quickly growing comfortable together. 'Do you have anything in mind?'

Harp grinned. 'Not a thing, Daichi, but we can palm it off, eh?' He tapped his own wristcom. 'Hendriks?'

'Yeah?' Hendriks sounded preoccupied; surfaced. 'Sorry, Captain. You wanted me?'

'You have any intel on what skillsets Ser Felli might have?'

'Crip. Sorry, give me a moment?' Gone.

Harp turned back to Daichi, still grinning. 'The sergeant will research the subject for us.'

'Ah.' Daichi relaxed a fraction. He and Hendriks had formed quite an alliance. If Hendriks or the navy weren't careful, he'd get poached.

Harp turned to C Block, still a shell. 'Back to work, I guess.' He might as well stay useful while he waited. Although... <*Blue?*>

<Harp-friend want>

<Ser Felli Harpan. Feldin Harpan offspring.>

<*Here*> Of course the Kraic were aware.

<Yes. He's maybe nearer your age.>

<Saw. Where now>

<Hopefully accepting cooler clothing. A Block cubicle.>

<On way. On way>

Harp tried to stop the grin and failed. <*Thanks.*> If Felli was staying, they might as well push him in at the deep end, to use a very Worlder saying. That way if the kid was going to run for the hills he might even go back with the next shuttle?

+++

Felli didn't run, at least not right away. He did reappear in some of his fancier clothes but only that first day, then he turned out for the next morning-meal, head held high, in the sand-coloured gear Harp and every other human here was wearing. When no one commented the kid subsided and at least looked calmer.

Their Kraic hosts – Harp had been careful to explain this was Kraic territory, even if a human was their landlord – made a point of eating with the humans, at least most of them did most of the time. Harp wondered if they had a roster; Big Red clearly understood public relations. The two species didn't necessarily tolerate the same foods but both enjoyed the outdoor meeting area beneath the overlapping awnings. Like a forest? Picking up a plate in the canteen, which had acquired walls if not yet aircon, Harp watched Blue skip up and welcome Felli, pointing out foods he shouldn't eat. The night before, the kid had stuck to foods he would have eaten on *Defiant*, even looking sideways at the local produce, but today he hesitated, sampled something, looked surprised then took a proper portion.

When one of its elders called Blue away Felli drew a breath, surveyed the scene outside the open doors where Kraic and humans shared the tables, humans on rough stools and Kraic on their tails, then filled the rest of his plate. Harp left him to it, only waved when Felli hovered.

Hendriks made a space then went on eating. Felli barely gave Hendriks a look as he took the spot, evidently not in the habit of saying thanks to the help. Oh no. Harp's place. Harp's rules. 'Sergeant Hendriks, meet my cousin Felli. You found him a job yet?'

Felli stopped eating. Hendriks smiled sweetly. 'Canteen roster to start, Captain, if you approve. It'll be cooler in there than on construction.' When Harp nodded Hendriks turned to Felli. 'You'll need to report to the head cook, ser. She's local, name of Sakar. She'll tell you what needs doing.'

'Um, Sergeant.' Felli stared at his plate. 'Er, when...'

Harp smiled too. 'When you've eaten, no rush, though when you have time you might take another look round then maybe tell Hendriks if there's anywhere else you think you could contribute. We like to use people's skills the best we can. Meanwhile, eat, you'll need it. Feeding all of us is a fulltime job.'

'Right. Captain.' Felli didn't seem to enjoy his food as much any more but he did eat it, he was a normal enough kid for that. Not to mention a Harpan, with the Family's calorie requirements? Eventually he squared his thin shoulders, remembered he was supposed to bus his own dishes – this time – and trudged back into the canteen block.

'Want to be a fly on the wall?' Hendriks fingers hovered at his wristcom.

'No, just alert me if there's any trouble.' Harp rose too. He had a meet with Big Red, then Sulis, then some more labouring, and Felli would either settle in or not. He wasn't sure which one *he* wanted.

He didn't see the kid again till suppertime.

'Captain, may I?'

No, the empty place wasn't an accident, even if the boy thought it was. Harp waved a fork, Felli sat, careful not to jostle, careful carrying his plate, mug, cutlery. Both ate. Harp waited for complaints, demands. According to Hendriks Madame Sakar had looked Felli up, down, grunted and assigned him table scrubbing, followed by feeding dishes into the solar-powered wash unit they'd "borrowed" from *Defiant*. Most of the new mech they were installing was solar powered, the obvious choice here. The kid had no idea how lucky he was; four days ago he'd have been dishwashing by hand. He probably wouldn't believe that if Harp told him!

But so far Felli wasn't talking so Harp left him to his thoughts, until they both reached for the insulated carafe in the middle of the table and Harp's arm out-reached Felli's. 'Caffee?'

'Please. Captain.' Felli held out his plain navy mug.

Harp poured for them both, added sweet to his own, watched Felli do the same. 'Still makes me feel spoilt.'

Felli stopped, mug in hand. 'What?'

'Adding sweet. I fear I've got addicted. Where I came from it wasn't usual.' Harp sipped and savoured.

'People here don't like sweet?'

'Not many could afford it.' Harp let his gaze roam round the nearby tables, knowing Felli's followed. 'A lot couldn't stretch to refills on their caffee either. Had to ration their water, y'know?'

'Oh.' Felli studied cheerful local faces, all with mugs before them. Found a sneer 'So they drink ours here?'

'Yes.' Harp dropped his voice. 'They know if they drink here their families can have more at home.'

'Oh.' Felli gazed into his own mug, but he'd dropped his voice too. 'I saw the vids you and my father put out on the casts. Was it really that bad here?'

'Still is, ser. What you're seeing here is one place things are improving faster than most.'

A frown. 'Because of you.' Why should that feel like an accusation?

Harp shrugged off his reaction. 'Mainly cos of the Kraic.'

'But they're here because you favoured this place.'

'I suppose. The land's mine. That made it easier to arrange. And I spent some years here, back when I was younger than you, so yes, I guess I caused it.' Harp stood up, caffee in hand. 'Walk with me?'

The youngster hesitated then stood and picked up his mug too. 'Why? Why are we walking?'

'Some things are better talked about in private. Let's check the perimeter sensors, save someone a job. When the winds come they get caked in crud, and I don't know about you but I could do with the exercise before I get into contortions.'

'Contortions?' Felli still sounded like he didn't trust anything Harp said but at least now he was listening.

'I'm muscling for construction at C Block again.' Harp pretended to sigh. 'Seems like no one else can get the damned plumbing to fit together in these rounded shells.' He laughed. 'At least that's what they say. I think they just like seeing me sweat.'

'*You* do plumbing?'

'Orphans learn to fix stuff.' They'd left the shade and now they stepped beyond the ring of buildings, open ground before them. 'I really wanted to brief you on the locals. I don't suppose I need tell you to regard this as privileged.'

'No, ser.' Did the 'ser' sound easier this time, or just sarcastic? Crip, the kid was like a foreign language.

'Good.' Harp tried for officer-to-private, that might sound less patronising. 'The locals you've met here are mostly happy about all this. They can see the benefits. There's the odd one of them not yet on board but you'll soon spot them, I'm sure.' Flattery maybe, but the kid wasn't dumb – he hoped.

'Are you saying some of these workers are a threat?' It didn't look like the kid had considered that at all; good thing he'd spoken.

'I doubt anyone *here* counts as one, and there's the navy and security presence, but let's say some folk may be happier than others?'

'About the Kraic being here, or *Harpans*?' The kid's head had dipped, Harp couldn't see his face.

'About the Kraic, not surprisingly, but yes also about Harpans, and World, and all the folk *didn't* come to their aid.'

'Till *you* did?'

Again with the snark? Was that it? Was Harp the interloper, claiming all the credit, here and World, as Felli saw it? Harp could see how that could happen. He'd unwillingly become the Family's poster boy. Quite likely Felli didn't like that any more than Harp did, but it still needed telling. 'Eventually, but there are a few folk over in the township aren't at all grateful, and I should warn you.'

'O-K.'

Harp wished the kid would look up, but then if wishes were rangers... 'Riverbend, the nearest township, is less than an hour away with the groundcars we have onsite, so I assume you'll want to visit. There's not much there yet but we lodged there at first, the locals live there, and some of us still head over when we're free, partly cos it's mission policy to stay on friendly terms. But there are things you need to know before you go there.

'One; you won't see too many kids, but it's best not to comment. That's cos a lot were kidnapped by the pirates, more than half from their two Orphan Houses but local families lost youngsters too. So it's a touchy subject.'

A slight stumble, maybe the pebbly ground, maybe not. 'I saw, about that, in the vids. I didn't know before, about the orphans.'

'Mm. I'm not surprised. I was kinda shocked to find out World didn't have any. We think the pirates targeted the towns with Orphan Houses, primed by Komar Regis. Best not mention that name here either. Anyway, back then Riverbend had a Nursery and a PreEmployment House. They left the youngest but the older ones were prime livestock,' Harp said grimly. 'The navy's still searching for them, and the kids from other places.'

Felli finally looked up. 'You said you lived here. You mean, in...?'

'PreEmployment? Yes, about four years.' Maybe Felli deserved to know more about him. Maybe that would help.

'But not the Nursery House?'

'No, I got moved around some.' He had his suspicions about that, not relevant right now. 'But on to the next thing you need to be aware of.' Harp thought to slow his pace, not sure how well Felli was coping with his first real taste of being in the open. Even early on the heat was fierce without the awnings. Next thing. 'Riverbend has a township council, headed by a mayor. You'll be familiar with the system.'

'Yes, I suppose.' The kid was definitely taking notice.

'I intend to replace most of the existing councillors, or at least let's say, encourage change come an election, and some of them will be resistant.'

A sideways look. 'You mean you're taking over there too.'

'No! No, that's not what I want. After all I won't be able to stay here forever. But I do want to leave them with an honest council.' How old was Felli really? How much should he tell him? Oh, just do it. 'The present mayor has too much power, including being able to bribe cronies with significant perks, some of which we're still figuring out. But we already suspect extra water rations have been involved.'

A grunt, so Felli got the gist, even if he didn't appreciate all that meant here.

'It isn't a new problem. Mr Tayla pretty much got handed the job from his father who was mayor here for years. We're still not clear enough about all the son's activities but we do know the son was aware of some of his father's games; it's possible he carried on where the father left off.' And maddening he couldn't prove it. Yet.

Felli stopped moving. 'So you're saying you want to change how the township works, and that's fine because the mayor and the council are crooks. But why should I take your word against theirs? Because you're "the hero"?' Felli's mouth had twisted. 'How do I know *any* of what you say is true?'

'Oh.' That he hadn't expected. 'You're annoyed people call me a hero? Not as much as I am, I assure you.'

Again with the lip curl.

'Look, Felli, I was in the wrong place at the right time and now I'm stuck with that too. It all started cos a Mooner taught me gun skills on a ranch, then couldn't pay his tithe, so I got drafted into Moon Militia, then someone transferred me to the navy. No one asked me what I wanted. That really sound like I *planned* any of this?'

'Ho-San says.' The kid glanced nervously at Harp then

switched attention to the bone-dry landscape. Maybe something there looked better. 'Whatever. If what you say is true, about this mayor and council, what sort of crimes are you claiming they're guilty of?'

Harp sighed, gave up. 'Believe me or not, it's the truth.' He drew a breath. 'Tayla Snr… liked children.' Would the kid understand?

The "kid" stiffened. Swallowed. 'Like, *liked*?'

'Yeah. Thankfully, from what I know and what we've found out since, he stuck to older kids. As I recall the Nursery Matron was a dragon. But that's bad enough, eh?'

'Yes. Did. Er. Were *you*?' A bit less doubtful? Maybe Felli thought even the hero wouldn't make this up.

'Happily, no.' Harp found a twisted smile. 'He kinda changed his mind when I broke his nose.'

'You? How?' The disbelieving frown was gone, replaced by what Harp judged was curiosity and morbid fascination. So he told him.

'Scratched him, tripped him up then kicked him in the face. After that I figured he didn't want to risk any more questions. I saved myself.' Harp breathed out. 'But I couldn't help others, cos no one here wanted to believe. Or maybe folk were scared to, the result was the same.'

'How, how old were you?'

'Ten. Eleven. Just after I came in. Crip, no, I only found out recently I'm almost two years younger than they told me.' Back to the subject. 'My point is I can't be sure how much Tayla Junior was, or is involved. There aren't many older orphans here left to ask and I'm sure folk would deny it. But I'm also sure he's very much his father's son; truth is my skin crawls when I see him. That makes me distrust the folk he's gathered round him. So I'd like you to be cautious, till we have more information. If our suspicions are right we have some major cleaning up to do before the township's fit to represent us humans to the Kraic, and ensure the Kraic will be safe here, which is vital to the joint alliance. Understand now?'

'Crip.' Felli stared round. 'Does my father know what you're claiming?' Ah, still doubtful.

Harp shrugged, trying not to feel offended. 'I assume so. We've talked, and Daichi sends regular updates.'

Lingering disbelief became more honest conjecture. 'Then why, why the stars did he want *us* to come here?'

'You and Ho-San? Honestly, I don't know any more than you. I'm guessing he wants to widen your horizons. The Family have pretty much ignored Moon for ever, haven't they? Maybe they want someone with a fresh eye, someone who'll be more familiar with the place in future.' Harp shrugged. 'Or maybe it's just public relations, or your father sending you on an adventure before you have to settle into a job.'

'Adventure, *that's* what you call it?' Felli kicked at a stone, it skittered noisily across the parched ground.

'Well, it is for me.' Harp grinned, relieved the awkward talk was done with. 'Bringing the first ever aliens to one of our planets, joining them here. You don't think that's something? Cos the people here do.'

'I suppose. Yes.' Another stone rattled then Felli moved on, watching where he put his feet. 'You really think he wanted us to know about all this?'

'Felli, you're Inner Family, more than I'll ever be.' Did the kid not see that? 'Moon will still be here when you come of age. Seems to me you knowing the place, and the Kraic, will be valuable to Ser Maxil and your father, when you're old enough to be involved in their decisions.'

'Oh.' They walked on, in silence now, while Felli thought, Harp pausing to check the green glows on each sensor stick, Felli not seeming to notice. 'So, you think I'm supposed to make friends with people here. And the Kraic.'

'If you want, and to be familiar with the climate. I'm not pushing you into anything you don't want. Just trying to make you realise this isn't...'

'A game? OK I see that. I suppose I could learn more about the Kraic, if they'll let me.'

Though maybe not so keen now to meet locals?

But that "Ho-San says" slipped out was telling; Felli

and his sister still had doubts, her especially. Depressing to think they distrusted him so much. Startling to realise he'd got used to the idea folk did trust him. Ah.

'Felli, it's obvious you don't know whether to trust me or not. I can respect that, you're old enough to form your own opinions and I'm guessing you've been raised to be suspicious. But I'm heading into Riverbend tomorrow. You can come with, or look around by yourself, as long as you take some security of course. But you can choose whoever suits?'

The kid didn't reply for so long, Harp began to wonder if he'd heard. But then he nodded. 'OK.' Another pause. 'I'll take Daichi.' Harpan arrogance returning in demanding Harp's most senior minder. But Daichi *was* a good choice. And perhaps in Felli's mind more loyal to the House than to "the hero"? Yes, Felli probably already knew Daichi, plus he'd have seen that Valt was tied up here, while Sulis was a local, therefore suspect. And Hendriks had already made it plain his loyalty was to the upstart Felli didn't trust yet.

So, OK, Felli would take Daichi into Riverbend, where no doubt Tayla and his councillors would welcome him with open arms. And Harp would trust his safety to Daichi, and hope Harpan genes, or training, had produced a kid with decent instincts.

Even if the kid considered Harp a liar? But he had to figure if he couldn't trust Feldin's kid to be leery of Tayla, he maybe couldn't trust him near the Kraic either. Crip, he should have talked to Red and Grey about that. Like it or not, his orders were protecting this alliance, and the Founder.

+++

So Harp dropped Felli in the middle of town and visited what was now *The* Orphan House, the two original 'homes' shrunk to one building. At least now Mik and little sister lived together, no doubt what they'd always wished for. He'd called in a few times; the kids there seemed to like it, the two remaining supers were thrilled and it gave Harp a welcome break. Unexpected bonus; it was surprising how much those kids could update him on life in the township.

By the time he saw Felli again he knew Madame Sulis was Madame Tayla's new best friend, that young Rill had twice dodged proposed "play-time" with the older Attina, in favour of time with Mik, and told Mik Tayla's daughter was "a snooty know-it-all he didn't want to see anyway". Mik had added a few remarks of his own about Attima; the girl had sneered at his little sister's castoff clothing. Harp wasn't about to repeat any of that to Felli though. He'd said the kid could make up his own mind, and meant it. Turned out he didn't have to wait very long, only till they walked out of earshot of the workers who'd returned with them.

Harp had mentioned he needed caffee. Now he detoured to the canteen module then outside with it beneath the awnings. Felli followed, sat then checked there was a space all round them, clear evidence that he'd been reared a Harpan. 'I met Mr Tayla, as you said I would.'

'Of course.' Harp sipped. Tried to relax. 'A town mayor isn't going to ignore a Harpan heir.'

'Mm. And Medam Tayla. And Mz Attima.' Perhaps a flicker of distaste? 'That girl... All right, I didn't like them. There were three other councillors I didn't like either.' Breath in. Breath out. 'I think you're telling the truth, about them.'

Harp let out his own breath too. 'Thank you, Felli.'

'I don't necessarily trust you, you understand,' Felli said stiffly, 'but I think you're right about Tayla, and probably about his council.'

'Fair enough. Which councillors did you meet?'

Felli's comments, teenage blunt, showed the boy wasn't dumb. He'd met several townsfolk, could remember names and faces, had opinions pretty much matched Harp's own impressions, and Daichi's intel. Harp inspected his mug. 'If you like, I can have Daichi send you the files.'

He could practically feel the boy's frown. 'You could have offered before.'

'But then you wouldn't have seen things with fresh eyes, and isn't that what you're here for?'

'Huh.' Frown turned to scowl; and a new inspection. 'You're as devious as my father, aren't you?'

Harp laughed and looked at him again. 'A compliment I don't deserve, ser. I think your father beats most everybody hollow.'

'Well, yes. Except Ho-San,' Felli said smugly, 'she's always onto him. I wish.' He stopped.

'You wish she was here too? A shame she couldn't, but perhaps she'll follow?'

'No, I doubt it.' Felli fiddled with his caffee, looked away again.

'I guess you'll have to settle for the com then.' They were pretty sure the kid already did, via *Defiant*, but to Hendrik's disgust he hadn't so far cracked some weird sibling code.

Felli sipped, placed mug on table. 'Gotta go, I'm supposed to be prepping supper.' A sigh. 'Mz Sakar wants to teach me to cook stuff.' A suspicious glance. 'I suppose you already can.'

'Not well, but I can manage some. It's a useful skill set.'

'Here maybe. Don't see me doing anything like that back home.' The youth rose and took his mug and himself away, to an assignment he maybe didn't dislike as much as he made out? He hadn't so far asked to change it.

18

Big Red, and Big Grey, joined Harp at the supper table, with almost-formal head-duck nods and an official update. Grey said the ground here was "resistant" but they were pleased to say they would soon be ready to receive the Seed, if Harp would call *Defiant* when they told him. Harp made his own formal request; to be allowed to invite the humans who'd come to the Kraic's welcome to witness the Seed's arrival. The arrival should be witnessed, and recorded, for Moon and World.

Once that was agreed Harp could relax and leave the details to Valt and Hendriks, no doubt with a word or two from Daichi. One of the best perks of being who he now was. The site acquired a buzz, both species got excited. Felli got impatient and short-tempered, Harp almost expected to hear "Is it here yet?" every morning. By the sixth morning the sulking, snapping – worse annoying Mz Sakar – hadn't abated, witness the unusually makeshift breakfast. Something had to be done. Come the seventh breakfast... 'No, they haven't sent a date yet, give me a break. You've been into town. Want another day out?'

'No.' Felli crunched on toasted wafers, the plain fare more evidence of unhappy cook.

'OK.' Harp turned back to his own plate. 'How about visiting the Kraic dome?'

The crunching stopped. 'Really? I didn't think I rated.' Across the table Daichi stilled, then went on eating. He, Harp and Hendriks had had meetings in there, twice since Felli arrived, and evidently that had rankled, but the Kraic hadn't asked for Felli. Till today, when Harp had.

'They're still digging, which can get messy, but they say it's safe enough now. This might be my last chance too. I don't know how protective they'll be once the Seed's installed, and I could be recalled any time Ser Maxil or your father want.'

'I suppose.' Shrugging casually. 'I wouldn't mind, if you want company.'

Ah, doing him a favour was it? 'Really? Good. Daichi, think you could talk Mz Sakar into giving Felli some time off? If she's not too busy?' And give her a day's peace? Somehow, Harp thought she'd do that.

But 'No, I'll go.' Felli rose. 'She's more used to me.'

'True, ser.' Harp refused to smile. 'It could be all day, tell her?'

'Right.' Felli collected his plate and strode away, not quite running. Harp could grin now.

Daichi wasn't. 'Good tactics, ser, but are you sure it's safe?'

'According to Big Grey it is. Besides if I go and don't invite him he'll be in an even worse mood, don't you think?'

Half a smile this time. 'Ser Felli is known to be impetuous.'

'No worse than most kids his age though, which he could be, given his position.'

'No, Ser, no worse.' Daichi rose.

+++

Visiting the dome was delayed when Harp had the inevitable "meetings". He eventually found Felli eating lunch back at one of the outside tables, slouched and scowling again, apparently with nothing to do. It was a problem Harp wasn't familiar with but he tried to dredge up some empathy, sympathy, whatever. 'Sorry ser, things always seem to come up, but I'm free now, if you still want to go?'

The kid rose gracelessly but the slouch straightened once they passed under the dome's archway. Harp admired the transformation, pure teen to born-Somebody. He figured it was ingrained, subconscious, Felli simply morphing into public-Harpan. There was no trace of petulance when he exchanged nods with Big Grey, and perfect manners when other Kraic flashed greetings, and when Blue appeared to act as escort.

Though that perfection did slip somewhat when they

reached the central atrium and Felli looked around them at those inner alcoves, each of which now had a tidy hole right in their centre and a corresponding pile of moondirt. 'You said digging, but I didn't think…'

'It surprised me too,' Harp agreed, though he thought it shouldn't have really. Eight alcoves they'd asked for, and there were eight tunnels. Sixteen Kraic, if he counted Blue an extra. 'Ready?' Blue had skipped into the nearest alcove.

'Yeah, I guess.' Though maybe not so unconcerned now.

Hm. 'Ever been underground before? It's bigger down there than it looks but you will have to bend. The Kraic don't need the height.'

'Huh.' Felli glanced up at Harp, seemed to think about… something… then squared his shoulders and headed over to Blue. Hopefully the kid wouldn't discover a fear of tight spaces, though Harp had told the truth; it wasn't as bad down there as he'd expected.

Blue of course hopped forward then dived, not bothering with its neck-screen. But then what needed explaining.

Ah. 'Head first is best,' Harp murmured. 'Want me to lead?'

Chin jutted. 'No.' Felli bent, discovered the hole wasn't a vertical drop but sloped, at about fortyfive degrees, and wide enough he could walk down it as long as he leaned back and kept his head and shoulders tucked forward. It was also easy to see the way, the surface light reflected off the pearly coating on the walls. The chin came down, followed by the necessary hunching, and the kid stepped forward.

For Harp, that meant bending at the waist. If Felli thought it awkward it was a sight worse for someone noticeably taller, not to mention wider at the shoulders. Though otherwise Harp too had ample room. The Kraic tunnel was essentially a pipe, wide enough two Kraic could pass each other. Which was happening right now, one adult passing Blue, the adult on what gravity would call the floor and Blue on what Harp thought of as the ceiling. Felli had stopped dead; Harp had to copy. 'Fun, huh? Shocked me too, the first time I saw it. Blue walked straight up a vertical in their Orbital. Useful though. I sometimes wish I could.'

The adult Kraic flowed sideways on to Felli, then passed him, then Harp, who twisted so he sort of bent around the tunnel, felt like he had turned into a semicircle. He was going to ache some later.

'It went straight up?' Felli was following Blue again, face forward, but he sounded shaken. He might have spent some time around the Kraic now but being so close, in such a confined space… that adult was as wide as Felli, would have been considerably taller standing, and those pincers weren't for decoration. Hell, they'd dug this tunnel, slicing into rock as well as soil. Facts that Harp had taken in but Felli obviously hadn't till this moment, when it couldn't be avoided.

Or disguised. Harp didn't think it accidental the Kraic seldom stood to their full height outside their dome, even if they were more comfortable closer to the ground. More information might be reassuring. 'Yep, that was my first meeting. The first time I saw them use tunnels too, although I didn't get inside one.'

The slope had flattened out, and curved. Felli looked back at Harp, or maybe at the retreating Kraic, and obviously realised they couldn't see the entrance any more. The wide eyes narrowed. 'It's still light down here.'

'Yep, that's the walls, the coating's kind of luminescent.' Being an Ambassador needed as many new words as being a Harpan, but maybe he wouldn't mention he thought the coating was Kraic spit, like that glue they'd used to fix the plantstuff to his cabin on *Defiant*. He could just imagine the reaction.

They followed Blue around the gentle curve until they reached an opening into its inward surface – one, alas, considerably smaller. One that wasn't there four days before when Harp was there last. Blue hopped into it then turned, bent double, head and tail both facing out toward the humans. That still made Harp blink. [ROOT TUNNEL NOW]

Felli, shuffled past the opening, had twisted back to face him, obviously puzzled. Harp took the opportunity to kneel and relieve his backbone and when Felli saw he copied, juggling his neck from side to side as well. 'Root what?'

Harp didn't need Blue's mental explanation, it was suddenly quite clear. 'Channels, to let the young tree spread its roots easier.' He looked at Blue. 'So the Seed is going in the middle, underneath the skylight?'

Blue hopped, not bothering with words, as if it should be obvious, which yes it was now. This whole building was a growing chamber, like a greenhouse only with the gardeners installed all round it and the too-fierce heat and light above it muted by the building. Till the tree was old enough to do without protection? Till the roots spread far enough to spawn new trunks out in the open?

Blue had tired of waiting. [MANS SEE NEST]

'Nest?' Felli swallowed, stars knew what the kid was thinking.

'Where they'll plant the Seed.' Felli had to know about that, didn't he? The whole site was speculating when it would be delivered from its storage on *Defiant*. Harp pushed a little. 'Can you manage the tighter space?'

Yeah, never suggest a teenager couldn't cope. The chin came up again. 'Of course.' A nasty smile. 'You might not though.'

'Guess I'll suffer it, it can't be too far and I'd like to see it. We might be the only humans ever will.'

Wide eyes. The kid's lips parted then closed again; it *was* quite a thought. When Blue contorted round again he followed on his hands and knees, no further hesitation.

Harp... made it through on knees and elbows, like a slider. Halted at the notion; no, he hadn't seen a single slider here since the Kraic had landed. Had the Kraic chased them off, or eaten them? Maybe he should ask about that. Later; Blue and Felli had outstripped him.

The smaller tunnel let him out into a better space,

spherical instead of tube-shaped and large enough even Harp could stand, just, once he'd slid down its curves. It also had eight entry holes around its "width". What was that word; circumference? And a larger one in the lowest point of its "floor". Harp pictured the Seed sending out eight roots to the sides, and maybe a larger taproot down toward the planet's core to find the water that no longer welled up to the surface? He was standing in the start of something unique, something momentous, that could change this world forever.

Felli was in the bottom too, still kneeling, staring. Suddenly he turned to Blue. 'Thank you, Ser Blue, for letting me come.'

[GO BACK] Harp thought Blue was relieved someone had broken the silence, the spell.

'Yes, please.' Felli edged upward again but Blue skipped off around the sphere's walls, chest high to Harp, and dived into a different tunnel. Thankfully a hole that wasn't the highest, about level with Harp's head. A brisk shove helped Felli into it before Harp pulled himself after.

They came out in a different alcove, surprise. Thanked Blue and Big Grey for allowing them such an honour. Emerged into the open air, the baking heat, and dived beneath the cooler awnings. In unspoken agreement they crossed to the cook module, poured caffee and came out again to settle at a quiet table. Harp sipped and let Felli gather his thoughts too.

'You think they're almost finished?'

'I'd say it can't be long now before Big Red'll be asking for their Seed.'

'It's a tree, that's right?'

'Yes.' Hadn't anyone *told* Felli?

Felli stared into his mug. 'It feels like it's a lot more.'

'It's a very important tree, Felli. Very precious.'

'And they showed us where it's going.' It was almost as if Felli wasn't happy about it.

'A sign of trust, don't you think?' Big compliment. Didn't the kid see that?

Felli sat up straighter. 'They trust you, obviously. But why me? Why not Mr Sulis? He lives here, and he helps more.'

'I don't know, Felli, but they chose to show you.'

'It wasn't your idea?' For a moment Felli's eyes showed panic.

Harp tried to reassure him; being singled out by aliens could do that to a person. 'Big Grey thought it was proper you got to see inside the dome.' Which Harp had understood could mean the tunnels, if Harp agreed, mind talk being so much clearer, but he wasn't going into that. Leave those sorts of revelations to his father. If Feldin wanted Felli to know that much, fine, but he wasn't about to blab that to a teen.

'I... So d'you know when it's coming?' Felli's speech was starting to lose its formality around so many Mooners. And perhaps the shortened phrases of the Kraic neck-screens.

'The Seed? I don't know. When they're ready for it, I guess.'

'Will I still be here?'

'I don't see why not. Do you?'

'No.' A breath. 'I'd like to see, y'know?'

'You and me both.' Harp downed his caffee. 'I can see Hendriks heading our way, so.'

'You're back to work.' Felli smiled. 'Do you ever take time off?'

'I went into the town only yesterday,' Harp pointed out.

'Yeah, to visit orphans.' Felli saw Harp look at him. 'Daichi told me. And arranging classes, for people to learn about the Kraic.'

'Mm, if they want. I want folk to be comfortable. New ways can take some getting used to.' Didn't he know it.

'Yeah, I see that. D'you think the adults will go?'

'I hope so. I can't force them. But without the real facts...'

'They'll hear rumours, yeah, I get that. But you *could* make them go, couldn't you?'

Hendriks was almost here, Harp rose. 'But maybe they'd resent it, and you can't force friendship. Folk have to decide that for themselves. Hendriks?'

Hendriks waved at C Block. 'Sulis isn't sure about…' Harp let himself be led away; wondered if Felli had understood; thought maybe yes he had, but as Ham would have said that ball was still in the air.

19

Big Red had finally named the day and *Defiant* was handling the transfer. Hendriks had printed more invites, even fancier than the first, hang the cost. And now at last the invitees – another Harpan word – were flocking to the village. Harp admitted he was nervous, only to himself of course. The public him was supposed to inspire confidence.

The private him was dithering, with reason. If anything went wrong... He'd stressed it was a momentous day, to be treated with respect, but if the Kraic were offended... Or the shuttle malfunctioned, or crip, the Seed didn't adapt to Moon, shrivelled up or grew stunted like the sorry trees he'd seen here...

So he stood and waited for the shuttle to appear above them, praying for a happy landing, then at least no one could blame the navy. Hendriks and Sulis were trying to calm the locals penned behind him. Daichi hovered on his left, as always totally impassive, if you didn't count a little stiffness this time in the shoulders? And young Felli flanked him on his right, and was the opposite, a mess of fidgets and overt impatience. 'We'll be able to see it, right? How big is it?'

'I don't actually know, Felli, it was wrapped up.'

That got him the scowl. 'You must have some idea.'

'The wrapping was bigger than Blue, but I couldn't tell what was inside.' Big enough to fill that nest chamber? That'd be one hell of a seed, but then it'd be one hell of a tree. If it survived the move.

Daichi stirred. 'ETA eleven minutes, sers. We should sight the shuttle any time now.'

'... There!' Felli looked pleased, maybe at being first. Harp wasn't admitting he'd seen it at least two minutes earlier, but that did rather confirm his sharper senses were a Harpan trait.

Except Harp thought the Kraic around him had also known sooner, at least as early as him. Something about the way some of those round heads had tilted, and a sort of tiny shiver had seemed to run right through them. All right then, this was it. Better make it good.

Surely a shuttle had never touched down so gently, even now their landing patch of dirt was flatter. He thought the ramp came down slower than usual too; avoiding vibration, or putting on a show? Because it was a show. Historic. Witness all this quiet.

The shuttle crew were in dress uniform today, the XO and Ngow here too, leading the way down. It was only after they formed up outside, making a corridor, that the remaining Kraic appeared, three each side that swollen, all-important bundle.

Valt's honour guard stood to attention. The XO and Ngow nodded. The Seed floated serenely down the ramp then hovered at about table height from the ground. If there was something supporting it, say one of Med Bay's carriers, Harp couldn't see it, but then the packaging was pretty bulky so maybe – and what did it matter how it moved, as long as it arrived without a problem.

The Kraic escort – Harp thought the oldest – ducked heads to Big Red, Big Grey then, crip, to him. He managed to nod back, vaguely aware Daichi had stepped back but Felli had just copied him. It was quiet behind him now, even the kids struck dumb this time. What next?

An anti-climax, of gargantuan proportions.

Big Red waved its front pincers; Harp deduced some mind talk, which of course other humans wouldn't realise. The Kraic escort ducked heads again then flowed forward. The Seed did the same. The other Kraic formed up, sides and rear –floated the Seed under the awnings, crossed the circle, and vanished under their arch. And that was that. Harp badly wanted to laugh, though he wasn't sure if that was shock or relief it was over.

He wasn't the only one taken by surprise of course, even Daichi had raised an eyebrow. Tayla looked if anything more irritated than confounded, and young Rill had hung his head, most likely disappointed. His father would probably need to have another talk about the dome being off limits! But the deed was done, and they were meant to party. Ah.

<Blue, will any of you be back out?>

<Big Grey comes. And me>

And a minute later they did just that, followed by what he was pretty sure were the six Kraic who'd just arrived. Harp surmised a handover, the original escort now officially off duty, as it were. They certainly deserved it. 'Welcome sers, and our thanks for your task completed. We have food, please, join us?'

Blue played host, inviting these latecomers to try foods it already liked. Sulis and Hendriks started conversations. Locals whose prized recipes were tasted and approved preened once more. Most humans were polite and didn't stare too openly across the circle, or remark on what they hadn't seen. At least not loudly or too near the Kraic.

Harp could admit he'd have liked to have seen more too, but what was, was. The Seed was something Kraic revered, not just precious, something... superstitious? So OK, if humans weren't meant to lay eyes on it, that wouldn't kill anyone, and it was here, in one piece and back in Kraic hands – pincers. Short of the dome collapsing it wasn't his responsibility any more, it was theirs?

Daichi offered him a glass, of wine. 'Compliments of the XO, ser.'

'Thank her for me if I don't, will you.' He didn't gulp, no he sipped like a Harpan should; quite composed. Noted Felli had joined Blue, probably asking questions no one else had dared. But Big Grey hadn't left him. *<Is all well, ser?>*

<Harp friend should join us when sun down>

Harp stopped, glass raised. Daichi's gaze sharpened. He took another sip. *<In the dome, ser?>*

<Invited> Big Grey's mind talk was as brief as his screen messages but this one was clear enough, and evidently private.

<You don't want the rest to know? They're bound to see where I go>

<Not join>

Oh great, he was to be the sole invited witness, that was going to please Felli. But anything the Kraic wanted was his duty, and it was surely safe enough. Even Daichi would agree he could go alone. Besides, he was hardly going to pass up on this experience; he might be the only human ever had it.

+++

Briefed via wristcom, Daichi looked grim but didn't argue, and had the locals nudged to depart an hour later, reasonably satisfied with the fact their new prosperity looked settled, happy with free food and drink and buzzing at the unexpected bonus; an actual image of the Seed's arrival, with its Kraic and human escort symbolising the alliance. Each copy was set in a small glassite block, expensive proof against erosion. And the things would stand, unaided, or be stored inside a matching mepal case embossed with both the Harpan H and Kraic equivalent, a stylised tree, above the date and the location. The earlier invitations would even fit into the lid. Hendriks had gone overboard, with a vengeance, but what the crip, they were impressive, and they made up for the let-down on arrival. Harp knew he would treasure his.

The village Circle cleared of locals and the shuttle lifted, with some more than happy crew onboard; they too had gifts to boast of. The remaining human residents relaxed at last and drifted to the outdoor tables, no doubt playing guessing games. And Harp? Made tracks for A Block and a shower. Cleaner clothes seemed called for and the light was fading.

Felli waited by his cubicle when he came out. 'You turning in already?'

Ah. 'No, I'm called across the way.'

'Just you.'

'Just me.' No, he wasn't going to apologise.

'Figures.' Felli's scowl got blacker.

Crip. 'If you want to talk, come in. Either way shift, will you? I need to get dressed. And you know as well as me we do as we're told, so don't sulk.' Harp stepped forward. Felli huffed then shuffled aside, but he did follow, flinging himself across Harp's cot. 'So you got invited.'

'Yep.' Harp dropped the towel and started dressing, in the usual sands. He'd have felt a fool in his dress blues, plus he didn't feel like he was representing the navy; the shuttle and Valt's people had done that part. It had already occurred to him he wasn't sure what he *was* representing; politics or something stranger.

Felli wasn't done. 'D'you know what for?'

'Nope.'

'Well, will you... will you tell me, after?'

Harp made himself stop rushing. 'Felli, I don't know if I'll be free to. You understand how things work.'

The trademark sigh was instantly replaced by the trademark scowl. Harp supposed it was understandable. He just wished Felli would grow out of all the ups and downs everyone else had to put up with. The youth stared at his boots. 'I guess. But if...'

'If,' Harp agreed, ran his hands through his still damp hair – how much longer had it got? – and shrugged. 'Got to go, Cousin.'

The 'Yeah. Sure,' as Felli followed him out didn't sound remotely sincere, the muttered, 'Have fun,' at the outer door more like sarcastic. They parted ways, Felli heading toward the canteen, presumably to scowl at Mz Sakar, who would react by making his mood worse. The kid was hard work sometimes, yet at others easy to get on with. Harp just wished he'd make his mind up how he felt about his newfound cousin. Every time the kid seemed to be softening something set the chip back on his shoulder. Harp was starting to think talking to his sister did it, the kid always seemed to come back in a mood; maybe it reminded him they were apart. But crip, that wasn't the case this time, was it, and Felli's farewell had sounded more like Harp was off to a funeral than a... sort of birth?

Either way, he was on duty. He straightened his

shoulders and marched across the circle, conscious of the stutter in the conversations. Yep, the farmboy was on show again, annoying Felli, and again not knowing what he'd gotten into. As for not making a big deal of this, Big Red and Big Grey were flowing out from their arch with a small escort and stopping just inside the awnings. Clearly there to greet him, making a display. So it *was* a big deal, and he guessed he'd better treat it like one. He stopped a few paces out and nodded. They nodded back, the escort fell to the sides, Big Red and Big Grey stepped apart. So he marched into the gap and let them lead him in, to whatever this was. And hopefully they wouldn't want to plant a human alongside the Seed.

+++

The light outside, muted inside the rotunda anyway, was fading, but there was still enough Harp could see the large hole in the centre of its floor; one that surely went straight down into the chamber he'd stood in a few days earlier.

Then he forgot all that because something... trilled. Except it wasn't a noise in his ears, it was more a vibration, inside his head. And it was coming from the bulky wrapping on the other side of this hole.

Big Red brushed his shoulder with a politely closed pincer. The Kraic were always careful about that little detail. <*Friend should unwrap*>

<*Me?*> Harp stepped back.

<Harp friend should welcome his new life>

His? They wanted a human involved. Cos this was a human colony? And cos worthy or not he was the human they knew. Crip. He'd told Felli he had to do as he was told. <*What do I need to do?*>

It was simple enough in the end. Big Grey loosened a strip of the fine fabric the Kraic spun from their trees, and offered the end to Harp. More nodding. Harp pulled gently and the fabric peeled off, layer by layer, like a bandage, till eventually...

The Seed was small enough he could lift it with both

hands from the mess he'd made around it, but a lot heavier than he'd guessed; very dense then. Oval, more like an egg than a seed, and the palest pearly green he could imagine.

Only he wasn't imagining, cos it was real. He was kneeling on the ground, surrounded by silent alien bodies. And it was making him dizzy, which was decidedly scary cos he really mustn't drop it.

Other Kraic came now, two at a time, tipping the dirt they'd saved back into the hole. Making a soft bed, part of him reasoned, a nest for the Seed. A nest the Seed wanted into.

He wasn't sure if he threw it or it leapt but one moment it lay in his hands and the next it was gone, Harp nearly after it, except Big Grey had caught him. Four short arms were wrapped around him, pincers closed up safely. Big Grey pulled him clear as that mass of fabric then more dirt was added, and he knelt there watching till the hole was filled in and the siren call inside his head had faded to a murmur.

When he raised his head, which took a while, he realised the Kraic were humming, and parading – dancing. Celebrating? – round the inner chamber. He had never heard them make that sound before, a sort of thrumming emanating from their stomach region. It was very soft, but he could feel it in his blood. It made him feel hotter, shaky. Distant. The rotunda shivered, everything was hot, and foggy.

+++

Harp woke on his back by the filled-in hole. It was an effort to sit up and he ached all over. Big Red was sitting, looking down at him. The rest had disappeared but at least his head was clear. Crip, so many questions. *<What time is it?>*

<Almost sun>

He'd been here most of the night? *<What happened?>*

<First tree speaks to first mans>

<A bond? Trees and humans?>

<Tree will grow now. Harp gives life>

'Yeah, OK.' Harp gave up on mind talk, it was causing echoes, and decided it was time to get onto unsteady feet. It pretty much felt like he *had* lost some of his life. Or like he had concussion, like he wasn't really in his body.

<Harp should eat, rest>

'You don't say.' He remembered his manners; no back-talking the alien brass. 'I'll do that, thanks, ser.' Sudden scary thought. 'Will you want me to do that again?'

<No, life shared now>

'Right.' He needed to think but he was tired. When Blue hopped to his side he put a hand on its back for balance; left it there when it began to flow toward the entrance, cos if he'd let go he wasn't sure how long he'd stay on his feet. Happily, if that was the right word, Blue seemed fine with helping him across a still-deserted circle – so no one else was up yet – all the way to A Block. A pincer pushed the simple latch – no fancy touches here – and his cubicle swung open.

'Where the crip have you *been*?' Hendriks wavered closer, reaching out to grab him.

'What?' Harp peered down at Blue. 'Wrong room, Blue.'

'No, it isn't, and don't you dare fall. I'm not big enough to lift you.'

Noises, from the corridor, and somehow Blue had disappeared, but Daichi's face replaced it.

+++

'Look, I don't know, exactly.' He was on his back again, too many faces looming. Daichi, Hendriks even Felli had ganged up on him, and Valt's medic in the background? Daichi looked quite fierce, for Daichi; sort of constipated. Couldn't have him thinking this was his fault. Harp struggled till he sat, his back against a pillow. 'Look, Ser Maxil sent me here to cosy up to aliens. There were bound to be some repercussions; let's accept we found one.' Daichi being the only one who knew of others. 'I'm in one piece, aren't I, just tired from pulling an all-nighter. Not the first time.'

Hendriks muttered, 'Cept you don't remember.' Felli was still quiet and the medic hovered in the background.

'Ser, you must remember something.'

'Sorry, Daichi. Must have fell asleep.'

Finally, a snort, from Felli. 'Sleep? It doesn't look it.'

Valt's medic shifted closer. Crip, the medic meant to take a blood test and this was no Harpan medic, sworn to secrecy. Daichi must be really worried, surely there were standing orders not to – and he wasn't sure he had the energy to "wish" a normal reading. Guess he'd have to find some.

Thankfully the medic didn't look shocked, just suggested a shot. Oh no. 'No boosters.' Crip, his head was spinning. 'Been there. Didn't like it. No.' Discussion, overhead, then blessed quiet.

+++

When he woke someone had left him a protein drink. Between that and the sleep he felt a lot more human, if a trifle groggy, so he got himself into the showers then went in search of breakfast. It turned out it was nearer supper, guess he'd really been that tired. The clearer head still painted him a pretty scary picture. One he couldn't keep to himself this time, but it'd be faster to brief Daichi and let him tell everyone else. That's what he told himself anyway.

It wasn't his intention to have to say these things to Hendriks, and Felli as well, but he somehow ended up cornered; it was either abandon food he seriously needed or get on with it. Daichi was their spokesman anyway. 'Now you're feeling better, ser…'

Daichi waited while Harp swallowed what was in his mouth, and reached the only possible conclusion. So what if he didn't want to talk about it. Something had happened and, and drained him. Maxil and Feldin needed to know, and telling Daichi, even with Felli hearing, would be less embarrassing than facing Maxil. So he told them as much as he recalled, and surmised; that the Kraic tree had drawn off energy when it was planted, and had wanted human energy because this was a human planet. 'My best guess; like the Kraic seem to have a bond with their trees.' Cos he wasn't supposed to blab all he knew about that either. 'So they hope this one could do the same with us.' He wolfed another mouthful.

'Best guess,' Hendriks repeated carefully.

Felli was less cautious. 'Bond with us, or just you?'

Oh for. 'How would that make sense, Felli? They know I'm not likely to stay here permanently. But I do think Big Red and Blue had a connection to a tree on their own planet.' Hang not saying too much. The last thing he wanted was for Felli to think Harp was making himself any more "special". The kid had just been starting to accept he wasn't doing it on purpose. 'I figure they used me cos I'm the one they're most familiar with.'

'And you're the highest ranking Harpan,' Hendriks murmured, so not helping. Naturally that had Felli frowning.

Harp jumped in to try to counteract that. 'Cos Felli's underage still? Maybe.'

But Daichi and Felli went on frowning, and no doubt they'd both discuss it, with Ser Maxil or big sister. Crip. Harp gave up and went back to eating, knowing he needed to replace energy. The others huddled round him, held a muttered conversation, none of which surprised him. Yes, the Seed was more than just a diplomatic gesture, as he guessed a lot of folk still thought it. And yes, their Kraic allies had become an unknown quantity, again. And yes, Ser Feldin might decide – as Daichi had just mentioned – that his only son was safer leaving. Harp agreed, a recall for the kid looked likely, never mind he wasn't happy it was being talked of.

As for Harp? They didn't say it but he could foresee a long interrogation in his future, now his mission to the Kraic was likely over. And another session with the Mansion medics. As if there could be any more weirdness left for them to find.

20

Harp was convinced Daichi had reported back to the Mansion even if – unlikely thought – Felli hadn't blabbed. But it was two days now and if there'd been a reaction nobody had told him. He didn't see how Maxil, not to mention Feldin or Mz Chan, could ignore it this long. They'd let aliens onto one of their planets then discovered they didn't know enough about the aliens' plans. Intentions. Capabilities? If that wasn't cause for concern surely knowing it had involved Harp again was, already the Family's "anomaly" as Feldin termed it. Harp was tempted to move Felli to Riverbend, but he was still officially under orders. Till that changed he guessed he had to sit tight and fake calm.

Of course, Felli, with no chain of command and a lot more attitude than any uniform allowed, didn't try to fake anything. Harp wasn't sure what the kid was het up about most; the Kraic, his own safety, or Harp back hogging attention as he no doubt saw it. Whatever the cause, the results were visible, and audible.

'Well, that's it, it's all over, isn't it, now you've planted the Seed.' The latest dig at Harp being singled out, once more in public, came at breakfast. Hendriks' daft remark about highest rank Harpan hadn't helped at all, however Harp had spun it. There'd been digs about that already. Now Felli jabbed at his food, then finally found something other than Harp to whinge at. 'My father's going to drag me back home, isn't he? Waste of time sending me anyway. I've hardly seen anything except this dump. *I've* been stuck here working in a stupid *kitchen*, with a bunch of –' Thankfully the kid remembered those he'd been about to insult were in earshot.

Harp tried to calm things down, again. Or at least stop the kid blaming *him*. Again. 'You're still here though, the Seed's in place, and the construction work's about finished. I reckon we could free up time for you to see somewhere else. Is there anywhere you'd like to go?'

Some vicious chewing was the only answer. Harp gave up.

But then, 'What's the point. The only interesting thing here is that volcano and it's out of bounds.' A sullen Felli jerked to his feet and stalked off. Hopefully back to his work assignment, but Harp wasn't counting on it.

Collar though, eh? It *was* off limits, had been since the mines closed, but… there'd been no warnings issued lately and the mountain had been quiet for ages, and Felli was getting looks. Folk here had relaxed, buoyed up about the Seed's arrival which they saw as proof they had a better future. Now, they glanced from him to Felli and pretended not to eavesdrop. They didn't need to worry too. So Felli needed to be distracted.

When there was still no word from World next morning, or at least no word Daichi was admitting… 'Felli.'

'Yes?' The kid half turned, at least he'd answered.

'I was thinking, maybe, if Ser Maxil and your father are still mulling things over, we *could* go visit the volcano?'

Lowered brows were better than a scowl. 'I thought it was off limits.'

'It always was, you know, except to those who worked there, so I never saw it either even when I lived here, cept off in the distance.' Harp took the plunge. 'But it's gone quiet again, and I always wanted to, and I figure its owner's got to be allowed. So, how about it? It might be the last chance for both of us.'

No answer for a moment, then, 'Why not.' A shrug. 'At least it might beat cooking.' Hardly Harpan-gracious, but more hopeful?

Daichi cleared his plate and rose. 'I'll organise a runner, sers.' And minders, that didn't need to be said. But last minute, so no one knew? Harp couldn't figure there'd be any danger.

+++

It took them two hours to leave, not bad considering.

Food prep, changing clothes, and packing spares – stars knew why Daichi thought they needed those – a checklist of assorted supplies. Oh, and a complete overhaul of their best runner. Harp supposed it could have been worse. He'd pretty much got used to being fussed at these days. Besides, Daichi was only taking two Security along. Positively frugal. No, there really wasn't any danger. Felli accepted the wait too, not even a scowl. Presumably it was so familiar it wasn't worth being annoyed about. At least it seemed to smother his frustration over the Seed. No one had been invited into the dome since Harp staggered out, and Big Red hadn't been out, which hadn't helped either Harp or Felli. But Felli's moods resurfaced once they left the shelter of the village in the distance.

Harp had made sure the kid had a wide brimmed hat like the one he wore now; thought Felli liked the novelty if nothing else, but that didn't last past the first few klicks. The fact Harp took the heat in his stride obviously fuelled the kid's renewed annoyance; burgeoning enthusiasm swung again to teenage-sullen.

To be fair, Harp reminded himself, the boy really wasn't used to this, had spent almost all his time here in the shelter of the barracks or the awnings. Harp might enjoy the runner's canopy and the breeze of their motion but it looked like even Daichi was wilting, let alone the much more pampered Felli. Yeah, but only Felli *voiced* discomfort. Maybe Felli realised that fact though. Five klicks out he suddenly shut up; his face spoke volumes but his mouth no longer shared it with them.

Sometime later quiet gave way to fidgeting, then questions. 'Aren't there any proper trees out here, at all?'

'Not big ones, it's too open. I think there used to be more, and there are still some farther south, they tell us, in the Canyons; I've seen pictures but I've never been there. You have lots on World?'

'Yes.'

'I should go find some,' Harp decided, 'see how they compare to Kraic forest.' Felli looked surprised; he'd probably assumed Harp knew more about World than circumstances had so far allowed. He should really plan to see more. If they'd let him. At least he was finally going to see Collar up close.

Their runner was way better than the Militia ever got, but it still took two jolting hours to bypass Riverbend and reach the base of Collar Mountain, and after another half hour, when the rough upward trail petered out, just past the main closed-up mine entrance and admin blocks, their driver gave up the fight and called a halt. Looked like they'd be doing the rest of the climb on foot.

While the rest milled about, Harp took the time to stand and stare. He'd always thought Collar was all browns and greys but now he could see some greener bits, some rusty orange, and a colour maybe six shades darker Daichi just called umber? The grey was surface dust hiding patches of black, a black all slick like it was oily, and the landscape higher up looked blacker, like a mass of jagged, broken towers on the skyline.

That was a way to go yet, all of it unfriendly, brittle-looking. Maybe not a good idea for Felli after all, but Harp was going on. This place *was* his now, and he'd always longed to be here, and he'd meant it when he'd said he wasn't sure he'd get another chance, not once the Family reclaimed him. One day maybe he would get to choose his life, not others, but he didn't see it coming.

Still, he edged Felli aside as packs were distributed. 'Look, you're not used to this and it's a lot to take on. Any time you decide you've had enough just say, all right.'

A huff, but, 'OK.' Maybe the unrelenting heat had made the kid see reason.

Someone *had* been past the workings, not too long back either; probably another risk assessment, govment wanting to reopen. Faint boot tracks offered maybe-easier routes. Daichi, in the lead, was quick to take them but it was a slog, a constant, winding climb between the baking sun and baking ground, the ground a mix of rock and soil at first then streaked with blacker ridges; cooled-down lava, giant drips of knobbly paint spilt down the hillside.

Harp stopped when he reached the tip of one such tongue of darker ground, recalling all those newscast images of red-hot rivers. What was left was more like frozen ripples studded with a mass of nameless debris. Harp knelt down and touched it; others copied. Touching lava. He figured they'd all seen the same vids, were making the same comparisons. Maybe wondering as he was what it would be like to reach the summit. Which felt pretty far yet.

+++

Two hours later Daichi stopped again to take a drink. The man and woman he'd brought along instantly copied, taking the same small sips. Harp wondered if Daichi was copying his own Mooner abstinence, or had been on Moon before.

Felli collapsed onto a rocky outcrop, panting, not yet reaching for his own canteen which Harp was pretty sure was almost empty. Thankfully, Daichi had packed spares, and Harp knew his was almost full. Besides, up here it was cooler.

Taking another small sip, mainly so as not to make the rest feel bad, Harp wandered, looking up to where the summit of the undead mountain beckoned. From below it looked like somebody had sliced the top off, with a buckled hacksaw, but he'd never figured Collar would be pretty.

Daichi crunched uphill to join him. 'How long now, ser, do you think?' Like being Mooner made him expert.

'I'd say an hour, about, if –' Harp shut up. Daichi understood though; if young Felli managed. It was really steep now. Then Harp realised *he* wasn't giving up, or going slow, he simply couldn't any longer. Collar called him. 'I'm sure it's do-able, but maybe I can scout ahead for an easier route.'

'Ser.' Daichi wasn't happy but they couldn't lose him on an open mountainside, and there was no one here to threaten either Harp or Felli.

'You'll see my footprints,' Harp reminded him, then shrugged his pack back on and headed upward.

In minutes it felt like he was all alone, he didn't even hear those behind. Maybe they'd stopped to rest; Harp didn't care, hadn't he always wanted to be here? He climbed on, faster solo, weaving over fissured ground, sluggish undulations, between black shards sometimes taller than he was. He'd escaped into a different world, if only for a moment.

When he'd learned other Harpans were weird as him he'd almost felt normal, sort of. But it hadn't lasted, had it? He could mind talk with the Kraic. OK, so maybe other Harpans might be able to now they knew? But now there was the blackout with the Seed and he was back to being odd man out again, unsure how Maxil and the rest would take it.

But he could have *this* before he had to face them. He pushed on, relishing a breeze that chilled his face, despite the sun, the drug-like sense of momentary freedom. The dust his boots disturbed – he guessed all that was ash – rose lazily and swirled about his legs, so that he couldn't always see the ground. The air felt heavy, crunching noises from the broken ground beneath his feet the only interruption. For this moment there was only him, and Collar. It was peaceful.

Then the ground vibrated.

Collar twitched, began to waken, maybe wondering what had disturbed it. Harp stopped dead, stared at his feet, the shaky ground. Vibration resonated through him till his heartbeat seemed to match the rapid rhythm. Part of him heard shouts, the rest was focussed on his bootsoles. When he thought to raise his eyes the peak above his head was spurting fiery sparks, and hazy ash had started falling, swirling round him. Newscasts had described the ash as dirty snow. He'd never seen real snow but that was cold, he thought. They'd said the ash up here would burn, and that too much could suffocate you, cutting off your air.

But Collar, waking, that was magical. It drew him

onward, almost running this time. No more choosing easy routes, conserving energy, he wanted *up*. To be there when–

A hiss. A roar. A *tongue* of fire poked over Collar's rim and lapped the rock, then spewed a crackling stream – that flowed toward him. Harp breathed ash and burning air, and smiled. Collar, coming out to greet him, saving him the last stretch of his journey.

'Captain!'

'Ser!'

'Max. Crip, Max!'

Felli's panic broke the spell. Harp stopped his forward rush, and realised the rest were shouting too. Crip, Felli – all of them could die here.

'No.' Harp found he'd raised his hand. 'Go back.' Then realised he hadn't spoken to the humans at his back. The lava flow slowed down, and spat, and then... retreated. Sluggishly. Retreating must have cooled its fire cos its edges darkened even as he watched; the angry scarlet morphed into a duller mix of greys and crimson. But it had *retreated*. No, he wasn't dreaming, cos the shouts behind had fallen silent.

When he turned, still dazed, he saw them lower down, four World-gold faces staring. 'Crip.' Last year he'd moved *Raptor* with his mind, now this year he'd moved *lava*?

21

There was no question of carrying on to the summit, so achingly close. The others waited like statues till he made it back down to them, a stumble here and there this time where he'd been so sure footed. Daichi's minions backed off like they needed distance. Daichi stood his ground, still quiet. Felli's mouth hung open. They had seen it too, he hadn't dreamed it.

'You.' Felli swallowed. 'You, er, have ash all over you. Aren't you burning?'

Harp grabbed that problem like a lifeline. 'Crip, I'm covered in the stuff.' He swiped at his clothes, his hair. 'Well, that was a close call. Sorry everyone, I shouldn't have brought you.'

Daichi recovered, at least on the outside. 'Not your fault, ser, I checked before we left.' Of course. 'There's been no warnings up here since we landed. I suggest we should head back though.' With a speaking look at Felli.

'Absolutely. You good to move a bit faster, Felli?' Harp tried to smile. 'Going down should be easier.'

Felli stared a moment longer then seemed to shake off the fugue. 'Yeah, OK.' The kid even smiled back, shaky but trying.

'Let's move then?' When had he got so used to faking being OK he didn't have to think about it?

They did make good time, partly cos no one spoke again till they reached the lower slopes and sighted the waiting runner, though the rest wasted time and energy looking back, pretty regularly. Harp didn't bother. He could *feel* Collar hovering above him, watching, holding back now as he'd wanted. As he'd told her.

If the others were scared he didn't blame them, especially young Felli. Only if they were panicking, what the stars was *he* feeling? Call it terror? Something pretty mindless anyway, cos he still wanted up, not down, and the only thing stopping him giving in to that... compulsion... was the need to get his younger cousin, and Daichi and the minders, clear to safety.

There was something seriously wrong with him, even worse than all the crazy he'd thought he knew about.

+++

By a sort of tacit consent they all pretended to ignore the unspeakable, made it back to the runner with no worse than the ground shivering under them a couple times, almost like it was teasing, and headed back. Daichi pulled ration packs from a cooler and munched stolidly at a rollup, after which nod to normality Felli ate two – Harp was impressed – and even managed another smile when Harp offered him a full canteen. Although his eyes stayed wider for a while longer. Security took their cue from Daichi; if their eyes kept straying round to Harp they pulled back quickly. Felli wasn't asking questions, nor Daichi, so perhaps the other two assumed their betters knew stuff they weren't cleared for. In the end the man drove and the woman dozed off. Or pretended to; her shoulders didn't say that. Harp quashed a sigh, settled back and tilted his hat brim to hide his face. And his thoughts.

+++

It was dark by the time they reached the village, the twinkling lights beneath the awnings and the sounds of after-supper relaxation welcoming them back to 'normal'. Hands raised in greeting when their runner whirred into a parking spot, but people stayed relaxed, so there was nothing outward to alarm them. Daichi jumped down first, looked to his team. 'Eat and sleep, yes?'

'Ser.'

'Ser.'

Blank-faced, the other two departed for the cook block. Harp assumed they'd got their orders; keep their mouths shut.

As usual Daichi waited for Harp, who needed food but

figured he should give the other two some space. 'I think I'll shower first, Daichi.'

'Ser.'

'Me too,' jerked Felli, so when Harp moved off the kid fell in. For once Daichi left them to it, no doubt an immediate report to Mz Chan took priority. Harp suppressed a growl, probably frustration. He'd survived having weird blood, cos that ran in the Family. And the navy had loved his odd reflexes, even if they never understood them. But the Seed, now this. It wouldn't be Felli who got 'dragged back' to World, would it?

The eye-witness still at his side waited till they were into adjacent shower stalls. Maybe the kid thought that more private. Maybe the kid didn't want to look at him while he talked. 'That, back there.' The hissing of the detox mist stopped conversation for a moment. Once things quietened, '*You* did that, right?'

Say no? Say it was, what, coincidence? Harp grimaced as he started scrubbing ash off. No, they'd seen him raise his stupid hand, even if they weren't near enough to hear. Daichi had kept quiet, but then maybe Daichi hadn't actually *seen* anything. No hiding this time though. Lava might change course, but reverse?

Felli had gone still next door, just waiting. Harp chose a sort of truth. 'If I did, I don't know how.'

'Really? Wow.' The scrubbing sounds resumed. Stopped again. 'You didn't look surprised though. Has it happened before?' No, Felli wasn't dumb.

'Felli, I'm sorry, but I'm not sure I'm meant to talk about this, OK?'

'What, it's like, part of the whole *Raptor* thing?' The kid sounded more curious now than scared. 'I do hear stuff, y'know. People think because I'm not old enough I'm deaf, but I'm not.' Harp could practically feel that chin rise, all that teenage indignation. 'There was something about *Raptor* and you. It sounded like they couldn't find another shooter. Is that the right word?'

'Gunner,' Harp said absently. If Felli had made that connection his elders had too. Mz Chan would reread

Raptor reports, Simshaw's complaints. Crip, he really *didn't* want Simshaw back in his life, but now he might not have a choice.

Felli only heard the spoken answer. 'Gunner, right. So you're like under orders.' The other shower turned off. 'It's a pain not being allowed to tell people stuff, isn't it? I'd go crazy sometimes if I didn't have Ho-San to share with.' A pause. 'I don't suppose you have that option either.'

'No.' Harp shut down and grabbed the scratchy local towels. He'd got spoiled on World; he wondered if all that was over.

Similar rasping noises next door. Maybe clumsier; Felli still not comfortable with this basic lifestyle. 'But Ser Daichi knows, right?'

Harps closed his eyes on that. 'He does now.'

'Ouch.' A shower door rattled. 'Does that mean you're in trouble?'

No point hiding in the shower, was there? 'Very likely.' Harp stepped out as well, the towel wrapped round him.

To find Felli waiting. 'With the navy? Because you do know my father can just tell them to eat vacuum?'

That was almost worth a smile, and a warm feeling, cos the boy sounded more cousin-ish; more... sympathetic. Sad to spoil it. 'I'm afraid your father will also be upset.' Especially about Felli being near him. 'Maybe it's best if you keep a little distance between us, for a while?' Like forever. Yeah, Felli's proximity, anything left of an improved relationship, probably needed to end. Harp had moved *Raptor*. Then mind-talked with the Kraic. Then *something* happened round the Seed and now, he'd halted lava.

OK, so far the things he'd done had sort of worked out, but he still didn't have a clue *how* he'd done them. Next time – he could do something a lot worse; hurt people. So Daichi was quite right to rush off and report, and Felli couldn't stay anywhere near him. Nor could anyone else.

His stomach growled, and Felli burst out laughing! 'You really need to eat, Cuz.' Still grinning, the kid headed for his cubicle, a slim young body in a towel, hints of the adult he'd be soon in the too-big feet and signs of gym-bred muscle. 'I swear you eat even more than me, and you didn't grab anything on the run back.'

'Hungry. Yeah.' Never mind the sky was falling, he would need to feed the yawning pit he called his stomach. He'd swear his calorie intake had doubled since he'd first left Moon.

Felli was waiting for him again when he came out into the corridor, like him dressed in the now familiar sands. For the first time – showed how distracted he'd got, even before today – Harp noticed Felli had taken to rolling the long sleeves back to his elbows. Like Harp? That wasn't good, not now, but he couldn't make himself tell the boy not to walk out with him, or sit beside him at an empty table once they'd got their meals.

Harp's hunger dictated silence for a while, then a walk inside for seconds, Felli at his heels. Maybe the kid didn't eat as much as him but he was definitely Harpan. Harp's jaw slowed at last; his gut had stopped complaining. Beyond the lights the land lay dark. World had arrays of what they titled mirror-sats, that cast what they called "twilight" on the night side; very civilised. But Moon had nothing but its sky. The lights around the circle stretched a little way but then surrendered to the darkness. It was quiet out there. And empty. Maybe people here would be safer if –

His wristcom shivered, signalling a call, tagged Feldin, personally. Here it was then.

"Max, we need to talk. Encrypt.' No greeting this time.

Harp pressed his thumb against the screen but then remembered Felli. 'Felli, I have to take this, so I'll say goodnight.' Maybe goodbye too.

Felli winced. 'My father? Good luck.'

'Mm.' Navy discipline made Harp bus his dishes before retreating to his cubicle. By then his wristcom was shivering again. 'Max, are you alone now?' This time he got a visual of Feldin looking ominously solemn.

'Yessir.' He decided to sit on his cot, before his legs gave out.

'Good. How is Felli?'

'He's fine, Ser. He doesn't seem worried.'

'Yes. He was there, I understand.'

'Yes, Ser, but he's not hurt or anything.'

'No.' Feldin's smile was rueful. 'I imagine he's asking questions.'

'Yes. He seems to think... what happened... relates to *Raptor*.'

'Ah, then he's excited.'

'Yes.' Harp drew a breath. 'Ser, I don't know what's happening, but I don't think he should stay.'

Feldin's smile faded. 'I appreciate the thought, but we want both of you back. There'll be a shuttle in about an hour. You'll both be on it.' Direct order, and as Felli pointed out his father was Commander in Chief. Harp nodded dumbly. *Defiant* would take Felli home, and him wherever Feldin told them. He guessed walking into the desert wasn't an option after all.

+++

Daichi came to announce the shuttle's approach. Predictably Felli, who hadn't wanted to come to Moon, now objected to leaving. 'I thought I was supposed to be here longer, ser. Besides, I want to see what the volcano does next.' Felli noticed Harp was silent. 'Oh. But I still don't see why we have to go right away. I mean, what will the Kraic think if Max deserts them? Won't they be offended?'

'Your father says it's urgent, Ser Felli.'

Felli sighed loudly, tried again. 'But Max is in *charge*.'

'Felli, I'm really just a figurehead.' Except Maxil Snr, and Feldin and Daichi and perhaps Mz Chan, knew he could also mind-talk. 'The major, Sergeant Hendriks and Ser Sulis do all the work.' Harp looked across to Daichi. 'But I should probably tell the Kraic I have to leave.'

Daichi hesitated, telling pause, then nodded. 'Yes ser, of course.' Protector, or jailor?

First, though, it seemed prudent to go back for his usual

second helping; Daichi looked resigned but he did have the Harpan stomach and there was no telling when he'd eat next.

A subdued Felli joined him in that too, and was still with him when he walked across to the Kraic archway. 'I need to thank them too, Max, for the tour and everything.'

'Yes, ser.' Harp tried to build a space between them; figured it might stop Daichi panicking about the youngster's safety.

Felli merely closed it. 'Max. This doesn't feel right.'

'I'm the reason, not you, ser. I'm sorry you got dragged into this.' Crip, he was a walking timebomb. Feldin and Daichi were understandably scared, wanted him contained and Felli where they knew he was all right. But wouldn't the boy be safer *not* travelling back with Harp? 'Perhaps if *you* ask your father if you can stay? I'm sure the Kraic would like that, and Sergeant Hendriks could act as your aide.'

The kid's steps faltered, then recovered. 'Forget it. If you're going, I'm going.'

And it wasn't his decision any longer.

Big Red registered [SURPRISE CAUSE]

'A Family obligation, ser.' He avoided mind-talk this time, far too dangerous. Who knew what he'd let slip.

[FELLI-OFFSPRING TOO]

Felli's cue to step forward. 'Yes, ser. I'd much rather stay but my father wants us.' Harpan breeding, training, trumped annoyance. 'I must thank you again for letting me see the tunnels, and for being so gracious. I very much hope to meet you all again.' The formal nod-bow Maxil favoured.

[WE TOO] Big Red turned back to Harp [WHEN HARP FRIEND RETURN]

A statement, or a question? Mind-talk had been magic, now it felt more like a curse. He couldn't risk harming the Kraic, any more than Felli or the other humans round him, but he had to assume Feldin wouldn't want him explaining that to the Kraic. It'd probably create a diplomatic nightmare. So he said, out loud, 'I'd like that too, ser, if I'm able.'

Felli gave him a look but stayed quiet. The two of them managed some polite chat for a few more minutes – Big Red sending mind-talk questions, Harp pretending not to hear – then thankfully he saw Daichi hovering outside the archway. 'Ser Daichi?'

'Sers, the shuttle's coming.'

So Harp gave Big Red a parting nod and walked back out into the oven, Felli close beside him. Hendriks found some stuff he said he needed signing off on. Harp confirmed them. Hendriks frowned when Harp was vague about returning and he had to say, 'It's orders, Hendriks. Major Valt is in command now.'

'Captain.' Still not happy.

'Thanks for all your help, friend.' Cos he might not see Hendriks again either. Whatever story Maxil Snr concocted, Harp couldn't see it featuring his freedom. More likely illness like with *Raptor*.

Finally Harp, Felli, Daichi and his Security boarded, the Family presence wiped off the map; so easy. Daichi was as bland as always, politely waving Harp and Felli to rear seats, like Family. It finally struck Harp the arrangement put Security between their charges and the outer hatch; protection could so easily become a prison. But Harpans didn't cause a scandal, even one gone crazy, so he would pretend as well, like everybody wanted. Everything would still look normal, if he could ignore the stiffness of the two Security who'd been with them on Collar.

The shuttle docked. The XO welcomed them. *Defiant* was already prepping for departure. No one asked the reason; it was orders. Harp thought he'd get locked away, for safety, but they stowed him in his G deck cabin, and invited him and Felli to a dinner. Daichi didn't argue. If he seemed distant maybe they'd assume it was because this recall was so urgent. Which it was, he guessed; a Harpan secret they would rush to bury.

22

'Felli. Enjoy your trip, my boy?' Feldin patted his son's shoulder. He'd come out to the semi-private shuttle dock to meet them.

Felli frowned, for once ignoring the inevitable 'casters, all kept at a distance. 'Did we need to come back now? I really wanted more time with –'

'Sorry, boy, it couldn't be avoided. Shall we?' Feldin cut him off and waved toward the private runner he had brought to meet them. So the Seed wasn't public knowledge here yet? Felli's eyes narrowed then he probably recalled that vids had ears, shut up abruptly.

Felli headed for the runner. Harp hung back, and Feldin noticed. 'Max.' Another public smile. 'Thank you for taking such good care of him.' Two meanings there?

Harp shook his head, aware of all those ears too, the casters' tec was bound to pick up something. 'He didn't need me, Ser. And he did his share of the work.'

'Work, you say? I must definitely hear about that.' Yes, Feldin would want to hear everything Felli could tell him, wouldn't he? But Feldin headed for the car with one hand firmly on Harp's arm.

It seemed only right to put a word in while he could. 'The Kraic like him. Your son is going to be a credit to you, Ser.'

Feldin, half inside the runner, seemed to hesitate. 'One hopes so.' Noticed Felli watching them and dropped the subject. 'Well, let's sit, shall we? Either of you want a drink?'

So Harp played the game, in the runner, on the underground platform under the Mansion, through the Security checks, past lower level staffers welcoming him back, up to seven then eight then nine, into the Founder's private quarters. There was a giant axe hanging over his head but they clearly wanted him to smile and pretend he couldn't see it. By the time he faced Maxil Snr his stomach was rebelling.

'Max, Felli, welcome back.' Maxil Snr inspected them both. There was no visible Security but Harp assumed surveillance. Not that he was going to do anything to bring them rushing in. Only, Maxil smiled. 'I can see you've both been in the sun. You must tell me about that later. But for now, Felli, I believe your father needs to talk with you.'

'About Max? I was there.' Felli's chin signalled willingness to fight. 'I don't think there's much point trying to keep me out of it.' The 'Ser' was so obviously an afterthought the boy might as well not have bothered.

'I see.' Maxil exchanged a look with Feldin, hovering behind. 'You appreciate this is a confidential matter?'

'Yes, ser.' Harp saw Felli's eyes had narrowed. 'Family keeps its secrets.'

'Yes, and this is something we need to *stay* secret, but young people are prone to, shall we say, let things slip?'

'Ser. I can keep my mouth shut, if I want to. And I will, I promise.'

Felli's father took him by the shoulder. 'Felli, this isn't something you can promise lightly.'

'I'm not a complete fool, Father.' For once the kid did look older than sixteen, and very like his father. 'Something's going on. Seems to me I know just enough I could put my big foot in it *without* meaning to, and I don't want that any more than you do.'

Harp closed his eyes. When he opened them again it was to find Maxil Snr looking at him instead. 'What's your opinion here, Max?'

His? Crip. 'I'd prefer you keep him away from me, ser. For his own safety.' He heard Felli's gasp. 'But he's right. He's sharp, and he's already seen enough he won't stop asking questions, so I think you need to talk to him, once you know more. Not necessarily right now though.' Better if they did all that once Harp was gone, and didn't have to hear it.

Feldin had walked round to where he could survey his son's expression; Harp thought that a mix, both pleasure and annoyance, very Felli. Maxil Snr... looked sympathetic? 'You're suggesting we treat Felli as Inner Family?'

Huh? 'Well, he is, Ser.'

'Actually, no.' Maxil drew a breath. 'Let's sit down, shall we? All of us.' Felli was first into one of the cushioned chairs, but only as far as its edge. That seemed to amuse Maxil but he chose a seat where he could focus on Harp. 'People assume Feldin's children are among our elite, and we have never disabused them. *We* assumed they would be. But in the strictest sense, the term Inner Family doesn't simply refer to our common ancestry. It also signifies genetic composition. You of course will understand that.'

Harp looked from Maxil to Feldin. 'Our weird blood, you mean.' But Felli had sat up; he didn't know that?

'That isn't a subject we share with minors, even if they have the markers. Not until they're mature enough to demonstrate discretion.' Maxil Snr had turned his gaze to Felli.

Feldin settled, also facing Felli. 'This is a conversation I didn't expect to have for some years yet. If ever. But Max maintains you are a credit to us. If you stay here now, we'll all require you to prove that.'

'Because you don't trust me?' Felli was gruff.

Feldin was equally blunt. 'Because you are still underage, and yes, frankly, because till now you have not shown that much discretion.' It was clear neither side was enjoying this.

Maxil Snr took over. 'Is it possible your experiences on Moon have encouraged you to grow up a little? Would you say that?'

'I. Perhaps, ser.' Felli faced his grandfather. 'Maybe I'm not always clever. But I've always kept my word.'

'Then will you give us your word that whatever you hear will not be repeated?' When Felli nodded Maxil sighed. 'Very well.' He turned back to Harp. 'Max, we owe you an apology. Unlike with my grandson, we have waited far too long to have this conversation.' A hint of humour surfaced in the darker eyes. 'At least we get to do the big reveal for two now. Felli, Max is already aware his genes are atypical for the average human, and that some of us, myself included, show the same genetic markers he does. He discovered that for himself somehow, when he was very young, but managed to hide it. Unlike us, Max didn't have the Family to keep that confidential. Max, *do* you know how you did that?'

'No, ser.' Big reveal, he'd said. They already knew more?

'You must have some idea,' Maxil pressed him.

'I… wished.' Harp felt himself shrug. 'I was a little kid, then later it just got to be a habit, wishing. Kinda superstitious.'

'Wished. Goodness me.' Maxil Snr shook his head. 'We'll leave it for now then. We found you, then saw the med reports. Those have been classified now, by the way. Anyway, there you were, my lost grandson, and you had all the markers for Inner Family status. We made that fairly obvious, publicly, as everyone expected anyway. But we waited to explain it to you properly because we didn't know you well enough to guess how you'd take it. And because, like Felli here, we weren't quite ready yet to share our Family secrets. You understand?'

'I was still a stranger.' And because, Harp thought grimly, you didn't trust me, any more than I trusted you.

'Exactly. I suppose we were all holding back, eh? So yes, Feldin and I watched you, and waited. We accessed your records from Moon. Daichi and Mz Chan sent us regular reports on your activities, and Feldin and I spent as much time with you as we could. We needed to know you better.' Maxil Snr paused. 'Young Emika had orders not to tell you anything either, something she grew increasingly unhappy about. Playing it safe was my decision, not your uncle's. I realise now they were right. We should have had this talk before we sent you off to Kraic IV instead of letting outside threats determine our priorities.'

All of which meant they knew something he didn't, but what? And all this talk about discretion hadn't helped him. 'Ser, am I a *danger*?'

'We don't know, boy. If you are… we'll deal with it, however we can.'

'Then what *do* you know? If there is actually any sense to all this, don't I deserve to know it?' Even if it killed him.

'Since Family legend has been at the root of everything, and seems increasingly more fact than fiction, I think it's time we share it, with both of you.' Maxil tapped his wristcom. 'Happily some of the source material survives, otherwise I'd probably have a lot more trouble persuading you to take it seriously.'

Across the room a large wallscreen dropped down, forcing Felli to twist round to see where everybody else was looking. Maxil tapped again, adding his thumbprint this time; what he wanted must have been *double* encrypted. 'Felli, this is your last chance to remove yourself. After this we will regard you as an adult, and a member of our inner circle. With the appropriate penalties.'

'I'm staying.' Harp thought the kid tried to hide excitement, probably so they would see an adult, but it wasn't working; he was practically vibrating. Feldin sighed. That sobered Felli. 'Go ahead, Grandfather.' Chin up. 'I won't let you down.'

'No. I don't think you will. Very well.' Maxil tapped once more, the screen lit. Harp thought everybody leaned toward it.

The small woman onscreen sat proudly in a throne-like chair that tried to dwarf her. She was extremely old, her ochre skin like parchment, her dark hair heavily streaked with white. Her features clearly labelled her a Harpan, but an ancient version as the darker hair attested.

Maxil paused the vid. 'Mai-San Har Pan, our original Founder.' Har Pan, Harp realised; two words the centuries had blurred together. Maxil Snr continued, 'Popular accounts say she liked to gamble, mainly high-stakes Havoc, and won the fortune she used to terraform World, then Moon, both barely habitable, way out on the Fringes as we called it then. They say she was "eccentric", claimed that she saw visions – psychic stuff that helped her beat the odds, and her opponents. Or as other versions put it, she was bat-shit crazy. For a long time, while we valued the results – what Family wouldn't want to rule two planets – we believed it was a makebelief but, well, in later centuries we had to think again. For now, I'll let you hear it for yourselves.'

The screen came back to life. Mai-San stared out at them, gnarled hands on padded chair-arms. The rest of her, what Harp could see, was covered by a high-necked tunic with embroidery all over it, clear evidence that she'd been wealthy when she made the vid, as were the many rings that decorated every finger, and what Harp assumed were real jewels in her hairdo.

But it was the face that captured Harp's attention most; those dark eyes glittered. He was suddenly glad she was dead and gone; he didn't think he'd want to meet her. Wasn't sure he wanted to discover what she thought she knew. Or what her genes bequeathed him?

'Honourable descendants.' A triumphant smile deepened age-lines. 'If you are seeing this then my time is over, and yours beginning.' She shifted slightly, maybe old bones aching. 'You have inherited worlds, their wealth, and power, and the source of energy to drive the ships that will protect you. And what greater prize is there than independence? I'm sure you're thanking me.' A sudden, shocking cackle. 'But all things have their price, don't they? Mine? They call me crazy. Yours? I cannot tell, but you will have to pay it, somewhere in the future. So, the bargain.

'I terraformed two worlds for you. Me. Certainly no one on Earth. Those bloodsuckers were too busy trying to sneak off before anyone else realised Earth was too toxic to save. Not even some conglomerate, greedy for food or ores. Just me and a few willing to bet on me. How could a simple spacer do all that, you ask? The truth is I had help that no one else could see and no one would believe in.'

She leaned forward. 'My visions led me to this world, a

dreary place, though there was water deep beneath the surface. My visions showed me what it could become. And if I took the bargain, sealed with our blood, I could leave Earth forever. How could I refuse?

'So a bunch of us changed planets, in the opposite direction, and that changed the game, and you, or what you might be in the future.' The dark eyes glowed. 'But heed my warning. If you don't evolve then one day you will lose it all; your wealth, your power, your very worlds will crumble.' The voice rose, and the face became more manic. 'So be warned. I gambled with your lives, and only time will prove who is the winner.'

The screen went black.

23

If Maxil or Feldin expected Harp to speak first they were flat out of luck. That was his ancestor? And 'Earth'? She had said Earth, hadn't she? Not *New*Earth. This was *before* NewEarth? Hadn't they realised; their ancestors never left NewEarth, never went there – chased some vision, for a crazy woman and a "bargain"! A wonder there was *anything* normal about him, and it answered all his fears; he *was* a danger to the others. He found he was on his feet. 'You need to lock me away, now.'

'No, no, Max, we need to tell you the rest. And you now, Felli. Feldin, perhaps…?'

'Certainly, Father, but maybe a drink first? Seeing that always leaves me needing one, so I'm sure the boys do too.' Maxil's version of Eda, male-voiced, produced a moving drinks cart. Brandy went the rounds except for a disgusted Felli who was given fruit juice.

Harp downed his in one. 'You say there's more to tell.'

'Oh yes. Some of it was recorded in private journals at first. We think those weren't shared till much later, probably about the time we realised we needed to seal our medical records. And the whole of it is shared only with our innermost circle. The real Inner Family.' Feldin looked at Harp, then Felli. 'Because as you might guess by now, if outsiders knew the whole Family might fall.'

Feldin topped off his glass – Maxil Snr hadn't taken more than a sip –refilled Harp's without bothering to ask. 'Long story short, Max, Mai-San had four husbands. You and my father are named after the most favoured. We like people to think they were consecutive but we suspect otherwise. Presumably, if you believe her version, she meant to maximise the chances of whatever "bargain" she'd agreed to, real or imagined. The records do show a startling, shall we say, interplay of those four original bloodlines, and we think the more they wove together, the more measurable the results became.'

Felli stirred at last. 'Like, our hair colour changed from dark to light?'

'Yes.' Feldin gave the boy a small smile. 'It's become one of the most recent markers. It's so easy to pick us out now, isn't it?'

Harp's turn. 'Because we're freaks.'

Feldin shrugged. 'That's one word. I've always preferred unique?'

Harp discovered he could still laugh, after a fashion. 'I seem to be that, all right, but I still say freak's closer to the mark. Or monster?'

'You may be different but there's nothing bad about you, Max. We've started to believe you're what Mai-San was telling us to hope for.'

'What, a second maniac? At least I don't have "visions", I suppose that's something to be thank –' Or did he? Was it all in his mind? That would almost be a relief, except he didn't see it. 'So I have these markers as you call them. But I can't be the only one.'

'Ah.' Feldin faced him. 'We can't really say, because there is more, isn't there?'

Harp drew breath; putting his cards on the table was all he had left, wasn't it? He swallowed half the second brandy; hoped it gave him courage. 'I *wished* for the blood tests to make me like everyone else. I still don't understand what I did.' He told them what little he recalled, walking away from the crash, being frightened by the medics' faces. 'I was a kid but I wasn't blind.' Another breath.

'Then I sometimes saw stuff more than others, or I heard when others couldn't. And I realised I healed faster. Back then all I wanted was to be accepted, I suppose, so I'd pretend I wasn't really hurt. Cos if I had a scar, that disappeared too, soon after.'

Felli leaned away, mouth open. Harp looked down instead, to see that Feldin's feet were moving slightly backward; he was leaning forward. 'Some of those traits *have* surfaced in us too, though not all at once. But I think you've already gone further, yes?'

When Harp raised his head he saw Felli staring at his father, maybe as breathless as Harp. 'You always said… it was good genes, and good medics,' Felli said faintly.

'Which it is,' his father told him gently. 'As a Family we're generally fit and strong, and seldom ill. It's helped us stay in power.'

'Only now,' Harp summed up, 'what I can do isn't about being healthy.'

Felli actually shook himself. 'So what can you do that we can't?' Maybe a familiar hint of umbrage this time; that felt almost welcome.

'I became a marksman, as they called it, good with weapons.' If he counted in that slingshot, and the turret. 'I suppose you'd call all that coordination. But it got me to the navy, and to *Raptor*.'

Feldin nodded. Maxil Snr said nothing. Felli practically quivered.

Spit it out then? 'They worked out I could handle *Raptor's* turret.' He saw Felli frown. 'Its weapons system, Felli. They say I cope with it better than anyone else, at least so far, and they may have to write prompts off my recordings. Then there was Simshaw.' Worth a scowl.

'Ah yes.' Feldin pursed his lips. 'We've kept an eye on the professor. There was one attempt to publish but we buried it, and the professor's funding, shall we say, lurched for a while? Hopefully that's the end of that but if need be we'll deal with it again.' Felli's eyes widened, but this time Harp was past caring. Feldin raised his eyebrows. 'So *Raptor* simply *proved* your superior reflexes.'

'Yeah. And something else.' If he was dangerous they needed to know everything. 'My pilot blacked out, and there were missiles heading for us, so I wished, and *Raptor* dodged. I moved it.'

'Without the physical controls,' Feldin guessed.

'Yes. I hid that. Then you sent me to Kraic IV and I discovered I could talk to Kraic, right?' Harp took another gulp. 'I guess it's all related, somehow?'

'I imagine. I can quite see why you kept quiet. Tell me, what changed your mind?'

'It's about more than me now. I could hurt people. And you'll want me away from the Kraic.' Crip, and the Seed, what harm might he have done there? 'But maybe now you know, I won't be the only one who can talk to them like that?'

'The telepathy? It does seem possible, knowing what we do about our bloodline. We have in fact been looking for contenders, planning to put them next to the Kraic and see what happens.'

Someone else able to talk to the Kraic properly after he was gone would help, surely. Crip. 'Could being able to mind-talk with the Kraic be what all this was meant to create? Could Mai-San's bargain have been with *them*?'

Feldin hesitated. 'If it was, they've never hinted at it. And you're past even that now, aren't you?'

'Yeah.' Harp sagged, defeated.

Felli's turn. 'It was amazing, Father, you should have seen… Max'd gone ahead of us. I think he was the only one not flagging. In fact.' Felli *grinned*. 'I kept thinking he got less tired the higher we went. Anyway, there I was getting my breath back, wishing I hadn't agreed to go, and sparks shot up into the sky, then the top of the mountain sort of cracked open and this steaming sludge started to ooze out. It looked black at first, then it turned, like, a darker red, and started oozing faster. I mean, I just stood staring. Only the crack widened and the sludge got louder, and the smell… Daichi tried to grab me but the ground had started shaking and he fell. I didn't, but I really thought we'd had it, and Max was up there in its path and I could only watch it happen.

'Only then he, well.' The kid looked round at Harp again and smiled, in delight. 'He raised a hand at it, and it sort of creaked. And then, wow, it tried to back up. Like he'd scared it off. It was the best thing ever!'

'No, it wasn't.' Harp faced Felli. 'It could have killed you all.'

'No.' A beaming smile. 'Cos you saved us.'

'Felli, I'm not convinced I did.' Harp looked at Felli's elders. 'I'm afraid I could have *caused* it, do you see? And if I can wake a volcano, what the stars else could I do?'

Maxil Snr finally rejoined the conversation. 'And there's the question. As far as we are aware – and we keep a very close eye – you are easily the most... developed, even though you're not the most recent birth. Which has led us to, shall we say, a working hypothesis.'

Felli saved Harp asking. 'You mean like a theory?'

'A hypothesis, young man, is an as-yet unproven theory. While we see indications, we don't yet have firm evidence.'

'OK, so you think Max is... what?'

Maxil didn't react to the tone. 'Consider what we know, boy. Before Max, it was almost unheard of for any of the Family to go to Moon. According to our records the last visit of any length was over two centuries ago.' The Founder looked at Harp. 'In those generations we've evolved, measurably, but it was an extremely slow mutation. Until now.'

Harp added two and two and got the inevitable four. 'You think living on Moon speeded things up?'

'It seems the only logical explanation, wouldn't you agree?' Maxil Snr started to shake his head, changed his mind. 'Historically, we have tended to regard Moon as an extra limb, something valuable enough to keep, but not as valuable as the main body, World. I think we may have made a grave error. I think Moon is an important part of... whatever Mai-San started.'

'But you don't know?' Harp scrubbed a hand through his hair. The damn stuff needed cutting, again. Without Emika or Stannis around he hadn't thought about his appearance in weeks.

Feldin once again took over. 'No, Max, we really don't. Remember that for centuries, Mai-San was considered at best delusional and at worst deranged. It's taken generations to rethink that.'

Harp could see that, sure. That vid was still clear enough to show the too-bright eyes, flamboyant gestures, and the shrill voice by its ending. *He'd* have thought the woman crazy.

Feldin was still talking. 'In any case it was well into our second century before anyone noticed some of us no longer quite matched the rest, and at first they thought the changes were some slow-acting disease. They spent decades looking for a cure before someone finally pointed out we were getting healthier, not sicker. Look at you. You say you've been injured. But have you ever been *ill*?'

'No, or if I have I don't remember,' Harp said flatly.

'Neither have we.' Feldin smiled suddenly at Felli. 'Or you, Felli, eh?'

'No.' The youth grinned. Then frowned. 'But, Ho-San.'

'Yes.' His father's reassuring smile faded. 'Ho-San had some childhood ailments.'

'O-K. Ho-San's been sick, so your hypothesis can't be right; we've just been lucky.' Then he looked at Harp. 'Except. Crip.'

'Yes, Felli. I'm afraid crip sums it up.' His father didn't smile. 'Max is living proof the Harpan bloodline *is* evolving. And now you know. You've always excelled at sports, haven't you? Max didn't have those opportunities but his talents found their way to other uses, like his skill with weapons.'

Felli nodded slowly. Harp sat back and listened. It almost felt like he wasn't there, like this was between Feldin and his son. Maybe it was, Feldin hadn't intended Felli to know so much, at least not yet, but the poor kid had stumbled into a crash course in weird. Not so different than him, except Feldin was trying to cushion the blow, where it felt like Harp was supposed to suck it up and deal.

Maybe cushioning the blow wasn't even necessary; Felli's face had brightened. 'You mean I could be like Max? I could do all that too?'

Harp shifted in his chair; Feldin noticed, switched attention to them both again. 'It's a possibility, but I'd guess not. Or not much more than you already can.'

The youngster sagged back in his seat. 'Damn. Because I didn't grow up on Moon.' Not dumb at all, young Felli, just clearly disappointed. Then he straightened. 'Is *that* why you sent us – me – over there? As an experiment?' Harp thought the kid half hopeful, half indignant. Feldin's turn to hesitate.

But Maxil Snr didn't. 'That was my decision, Felli. You were old enough the trip wasn't going to cause awkward questions, and young enough ...'

'I might still be affected by whatever Moon's done to Max.' Felli shot his grandfather a less than friendly look. 'You didn't think it was worth going yourself, because I'm still growing and you're not.'

'And if nothing else, your visit *has* matured you, hasn't it?' Maxil Snr smiled and raised his eyebrows.

Felli didn't smile. 'So I was an experiment, only I wasn't there long enough to show any results. Oh. Just how long did you mean for me to stay, Grandfather? A year? Longer?'

Maxil Snr looked approving. 'Well done, Felli. Yes, I intended a longer stay, before Max's latest... talent... emerged. How would you feel about going back, now you know why?'

'You mean I have a choice?' Harp figured that wasn't so much teenage petulance as a more adult dislike of what being a Harpan really meant, that constant lack of freedom that he too had had to cope with. Because if Maxil Snr wanted Felli on Moon, even for the rest of the kid's life, there wasn't much Felli could do about it. Feldin's face confirmed that. Felli's father might have power but he wasn't, yet, the Founder. Neither World nor Moon were a democracy, however prettily they wrapped it.

Only Maxil Snr surprised them. 'If you don't want to go back now I won't insist. I think you may finally be ready to make your own choices, as a real member of the Inner Family.'

Felli blinked. So did Feldin, though he tried to hide it and he left his son to answer. 'Er, can I think about it?'

Maxil Snr nodded. 'Of course. It's sensible not to rush into things, whenever possible. Meanwhile, we should address Max's concerns.' His voice got brisker somehow. 'You believe you're a danger. Who to?'

'Potentially, anyone.' Harp tried to match Maxil's tone, like this was all... hypothetical. 'Moving *Raptor* was bad enough but at least that was in vacuum, and I did protect my crew. When nothing happened after I thought... but now. I moved molten rock! I don't know how. I didn't even mean to. That's a whole new problem.'

'Yes.' Maxil Snr studied him without the rising panic Harp was feeling. 'You grew up on Moon, with mutations we were already somewhat aware of. You concealed the genetic markers, every time you had a routine medical, yes?' Harp simply nodded. 'Admittedly that wouldn't have been as many times as here, since we've established you were never ill, but that you *could* conceal it was a clear indication, if we'd only known, that your mutation was more advanced. It's possible the early traumas, your kidnapping then the crash, accelerated things,' Maxil said thoughtfully. Harp froze. The Founder's face was quite impersonal. Harp might not have been a deliberate experiment, but he figured he was under the microscope now, with a vengeance.

The old man wasn't done yet either. 'Did you become aware of any *other* differences, between yourself and other Mooners?'

Crip, he'd never thought to analyse himself, but Maxil wasn't going to stop, was he, not till he'd wrung out every tiny detail? Details Harp was only now perceiving, though he guessed they'd always been there. 'Heat.' He stared at Maxil, vaguely conscious of Feldin and Felli paying close attention. 'I could stand the heat better than most.' Maybe better than any? 'I don't think I burned, in the crash. I don't think I was hurt, at all.' Why hadn't he ever seen that? Cos he was scared to? 'And I could live on less water.' All those times he'd shared with Bays, or others in the Orphan Houses. 'And, I think I was more comfortable round the prairie fires.' His clothes had charred that day; he hadn't. 'I don't see how that links with *Raptor*, but it maybe does with moving lava?'

'Yes, the lava seems a more extreme example. I wonder if it signifies a growth spurt, or just a more blatant demonstration of something that was always there.' Maxil's face was *still* impassive. 'Perhaps *Raptor* wasn't directly related, but a different aspect. Though I'd hazard a guess it is related, generally, to your mental powers.'

'I'm abnormal,' Harp agreed grimly.

'Not for us', Maxil told him, 'and I'd go with paranormal.'

Harp waved off semantics. 'And dangerous, enough you should think again about sending Felli back to Moon and putting him at risk too. In fact you shouldn't send anyone till you see what happens with me. Was Mai-San always crazy, or did Moon do that too?'

'My boy, Mai-San may or may not have been mad, but the more I find out, the more I wonder if she was anything but.' Maxil went from calm to solemn. 'Was it mad to make some bargain with stars-know-who, or what? It gave us two planets after all. And I don't believe you're mad. I think you're very sane, but you could finally show us what it's all been about.' Then Maxil smiled; Founder calculation disappeared and perhaps a grandfather resurfaced? 'I have no intention of locking you up in a padded cell, my boy, or strapping you down on an examination table, as I can see you imagining. You are not a specimen, you are an honourable young man, and one your Uncle Feldin and I both like. You have my word we will not harm you.'

'And mine,' said Feldin quickly. 'And, I suspect, Felli's?'

'No!' Felli blurted out, 'I wouldn't!'

Maxil's eyebrows rose once more. 'Even though, as I recall, you didn't exactly welcome Max into the Family.'

'That was before. I mean, there was all the fuss, and...' Felli gulped. 'I didn't know him then.'

'Good, good.' Except Maxil Snr exchanged another look with Feldin. Felli missed it; Harp didn't. Somebody was going to keep an eye on Felli, Feldin's son or not. Because that response said Felli *had* once wanted to hurt Harp?

Maxil Snr continued, 'Well, I think we've enough to go on with.' To Harp. 'Mz Chan is the only other person who will be privy to what we've discussed. I promise her loyalty is absolute. Other than her, we four.' He turned his gaze on Felli. 'Will be the *only* Family, Inner or otherwise, to know so much. Unless or until I decide it's necessary. Understood?'

An order, from their Head of House. His audience gave the formal nod.

'Then if there's nothing else.' Maxil sat back, subtly dismissing them all. Harp, eager to leave, rose at once.

Felli didn't. 'But, ser. Ho-San.'

Maxil's face blanked. Harp knew that look, he'd seen it on vids. Crip, in mirrors. Maxil was hiding his thoughts behind a polite mask, which meant Felli's outburst was significant, and possibly unwelcome. He recovered fast though. 'Ho-San? You wanted her to go to Moon as well.'

Maxil's sigh was so slight maybe Felli didn't notice, but Harp thought Feldin did, and maybe shared the… sorrow? Maybe Feldin meant to answer, but *his* father stopped him with a gesture. 'I asked both of you to visit Moon because I thought you would be more comfortable with your sister along. I know you're close. I was also aware,' the old man added drily, 'that you were not as comfortable in Max's company as I could have wished. Thus Ho-San would have spared Max some of *your* company. Daichi had orders to keep both of you clear of Max if he thought that advisable.'

Felli stared at his boots, but didn't protest, obviously knew his actions hadn't always been what they should.

'Happily, your going out alone and spending more time with Max has clearly allowed you time to rethink your opinions.' Maxil watched the boy, who sat so still now. 'I believe you now accept he is neither a fake, nor ambitious?'

'Yes, ser.' An even smaller voice now, and a nervous glance in Harp's direction.

Harp shrugged, and smiled. 'I don't blame you.'

Maxil Snr wasn't done. 'So now you know. Annoying though it was, not to mention ill-mannered, it wasn't strategically important when your sister pretended to feel ill in order to avoid doing as I asked, thereby leaving you to travel offworld alone. Ho-San *is* fully grown, making it unlikely she will develop further. And those childhood illnesses...' The Founder waited.

Felli paled. 'She doesn't have the markers.'

'No. The mutations have been known to fail, even in the direct line. Sadly, that means your father and I will probably never be able to tell her any of this. The general populace, unsurprisingly, have always regarded her as Inner Family. There is no indication she has ever suspected there is so much more to that than the privileges she enjoys. But then nor did you, young man, until this meeting?'

'No. So I'm Inner Family.' Felli swallowed. 'But Ho-San only thinks she is.'

'I'm afraid so.' Maxil was trying to sound sympathetic but Harp had to wonder. The older man still sat back, no leaning in to Felli.

It was left to Feldin to lay a hand on Felli's shoulder. 'Your genes are like mine. Ours. That makes you Inner Family in the secret sense, which Ho-San cannot be. You see that? And not all our relatives who do have the markers fully understand. Most merely believe us fortunate; a superior strain if you like. Only a very select few have heard Mai-San's warning. And now, well, no one but we four and Mz Chan will know how far things have progressed, and even we don't know where we go next? Being *not* one of us, Ho-San cannot be allowed to share this knowledge. It's too dangerous. Do you understand why?'

'Because it would make us targets,' Felli said dully, 'so we don't tell anyone who isn't. Even my sister.'

'Yes.' Feldin's turn to sigh. 'I knew eventually you

might have to know too, have to keep our secret. I didn't think it would be so abruptly. I am sorry, son.'

Maxil Snr stayed aloof; the Founder. 'Since you know so much now, we may as well finish it. Your sister will no doubt inherit a great deal, if only because your father feels an irrational degree of guilt at having to exclude her from matters that will never concern her. But he cannot choose her as his heir; she will never be eligible.'

Harp thought he'd jumped; *chosen* as heir?

Maxil wasn't finished. 'She lacks our inheritance, and the vested interest in extreme discretion such a role requires. It's probably fortunate outsiders will probably not be shocked when someone else is eventually named.'

Feldin winced.

Felli's mouth, shut tight, fell open. Their Founder had just all but stated his granddaughter wasn't, in any case, his choice to take charge of their worlds.

Sadly, Harp thought he might be right. She hadn't struck him as a politician, or indeed the grownup Felli thought her. Merely growing up would never have been enough anyway, would it? Ho-San wasn't one of Maxil's "paranormals". The Family's need to keep that secret meant they'd never risk letting her in on it.

And he'd thought *he* didn't know enough.

24

Back in his own quarters, Harp slumped in his chair, caffee in hand. He'd declined another brandy when his Grandfather offered. If he was stressed why shouldn't he be? He'd thought he was adjusting to being a Harpan, to finally being around folk who were like him. That he wasn't so alone any more.

Now he was an outsider again, more than ever. Crip, he wasn't human. Because he couldn't read it any other way. Oh, Maxil and Feldin had been careful not to say it. Maybe trying not to frighten Felli, maybe trying not to scare themselves. But there it was, that word. Mutation.

Was that why Mai-San had travelled far from other normal-human worlds? Had she known back then? Though how it began didn't feel as important right now as how it was changing everything he knew about himself. He felt for Felli, but right now he needed time alone, for being selfish.

He told Eda he didn't want anything but she still flashed a suggested dinner menu onto the screen on the opposite wall so he supposed he ought to eat, his stomach was an empty cavern again – another "signifier" he'd been born with. The menu was from the Family restaurant. If he didn't fancy it he could ask for anything he wished.

Except for being normal.

Enough. 'It isn't like you've changed overnight. Crip, you were always a freak, so stop whining, you might as well enjoy it while you can.' So he ordered dinner, it arrived soon after, and he ate it all. He'd take the blasted brandy too, a lot of it, and go to bed and hope it sent him to oblivion until the morning.

+++

He didn't remember falling asleep but waking wasn't pleasant; he didn't recall ever having a headache before.

Maybe Maxil's "fortunate genes" didn't recognise being hungover as illness. They sure weren't doing anything for it. But in another way at least his head had cleared. The fog of indecision he had left the meeting with had lifted. If Maxil Snr wasn't going to lock him up it had to be business as usual. Even if Daichi might have orders to put him down for good if he got to be too much of a risk.

And that meant, things to do; the office.

First, leave messages for Maxil and Feldin, to assure them he was still playing the game and would copy them his revised itinerary once he sorted it out. Then a pass through his office downstairs, to see how Moon Aid was doing in his absence. Then, maybe he should suggest he returned to Moon as Big Red expected, so the whole Family didn't seem to insult the Kraic delegation.

If Maxil would agree to that, it might be safer if he *stayed* on the smaller planet. Unless staying where he'd "evolved" faster was an even greater risk? Had Maxil thought about that? Crip, messages wouldn't cut it, at all. 'Eda, can you set up an appointment with Ser Maxil and Ser Feldin, asap?'

+++

Apparently asap equalled the next day. So much for always being there when he needed them! But even if *his* world was disintegrating around him Mooners still had *their* problems, and it was supposed to be his job to solve them. Harp settled into his office chair, woke all his screens and tried to fill the time with something useful.

It looked like Feldin had signed off on regular shipments and such, but otherwise from what Harp could see he'd left everything to the folk in General Admin. Goods and services were still moving, but anything outside the established "rules" had been sidelined "for later study". That was now a mountain. Ah, forget Mz Chan's objections.

Harp put in a call to Stannis.

+++

If Stannis was surprised he didn't show it. Nor did he show any pleasure when he stood in Harp's office. But that might have been cos he'd walked into a stream of navy curse words; not the greeting Harp intended but for once his temper had erupted. 'Apologies, Stannis. That wasn't aimed at you.'

'Don't mention it, Captain.' Crip, captain, not Max. Stannis was wearing brighter colours than he usually chose to work in too; a subtle message but Harp got it. The man hadn't assumed he'd been recalled to his job. That easy smile was the superficial Stannis he'd met first, no longer trusting.

His job then, to put the real smile back, to prove he trusted Stannis? 'I've messed up. I had no idea I'd be away so long and I didn't realise so much would mount up. Now I'm afraid we're in for some late nights if you can manage that, especially since I don't even know if I'm back for good.' Harp scowled back at his screens. 'On top of all that, I left someone in Admin a task it looks as if they never started.' Harp scrubbed a hand through his hair – *still* needed cutting. 'The navy are searching for those missing kids but I wanted a full list of who's lost, and any next of kin, if only to know who to notify down the line. But all I have here looks like a very approximate headcount, not even a confirmed total!'

'Ah.' Did Stannis relax a fraction? 'Would you like me to contact Admin?'

'Please. I'm pretty sure you'll be more polite about it. Caffee before you start? And welcome back. At least I hope you're back. Sorry I wasn't in touch sooner, things got a bit involved.'

There, finally, the real smile. At least he had one thing in his current life he'd put right, ending Stannis's doubts. He could trust Stannis to find the missing data, and to sweet-talk some of those he'd left in limbo. Right. Time to stop throwing a tantrum and think positive.

+++

Or not.

Things did seem ok for the next several days. Harp talked with Maxil and Feldin again and walked out with no immediate plan to return to Moon, or go anywhere else. He even, he thought, had persuaded them not to send Felli back, till they had more intel on the Kraic's motives.

With long hours and Stannis's help he was starting to make inroads into Moon Aid's backlog, largely the hundred and one requests, offers and complaints Admin hadn't considered routine enough to handle.

He'd overheard – that Harpan hearing – Stannis's very "polite" exchange with Admin about the missing data, so he knew Stannis had people down there chasing records like their lives, or jobs, depended on it.

He'd even found time for a haircut, before anyone started a rumour something was wrong cos he wasn't his usual dumb, "pretty" self. Ugh.

On the brighter side, Felli had turned up at the office that morning, curious about Moon Aid then saying he'd like to help. And Felli was a Harpan, and the kid could charm folk when he wanted. So Harp had sat him down at a spare desk, sketched out a generic thankyou message to give him a base line, then handed him the list of all the folk who'd sent him pleasant messages, the offers, the significant donations. 'Contact these on Moon Aid's behalf? Apologise for keeping them waiting if it seems right, or whatever. Use your judgement?'

Felli blinked, swallowed, then got to it. When Harp sneaked a look the kid was varying the wording he'd given him, so the replies didn't look so mass produced. And he'd already had the sense to ask Stannis when he wasn't sure about something. Harp figured the novelty would wear off by the end of the day, then the kid would remember he had friends and pleasanter pursuits, but till then at least they were getting more done.

+++

'Felli?' Ho-San appeared in his bedroom doorway, looking murderous. 'Why haven't you answered my calls?' Her forward movement stuttered. 'And where the crip are you going dressed like that?'

Felli tried for nonchalance. 'Just looking the part, San. I'm spending the day.' Like yesterday. 'In Max's office.'

'Oh? Not so bad then. Thinks he's won you over, does he? Maybe you'll finally find something useful.'

Felli couldn't stop a wince, good thing she wasn't looking. She'd sent him off to Moon with clear instructions to unearth some "dirt" on Max, and cursed him when he hadn't. And she knew a lot of words you'd never guess in public. Then she'd found some new ones when he'd owned up he was starting quite to like his older cousin, now he'd got to know him.

Now... he knew so many secrets that would earn him her approval, but he'd promised not to tell. He wasn't used to keeping anything from San, even if he'd grown up knowing how to. But he'd promised. And besides. 'Honestly, Sis, I don't think there's any dirt to find.'

By that time Ho-San was flitting around his room, touching his stuff, flicking at things the way she did. She paused to sneer at a message on his bedside screen, an invitation from a would-be friend she didn't favour. In the past he'd mostly turned the fellow down to keep the peace. Today he'd been considering accepting. Better not to mention that while she was in a temper?

Then he saw her stop. She'd reached his Mooner plaque, the image of the Kraic and the Seed arriving, that he'd given pride of place among his trophies.

'Ah look, you brought home a souvenir. And there's you, next to golden boy himself, like besties.' Ho-San turned round, slowly, till she faced him. 'Tell me you haven't actually fallen for the poor-orphan act. You can't be that stupid.'

'Sis, he looked out for me, and seeing him on Moon was different.' Felli grabbed his wristcom, with the office clearances that Max had sent him. Remembered he had wanted to be early to impress Ser Stannis. Edged toward the door. 'I wish you'd gone, then you'd have seen too.'

'I wish I had as well, if letting you go alone let him mess with your head.' She saw him hovering. 'Oh run along, do. Wouldn't want you to be late for work, would we?'

Felli still hesitated, torn between fight and flight. Speak up for Max, and himself, or dodge the sort of face-off with San he hadn't had for years? The mood she was in he had zero chance of talking her round, so maybe later was better? 'See you this evening then? We're having dinner with Father, remember?'

'Mm.' Ho-San came to join him and they crossed his (relatively) small apartment; add-on to his father's, that he'd got when Ho-San had moved out as soon as she achieved the magic adult-twenty. Now, she had a bigger place on six she called her hovel, that she'd taken over when another cousin suddenly departed. By the time they reached his outer door her sour mood had melted; quick to anger, but she soon forgave him, that was Ho-San. She had even found a smile. 'I suppose *Father* wanted you closer to new-cousin.'

Felli laughed, relieved. 'Of course. And honestly, you should have gone to Moon. It was a rush. The land, the people... If Father lets me return once,' – crip – 'once the Kraic have settled in, I'm going to drag you along too.'

Ho-San smiled back. 'If there's a next time, maybe I'll let you. And maybe you should tell me more about it, and why you've changed your mind about new-Maxil. Maybe I *should* take a fresh look.'

'You really should, Sis. He's well, something special. Even Grandfather thinks so, and he's no fool, is he?'

'True. Well, I'll see you tonight. And don't ignore any more of my calls!'

They parted ways, Felli with a bounce back in his step. It was their first meeting since, oh, since everything he thought he knew turned upside down. In one way at least it had gone better than he'd feared. He wasn't exactly happy about keeping so much from the one person he'd always confided in. Maybe he could talk Father into telling her something? But for now, a Harpan's word was his bond, and he'd just proved he could keep his, hadn't he? Though he'd have to be more careful not to slip up the way he almost had at the end.

+++

To Harp's surprise Felli was back. He'd even toned down on the flash, and gone straight back to work like he meant it. Suddenly it felt like the three of them were a real team.

Till Stannis, who'd been down the way in his own space, walked in on them. 'Captain.' Stannis was more formal around Felli.

'Mm?'

'They're still checking, but I think I have a complete list of the lost children.'

'Really?' Harp paused the complaint he was personally investigating. 'Transfer it to my desk?'

'Yes, ser.' Only Stannis glanced at Felli, who had stopped to listen.

'Whatever it is, spit it out. Felli understands discreet.'

Felli looked pleased. Stannis didn't but continued. 'There are some anomalies. They may be clerical errors but I thought you might like to see them?'

'OK, show me.' Harp exchanged his desk for an easy chair and nodded at his wall screens, easier that way for everyone to see it. Felli closed his screens and jumped to join them, obviously keen to be included.

Stannis took over Harp's desk and brought up several new files: names and ages, dates, locations; relatives, for those who'd had them. Felli, who had fidgetted at first, grew still and quiet. There were a lot of names, more than Harp had known too.

'Sers, most of this is straightforward enough. Compiling alphabetically wasn't much help with identification so I got them to cross reference according to gender, age, physical characteristics and last known location. The last threw up something unexpected. As I said it could be something or nothing…' Stannis's hand moved, two names brightened. 'A Pre Employment House – have I got that right? – in a town called Riverbend, listed two twelve year olds among those kidnapped, but according to earlier House records they'd left, several months before. At first I assumed they'd just been listed twice, a simple clerical error. But when I chased it up I couldn't find the second placement.'

Felli frowned. 'So they *were* kidnapped, but you don't know where from? Is that important?'

'Ser.' Stannis kept his eyes on Harp. 'I couldn't trace the placement they're supposed to have gone to. As far as I can ascertain, it doesn't exist.'

Harp met his gaze. 'Now, or never?'

'I think never did, ser. With your permission I'd like to search their local records. But there's always the possibility I'll cause some local offence, and I know you prefer to be careful about World-Moon relations.'

'Do it. Keep Admin out of it for now, and if anyone does complain refer them to me?'

Stannis left without comment. Felli made up for it. 'Did they get the address wrong or something? I mean, they'd have to be somewhere, with someone.'

'Stannis is very good at what he does.' And like Stannis, Harp smelt a slider. Especially in Riverbend. He forced himself to relax, no point borrowing trouble too soon. 'We'll see once Stannis has more intel. Till then…'

'I know. Back to the grind.' Felli grinned though and he didn't dawdle as he strode across the office. 'I've almost finished the thankyous and such. Ser Stannis said he'd reroute any replies to his desk, and pass them on to whoever's job it was next. So I'll be free for something else tomorrow.'

'You want to come back?' Harp didn't hide his doubt. 'I'll understand if you'd rather spend time with your friends. You must have missed them, and you've already done a lot.'

'Nah.' Felli studied his own screens. 'They're a bit

boring these days; same old, you know? I'd rather do something useful.'

Like the boy would still rather talk, and dress, more like Harp? Like right now? Maybe Felli was changing more than outwardly, now his life had got more complicated. Harp was touched by the implied compliment but the youngster would do better with another template. Maybe Feldin could find him an interesting role somewhere else? Meanwhile, though, no one was forcing Felli here and he could use the extra hands a while longer.

Harp turned back to work as well. 'Stay as long as you like. I appreciate it. I'm sure Stannis does too.'

'Mm.' Pause. 'My father didn't approve you employing Ser Stannis, did he?'

'Oh?' Ouch. Felli had said people forgot he was around.

'He's really good though, so you were right.'

'He's very able, yes. Easily the best candidate I saw.'

'Mm.' Apparently that ended the topic. They worked on, in comfortable quiet, Felli handling the 'friendlies' as he called them, Harp the not-so and the public stuff he hated. Stannis fielding follow-ups, the day to day, the comp search into Riverbend's old records. Which were likely pretty slapdash.

Things stayed relatively peaceful. Harp felt tired, occasionally angry. Somewhere in there Felli hinted at a fallout with his sister, didn't give out any details but he likely felt uncomfortable now he had to censor anything he told her. Stannis stayed urbane, and eased Harp's workload where he could, once physically barring an unscheduled intrusion. Felli grinned and said he saved their sanity. Harp didn't argue.

No one smiled ten days later when the older man reported back on what his comp search had uncovered.

'I went back ten years, then extended that to twenty. There were nine similar anomalies in the earlier decade, and twelve in the last. Six in the last four years,' Stannis finished.

Harp stared at the big screen. 'Do you happen to know when the older Tayla died and the younger became mayor?' Beside him Felli jerked.

'Four years ago, ser.'

'And almost two a year vanished since.'

'Yes, ser.'

'Max?' Felli looked between them. 'What's it mean?'

Stannis hesitated. Truth be told, so did Harp, but the boy had earned the truth. 'Remember I talked to you about problems in Riverbend?' Harp had to wonder what else Stannis now knew about the town, and the Taylas, but he would leave that talk for later. 'You met Mr Tayla.'

'Yeah. Creepy. So he took over from his father four years ago?' Felli's eyes widened. 'And the number of missing kids, who maybe *weren't* kidnapped, doubled? You think *both* Taylas could be involved?'

'You'll recall I told you Tayla Snr preyed on the older kids. I'm thinking now, maybe that wasn't all.'

'You think he did something? Then made it look like they'd moved on?'

'If, say, they tried to cause trouble, after…'

'But you didn't think Tayla Jnr was like that.'

'No, that's where it doesn't make sense. Sergeant Hendriks – sorry, my aide on Moon now, Stannis – is a menace around comps. He found nothing to suggest Tayla Jnr was into children that way, but he was still digging into the finances when we left. Hm. I should check he's still on that. But we have six kids gone missing, all from the same place, since Tayla took office, and some suspect credit.' Harp swallowed bile.

'Kids, and credits.' Felli licked his lips. 'You think he *sold* them?'

This time Stannis answered. He'd forgotten to stay formal. 'From what Max said, the motives might have varied, but if the son didn't have any more urgent reason to get rid, maybe his motivation was the creds. Maybe he just stole the method from his father?'

'Crip.' Felli slumped in his seat.

Harp nodded. 'And maybe, just maybe, that's where the damned pirates got the idea of buying wholesale? We found our lead. Tayla has got to know who he deals with!' He was on his feet. 'I need to share this with Navy Intel. And Hendriks. He needs to find some solid evidence so we've enough to pull Tayla in for questioning.' There was finally *something* he could do to find the missing children.

25

'Max, I'm not sure that's a good idea.' Feldin swapped a quick look with Maxil Snr, a longer one at his son. 'And no, Felli, you're definitely not going back there right now, whether Max does or not.'

'But Father, if Max is going. Besides this will upset Mooners, perhaps Kraic too. I could be a, a calming influence.'

Feldin's lips twitched but he managed to control them. 'Very thoughtful, Felli, but hardly worth the risk.'

'But.'

'No, son. You'll have to settle for knowing more than you should. I should really send you off before we –'

'Father!'

This time Feldin did allow a smile to surface. 'Then listen, learn, and keep quiet?'

'All right.' Not that the sigh meant the kid'd given up, just that he was learning when to pick his battles.

Maxil Snr took over, back to business. 'Max, tell me again what we gain by risking your safety. Navy Intel can deal with this.'

Logical, cold-hearted Maxil, who regarded Harp primarily as useful, so what was important enough Harp was insisting he should be the one to deal with what the Founder'd termed "Riverbend scandal". But that very unimportance, in a Worlder mind, proved Harp *should* be there, not some clueless Worlder.

'Ser, Navy Intel could arrest the whole town and it wouldn't be enough cos all they'd be were interfering strangers. There's also the people didn't go back. I do need Intel, and perhaps Militia, to trace those. They might talk more freely now the place is behind them. But the navy don't understand Moon, the orphan system is as foreign to them as Moon, and they sure as death don't understand the ins and outs of Riverbend, or Tayla and the council.'

Maxil actually shrugged. 'That sergeant of yours does.

He unearthed the evidence, and he sounds a capable young man.'

Harp checked his first response; Maxil wanted facts. 'He's still not Mooner and he has no background there. I do, and Tayla knows that I'm in charge there now. That made him nervous, and others doubt him. I can use that to get his cronies to spill their guts if he holds out.'

'You still think this Tayla fellow isn't the only one involved.'

'I don't see them getting away with it so long otherwise, do you? But I own the land they live on, that's a lot of pressure.'

Maxil pondered. Harp crossed mental fingers. 'So in your opinion an eminent Harpan taking a personal interest will impact more than the navy. You realise the navy have considerable expertise in getting answers from unwilling subjects?'

'Which I'll use, ser, if I have to,' Harp said bleakly, 'but from what we've found these people have been lying for decades. Plus, honestly, I expect there'll be some folk, innocent or not, who'll simply refuse to believe what we say, while going in too hard would cause unrest and only hamper the investigation. And make leaks more likely, to whoever's guilty. And might impact Kraic relations?'

Which point Felli got another shot in. 'They'll trust Max, Grandfather. Letting him handle this will keep the peace where sending the navy will look like an invasion!'

Feldin stared at his son as if he'd never seen him before, but Maxil nodded slowly. 'Good points, Felli. I can see your time with Max has taught you some strategy. But Max is a significant factor to more than Moon's future. With all that's involved, would you still advocate letting him go?'

'Yes ser. Moon is, like, Max's planet, even more so now.' That chin came up. 'I don't think you could stop him going. But if I can't go with, I guess I could help out in the Aid programme with Ser Stannis until Max gets back, and make sure nothing there upsets things.'

Maxil and Feldin exchanged another look; Maxil

finally nodded. 'Very well. Felli will keep Moon in general sweet, ensuring Moon Aid doesn't falter.' Felli gulped then nodded. 'Max, I suppose you'll do as you wish, but you'll take extra Security.' The hint of a smile? 'And no sneaking off to help repair anything this time.'

'No ser.' Tell them he hadn't even known he *had* been sneaking off? No. 'Thank you, ser. I'll ask Daichi to keep you updated.' As if he could stop him.

'Of course, and talk to us yourself when you can, so we all know you're safe?'

'Yes ser.' Maxil settled back into his chair so Harp rose to leave.

A lot to do now.

+++

Four hectic days later he was on his way back to Moon, on a superfast this time, the smaller, "discreet" craft crammed with a reduced four-man crew plus Harp, Daichi, no less than nine Harpan Security and a foursome of the navy's Intel. Oh, and cargo; weapons, multiple encrypted coms and comps, body armour and all appropriate spares, wedged in anywhere they'd fit.

Harp had no objection to the weapons. Well, he was at least officially a gunner, and pretty sure half his Security were ex-Marines. But his priority was the encrypted gear. He needed information but he didn't need anyone in or outside Riverbend knowing he was coming after them. Because if Maxil Snr and Feldin thought he'd sit back and leave this to the navy, they should recall he was navy too, and this wasn't his first battle.

Harp only hoped Hendriks was restraining himself. When Hendriks knew something he always wanted to know more and Tayla was a steer they needed to sidle up on.

So it was a relief to see Hendriks looking relatively calm when they landed in the Kraic village. 'Major, I'm afraid you haven't got rid of me after all.' Valt might not know as much as Hendriks but her rank took precedence.

'Captain.' She smiled as she nodded. 'Welcome back. Big Red was asking after you. It'll be delighted.'

Hint received; play nice with the visitors. 'Oh? Good. All well?'

'Yessir. Very quiet.' Though the eyebrows questioned.

Hendriks stepped up, not so deadpan. 'I have the files you requested, ser, whenever you're ready.'

'Thank you, Hendriks, in a moment. Will you help Ser Daichi's people get settled in while I visit the dome?'

'Ser.' Hendriks counted heads, blinked. 'A few might have to double up.'

'Do the best you can. Daichi, you coming?'

'Yes ser.'

Of course. He'd hardly left Harp's side, even on the way. Catch him letting Harp alone with aliens. 'It's a friendly visit,' Harp said gently as they crossed the circle.

'Yes ser.' Deadpan.

Harp gave up and focussed on the dome where Blue was hopping on the spot and Big Red just emerging from their tunnel. Maxil Snr thought the Kraic delegation was going to be kept out of the loop. Harp had other ideas. 'Big Red. Blue.'

[HARP FRIEND WELCOME]

'Nice to be back. I hope everything's going well? How's the Seed?'

[SEE]

'Thank you, I'd love to.' That much took them through the tunnel, Daichi like Harp's silent shadow. 'Oh, wow.' In the centre of the dome floor a small spike – shoot – peeped from the ground, already as high as Harp's knees. Pale green with streaks of pink and yellow, stick-like, bar the feathery tendrils at its tip, so fine they waved each time the air moved.

[SEED IN SUN]

'So I see. That's very fast.'

[SEED EAGER] A breathtaking reminder the Seed wasn't just a plant, the dome not so much a garden as a nursery.

Harp exchanged a few more spoken compliments, he

and Big Red both careful not to say too much in front of Daichi. Then Big Grey arrived to join them, and Harp dropped the voice-talk. This way he'd be clearer, and Daichi couldn't stop him blabbing what he'd say were Worlder secrets.

Silent explanations: Riverbend, and Tayla. Harp spoke compliments between, Big Red flashed updates, soil additives they'd ordered. Harp explained the missing children, years *before* the pirate influx. Mind-talk was so easy, so much faster. Big Red understood the nuances.

<Pirates Tayla>
<Yes, I think so too>
<Find Tayla. Intel. Young, find pirates>

They were in complete agreement; Kraic would give assistance as and when he needed. First objective dealt with. Both sides nodded formally. Daichi looked suspicious but he kept his mouth shut. Then whatever he was thinking probably went off to vacuum, cos the Seed had started swaying more, in Harp's direction, then curved down, the tendrils stretched towards Harp's knees, then seemed to hesitate.

Harp found he'd done the same, a hand extended, not quite touching; sensed Daichi shift behind him. Only Big Red flashed [TOUCH. SEED RECOGNISES]

As soon as his fingers brushed those delicate wisps they stroked like silk threads. Harp felt its pleasure, hoped it felt his wonder. He could finally believe it really might rejuvenate his planet.

26

Stannis had been careful not to comment when the captain said he had to return to Moon, despite the fact he obviously hadn't expected it so fast. Didn't comment when the captain told him Ser Felli had volunteered to help out in his absence. Nor when on his first day there alone with Stannis, Felli blocked a call from his big sister. Sibling spat, or more? And did it really matter?

Of course, no comment didn't mean Stannis didn't think furiously. Max had flipped over those missing youngsters. Yes, that had to be the reason he'd left. Or was there more? Speeding through the office messages – and passing off to Felli those who'd be most flattered by responses from an actual Harpan – Stannis scanned the cast list, as it were, and planned the covert searches he would make that evening from his own encrypted system. Safe, he hoped, from friends *and* enemies, the way he liked it.

He could do a lot with it, but what he couldn't do was keep close enough tabs on Max. He'd gained some small measure of access but he'd given up, for now, on earlier attempts to hack the captain's private conversations. He suspected there was more than Mansion expertise involved, those firewalls had a different feel. It was frustrating. But he still had others. Nothing sending up alerts so far, but maybe he'd go over them again this evening. Felli said he'd need to leave, a dinner with his father.

+++

'Caffee in the lounge, you two?' Feldin rose from the dinner table, fairly sure Felli *hadn't* shared anything with Ho-San. Very good. 'Or one of your fizzies, Felli? I think we have some.'

'Caffee, please ser.' Felli noticed Ho-San's head turn. 'I guess I've got used to it. There weren't any fizzies on

Moon, and the water tastes different, so caffee was pretty much it.' He pulled a face. 'I couldn't drink it like Max though.'

'Nor me,' Feldin admitted. 'I imagine it's something he picked up in the navy.'

Felli looked doubtful. 'I don't know ser. One friend of Max's on *Defiant* drank his with about six different additives, and Sergeant Hendriks favoured it so weak that it was practically water.'

'Oh, I'd forgotten you'd spent time with Max's sergeant. You'll have to give me your impressions, sometime. Thank you, Kato.' They had reached the lounge. His Security-disguised-as-houseman was already setting out the caffee tray, and the mints Ho-San liked. The city lights outside the full-length wall of one-way glassite faced them, an impressive sight and one he could be proud of. As he was, these days, of Felli?

Ho-San added cream but Felli took his black, with sweet. Ah. Taking Max as a role model was changing his son, probably in more ways than he, or Felli, yet realised, but on the whole Feldin judged it a bonus. His own father would no doubt be pleased by it too, as he had been to discover Felli had done chores on Moon instead of loafing. And the fact he wanted to involve himself.

Though Feldin wasn't entirely sure he wanted his son getting too friendly with someone like Mella... Feldin shook away that reservation, brought his mind back to this hour he'd carved out for his children. Ho-San seemed to be taking new interest in the wider universe. Maybe Felli's excursion had finally made her more curious as well?

'Yes, Father, Felli sent me vids of the Kraic. They looked so odd. It made me wonder what else was out there.' Ho-San described what she'd discovered so far, largely for herself, she said. She frowned. 'Our Diplomatics didn't seem as knowledgeable as I'd expected. Given this new alliance, should we have more of the Family in that department, rather than nobodies? I can suggest one or two might suit.'

'You're quite right, and by all means send me your suggestions.' Ho-San was thinking of diplomacy instead of fashion? Feldin was tempted to think Max had given both his children new directions. It was too soon to assume, but the possibility was pleasant. 'Your grandfather and I have been discussing some changes in that direction, but we don't have anyone seriously qualified for Diplomatic.'

'Except Max.' Felli grinned at his father, quietly enjoying what he wasn't saying out loud. There was nothing like the thrill of knowing secrets, was there? And the bigger the secret, the better it felt. Till one grew old enough, and tired enough, that the excitement faded. Feldin hoped his son could stay excited for a while longer.

'True, poor boy. That's why we had to send him back, though his public appearances here have been very well received. From all accounts he's done a good job with the Kraic too.'

Ho-San sipped. 'I do admire the way you and Grandfather invented the Moon Aid persona. It certainly boosted the man's image.'

'Stars, no, wherever did you get that notion? That was all Max, it was the first thing he talked about when he found out we were setting up interviews, though it's been good for the whole Family's image. We've been remiss in our treatment of Moon. It's actually helping to right *our* wrongs.'

'So that's why Felli's been in Moon Aid too? But Father, does he have to spend so much time down there? I couldn't even get a call through to him the other day.'

Ho-San would probably have been even more indignant if she'd been looking at her brother instead of her father. Felli never could lie worth a damn. Feldin strongly suspected her call not "getting through" was more Felli's doing than some admin's.

Ho-San wasn't finished. 'I'm sure Felli will make it look good for you, but surely he can do it without being there all the time, and miss out on his fun. And I've heard all kinds of things about this man New-Cousin hired.' She glanced pointedly at Felli then chose not to say more.

For once Feldin chose to be more forthright. He'd promised himself he'd make an effort to treat Felli differently. 'I suspect your brother has heard the same gossip, eh, Felli?'

Felli shrugged. 'There's talk, yeah.' Another Max-word. Several had crept into Felli's language, into general usage too. Even his father had acquired some. 'But Ser Stannis is very good at his job, even I can see that, and I think Max trusts him. Well, he's left him there in charge. I'm just a volunteer.'

'But it's so beneath you, Felli, acting as some no-one's lackey, and you can't enjoy it.'

'Well.' Felli scratched his neck. 'Sometimes I do, and mostly it's at least interesting. And it's doing something worthwhile, y'know?' The poor boy looked embarrassed.

He positively blushed when Feldin said, 'Ho-San, I think we have to accept that Felli is growing up, and perhaps putting what needs doing ahead of amusing himself? But if you feel put upon, Felli, don't hesitate to come and talk to me. I'm very happy you volunteered, but I'm not forcing it on you.'

'Of course not, ser.' Felli frowned at Ho-San, rare occurrence. 'I do know what I'm doing, Sis. I don't need your protection.'

Ho-San's lips twitched. 'Oh, well, if you're all grown up, I guess my work is done.'

Feldin laughed at them both, and the talk shifted to coming engagements and Family gossip, which Ho-San was always up to date on. When Felli left, citing Ser Mella's habit of making an early start, Feldin was slightly surprised to see Ho-San linger. He and his daughter seldom seemed to spend much real alone-time now she'd gotten older, yet another thing that he regretted. Now, she watched her brother leave before she turned back to her father. 'Are you sure letting Felli get so... so *enamoured* with Maiso's son is a good thing, Father. How much do we really know about him?'

'If you're concerned about Max's character I can assure you we vetted him very thoroughly. He's an exemplary young man. And if you're concerned about Felli's safety, well, Ser Daichi hand-picked his own team, and Max himself has combat experience. Felli is probably safer than he's ever been.'

'Even after the attempts on the man's life?' Ho-San looked unbelieving.

'Ah.' Feldin waved that off. 'An initial hiccup, no more. Things have settled now.' He wished.

'I still don't like it.'

'As I said, Felli is growing up. We need to allow him to make his own choices, especially if he's to play a role in the Family's affairs, which I think he now aspires to. He's certainly impressed recently.'

'Mm. Do you think it will last though? Felli's enthusiasms always have a time stamp, don't they?'

'Well, time will tell, won't it?' Feldin said it lightly but concealed annoyance. Anyone would think Ho-San didn't want the boy to grow up. Ah – was that the problem? Felli had spent much of his young life following where Ho-San led, but now their paths had split. Over Max? Was jealousy prompting these complaints?

Feldin made the appropriate noises till his daughter left but sitting down again, alone, he could admit that her reactions disappointed. It would be a shame if she didn't change her opinion of a cousin she should think so much better of. Well, Felli had come round. Perhaps once Max returned his daughter would too.

27

Harp's first thought: Tayla didn't look scared enough. Surprised, yes, but guilty, not enough. Something crawled up Harp's spine and latched on. No way should Tayla be so *unctuous* when he found Daichi and the navy on his doorstep, even if he hadn't spotted Harp yet.

So Harp stepped forward from the shadows. This time Tayla's face went thinner. 'Captain Harpan? Is something wrong. It's late, and there's so many of you. Oh, come in, I shouldn't keep you out here.'

Harp didn't answer. They'd agreed he'd be the silent partner, the intimidating presence; leave the talk to Daichi and the leading Intel. He let others enter first as well and watched them as they herded Tayla to his kitchen till he fetched up on a stool somebody placed with space all round it. Still unsettled, Harp picked out a spot against the wall, behind him.

Even then the confrontation stayed off kilter, to Harp's way of thinking. One accusation and Tayla simply looked resigned, and owned up. 'Can't say I never expected you lot, sooner or later. But if you could look after my family I'd be grateful.' He obviously saw their reactions. 'Look, you gotta understand, I inherited this mess, I didn't start it. By the time I knew how bad it was I had a daughter, and they said she'd stay safe long as I cooperated. Said they weren't greedy. One here, one there, the same m'father gave them. Little earner, they called it, to top off the merch they channelled through my store. But if I din't deliver they'd take the nearest. My own daughter.' He twisted round to Harp. 'You see, Captain, don't ya? M'father might have chose it, but I didn't.'

Perhaps the Intel relaxed. Harp didn't. But the Intel did stick to his questions. 'So who are "they"?'

Tayla turned back. 'I was never sure, not till the big pirate raid. Then I figured it was them all the time, right? 'Specially after you lot put out that wanted notice. It made sense then, you know? How they were always so sure they wouldn't get caught?'

Harp caught Daichi's eye from behind Tayla's back and mouthed one word. Daichi's face went even blanker but he followed up. 'What wanted notice?'

'For that Worlder, name of Regis. He was here one time, see. I wasn't supposed to see, I don't think. He came out their lander, saw me and scuttled back in. But I'm good with faces. I remembered when I saw his picture.'

'Regis the traitor.'

'Yeah, that one, but I didn't know that, not till you found him out.'

There were more questions. How were messages passed. By hand. How often? Varied. Descriptions for those Tayla had met. His description of Regis was accurate, but he could still be lying about the rest. Harp listened harder when they got to the "handovers" as Tayla called them.

'Riverbend councillors've always had clearance for the mine compound, long as its aboveground. Course, if we ever wanted to go under we had to have an escort. Not as if we needed to, but m'father started meeting his damn contacts up there instead of in town. No one thought it was odd if we went to check everything was all right with our people, especially near election-time, 'specially when the mountain started smoking. So when they shut everything down I told the manager I'd go up when I could, check the compound, see the Admin modules weren't broke into or damaged. Not that they left much worth checking, even the pirates weren't interested. But it explained me going.'

'You've been up there since it closed then.' The Intel looked unimpressed. 'Anything from there would be tagged, so if we search your house and business…'

'You won't find anything from up there, sir. But it was still a good place to meet, they didn't even have to fake being miners anymore.'

'So you meet the pirates at the mine's Admin compound.'

'Yessir. I'd stash what they left a bit at a time in the modules till they sent a ship to collect. It was my insurance too, cos they couldn't get at it without me, cos of the retinal scan, so it stopped them double crossing me. Someone'd come into the store and pass me a note, old style, when to go. Fact, I was up there only last week, adding the last load and arguing a price. Hey, that Regis guy was there then, lurking around back till the other guy yelled at him to help.'

Harp wondered if Daichi too was thinking about the footprints they'd followed.

The Intel had picked up on something else. 'The last load, that mean there's a meeting due?'

Harp was almost sure Tayla had stopped himself smirking, never mind he sighed. 'Two more days, sirs. Tell the truth, I was worried, what with the navy setting up with the aliens for good now. I was starting to think about getting out while I could, taking me and mine and making a fresh start with what I'd got saved. But now, it's finally over. I guess I'll do whatever you want me to.'

They locked Tayla in his own cellar, after a thorough search confirmed there was no convenient bolthole and anything resembling a weapon was removed. In the end, Tayla's family gave them more hassle than Tayla. Wife and daughter both threw tantrums. Attima screamed and Madame Tayla called them filthy liars, blamed it all on Harp. At which point Daichi bristled and they found themselves escorted none too gently to the daughter's bedroom with a pair of Harp's Security on guard until their future was decided.

When they could hear themselves talk again the lead Intel finally relaxed, 'A success, all things considered. Thank you Captain. We'll need to interrogate them all, but we already have enough to mount a mission.'

'If we believe him.' Harp had wandered, poking into cupboards other Mooners would have gaped at. According to Sulis, and Hendriks, the Taylas only invited close friends farther than the much plainer room next the front door Tayla had tried to show them into. He was amazed they'd hidden so much so long. Hm. An inspection of other council homes might be informative as well.

The Intel stayed more optimistic. 'You said the father was at the root of a lot, and pirates threatening family members is as old as the stars.'

'Yes, but.' A hunch wasn't evidence, not even logic.

'We'll carry on digging, ser, don't you worry, but right now this meeting on Collar is our priority, don't you think?'

Now they were humouring him, but he could hardly blame them. 'Just, don't trust him.'

'No ser.' The guy looked serious enough. Harp just had to hope he was. Now, they had two days to keep a lid on Tayla's arrest so the pirates turned up at the mine. With Regis? Oh, he so much wanted Regis to be with them.

+++

Felli tried calling again, waited another hour, tried again then decided it was time to panic. Only who to call? Not Father. If he caused an uproar over nothing…

'Sis, I need some advice.'

'Oh?'

Felli relaxed a little. Ho-San didn't sound annoyed so at least he hadn't interrupted something urgent. 'Ser Mella hasn't turned up to Max's office. He's usually here hours ago.'

'So? Have you called?'

'Of course I have, several times. It's like no one's there.'

'So?' Not so patient.

'So what should I do?'

A pause. Maybe Ho-San was finally taking him seriously. 'He's really disappeared?'

'Yes!'

'Hm.' She still didn't sound very concerned. 'Have you checked the office accounts?'

'What? No, I'm sure he doesn't steal.' Was he?

'The man does have a rep, I said as much to Father.' Another pause. 'You'd better tell him.'

'Father? It didn't seem that important.'

'But it might be, and he'll know what to do, won't he?'

'I suppose.' Felli licked dry lips. 'OK, I'll do that. Thanks, Sis.'

'Better safe than sorry, especially when you're dealing with a crook.' Ho-San's screen went black. Felli supposed, now he'd asked, he should take her advice. He hoped he wasn't getting Stannis into trouble.

+++

'So I thought I should tell you ser.' The boy's image looked uncomfortable, he obviously liked Mella. Growing up too fast could be a slap in the face, as Feldin had feared. But his son was right, this did bear looking into.

'When did you see him last, Felli?'

'Yesterday. I left him in the office, he said he was staying late.' Felli looked miserable. 'Should I have stayed too? He told me to go, said I'd done enough.'

'No, you had no reason to. You aren't Ser Mella's minder.' Someone was though, so why hadn't he heard anything from Security? 'I'll have it looked into. It's probably nothing but you were quite right to tell me. In the meantime I'll find you someone capable of filling the gap in Max's office, if you feel you can supervise their efforts, since you know more?'

'Of course.' Felli sat straighter. 'Anything I can do.'

'Good man. Let me know if there are any more problems, otherwise I'll leave you in charge.' Feldin signed off. Only later did it hit him; it was the first time he'd ever called his son a man, not seen him as a child. It was both a cause for pride, and sadness.

28

With half Valt's uniforms, plus a bunch of locals Sulis swore were safe, they basically locked down the township. Patrols. A curfew. Coms that suddenly went haywire, courtesy of Navy Intel. Hendriks would have loved it. Sorry, nobody was leaving at the moment, even to the Kraic village. The story was quarantine; Madame Tayla had contracted what they feared was an infectious disease, probably brought in by the influx of naval personnel. Who would also be staying put till it was settled.

That spawned a rumour the disease originated from the Kraic, why their site was shut down too, cos humans there were dying, horribly, but politics was keeping it a secret. There was nothing Harp could do about that, but at least Big Red knew the truth, so he spent most of the first day assuring townsfolk the situation was under control, they were just waiting on navy medics signalling their treatments were successful. Yes, Madame and daughter were in the best hands, and the rest of the family confined to quarters only to protect everyone else.

He rose on day two thinking whether they caught the pirates that night or not, come the next day he could at least tell the town the truth and end *their* worry. Tonight, Tayla was meeting the pirates, but with a security collar under his scarf. Harp thought the Intels had rather enjoyed demonstrating what would happen if he didn't do as they said.

So they were set. One team had left town the first night, to infiltrate the compound and the area above the mine entrance. Harp was going up today, in the second group. So was Sulis, who'd insisted they'd need someone familiar with the layout. The four Intels would be going up last, in Tayla's battered cargo-runner, Tayla driving and the Intels hidden by the tarp that normally concealed cargo. They'd be cramped, and would sweat buckets, but they had insisted, obviously wanted closest to the action. Harp figured they'd regret it by the time they reached the compound.

+++

They'd given Tayla a one-way earpiece and tagged him with a minicam, so up on Collar Harp could watch the runner jolt toward him, listen as the Intel leader gave their bait a final warning. 'Remember, turning State's Evidence is your only hope of leniency. If you mess up now everything you've done so far goes out to vacuum, and our high-sec prisons make this place look like a palace. So get out, open the gates, and act normal.'

Harp took the opportunity to check his rifle as Tayla climbed out. It felt superfluous with Daichi there, both of them some distance above, nearer the huge down-ramped mine entrance, but in the still night air Harp could clearly hear the thud and scrape of Tayla's footsteps. He could see everything too, with or without the scope, since he could witness every camra-view across the compound on his wristcom. Tayla's wasn't the only body-camra, navy engineers had set the tiny optics up all round them. Intel had brought their own mine passes too, something else they hadn't told Tayla. They only wanted him down there to reassure the pirates.

Tayla had sworn he always got here first, parked up at the site manager's module and waited till someone came. The engineers who'd done a recce said he had a comfortable nest in there, a solar lamp, some bottled water and a cushy chair. The desk was gone, they said, the tec in that more worth removing. Tayla said he was supposed to leave the door ajar to show the pirates it was safe, so the camras that fed Harp's wristcom showed him Tayla unlock the compound gates, drive across the open ground inside and park outside the module, farthest – maybe quietest? – building from the black depression of the entrance to the mine shaft proper, clogged up by a slew of battered miner-runners parked inside its looming shadow since the shutdown.

Tayla stuck at the module door a while, head down, but then Harp heard the lock release – both in his ears and his earpiece – and Tayla stepped inside. His bodycam shut off, perhaps the module cut the signal, but a flicker, then a muted glow along the crack outside confirmed he'd primed the lamp.

And now they waited.

+++

Two hours passed in silence. There was still another camra now, high in the module, so they watched as Tayla sat there, drank some water, didn't seem to realise that it was watching. Tayla didn't fidget, which was more than Harp did. Someone outside clipped a rock and sent it skittering downslope behind the module. Everybody held their breath, then breathed again when nothing happened. Someone would get bawled out later.

It was strange being the civ, the spare part, and annoying cos he'd had to agree to wear the dumb vest and still stay back up here till they'd caught the pirates. Thank the stars he had enough clout to make them bring him along cos there was no way he was missing this. Not least cos he didn't trust Ser Tayla, *and* he suspected Collar might behave better if he came.

He'd tried not to think about that at first, tried not to believe anyway, but when it came down to it he'd proved Collar *was* aware of him. She hadn't reacted this time, not obviously. All he'd got was an impression-of-a-feeling, not unlike he got from Kraic underneath their mind-talk, but he thought Collar liked that he'd come back, was maybe tolerating all these other humans. He would hope so cos of course he couldn't warn them.

Three hours now. The small movements those still in the runner would be using to stop themselves seizing up couldn't be working worth a damn by now. Pretty soon they'd either have to get out, or be unable to move in fast when they needed, the whole point of them being down there. But it was up to them. Harp had to assume they knew their jobs.

Finally, a noise that wasn't wind or shifting pebbles; someone else was coming. Heads half visible to Harp's keen sight sank down, relying on the camras.

This runner came in without lights, and across the slope not up. Bigger than average and sprayed a patchy black and grey, and maybe rust, or orange, reasonable camo. Had it come from a ship or been hidden somewhere on the mountain? He hadn't heard a ship land.

A bulky figure opened the gates Tayla had left unlocked then jumped back in. The pirates were cautious enough to park several paces short of Tayla's runner, but the hidden Intels would still be able to stop them retreating. Six got out this time, all wrapped up and faceless – Harp couldn't tell if they were men or women – wasted no time getting inside, although the last one stumbled for a moment. Something…

The module door slammed shut, reminding Harp to switch his wristcom to the interior camra. Where Tayla still sat down? The pirates, faces still concealed, weren't moving either, and there was no sound – no one was talking?

'Daichi, something's off.' He got a soft grunt, Daichi's eyes fixed on his own com, so they both saw one shape reach into a pocket and pull out a navy-issue cuboid. Vacc it! Next thing they had only static. 'Crip, a jammer?' Harp half rose.

Daichi grabbed him one side, Sulis from the other. 'No ser, let the –'

Tayla's runner, and the Intel guys inside it, turned into a roaring bonfire, must have killed them instantly. Yet nobody ran out the module.

Valt was shouting in Harp's ear for her forces to converge, her armoured engineers racing down the slopes with weapons powered. The leaders kicked the module door in, others followed, crowding through the doorway. But some instinct had Harp looking left, toward the mine itself, and so he spotted furtive movement that way. 'Daichi, over there, see?' Daichi didn't have Harp's eyesight. 'One, no two. How. There, behind those miner runners. They've come *up* from somewhere. Crip, they had a tunnel!' One that Tayla must have known about. Harp rose, full height. 'Valt, get everybody out!'

The office module went up too, with half Valt's engineers inside, while those outside who'd hesitated when Harp shouted all went flying backward in the shockwave, some not rising.

This time Daichi's reaction beat Harp's. 'Any medical, down there. The rest converge on Gunner.' Harp's inevitable call sign.

'Not up here, there.' Harp started running down, toward the entrance. He couldn't see the pirates any longer but there was only one place they could have gone. No wonder Tayla was so calm. This wasn't some last-minute plan, it must have been agreed for ages. Harp had let the navy override his gut reaction and now half of them had been cremated! When the ground beneath him shivered he yelled, 'No,' without a thought, but Collar stilled and gave him clear passage.

Rattling steps behind him now. Daichi, more. Daichi cursing, probably cos Harp outran him, but the entrance to the shaft loomed up ahead, a giant, square-jawed maw in almost total darkness. Harp only remembered the others couldn't see it when he heard them stumbling after. There, a smaller, even darker patch ahead broke up the plainness of the drop-down outer doors. A people-access like a warehouse, somewhere Tayla said he couldn't access.

He was going to throttle Tayla.

'Ser. Captain.' Daichi caught up as Harp flattened himself beside the smaller opening. See, he did know what he was doing. Sort of.

This time round Harp used his throat mic, murmured. 'At least two. Neither was Tayla, but he must have got them in.' He remembered his rifle, decided he preferred hands free. Probably not a good idea anyway; the ricochets... He tucked it out of sight beneath the nearest runner.

'Ser, I'm down to six.' The ever-stoic Daichi didn't actually add, "and one is Sulis" but no doubt he thought it. 'How sure are you on *their* numbers?'

'Worst case is seven of them to six of us, but I'd go with less. I'm not letting them get away.' Even if he had to go alone.

'No ser.' Daichi probably wanted in just as much. 'But I need you to –'

'Daichi, you *know* I have better night vision without lenses than you do with.' Behind them Harp heard Sulis suck in a breath. 'So I'll take point.' Hopefully Collar would too.

Through the hatch, slid to one side so he wasn't outlined in the doorway. Daichi's professionals did the same then Sulis copied. In here was a "corridor" at least three times Harp's height and ten times wider, more for mech than people. He could make out smaller, even darker openings bored off to either side, and wondered if the rest could.

Outside, even smaller sounds had carried. Here they echoed, couldn't be concealed, so Harp moved faster; forward and toward the left was where the sounds were headed. Bypassed several openings, no echo. Finally, a tunnel *with* an echo. Cautious now, Harp stuck his head in.

'Ser!' Hissed in his ear.

'Trust me, Daichi.'

'Ser.' When Harp moved on, the other man fell in behind again, a pulse in one hand while the free one *signalled* quiet. He'd been right; Daichi was ex-navy. Told himself not to feel smug.

Corner coming, slow, drop onto a knee, assume anyone in wait would aim higher. Clear ahead, a longer stretch of tunnel, then a T, and damn, a single, lurching figure, a tailender, swinging left, the face uncovered and in profile for the merest second. Regis, here, when he'd left the blasted rifle! Harp's hands flew to pull his pulse but he had gaped too long, his vaunted reflexes for once had failed him; Regis had escaped around that distant corner. 'That was Regis!' Harp *leapt* forward this time, done with caution.

Frantic footsteps, then Daichi murmured in his ear, 'Positive ID ser?'

'Yes!' They'd all have heard that, Sulis cursed, they all raced forward.

At the turn Daichi put a sudden spurt on, caught him up and hauled him back – Harp figured everybody heard those stumbling footfalls this time, not that far ahead now. Only Regis? So the rest had run and left their weakest to catch up, or not. Where to though?

Damn they had a plethora of choices and that multiplied the echoes. Lost again, Daichi had to let Harp pass. Harp hesitated too, ears straining. That way. Why though? 'Sulis? Where could they be heading? Anywhere important?'

'Sir, not really,' Sulis panted from the rear, 'but we've tended left, they could be trying to circle round us.'

Crip. 'Can they get out, back to the compound?'

'Could do, if they know the way.' A pause for thought, or breath. 'They'd need a miner though, the plans are useless, way too many alterations this way.'

Harp could well believe that. He was twisting, turning, trusting to his ears to guide him. 'Daichi? On or back?'

Daichi's answer was a question. 'Sulis, which is quicker?'

'On, I'd say.'

Harp speeded up; they'd left the injured out there. 'Daichi, warn the medics.'

'Done, ser.'

So they ran. Collar stayed inert, or maybe watchful. Regis sounded close now but Harp couldn't hear any others, maybe they'd outstripped him. Then a clang, of something large and metal-sounding, rang along the tunnel, made Harp wince and stumble. Super-ears weren't always an advantage. 'What the.'

Sulis's voice huffed, 'That sounds. Like a blast door.'

'Got it.' Like a fire door, like the distant entrance only smaller. 'Are there many?'

'Couple hereabouts, to shield Main Vertical.'

A down shaft? Would the pirates aim for lower? Seemed unlikely. 'If they're lower can we trap them?'

Sulis sucked in air to answer. 'Dunno, maybe? If we can wake the main boards?'

'Good idea. Think about it.' Meanwhile he was certain they were gaining. 'Daichi, you hear Regis yet?'

'*Yes,* ser.' Daichi sounded positively eager, not at all Daichi any longer, showed a tendency to want to pass again, but Harp knew he could outrun them all; he *was* a Harpan.

A second clang, and close enough the echoes stabbed Harp's ears. He gasped and staggered. Someone caught him till he steadied as he tried to block the sudden biting pain and carry on. They must be *very* close now.

Two more turns. Another opening; the full length mepal barrier gaped just enough for them to duck beneath, their weapons at the ready. Maybe twenty paces in Harp saw the sealed shaft-head Sulis must have meant, a massive, disc-shaped hatch more like a table than an entry. Still locked. And on the edge, head down, his elbows on his knees, sat Regis, thin chest heaving. When his head came up their weapons were already trained on him, but he just sat there, looking beaten.

Sulis cursed but had the sense to stay behind the rest. Daichi waved his team in, one pulled out restraints. Harp took a moment. Regis, finally. And intel; on the pirates, on the stolen children.

Now he was in he could see past the raised seal to a farther blast door, also partly open, so the pirates must have run right through and Regis couldn't keep up. But leaving him here would mean leaving two people to stand watch, and splitting their own numbers.

When Harp resurfaced Regis was restrained at wrists and ankles, watching Harp. Cowed enough to tell them where the pirates had been headed? 'Where are your friends off to, Regis, now they've left you to rot?'

No answer. Just that sullen stare.

Then someone spoke, but from behind him. 'Oh, we're heading out, *Ser Harpan*. Soon as we're all done in here. Drop the weapons.'

29

Daichi and the rest had frozen, looking past him. Harp drew breath then turned. 'Hoik, you always were a sneak.' An adversary he'd almost forgot, it seemed a lifetime since they'd fought, and Hoik's dishonourable discharge. But now the man was standing just inside the blast door they'd come in by, a pulse jammed into Sulis's neck.

Farthest away, two of Daichi's people still flanked Regis, guns still pointed that way. Closer, Daichi might think Hoik had missed him edging Harp-ward. Something in his face made Harp think Daichi knew who Hoik was, maybe from the navy's records.

'I said drop 'em.'

Nothing happened, so Daichi hadn't signalled. So Harp said quietly, 'Please.' Because the question was, was Hoik alone? He'd bet against it, Hoik had always been a bully, and a coward. But if not where was his backup? Play for time then? 'Hello, Hoik. Come back for Regis?'

Regis groaned. He didn't move. That said a lot.

Hoik grinned. 'Hm, I'm not sure. Would you give him up, in exchange? I'm not sure you would, but if you did… I wouldn't have a real hostage, would I?'

'So you want safe passage. I suppose I might arrange that.'

Hoik had lost mass since the navy threw him out and was a world away from spit and polish, an unshaven jaw and greasy looking hair pulled back behind his neck, stray hairs come loose while he'd been running. But he was still smirking over Sulis's shoulder. 'Oh, we have safe passage. And a bonus when we get there.'

'A bonus.' Harp considered. 'You expected me.'

'Yeah, didn't know *that*, did you? Zorr said they'd keep you safe. I bet they wouldn't, and he *wanted* me to be right, didn't he, *Private Harp*? You lost him a ship, and almost got him caught. Man like him don't forget. He got even madder when he watched, and realised you wasn't even a proper Harpan, not back then. Then someone worked out you were the Militia kid did for one of his before he even knew you existed. After that you were a dead man walking.' Hoik spat. 'Course, now *I* know how you passed the navy tests, don't I, *Captain Harpan*?'

'I passed those for myself,' Harp said evenly. 'Just like you failed.'

'I failed cos of you.' Hoik looked past Harp, gripped Sulis's shorter hair and ground the gun into his head. Sulis clamped his lips, eyes narrowed. 'Now, now, no getting in the way of our little reunion.'

Daichi had stopped; Harp felt still air at his back. The man was maybe just a pace behind but Harp kept his attention on the man before him. 'All this, for me?'

Another smirk. At some point Hoik had lost a tooth. 'We had the contingency plan. And we had some tidying up to do anyway.'

'Tayla.'

'Yeah. Zorr told him we'd see him right if he helped get you here.' The smirk Harp knew of old. 'We did.'

'So is the bonus for killing me, or taking me to Zorr? I guess I'd be a better hostage than some miner.' Don't let Hoik see you know Sulis.

'Oh, not some miner, Captain. Tayla said this one's a favourite.'

'Really? Nowhere near as valuable as I am though, right?' Harp willed Daichi not to make a move. If Harp could swap with Sulis, get in closer…

'True.' Hoik sneered at Sulis. 'Might as well leave him, eh? Well, it's been nice to chat, especially with everything recorded for the boss to watch. But all good things, as they say.'

The farther blast door slammed down, stirring up black dust at their feet. So Hoik did have backup. The echoes sliced into Harp's head again; somehow he hid it. Hoik was edging backward to the gap behind, still open. 'The camras here'll work a while longer, proof, like. Cos there won't be much after, eh?'

Harp's brain was aching but Hoik's gloating pierced the headache. He began another furtive scan of his surroundings. 'So I'm staying here, between two blast doors. How about you let the others leave, including Regis? Zorr might even like that, right?'

'Ah now, *Captain*, still playing hero?' Hoik was hunched, backing out, gun still touching Sulis, who was breathing faster. 'Think you'll die like one?' Hoik gloated. Then his face became a snarl. 'Maybe a hole or two will change that, eh?' Hoik shoved at Sulis and his gun dipped lower, aiming for Harp's legs.

But Sulis spun, lashed out a miner boot; Daichi leapt for Harp. The gun went off, a second shot. Daichi toppled first, then Sulis.

'Oops.' Hoik scuttled through the gap. That blast door crashed into the rocky floor, and trapped them in here.

Daichi's people were grabbing weapons and converging on the wounded. So was Harp. Both men were breathing, although Sulis had already lost a lot of blood, but Harp's relief quickly gave way to the urgent need to find whatever explosives Hoik had planted. Cos that was the only thing made sense. Zorr wanted his revenge, on vid, and something bad enough it would repair his loss of face and maybe warn off others.

Harp had to admit, bringing a mountain down on an enemy's head would be a warning to any rivals. But had the pirates factored in that Collar was volcanic; that the damage might not just be here, in this tunnel, even in the mountain? Riverbend, the Kraic, and the Seed could be in danger too. Would *Hoik* get clear even? Crip, he should have said that, gained a bit more time.

No point telling Regis to help, the man was rocking to and fro and useless. That left four of them still standing, one of whom was helping Sulis and would have to stay there while the farther two stood guard on Regis. 'OK, you two, there's a bomb. You start the other end.' And he'd work back toward them.

There were wires near the ceiling. Harp prepared to climb.

'No, ser!' the only woman with them shouted, 'they'll be trip wires. Touch them and whatever's there will blow.'

Harp froze, his fingers hooked into a crevice inches from a wire, let his fingers open, dropped back down. How long would it take Hoik and whoever to get to where he thought it safe to push a button? 'Right, no wires. Can we get to cover, in the vertical?'

That caused a flurry. Harp stayed back; he didn't have the training. The woman seemed to be in charge now– damn it he'd forgot her name – was pushing at the seal-locks. Cursing. Harp backed off to check his wounded.

Sulis's eyes were closed. So were Daichi's, but he was propped up against a wall. His man had applied field dressings, wasn't that a familiar sight. 'Ser,' Nod. 'The boss was hit in the shoulder, not fatal.' Thank the stars. 'But the civ's not good; a shot to the neck, tore a chunk out.'

Daichi blinked up at Harp. 'Bomb?'

'Fraid so. Your number two's trying to open the vertical.' Sudden thought. 'I should have tried the blast doors too.'

'Don't bother.' Daichi waved his able hand toward the switch box bolted in above his head. Harp hadn't looked that high before. They had already opened it, inside was just a mess of melted wires. Daichi hadn't looked away from Harp. And had gone stiffer. 'Ser, I regret I have failed you. It has been an honour.'

'Nonsense.' The anguish on Daichi's face was obviously down to his wounds; he *never* showed that much emotion. 'It's my fault for walking into the vaccing trap. Will *our* camras transmit?'

'Till they sealed the blast doors, that would cut the signal. But they'll know enough.'

'Good.' They'd know to look for Hoik, if the fool didn't blow himself up with them. And if Harp was going to die at least he was in good company, however much he wished they weren't here too. He should say that, but he was a dunce at speeches. It would probably sound feeble and they wouldn't think he meant it. What the crip, their wristcoms would die with them, no one else would ever hear.

Collar... growled.

The others jumped, looked up, around, but Harp looked down. The ground stayed stable, but the growl said anger. Collar would already know about explosives. Harp's mouth twisted. 'Don't suppose you're happy either, huh? But if there's any way you can help.'

Anger shifted to... confusion? Collar didn't understand. Or couldn't help? But then a shiver of awareness bled from Collar, into Harp. Somewhere out there Hoik had pressed his button, and the signal raced toward them. There were maybe milliseconds–

Collar roared. The rock, those blast doors, vanished in a wave of searing white then choking black then muted glow. Then there were cracking, creaking sounds, then crashes, fading into patterings, then eerie quiet.

Then coughing?

Harp discovered he was wrapped around Daichi, who was gasping, staring up at him in pain and probably in shock. 'Sorry.' Harp jumped to his knees. Daichi didn't look to have new injuries, just dust and splinters Harp hadn't blocked; looked almost like there hadn't *been* a huge explosion, just the lights had failed.

But of course there had. Once Harp looked round the evidence was there, the debris, melted rock, the buckled blast door and a glimpse of fallen rock behind it. All of that, *everything*, at least ten paces from *him*.

'Crip.' All right, he'd shielded Daichi and it looked as if Daichi's guy had done the same for the recumbent Sulis, and the four of them were still alive. Unhurt? He thought so. Everywhere was fallen rock, except not *here*. It looked, it looked as if they had a force field in here, with him at its centre. He'd done it again, hadn't he? What other explanation was there? Either that or he had prodded Collar into making them this little cavern. His brain caught up. They'd survived but what about the other two Security, and Regis?

The sealed vertical, beyond his magic circle, was beneath a mass of rock, part-solid and part-melted. No way Regis or the others had survived. If he had only known. The anger crackled through his veins – at Hoik, at Zorr, at his own ignorance. What was he? Every time the craziness went farther.

'Max?' Daichi sounded strangled; Harp swung back. The man was open mouthed. 'You're, all. You.'

Harp gasped as well. The anger crackling along his skin was more than mere anger this time, it was real. That glow was red and gold electric shimmers, dancing on his arms, his chest, his thighs. They didn't hurt, in fact he felt like he'd been super-charged. Was this what held the mountain back? His body thrummed with energy, like it was overloaded, looking for an outlet.

Outlet! Harp surveyed the buckled door, it felt like he was floating. 'We still need a way out.'

Daichi swallowed, stared past Harp at devastation they'd impossibly escaped. 'Yes ser, but they'll bring in reinforcements, maybe miners. Soon as they can bring in the equipment.' Unsaid; maybe not before they had no air left.

'No need to wait.' Harp held out his light-show hands. 'I think.' Sparks flew, a heady power that didn't hurt. 'I think…' He walked toward the sagging blast door, raised the hands. The colours swirled around his fists then up his arms, energy threatening to scorch him from the inside out. Except it wasn't. Red and gold reached out and wove together, rock and mepal started melting.

The bomb had brought a lot of mountain down but Harp regained their tunnel at about a hundred paces out. Maybe Collar had managed to contain some of the damage, even while *he'd* been pushing it away? But now here he was, back in undamaged tunnel. Only the black dust, still making the other three cough – not him cos any dust burned off – proved it was real. And of course the almost-Kraic rounded tunnel at their back, still glowing.

The last Security, gone partly deaf but in one piece, had carried Sulis out and laid the man back down to check his dressings. Still avoided Harp, and hadn't said a word yet even to Daichi; couldn't blame him.

Daichi had managed to walk. Now he sank down, leaning on a cooler patch of wall, head tilted back and breathing shallowly. He wasn't talking either. So what now? Harp raised his hand, then choked a laugh. 'Daichi, your wristcom still working?'

Daichi's head came round till he could see Harp's wrist, the wristcom sagging, melted, like the rock. The wrist beneath still perfect. Daichi laughed! Then winced cos he was forced to lift his injured arm to send a message.

While that went on Harp wandered off, touched rock and sent a silent thanks to Collar. Collar purred, it felt like. Like some giant feline, paws like silk when she was happy, claws like razors when she wasn't. Vaguely he could hear Daichi talking, hear somebody out there responding. Hear the giant entrance door release, and navy runners, not those older ones, race in to find them, homing on Daichi's wristcom. Hear the fuss when someone took the wrong direction and they had to backtrack. Hear Valt cursing, she was still alive then. Hear her inform Daichi they were almost with him. Asking after 'Gunner', was he injured?

'Ser.' Daichi eased back to his feet. 'They're close. Can you...?' He was gesturing at Harp.

'Oh. Yeah.' He hoped. Those colours were still washing over him, weren't they? Only one way to find out. He focussed on his hands and *wished*. The heat waves dimmed but didn't leave completely. What more could he do, and quickly? Excess current. Hm. He laid his palms against the tunnel wall and offered. Earthed the current. That worked; power flowed into the rock, and left him feeling very empty.

Next thing he was on his ass, back slammed against the wall he'd leaned on, gone from wired to exhausted. Movement. Noise. If he closed his eyes they'd maybe leave him for a while. But he forced himself to listen.

Valt was questioning Daichi, who was being very

careful with his answers. Daichi's guy was handing Sulis over to a real medic and describing what he knew of his condition. Same Security accepted water then stepped closer to Daichi, like Daichi was his safe zone. No, they both confirmed, nobody else had made it, Daichi adding they'd been very lucky. He thought 'Gunner' was a mite concussed. Yes, who'd have dreamed the bomb would be so badly built it blew the hole that freed them?

Harp felt his lips twitch. Yeah, a nice, neat, rounded hole, straight from the explosion site to the only safe tunnel? Valt didn't comment but no decent engineer would believe it. Feldin would have to issue another gag order, fast. He'd better tell Daichi to make that call too, if he hadn't already thought of it.

Daichi allowed someone to immobilise his arm and shoulder but refused a shot. The man really was invincible, and stubborn. Sulis was being loaded onto a runner – wonderful how much he could 'see' with his ears – and Valt and Daichi were heading his way; the peace was over.

'No really, I feel fine, Major, just need some sleep. How's Mr Sulis?'

'We're pushing plasma, ser. We'll know more once we get him to the village. Can you walk?'

'Of course. I was the lucky one.' Harp dragged his bones up the wall then swayed till Valt caught his arm, saw her mouth open as she saw the state of his wristcom. 'Weird, huh. Don't know how it happened but better that than me.'

'Yessir.' Valt stared into his eyes. Ah, yes, concussion, that excuse again. 'Ser, you need to stay awake a little longer.'

'Yes, of course, Daichi warned me.' Daichi didn't comment. 'Thanks for reminding me.' He walked. Daichi followed. 'Daichi, I owe you for that shoulder.'

'My job ser.'

'Oh, I think we've gone past that, don't you?'

Did Daichi smile? 'All over now, ser.' Eyes everywhere though. 'Let's just leave, shall we?'

Daichi couldn't know Collar was unsettled. Was there some other threat? Oh, Hoik. Had Hoik been found? Or had Daichi realised he didn't like being underground? Harp quelled the urge to tease; Daichi was allowed *one* weakness.

It was light again outside, the air blessedly free of dust. Not-Harpans stopped coughing. Other things calmed down once they were en route to the Kraic village. Not Riverbend, considered suspect. And no, they hadn't picked up Hoik, and wanted Kraic and the navy to protect "their" Harpan. Harp's mind drifted. Hoik would be long gone, but had the Kraic been affected by the bomb? Would *they* survive if Harp exploded energy around them? Or whatever else he might do next?

'Ser?' A medic prodded him awake, again; couldn't Daichi have come up with a story that let him sleep? They kept wanting him to drink too, he didn't need that either. It was getting irritating, all he wanted was to go back underground and sleep until his body had recovered.

Only that was out, so he supposed he'd better work at being Captain Harpan and display some manners when they reached the village.

Any etiquette he'd learned imploded when he saw who strode toward him.

Stannis, here?

30

'Max! Captain, are you all right? They wouldn't tell me anything, and when they brought in those body bags…'

'I'm fine.' Amazingly Stannis looked dusty, which struck Max as very wrong. Stannis was *always* elegant. 'Has something happened?' Crip he wasn't thinking clear enough yet. 'Felli…?'

'He was all right when I left. Probably mad at me for leaving him in the lurch but that's all.' Stannis looked Harp up and down. 'You are OK.' Like he was surprised, shocked even. 'I was afraid I'd be too late but obviously you didn't need me.' His gaze slid past, onto Daichi, arm immobilised, then Sulis's cradle being lifted from another runner. 'Well, not now. But I couldn't get through, not even a flash-send. And by then I didn't know who to trust.'

'Reach me?' A new medic was nudging Harp into the shade of the Circle and the nearest table. He'd allow it was a relief to sit down again but he needed to focus. 'When, Stannis?'

'Three days ago, four now. I even tried to contact Ser Daichi, but it was as if all the local coms had gone dead. I was afraid something had already happened.'

Logic surfaced; the lockdown at Riverbend, no coms just navy frequencies, on mission. Stannis had been trying to reach him, then come all the way to Moon to find him? 'Stannis, I'm sorry, I don't understand.'

Stannis pushed a hand through his hair. Harp didn't think he'd ever seen the man do that either. 'I picked up another encrypted message, from World to Moon, using the same code as before. I could only unravel part of it but enough to think it was about you leaving World again. And it went to the same area on Moon as before.'

Tayla's code? A message to Tayla, from *World*. Harp felt colder. Someone on *World* had warned Tayla he was coming, in time for Tayla to inform his pirate buddies. Someone on World was responsible for what had happened back on Collar, for their dead and wounded. The way Daichi was looking at Stannis, no prizes for guessing *his* chief suspect. This was a mess; but he guessed he could survive on caffee for a little longer. Harp looked round him at the hovering bodies. 'Could someone rustle up some caffee for us? And some food?' Inevitably he was starving, little wonder he was drooping. 'Daichi, vaccsake, sit down too, you're swaying. Oh, and someone check if Major Valt's reporting all this to the Founder.'

At least that caused an exodus, now only Stannis hovered. 'You sit too, and tell us everything again.'

They ate. Daichi one-handed but neat, Stannis little, Harp a lot. What Stannis had already blurted pretty much covered it. He was coy about how he'd managed to get here so fast – Harp guessed some contact from his less legitimate life – but the rest of his story hung together. Harp's Security wouldn't believe it of course, nor the Mansion. They'd double check every breath Stannis took. But to Harp's tired mind it added up. The man had raced to the rescue, didn't find Harp in Riverbend and tried the next logical location, the Kraic village, where the navy hadn't liked him turning up and had prevented him from leaving. Not that he'd have known to go to Collar, that was mission-secret.

Because Stannis couldn't have known about the mine, the ambush. Could he?

'I'm done. I'm off to bed.' Harp rose, stomach satisfied at last, mug in hand. 'Stannis, I'll see you when I wake up. Daichi, get some rest too. That's an order.'

'Ser.' Harp just knew Daichi would ignore that, but was too tired now to argue.

Block A. He debated a shower but his cot was all he really wanted, with some dark and quiet…

+++

The Seed was trying to tell him something, but it didn't have much language yet so he only got impressions. Seed was anxious that he rest, replenish. Seed would talk to Collar. Everything could… wait? Till Harp was… ready?

+++

Hendriks tried to wake him gently; didn't work, he jolted from the cot and almost strangled him before he realised it wasn't Hoik or Regis. 'Sorry Hendriks!'

Hendriks swallowed, carefully. 'Sorry ser, but a superfast's here, under orders from the Founder to transport you back to World, asap.'

Of course it was. There were so many reasons the Family would want him where they could see him, weren't there? It was only what he's been expecting, yet again. But first. 'How's Mr Sulis? Has his wife been notified of his condition? Is she being brought out here? And Daichi, how's he doing? Crip, I need to see Big Red before I leave.' To check that the explosion hadn't scared the Kraic. To find out... had he dreamed or had Seed tried mind-talk with him, while he lay here sleeping?

Hendriks morphed to panicked. 'Harp – Max. Crip' a breath. 'OK, the superfast commander's shit scared of taking too long, said no one told him he couldn't drag you onboard if he has to. The Kraic said to let you know they're not at all concerned about events except for your wellbeing, and that you should do whatever you need to.' Hendriks finally consulted his wristcom. 'Mr Sulis has been transferred to the Orbital, where they have a regen tank, and Ser Daichi is organising your departure. That part's going smoothly, as you would expect.' A flash of humour. Hendriks meant Daichi wasn't happy so his folk were jumping. Probably the stupid fellow still refused to take the shots he needed.

'All right, I hear you.' Harp scrubbed a hand through his hair. 'So I'm leaving.' He was a Harpan, like it or not. 'But I'm showering first, I'm filthy. And I'm damn well having breakfast.' Lunch, whatever. Both.

'Yessir!' Hendriks backed toward the door. 'I, er, I'll tell the kitchen, shall I?'

'*Thank* you.'

+++

So here he was, back in the same stripped-down superfast, Moon Orbital shrinking out the port, his real homeworld dwindling behind it.

They weren't as loaded on this return journey. Two Family Security, who hadn't been on the raid, were left behind to "oversee" the navy's questioning of Medam Tayla and the township's council, all now loud in their objections.

And of course they didn't have the Intel people any longer, all four killed in the explosion on the surface. So they had the reduced crew, himself, Daichi, the Security who'd cared for Sulis, and Stannis.

What they didn't have was a regen unit, so Daichi was going to suffer, arm and shoulder still disabled, till they got back to the Mansion.

Daichi and that younger minder, name of Kerit – Harp had *finally* remembered – were the only two alive who knew exactly what had happened in the mine, how Harp had melted rock to get them out. There was still Sulis though, who knew a little, or suspected. Harp had slipped up there, reminding Daichi his eyesight was abnormal in the miner's hearing. But Harp thought, he hoped, the Mooner would keep quiet. Not least because Harp feared for that good man's safety if he didn't and the Family discovered. Face it, Harpans were obsessed with keeping secrets, even him.

Like what was taking him to World, again.

Cos everything he'd thought he knew had changed. Again.

Meanwhile, the crew weren't asking questions, not even about the empty seats. Daichi was finally dozing, those stiff muscles gone slack now Harp had insisted he took a shot, and one of the crew sleep-pods. Kerit was still awake, just, but never looked in Harp's direction, a reaction those who got too near him these days all too often copied. The remainder were either piloting, asleep in their seats or as near off-duty as they would be till they landed, bar the crewman keeping watch – she thought discreetly – on Ser Stannis Mella, sitting very quiet in the rearward seat he had been shown to, pretty much as far from Harp as they could manage.

Stannis swore he'd followed Harp to save him from the ambush when he couldn't reach him. Daichi's actions made it clear he didn't trust that.

Harp? He'd trusted Stannis and his instincts over Family Security. Now? Could he still?

He sat and thought it through. At least this time he had some solid data. Regis was a goner. At tremendous cost, but finally Harp's crewmates were avenged. He'd stomach that part if they hadn't also lost whatever Regis could have spilled about the pirates.

So Regis as a threat was gone but Hoik, and Zorr, made bad replacements. Hoik had always hated him; now – he'd lost face with Zorr, and lost his "bonus". He'd be rabid, and with Zorr involved that could put *anyone* in Harp's vicinity in danger, Family to perfect stranger.

But there had to be another traitor, back on World, connected to the pirates. If Mz Chan could track *them* down there was another source of information. Hopefully she could accomplish that before whoever-that-was came to kill him off as well.

Add the threat to life he presented and it got ridiculous. He was what, a sort of human battery this time around? Could suck in power or whatever – without even meaning to – and let it out again like an explosion. He had bored a steaming hole, in Collar. Even less believable, now he had time to think, she'd *let* him!

Face it, he was drowning in "connections", all of them abnormal. To the Kraic, to their Seed, now Collar. He wasn't sure he should return to World. The pull he'd always felt to Moon, his real home, felt stronger, and he didn't know who he could trust on World, not now. At least on Moon he knew who not to turn his back on. But he didn't get to choose. For good or bad he was a Harpan, so he had survived again, but how much longer could he dodge the missiles when there were so many, blazing in from all directions?

Missus Destra always said how "Life was what you

got". He'd bet the superfast she hadn't meant anything like this.

+++

Mz Chan personally met the superfast, with three armoured transports and a whole squad of blank-faced Security. Daichi got summarily removed by the Mansion's own medics, hopefully straight into regen. Stannis was "escorted to a debrief, ser". His air of resignation said he fully understood it wasn't invitation as he climbed into the second transport, but Harp couldn't in all honesty object. He understood Mz Chan was being cautious.

Harp got Mz Chan, herself, four more minders and a driver. No one spoke, except to ask him if he'd any injuries – of course he hadn't, only everyone around him. Harp bit his tongue, remembering even Chan might not know that truth about him, yet. No doubt she would though, once his grandfather decided what to share and what should be kept quiet after he explained the gory details.

+++

He'd actually forgotten his Security wore concealed body-cams, but at least it saved *some* explanation. Though how they thought he could explain what they were watching now…

Kerit's focus had stayed largely on Sulis as he worked to staunch that shot to the neck. Daichi's, naturally, had been mainly aimed at Harp, and showed without a doubt how when the bomb went off the stretch of tunnel they were trapped in had collapsed – except that perfect circle. Sphere? Harp dead centre.

The images got more muddled after that, Kerit's camra obscured because of carrying Sulis, and Daichi's wobbling when he staggered. But they showed enough; Harp, walking forward, hands outstretched, emitting waves of red-gold 'fire'. The buckled blast door melting into liquid goo that oozed first down then sideways – Harp had missed that – like it wanted to avoid him? And of course the wall of caved-in rock behind it simply disappearing to provide the brand new tunnel he'd so obviously caused to get them out to where the tunnels proper had survived and backup found them.

When the vids shut off the room stayed quiet for some time. Harp sighed and poured himself another coffee; no way was he speaking first. Harpan precedent, as far as he could tell, was for recording everything relating to the "bargain" that had gifted them two near-habitable planets and genetically changed them. So yes, they'd be recording now, for future generations, even if they locked it all away immediately after.

Maxil Snr eventually broke the silence. 'Did you have *any* inkling you could do that?'

'No ser.' And he wished he couldn't, even more now he had watched it.

Maxil nodded slowly. 'Do you think you could repeat it?'

'I've no idea, since I don't know how I did it.' Harp held onto temper. Maxil Snr looked *hopeful*. Then he got it. Maxil looked at what he'd done, the dire results, and saw a weapon, as he had with *Raptor*. And not just against the pirates, but NewEarth as well, if he was right about it still existing. The Founder wanted the ability to rain destruction down on other humans?

His face revealed too much cos Feldin looked from Harp to Maxil, maybe shocked, or maybe panicked. 'We do understand you're upset, Max.'

Upset? Harp forced himself to sit back and *not* crush the expensive glass, which it suddenly occurred to him he might. Well, he seemed to be able to trash anything now. Or maybe melt the thing. So, softly. 'So far.' Maybe softer. 'Every time someone tries to kill me, either someone else gets hurt.' Or dead. 'Or I do something impossible. Something I can't control. People *died* trying to protect me. And we still don't know who else is involved, do we?'

Feldin looked abashed even if Maxil's face didn't change. Harp felt his anger growing, gave up trying to suppress it. 'I don't –'

The outer door slid open. Being Harpan, he and both his elders heard it from two doors away. 'But Kato, Max is here. I'm sure he'll say to let me in.'

Harp thought Feldin looked annoyed, then resigned, then possibly relieved? Harp guessed because the interruption had at least prevented the collision that was brewing. But Harp wasn't going to be a deadly weapon in another's hands, especially the Founder's.

Still, the atmosphere had lightened. Temporarily perhaps but still a respite, so the storm he now foresaw could wait a little longer, while both he and they adjusted to his latest, strangest-yet mutation.

Sure enough, when Feldin glanced at Maxil Snr the older man abruptly nodded. So his son called out, 'It's all right, Kato, Felli's cleared to join us.'

'Father? Oh, Grandfather.' Felli looked taken aback, but it didn't last. 'Max, everything OK? I didn't see any of your usual Security.'

Both Maxil and Feldin frowned, so Harp took it on himself to reply. 'Daichi was injured, but it's not life threatening, and the rest,' – what was left – 'are probably sleeping.' Or debriefing. No point yet telling the youth some were dead; he already looked anxious enough.

'I knew it.' Felli looked Harp up and down, apparently checking *him* for injuries. 'But you're OK?'

'I'm fine.' Harp found a smile; wasn't Felli's fault he'd been so angry.

'But *something* happened.' Felli looked expectant.

Feldin interrupted. 'Whatever makes you think that, Felli?' Maxil Snr didn't look pleased but Feldin... more curious.

The youth looked scornful. 'I knew something was up as soon as Mz Chan rushed off. I only had to keep a cam on the Security checkpoints to see Max arrive, and if Mz Chan thought she needed to collect him...' Felli shrugged.

Now Maxil Snr leaned forward. 'You keep tabs on Mz Chan.'

Felli's chin rose. 'Have for ages. The first I ever knew anything was wrong was when I spotted extra Security. So I set my AI to scan for things like rescheduling and increased activity.' The youth assessed the stares and smirked. 'It's easy once you think.'

'I see,' Feldin said faintly, 'and how long is "ages"?'

'Oh, two years, or a little longer.' Was that a blush? 'I might have increased surveillance after Max arrived.'

Harp hid a real smile this time. Felli had been watching him as well, perhaps with changing motives? And had come up here to make sure he was well. But how much would Feldin allow him to know?

It turned out Feldin chose to treat Felli as adult again – or as that trusted Inner Family – so the youth got briefed on Tayla, the botched raid, even the latest attempt on Harp's life. But not how Harp survived. At that point Maxil Snr put it down to luck, to Harp and Daichi being clear of the blast site. Harp could own to being thankful. Airing the threats to his life was bad enough, he'd as soon as few people as possible knew how truly alien he was becoming. After the look on Maxil's face earlier, he'd prefer not to let *anyone* learn if more impossibilities attacked him.

By that time he'd had enough, all he wanted was to fall into bed. When he rose and excused himself Felli jumped up too; wanted to "report" on Moon Aid, and about Ser Stannis "going missing", which they *hadn't* filled him in on. Felli was right, they didn't tell him enough. It didn't feel good, but for now Harp dodged the problem too. 'Oh yes, I believe Ser Stannis is fine too, but occupied elsewhere.'

'You knew?' Felli frowned at the minders outside pretending to be deaf. 'I wish someone had said, I was hunting all over.'

'I believe it was rather sudden. I'm sorry they left you to hold the fort.'

'Oh well, Father sent me a couple of office types, so we

muddled through where we could, but you'll probably need to check everything now you're back.'

'I will, I promise, but tomorrow?'

'Oh, I didn't… You'll be tired.'

'Frankly, I'm asleep on my feet,' Harp admitted, 'but you've done more than enough. I'll get back to work tomorrow. If you have time maybe you could update me then?'

'Right. First thing as usual?'

Harp found a fervent wish to say midday or later, but duty made him answer, 'Fine, let's make it oh-six-hundred.' He should get it over with and give the kid his life back.

31

Felli was up and dressed well before oh-six, slightly shocked at how eager he was to see Max again. Really, it felt like he'd known new-cousin for years. And liked him a lot more than some he'd known much longer.

After a quick breakfast he called up a screen to give today's "uniform" a final inspection. That was what Max called his office outfits. Actually, he'd reached the conclusion Max saw almost all his clothes like that; navy uniforms, office uniforms, public uniforms. The guy probably organised his wardrobe that way. But it did work. Max and Ser Stannis always looked well turned out, in charge, grown up. Felli was starting to think maybe people were looking at him differently too since he'd changed the way he dressed, and maybe copied Max's manners just a little. So he supposed he was wearing a uniform now too. He grinned at his image then shut it down. Time to go, if he wanted to be first there.

Which was when his entry signalled an arrival and his AI told him that his visitor was Ho-San. Had she noticed he'd become an early-riser? 'Hi Sis. Come on in, but I'm just leaving.'

Ho-San swept in to meet him as he reached his tiny foyer. 'I assume the totally boring clothes mean you're still slaving for new-cousin.'

'Yes.' Felli quashed annoyance. Ho-San had been nagging him for days for being "unpaid labour", and frankly it was getting old. It wasn't as if he'd asked her to help, given she still didn't seem to like Max, or even believe in what he was achieving. 'Max just got back and I promised an early start.' It actually felt good to say that, like he had a role to play, a purpose. It was a shame Ho-San didn't see he was growing up, like Father had.

Except perhaps she was beginning to? She'd frowned, but now she raised her eyebrows. 'Cousin Max is back? From where?'

'Moon.' Felli's fears, eased last evening, rushed back into focus. 'Someone tried to kill him, again.'

'I gather he escaped though?' Ho-San turned around to follow him into the outer corridor. 'He wasn't hurt, at all?'

'He didn't look it.' Felli had to wonder though. Max had the Family genes, and more. If he had been injured, could he have recovered on the way back? Cos if anyone could it was Max. The thought was unsettling, he discovered, even after seeing him in one piece. 'Daichi's hurt though, he's in Sick Bay but he'll be OK.' He hoped.

'I *like* Daichi,' Felli finished, then rethought – he'd got to stop at least sounding like he was whining, it wasn't grownup, was it? On which subject, 'Who d'you think they'll send as a replacement? Lin would be good.'

Ho-San cast him a look. 'Just because she flirts with you, despite being ten years your elder, doesn't make her first choice.'

He wasn't blushing, was he? 'I just meant Max would probably like her.'

'I'm sure Mz Chan will send someone suitable. Though considering the times that man's been attacked whoever she chooses might not be so happy about it.' Ho-San walked beside him, thinking for a moment. 'I still think he's no prize, Family-wise, but I don't like those attacks.' She joined him in the crowd-sized grav-chute, built to take Security around their charge if needed. 'How is he coping?'

'Oh, it's Max, he seems to take everything in his stride, but then he's navy after all. He's been in battles.' And he couldn't tell his sister Max was way more special, he had promised.

'Hm.' Did Ho-San look conflicted? 'I have to admit I can't imagine a worse way to be thrown into the Family.' *Was* Ho-San rethinking her opinion? 'Not growing up with us is bad enough.'

Felli took a breath. 'If I was him I'd be a gibbering wreck but he's... look, he's a great guy, Sis. If you'd only give him a chance, get to know him. Grandfather's besotted, Father too, and I know Cousin Emika still checks even now she's left. Everyone who gets to know him likes him!'

Ho-San studied his expression. 'You really care about this, don't you. It's not just a crush.'

Not so long ago Felli would have hotly denied "caring" about anyone or anything, and "crush"? – ouch. But he didn't hesitate. 'OK, there might have been a bit of a crush, once, but I grew out of that on Moon. Now, I admire him, and he's a friend, and, and, I want you to be one too. It's practically the only thing we've ever seriously disagreed on, and I don't like it.'

'Well. All right.' Maybe she took a breath too. 'I'll try. How's that?'

'That's great.' Felli felt his mouth stretch wide.

Then Ho-San's shoulders straightened, always signalling decision. 'How about I go down with you now? Just to take a look, say hello, nothing more. After that I'll leave you to it.' When he nodded, speechless, she went on, 'I'll need to rearrange my schedule, but that'll only take a moment. We can stop by my apartment on the way down, can't we?'

Felli's first thought was that would make him late, but what the crip. It was on the way, as she said, and this was surely worth it. 'Yeah, sure.' Call Max to say he'd be delayed? No, better make it a surprise. Max was probably as wary of Ho-San as she was of him.

In any case Ho-San was quick, vanishing into the room she called her study and returning in minutes rather than the hour Felli half-expected. Not stopping to gossip signalled how seriously she was taking this, but then once she made up her mind his sister always did forge ahead. Maybe she saw it as getting it over with to clear her conscience, but she wasn't changing her mind and a brief hello, a first small step, sounded a good approach – enough to show she was willing to thaw, but not enough to get too awkward? When they reached the third floor Felli practically leapt from the chute before he remembered to be adult. 'This way. Well, I suppose you knew that.'

'Yes.' Ho-San strode forward. 'It's Uncle Maiso's old suite, isn't it? I always wondered why it was shut down so long.'

Felli hadn't till that moment, but it seemed obvious now he did, 'I'd think Grandfather must have always been hoping, y'know?'

'I guess.' Evidently even Ho-San was picking up a few Moon-isms. 'I heard they vacc-sealed the whole suite so it should at least have been useable.'

'It's fine. They've updated the desks, but Max says he thinks it's pretty much as Uncle Maiso must have left it.'

'He hasn't changed anything else?'

'No.' Felli's steps slowed as they approached the office entry. 'I think maybe he likes that it reflects his father, a kind of link. I mean, if we'd never known *our* father, except in images…'

'Yes, that is rather sad.' Ho-San straightened. 'Well, in we go?'

'In we go.' Felli swiped the panel, which slid open to his code, and decided to play tour guide. 'Ser Stannis usually mans the desk in there when Max doesn't need him close. In there's a kitchen, that's pretty glam, Max sometimes still calls it the galley. Then the washroom. That door's only storage at the moment. Then we have the inner office, Max's workspace – oh, hi Max, you beat me.'

Max was at his big desk, screens already loaded, looking up and visibly surprised to see them, or surprised by Ho-San. 'Mz Ho-San, good morning.' The Mz said it all, didn't it?

'Good morning, Cousin. Felli had been enthusing about your brain child. I admit to being curious about it.' Ho-San hovered in the doorway.

'Of course, welcome. Maybe Felli should show you what we're up to, he's more up to date than I am right now?'

So Max was being cautious, understandable when Sis had always been standoffish, but if Felli could just get Ho-San to *see*. He crossed to the smaller desk. When

Max was out he often joined Ser Stannis in his office, but today he wanted Max close by, to hear. 'Anything you'd like to start with, Sis?'

Ho-San stepped in to join him. 'No, you choose.' She took the chair he waved her into, settling as he leaned in past her, calling up some images of Moon, then facts and figures.

Ho-San looked, and listened, and eventually asked a question Felli could pretend he couldn't answer. Max, appealed to, crossed to join them, looking more relaxed when Ho-San's questions were insightful and her comments were approving.

Half an hour later Max had called for caffee and the three of them sat down, like cousins, actually chatting. Felli talked about the Kraic. Ho-San asked questions, some of which Max answered too. Her brief 'hello' became an hour before she finally recalled she had appointments, used the washroom and departed, almost smiling. Felli thought it was a seriously good beginning.

+++

Harp was still sitting, hoping Ho-San's change of heart would last – if only for Felli's sake – when Mz Chan's call came through.

'Ser Mella is requesting to speak to you, Captain. In fact he refuses to speak to anyone else.' Mz Chan did not look happy. 'I'll get answers, eventually, but it might be quicker if you agreed? I am not prepared to risk putting you in close proximity with the prisoner, though he has been searched, but…'

'I'll come, of course.' Harp wanted to see Stannis, still by no means convinced of the man's guilt. Or was willing to believe it. Belatedly he thought to ask, 'Where is he?'

'Interrogation level, ser,' Chan said crisply.

'Which is?' Harp said gently.

'Ah, Sub-level three, ser.' If Mz Chan looked awkward so she should. There were levels here Harp hadn't known existed? Not included in the tour he'd taken. Yet more secrets. What else had his Family not shared; he'd need to find out. Later. Now…

'I'll find it.' Harp started to sign off then thought again. 'Please don't do anything else till I arrive.'

Mz Chan's image blanked out without a yes or no. Was Mz Chan still under the impression she gave the orders, outside Maxil Snr and Feldin and presumably the navy brass? It occurred to Harp Mz Chan hadn't yet fully understood Harp now obeyed orders, from anyone, because he chose to. But then why should she when Harp was only now realising that himself? He might be part of the Family, but those same genes were also increasingly separating him from them. If he was dangerous – and he was – he needed to be his own vaccing judge and jury from now on. Not Maxil's superweapon, even against outsiders. He wasn't at all sure he could walk that tightrope but the more he learned, the more he knew he had to try.

Right now he was more inclined to listen to Stannis than Mz Chan, and make his own decisions.

+++

When Harp looked through the one-way obs window, Stannis sat behind a bare mepal table, wrists mag-locked to its upper surface. His feet, visible beneath, were even set in mag-boots. High-sec, navy brig equipment, blatant overkill since Stannis was a civ and hadn't fought them. They'd taken away his clothes too, put him in a garish yellow jumpsuit.

It was the first time he'd ever seen Stannis look dishevelled, the suit still packet-creased, his hair all rumpled. The man was scowling too, at the table top, or maybe his tethered hands. Or using the table's polished surface as a makeshift mirror? That would be more Stannis, but if so it must be really irritating not to mend what he was seeing.

'What exactly have you done so far?' Harp kept his gaze toward the window.

Mz Chan stepped up beside him. 'Standard procedure, Captain. Strip. Cavity searches. Scan for implants.'

Ouch. 'Find anything?'

'Not yet,' Mz Chan admitted, 'but we can't rule out programmed compulsions. So I can't allow you –'

Harp... twitched. Only realised because Mz Chan blinked and fell silent. But really, this had been coming, hadn't it? 'I appreciate your concern, Mz Chan, but I believe I'll make that decision.'

'Ser, I –'

'No.' Harp stepped back from the thickened glassite. Peripheral vision warned him two of Mz Chan's suits had stirred too. Anticipating orders? Harp was vaguely conscious of annoyance, and it didn't somehow feel surprising when they stopped abruptly, eyes gone wider. Looked like he could now create that bubble round himself at will – or rather without thinking – even make it smaller this time so that he alone was now inside it. He suppressed a sigh; it'd be nice to know what he could do *before* he did it, not in hindsight. Now there'd be more people giving him a wider berth.

Meanwhile the suits and Mz Chan were immobilised, even the tec recording Stannis. So how many obs-circuits had he'd tripped; how many more Security were rushing to defend their leader?

And could he undo what he'd done? The trouble with acquiring new "skills" was they never came with a manual.

So try the simplest approach first?

He crossed to the exit, which slid open for him – despite the fact he'd been irritated Mz Chan hadn't seen fit to give him the codes– and took three steps left. That put him outside Stannis's next-door cell. Feeling rather silly, he *wished* that panel open too, but felt better when that worked. Leaving the obs room must have done something too, he could hear exclamations and Mz Chan was snapping orders. Seemed his Harpan-hearing had improved again. Hm. How about from inside the cell?

He stepped inside and tried to think a polite request to

the panel, maybe it could close till he asked it to reopen? This time felt surprisingly comfortable. Maybe all that mind-talk with the Kraic prepared the way?

Well, it had closed, so he would hope.

'Max? Thank the burning stars.' Stannis had finally looked up. 'I know this doesn't look good, but I swear.'

'Just tell me.' Harp sat across the table, realised his chair was mag-fixed too, presumably so nothing here could become a weapon. His longer legs objected being cramped and he'd un-fixed the chair and pushed it back before he'd consciously decided, while a sudden silence from next door – he *could* still hear – confirmed Mz Chan had seen it. Now perhaps she'd get the message that *this* Harpan couldn't any longer be controlled, at least without risks he really hoped she wouldn't take, considering even he didn't know his limits any longer.

Stannis hadn't noticed. He drew a breath, tried to clasp his hands together, and winced? This was ridiculous. It was so unlikely Stannis could do him any damage. Harp "asked" the wrist-locks to release as well. This got easier each time he did it.

Stannis closed his mouth then rubbed his wrists. 'Thanks, the damn things were cutting off my circulation. OK, I suppose I should begin with a confession.'

Harp felt himself go still, finally *felt*… forces… inside him come into focus; had to struggle for a second not to do anything else on instinct. 'A confession?'

'Yes. Oh, nothing dreadful.' Maybe Stannis saw something in Harp's face; he talked faster. 'But I kept tabs on what you were doing as soon as I realised you were suspicious of Eleanora. I might also have.' A tiny pause, perhaps another reassessment of Harp's mood. 'I copied anything interesting to my own files. Any dirt on Eleanora was potentially useful to me too, you see?'

Harp sat still and listened. Stannis swallowed.

'But what you were finding seemed to point more to Sirena's branch of the family. I figured Eleanora could still be behind it, but the more I dug, in my own time, even those businesses you weren't happy about were linked to Sirena, or her husband. I couldn't find any evidence Eleanora had ever done more than glance at the balance sheets, and their safety records always looked good, on the surface; no recorded disputes, just a boringly productive sideline. I started to think Eleanora wasn't party to what was going on. Which left me asking if she was the strongest suspect in the threats against you. Much as I'd have liked to think so.'

'But you didn't pass on any of this information?'

Stannis shook his head. 'I was stuck. You'd hired me but why would you trust me. I'd used intel from your office, and from Mansion Security. If you knew, I figured I'd be fired, which would be social ruin, plus I'd then lose access to more intel. And after your Security thought I rigged the ambush at that school, well, admitting anything felt dicey. So I kept my head down. But I went on looking.' Stannis licked dry lips. 'A while back... I arranged a meet with Eleanora.'

Someone started banging on the door, someone else on the one-way window. Harp's brows twitched, and the sounds receded. That was better.

Stannis was distracted for a moment by the sudden quiet then recovered. 'I'd researched my... grandmother, you see, when I was younger. I wanted to know the woman who'd thrown my mother out; some vague idea I'd avenge her.'

'By stealing from your mother's sister,' Harp said quietly. It looked like the cell door was obeying him, and whatever else he'd done had either shut those outside up, or muffled their objections, so he focussed back on Stannis.

Who shrugged. 'That was how I started out. Mother never had anything good to say about her family and from what I could find out Suniya never tried to help her, acted pretty happy my mama was gone.

'Maybe I shouldn't have taken as much as I did,' he admitted, 'but she was so greedy, and so gullible. But I learned a lot about House Regis, and Eleanora's fixation on loyalty. Not so surprising once you knew Eleanora's elders almost bankrupted them. So my mother's "lapse", as Eleanora called it, counted as betrayal, and if I'm right what made it worse was mama used to be the favourite. Eleanora tried to hide it but I think she'd hoped mama would rise up the ranks, as it were.' He sat straighter. 'My mother might have fallen for a bad lot, Captain, but she did have loyalty. She could have left my father, but she didn't, and I think Eleanora considered the rest of her offspring idiots, because after that she very much kept the reins in her own hands. Your Security saw that as suspicious, but I thought, maybe she didn't trust the rest of them not to mess up?'

Harp pulled them both back to the present. 'This is interesting, Stannis, but how is it relevant?'

'I think Eleanora thought she'd finally found another heir in Komar, who at least had cunning even if he'd rather cheat. But now she's had to discard him too, and she's getting older and she still has no successor.'

Light dawned. 'You let her see *you* as a possible heir?'

'Yes,' the other man said simply.

Harp followed the logic. Stannis was clever, financially able, adept at persuasion, and had proved he could charm World Society. Yes, luring him into House Regis might give Eleanora a much more capable successor, even reason to "forgive" her long-lost daughter? And, bonus, see a member of her House positioned closer to House Harpan. Oh yes. 'What did you ask, in return?'

'I told her I thought her House *was* deep in what was happening to you, but if she helped me find out more, I'd consider a position inside House Regis, provided that included mama. I pointed out I didn't need the family, financially, and showed her I knew enough I could hurt her more than she could me if she tried threats,' Stannis said bleakly. 'It's not often being the black lam is a benefit, but... I pointed out any harm to you that traced back to House Regis would rebound on her, guilty or not. So either way was a win-win.'

Stannis hesitated. 'Frankly, I thought the benefits, material and political, would be the deciding factor. I'm sure she's rationalised it that way. But I'm starting to think a yearning for family had more to do with it. In the end I think I appealed to her emotions.'

Eleanora longed for her lost lams, and Stannis had offered a path that needn't reveal that weakness? Harp couldn't say he'd seen any sign of it, but who knew.

Stannis wasn't finished. 'She hummed and hawed but really she pretty much jumped at my offer. She's not pleased with Sirena anyway, clearly doesn't rate the husband and she's furious Komar has damaged the family, a far bigger betrayal than my mother's. With the evidence I already had it was easy to convince her Sirena could have done a lot more than help Komar escape trial, and when I showed her the vids of those factories, she was actually speechless for a moment. I think that was the final straw. She'd been trying to curb what she thought were just Sirena's tantrums. Now she's ordered full surveillance, com taps, the lot.' He grinned. 'She even gave me the codes. Turns out Komar set up some hidden stuff that proved they were still in touch, despite Eleanora forbidding it. But the clincher was two of those encrypted offworld transmissions went out just before attempts on your life. I think that really scared her. And while she didn't see you as an asset, I don't think she wanted anything to happen to you, you know? You were a lost heir.'

Like Stannis. Yes, Harp got it.

'There was a mass of on-world stuff to sift, that alone took weeks, but eventually her people singled out a few messages, apparently innocuous, till they confirmed those weren't from the businesses they claimed. No one's managed to pin down the real sources yet, but,' Stannis sagged. 'When I saw another, to Sirena, followed by another coded message offworld, almost certainly to Komar, then I added in you'd gone again...'

'You tried to warn me.'

'Yes!' Stannis reined himself in. 'Your Security wouldn't have trusted me so I couldn't go that route. I couldn't even get anyone to tell me where you'd gone, though it had to be Moon, didn't it? If you'd still been on World I'd have traced you. So like a fool I chased after you. I knew it was stupid but frankly you've dodged death so many times already I thought your luck had run out.

'And after all that I wasted my time because you coped without me.' Stannis looked disgusted for a moment. 'All I did was get myself arrested.'

'Mm.' Harp rose. 'I think I need to talk to Medam Eleanora. Oh, there.' The mag-boots folded down into the floor, releasing Stannis's feet, now left in matching yellow softsoles. 'You still have clothes at the office? Good, you can shower and change there, after you call to arrange the visit.'

32

'Captain Harpan, this is a pleasure, of course.' Though Eleanora didn't look that pleased. Harp wondered how much of the stiffness was meant to conceal her new alliance with her grandson, which she probably assumed he didn't know about, and how much was simply Eleanora.

He tried a smile. 'Medam, I thought it was time we got better acquainted.'

'Indeed.' The woman glanced from Harp to Stannis, saw something that reassured her and returned his smile, if thinly. 'Would you care for caffee?'

'Thank you.' Harp consoled himself with the thought she was hardly likely to poison him in her own parlour, or with Stannis as a witness. And if she did, well, he wasn't even sure poison would work any longer.

They maintained the stilted politeness till the caffee arrived, by human hand, and Eleanora shooed the minions out, but Harp finally saw Stannis relax when she prodded at her wristcom – suitably bejewelled – and a red light glowed above the entry. 'There, now we won't be interrupted. Nor recorded.' Maybe Medam relaxed then too. Harp didn't, but he didn't think he showed it. Eleanora frowned at Stannis. 'I was informed you were under Mansion arrest.'

'A misunderstanding.' Harp waved it off. 'And no longer relevant, but our Security would probably be happier if you could confirm Stannis's reading of recent transmissions?'

'Ah.' Eleanora abandoned her glass for Stannis's expression. 'Very well. I can confirm a recent encrypted message to my daughter Sirena apparently resulted in an immediate transfer to a point in space near Moon.' Another glance at Stannis. 'My reprobate grandson read this as a threat to you, Captain. I myself,' Medam looked slightly peeved. 'Was not aware you were going offworld.' A sniff. 'Nor that my grandson would rush off without taking better precautions, or asking for help.'

Stannis looked shocked. At the suggestion he should have asked *her* for help? But at least Harp could assume his own Security had kept *his* activities quiet. 'But you don't know where the message originated.'

'We didn't then, Captain.' This time Eleanora's smile was more shark-like. She watched both men sit up. 'The transmission was inside the Mansion.'

Harp's heart missed a beat, or so it felt. 'You can prove that?'

'Yes.' The older woman stared back.

'Could you track where?' Because the Mansion was bigger than Riverbend, much bigger with those blasted sublevels, and it had *layers* of Security. Even knowing which floor or wing would significantly narrow a search.

'My staff estimate the fifth level or above.'

Harp closed his eyes, partly in relief, partly dread. That might absolve the general admin staff. Most of those, like Stannis, came in from outside and didn't have clearance to go much higher. Of course one traced call didn't eliminate all the staff, or visitors. But they could check such visits, he was sure. Only that left… When he opened his eyes again Eleanora was sipping her caffee, watching him over her glass. He needed more. 'I assume you can provide the approximate times the calls went through. Could you trace any of the previous calls to the same location?'

The old woman looked approving. 'We are attempting to do so.'

Stannis was the one who looked annoyed. 'Why didn't you—?'

'Inform you? Was I expected to know you had gone on a fool's errand, without telling anyone? Perhaps in future you will.'

'Yes, sorry, Grandmother.' Stannis stopped, Eleanora looked blank. She didn't refute the connection, and she'd called him "grandson" first, but it seemed to halt the conversation.

'Mansion Security could assist,' Harp said mildly.

Eleanora fixed on Harp again. 'And how can we be sure none of them are involved?'

Crip. 'I trust Ser Daichi, absolutely, and Mz Chan.'

'Do either have the skills required? No, they'll bring in subordinates.'

Eleanora obviously felt Harp needed teaching to suck eggs. Time to demonstrate he didn't? 'No, Medam, they won't. I'll advise them, but I'll bring in my own specialist.'

That earned him a sharp look, 'One you can trust with your life? And apparently my grandson's?' No bet which she thought important this time.

'One hundred percent, medam. If you have a secure comp, one with offworld range? It'll be quicker than waiting till I'm back in my own office.' And a demonstration of trust Harp really hoped would prove justified.

+++

Fifteen very long hours later, this time through the Mansion's com, Hendriks finally admitted he was getting somewhere, confirmed, of sorts, by Mz Chan and Eleanora's Senior Security – still eyeing each other sideways. Apparently linking Hendriks into both Eleanora's and the Mansion's systems, via *Defiant*, had been the "vaccing pain in the ass" that had taken the rest of that day. When it became clear nothing was going to happen fast Eleanora had gone home, and Harp had forced himself to use the wait to make inroads into his Aid backlog. Happily, with both Stannis and Felli to hand he'd at least made progress on that front. When the day ended without news from Hendriks he ordered Stannis home and Felli up to his side of Feldin's apartment; everyone needed rest anyway. Then he left Eda to whatever she did alone and trailed upstairs himself, thinking that come morning he should ask Feldin to find somewhere Felli needed to be, to keep him out of it.

Eda woke him in the early hours with news that

Hendriks had control of the systems and 'has stopped complaining, Captain, though a lot of muttering continues'. Eda sometimes felt more human than he was. But finally the sergeant was reporting progress.

Harp had settled on his downstairs office as the logical place to play host to all interested parties, some of whom Mz Chan would *not* have wanted going higher. Mz Chan was keeping Maxil Snr and Feldin in the loop but Harp had dissuaded her from increasing security. Tipping their hand before they were ready wouldn't be clever.

Mz Chan joined him and Daichi in his office. Stannis arrived next, Eleanora not far behind, watching everything with interest. Harp figured she was keen to work out how much clout Harp had established, how much power. And how comfortably he worked with Stannis? Eleanora, Harp was guessing, had that sort of mindset; never switched off, never focussed on only one thing at a time. No wonder she'd want Stannis in her House; she could well see him as a younger version of herself. Certainly, both of them were impressively calm when Hendriks came onscreen, more-than lifesize torso flickering on Harp's main wall screen.

'Apologies for the visual, the perils of long distance. Can you at least hear me?'

Hopefully he saw Harp nodding cos he didn't wait. 'Right. Of the five confirmed messages at least three definitely came from your fifth floor. If you have the schematics I can probably give you a better fix.'

Mz Chan leaned forward at Harp's back. 'The House does not release any details on the Mansion. Certainly not over com.'

Hendriks sighed, loudly. How often did he forget he was navy these days, not civ? 'Then that's the best I can do. You'll have to take it from there.'

Harp cut in before Mz Chan tore his friend off a strip. 'That's fine, Hendriks, just send them?'

Another sigh. 'OK, but you'll let me know.'

'I'll let you know, when I can. Thanks.' Harp cut the feed before Hendriks pushed his luck any further. 'Mz

Chan, I need this to be discreet, not a horde tearing the floor apart. In fact no *visible* Security at all.'

Mz Chan was already rising. 'I assure you, Captain, we have suitable personnel onsite.'

'She means your sleepers. Didn't you know?' Eleanora's smile was wolfish. Mz Chan looked annoyed. Eleanora ignored her. 'Most Houses have them, Captain, people planted in nondescript roles in case they're needed.'

'Ah.' Harp eyed Mz Chan with less than favour, let her see it. Spies. He supposed it made sense, but it was yet another secret his Family had chosen to keep. Enough. But for the moment... 'Can we rely on *them* not to be involved?'

Mz Chan chewed lemons. 'You have my word, Captain.'

He supposed he had to trust someone. 'Very well. Do it.' And if Mz Chan didn't like him giving her permission in front of outsiders, tough. But it looked like she'd decided to live with it, so locking her out of her own interrogation room had done something useful. Still, he backed off, slightly. 'Quiet is more important than speed, agreed?'

'Yes, ser.' Mz Chan left, already tapping on her wristcom. There'd be nothing verbal, sensible precaution.

Harp slumped back, hoping he looked relaxed. 'So now we wait, I guess. Would you prefer to return home, Medam? No? Then breakfast, perhaps?' Because he'd missed his own, a handicap these days, and probably why he was starting to snap.

At once Daichi murmured to Eda, the only one of them who sounded cheerful. Daichi looked particularly bland. Maybe wondering if by nightfall – cos this wouldn't be quick – he'd be landed with arranging guest quarters for Eleanora, and Stannis, not to mention the Regis Security Harp had dumped in the ground-level Main Security Station. Neither Maxil Snr nor Mz Chan would like that either, but if Eleanora really was an ally they could hardly insult her, or her grandson, by throwing them out.

Harp was mulling over options when Eda chimed. 'Captain, Ser Felli is requesting entry, and wishes to know why his codes aren't working.'

'Crip.' He'd meant to call Feldin. Being awake so early had put it right out of his mind. 'Er. Voice only, Eda?'

'Certainly, Captain.' She gave him more, a one-way vid of the corridor, and a frowning Felli.

'Felli? Sorry, I meant to warn you the office will be closed today. I'm just on my way out.' Harp winced. It wasn't a good excuse.

'Closed?' The youth's head jerked up, so familiar. 'It doesn't close just cos you're not there. What the crip's going on?'

Let him in, to see Eleanora? Probably not wise. 'I'm sorry Felli, this time I can't tell you.' Inspiration. 'Maybe you should ask your father.'

'Don't think I won't.' The youth glared into the camra, turned on his heel and stalked away.

As Harp winced again Stannis half rose. 'Maybe I should…'

'No. Ser Feldin should decide how much to tell him, Stannis. I'd rather keep him out of it but it's not up to me now.'

33

Felli strode from his father's office in an even worse temper. He'd intended to make a start on the next round of appointments, now that Max was back. He'd got up *extra* early, to show everyone, including Ho-San, how committed he still was. And now he'd been shut out?

What's more, Father wouldn't tell him anything either, though it was obvious he knew something. Why else that cryptic warning to avoid the fifth floor, when he was hardly likely to go there anyway? Felli wanted to throw things. Or damn well *go* to the fifth floor. All of which would only prove to Father Felli *was* the kid they shouldn't confide in. Being grown up was harder than it looked.

At least there was one person up here who didn't mind him letting off steam.

+++

'Shut you out?' Ho-San repeated.

'Yes!' Didn't anyone listen today? 'Something's going on on the fourth but no one will tell me crip. Do *you* know? I'm worried there's another threat to Max.'

Ho-San still didn't look concerned. 'Why would Max spend time on the fourth floor. He's probably never set foot on it. Besides, well, when has Father ever told either of us everything that goes on?'

'He does now, cos-' Crip, he couldn't explain what had changed. 'Cos he said I was growing up, and promised.' Even to Felli that sounded lame, but at least Ho-San looked sympathetic this time.

'Yes, all right, but I doubt that means he's going to tell you everything, does it? Though I do sympathise. I'm older, and I know he still doesn't with me. Anyway, you don't actually know Max is at risk, do you? It could as easily be some problem on Moon, or with the Aid programme. That would involve both Max and Father.'

'I suppose.' Felli threw himself into one of Ho-San's contorted chairs and tried not to sound sulky. 'But if it was I'd *know*.'

Ho-San studied his face. 'I don't suppose you've dealt with the finances. That was Ser Mella's role, wasn't it?'

'Partly.' Felli saw the way she watched him. 'But Stannis isn't the problem. He's not even… here.' He swallowed. Stannis vanishing, Max saying the man was occupied elsewhere. Surely not.

'Ah.' Ho-San was trying not to, but "I told you so" was on her face now. 'Embezzlement isn't a threat to new-cousin, even if it impacts his programme and his public image, but if Father *and* Max want you to stay out of it, you need to respect that, yes? I'm sure they'll want to keep it quiet.'

'I guess.' Felli scrubbed a hand through his hair. 'Maybe.'

Ho-San clearly saw rebellion. 'Butting in never does any good, Felli. Who knows what you might upset. Look, if you'll keep away for now I'll see what I can find out, if only to stop you fidgeting. Deal?'

Felli's mood improved, Ho-San found all the rumours and the gossip. She was bound to know someone who knew *something*. 'Really? That would be great.'

'All right, I'll ask around, discreetly. As soon as you leave. People won't tell me anything if they think someone else is listening in.'

Felli wanted to stay but he supposed she was right. It wasn't till he hit the corridor outside her apartment it occurred to him there was nowhere else he wanted to go, that all the things he'd previously filled his days with, before-Max, felt, well, pointless. In the end he went back up two floors to his suite, ate a second breakfast, felt a little better after that and told himself he could be patient if he chose to. Besides, while he'd agreed not to pester anyone till Ho-San had news, that didn't mean he couldn't keep a long-range eye on things, did it? His system could still monitor Mansion activity.

It was almost fun, even now, sitting back and watching

what went on lower; always had been. He'd started when he was ten, not fourteen. Not very seriously, but he'd, well, *upgraded* stuff when Max arrived so now his AI duly filed its observations. Felli sat up. There was a low-level schedule change logged for the fourth floor. But it was only cleaning staff, according to their outfits. Only they weren't cleaning, just pretending to? An unofficial search? How long before Ho-San found out about that?

+++

Daichi was back. The man still looked pale, but it was good to see him raise an eyebrow at his interim replacement, whereupon the woman stepped away, without a murmur.

Then they spent more hours waiting.

Harp arranged caffee, then lunch, more caffee. Eleanora used his washroom; probably as well he'd mental-locked the walk-in wardrobe, just another undiscovered talent. Eleanora poking into his spare underwear *wasn't* an image he needed. Being able to "ask" Eda, or the wardrobe, so discreetly was a skill he could get used to, if it ever stopped being scary.

In the background Stannis, imperturbable as ever, was managing to field calls. From the outside things must still look normal. From in here, everyone bar Eleanora and her grandson was on edge now. But eventually Eda chimed. 'Captain, a call from the fifth.'

'Put it on speaker please?' The rest sat straighter.

'Captain?' A female voice he didn't know but obviously knew him. 'Officer Tan, ser. We've found a backdoor a level above, in one of the housekeeping data storage units. We're trying to track the source but meanwhile we've sealed the corridor and called in forensics.'

'Very good. Please update us when you have more.'

'Of course, Captain.'

Daichi was on his com before the call ended, it sounded like he was increasing Harp's Security here now the steer was out of the pen, as it were. Harp didn't see much point, but didn't argue. If it made Daichi feel better, after what he'd been through…

Medam Eleanora consulted her wristcom, presumably updating *her* Security, and Stannis went back to answering calls, so Harp tried to look as calm as them. Except the Mansion didn't feel secure now, and while *he* might be the target there were an awful lot of other people all around him. 'Maybe I should leave the Mansion.'

Daichi gave him that look. 'To where, ser?'

'Crip, I don't know, but I could be putting everyone in danger.'

Daichi didn't even look up. 'World or Moon, you're still the target, Captain. Here we can protect you better.'

'I suppose.'

+++

Ho-San watched her screen as more-obvious Security arrived at the cupboard. She wasn't sure what they were doing but Felli was right. She put a call out to her brother, slaved her sixth-level comp into Main Security.

Felli popped up on her second screen as she continued to monitor, switching his gaze from something *he'd* been looking at. 'Hi Sis, you got anything? What have they found in that cupboard?'

So Felli also knew about the cupboard. Ho-san was impressed; it seemed Felli *was* finally growing up, and taking notice. 'No one I've talked to so far knows, but one of the lessers,' as she'd always called all less-related Harpans, 'is complaining Security are keeping him in his room.' The images on her screen shifted. Ah. 'It looks like they've found something, but no one's being told to evacuate, so it can't be dangerous.'

'No. No, I guess not.' Felli's eyes strayed. 'But there's two Security teams outside Max's office now. And Medam Eleanora's there. She came early this morning and she hasn't left.'

'Oh? Medam Eleanora Regis is in Max's offices?' Felli's news added another dimension to what she *had* seen.

'Yes.' Felli turned back. 'I'm going down there!'

'Not a good idea, Felli.'

But her little brother was already rising. 'Daichi's back, and if Max wasn't in danger Daichi wouldn't have increased his protection, so I need to be there.'

Ho-San sat, the blanked screen mocking her assumption she could always handle Felli. Damn new-cousin. Calculating the scant minutes it would take Felli to reach the third level, no doubt at a gallop, she sighed, then opened the bottom drawer of her desk, removed the false base and placed her palm on the hidden seal. The space below slid open.

34

In Max's office they waited for more intel, this time on what, if anything, forensics might discover. In short order the Security above, now headed by Mz Chan, informed them of the long-distance com unit, very miniaturised, very well hidden, and capable of micro-burst signals as far as Moon. They were now checking for self-destructs, boobytraps and the like, had already disabled two destructs inside the *cupboard,* and were now removing the entire storage unit to a reinforced room in the sublevels, "in case".

Harp didn't envy those handling that.

Meanwhile forensics had been gathering "samples", which they were transferring to their own sublevel haunts, and would report on progress as they found it, though that also would be hours.

That was when Feldin turned up. Eda sent out more coffee. Everyone was getting hyper but Harp took it anyway. His neck itched. Something somewhere didn't feel right; what were they missing? When the next call chimed he actually jumped. He didn't think he was the only one, but no more coffee. 'Eda?'

'Another call from Forensic Officer Tan, Captain.'

'OK.'

Officer Tan's round face was flushed. 'Captain? We've found a hair, caught under the comp.' She stared at Harp as if he should find it significant.

'I'm sorry, what?'

'Underneath, Captain, stuck to the casing.' She drew breath, spoke slower for the dummy. 'It got there with the casing.'

'I... see.' Harp did now. 'Can you pin-point whose?'

'Ser, I... ser, it's definitely Harpan. We've been waiting for Mz Chan to access the House database but I promise I'll inform you as soon –' Her head jerked sideways, somebody was shouting. 'What?' She disappeared!

'Officer Tan!'

It was probably only minutes before the woman reappeared, but it felt like hours, and this time she was shaking. 'Ser, we got a match. It's, it's Mz Ho-San?'

Feldin, next to Harp, was saying, 'No, it can't be, officer.'

But Eda interrupted, no chime this time. 'Captain, an unknown device has activated in your wardrobe. I would advise…'

+++

Harp found himself on his feet, the noise around him distant. Everything felt slow, almost leisurely. He could feel Eda's "device'", sense it had been dormant, had been woken. And the powerful energy – explosive – at its centre.

He could block it now of course, the way he had in Collar's tunnels; form a sealed sphere that would save all those inside it. But the blast would then push outward. Collar's blast had travelled. Here, in the Mansion, it would funnel through the corridors and open spaces, breaching walls, much flimsier than rock or lava. Outer walls could fail, floors above be weakened. He'd be safe but others, Felli…

He was in his corridor before he knew what he intended, pushing anybody in his way aside, become a blast of air that threw them back into the office, then a second one that slammed the panel closed between them.

Then he was alone inside the washroom, and the only thing that he could see to do was not to push *away* the bomb he sensed but to attract it, *swallow* it, so that it couldn't reach to others.

35

Felli tried to pick himself up when the floor stopped shivering, fell against the corridor's wall and decided to stay on the floor till he was OK to walk. This felt worryingly like when the volcano had knocked everyone but Max off their feet.

Max! Felli shoved himself up again and stumbled forward, leaning on the wall for balance. He'd reached the ground floor, close enough to the office he'd seen Security ahead when he rounded the next corner. Some of them were still struggling to find their feet too. That made him feel better, he wasn't the last. Which was probably childish but hey, it helped. Unless they were slower cos they were nearer the explosion?

OK, get down there and make sure Max is all right this time too. Felli's brain started to work at the same time his legs, or the ground, steadied. World didn't have any volcanoes – at least none he knew of – but they'd found a "device". A bomb then? Maybe it'd gone off after they'd got it down to the sublevels. They'd have had shielding. That must have contained the worst but it had still shaken the building. In which case Max was alive, same as he was, but he acknowledged a need to see that for himself. If the grim looking men and women out here would let him by.

When the entry panel ahead slid open it was a relief to see Daichi. The man had clearly come to check on his teams and he wouldn't be out here if–

Then it wasn't reassuring any more cos Daichi swung, saw him and pulled his sidearm. 'Whoah, it's only me.' Felli stopped dead, trying not to shake. 'Ho-San told me we were restricted to wherever, only I was worried so...' Daichi hadn't lowered the gun. The rest of them were focussed on him too; not one was looking friendly or indulgent.

Daichi's face was especially blank. 'Mz Ho-San told you what, exactly?'

Felli gathered his wits. Something was wrong, but Daichi needed intel. 'I spotted the people searching, and Ho-San said she'd try to find out what was going on.' Felli faltered. 'She didn't think it was a bomb, but it was, wasn't it? Is anyone hurt?' The bomb hadn't been up here or Daichi wouldn't be standing, even if everyone was spooked. Although, if Ho-San hadn't thought there was a bomb, why had she been so keen Felli didn't come down?

Daichi had lowered his gun though, so Felli could breathe again. 'Where was Mz Ho-San, ser?'

'In her apartment.' Felli frowned. One of Daichi's people had glanced at her boss, raised her wristcom, tapped a bit then ran toward the chute Felli had come down in. 'What *is* going on?' Cos he *was* a Harpan, and tapping meant the woman didn't want to be overheard.

'You'd better come inside, ser.' Daichi gestured to the office.

'Stannis?' Finding Ser Stannis inside relieved any doubts Ho-San had raised, and Felli remembered to bow to Medam Eleanora; he should have recalled she was here too. His father was a surprise though, especially how pale he looked, but then he saw now that the rest were. 'Father?'

Daichi murmured something to his father, who nodded. Daichi left. Father waved at a vacant chair. 'You're sure Ho-San was in her apartment?'

'Yes ser, it was behind her onscreen.' Felli held his tongue and waited.

'Do you know if the AI here log visitors?'

Odd question. 'Let's ask?'

Eda spoke before he asked, like she was waiting. 'I have a complete log, Ser Feldin. Recent entries to the Captain's washroom were himself, Ser Stannis, Mz Ho-San, Ser Felli and Medam Regis.'

Eyes shifted, from Felli, thank the stars, to Stannis, quickly on to Eleanora, who sat up abruptly. 'I most certainly did not –'

'The Captain sealed his wardrobe before Medam

entered,' Eda continued, apparently unimpressed by rising tension. 'And Ser Stannis accessed only the section furthest from the reading, *and*.' A slight, very un-AI stress? 'While I have no visual, audio-reconstruction suggests Mz Ho-San removed a small object from her person, though I could not observe what it was, or what she did with it. I am currently rectifying those failings.'

'Thank you.' Felli's father licked dry lips. 'Can you trace the Captain's current whereabouts?'

'No ser.'

Felli gaped. 'Eda, you must know something.'

'Ser, the Captain entered the washroom nought point two six seconds before the device exploded. When I transferred an emergency camra he was no longer there.' A pause. 'There is residual evidence of his presence in the area but no evidence he... departed.'

Felli swallowed, had another thought. 'His tracking implant, Eda. Can you find that?'

'No, Ser Felli.' Eda's voice was softer. 'The Captain's tracker ceased to function nought point one four seconds before the explosion.'

Felli's chin rose sharply. 'It shut down *before* the bomb went off?'

'Yes ser.' Pause. 'That does not equate.'

'No, it doesn't.' Felli swung to face his father. 'Could Max *do* that?'

Father froze, then glanced at Eleanora. Felli got that message, Eleanora didn't know their secrets, or that Max especially was an impossible-survivor. Only she was here, observing.

Eleanora snorted, rose. 'I see my part is over. If there is anything House Regis can do...' Eleanora glanced at Stannis, who was staring blankly at the corridor where Max had vanished. 'Perhaps you will allow Stannis to contact me with any news.' The old woman nodded formally, to Father then to Felli. 'My condolences. The Captain was an honourable young man. I'm sure many will mourn him.'

Felli held his tongue till he was sure she'd left the

whole suite, then couldn't any longer. 'Father, Eda said *before*. Not after, and we know he beat the bomb in Collar.'

'Yes, but then where is he, Felli?' the door reopened, Daichi appearing. 'Daichi, have you found anything?'

'No ser.' Daichi looked as shell-shocked as Stannis. 'Felli is right; the captain did save himself there, and those near, but in the mine that caused a circular safe zone, while outside that the blast affected everything for half a klick. Here – I've checked, ser – the bomb has had almost zero effect outside its location. My team report even the washroom sustained minimal damage, only an odd blast area from the wardrobe, where only half the contents are incinerated, towards the door.' Daichi looked bewildered.

'Where Max must have been,' Felli butted in. 'The blast went *to* Max!'

'Ser, a charge can be directed,' Daichi told him gently.

'Yes, but not this one, Daichi. No one could have expected Max to be there at the exact moment, whether he knew about the bomb or not; it had to be aimed at the whole suite. We need to –' Felli tried to breathe and swayed, till Father pushed him back into his seat. '*Ho-San* did this?? But she'd finally started liking him. And she'd have killed you too, and Stannis and Daichi, maybe hundreds more around you. Is she crazy?'

'Felli, I don't know.' His father rose from his side. 'But if she did this, we'll find out, I promise. Daichi, have we found my daughter?'

'Mz Chan has taken a force to the sixth, ser. We should hear very shortly.'

'Very well, we may as well wait here then. Is there *any* news on the Captain?'

'No ser, nothing. All the damage is confined to the washroom. But the blast pattern there left a silhouette on the wall. I'm afraid that resembles the Captain, ser. It looks like his body stopped the blast reaching farther.'

'The blast didn't go any farther.' Felli only realised he was grinning when the rest stared, but really. 'Don't you see? A normal explosion wouldn't behave like that, would it? That means Max controlled it.'

Father's hand fell on his shoulder. 'Felli, if so I'm afraid that also means Max took all the blast on himself. He saved us, but in doing so…'

'Well, I'm not going to believe he's dead till I see proof.' Felli looked Father in the eye. 'You shouldn't either.'

Father tried to smile, failed. 'Then I won't, not yet. But now, I need to brief your Grandfather.'

'I'll come too.' If they were going to talk about Ho-San maybe he needed to.

Maybe Father thought the same, he didn't argue. 'Come on then. Ser Stannis?'

Stannis finally looked at them. It was like the man had forgotten they were there. 'Ser?'

'I trust you'll keep all this to yourself?' When Stannis nodded Father looked around the office, gestured helplessly. 'It seems no one outside ourselves and Security are aware there was a bomb. I expect Mz Chan is circulating a reasonable cover story that will reach you shortly. Perhaps you could keep things running here, till we decide what to do next.'

'Yes ser. Is there really a chance…?'

Felli couldn't not say it. 'Stannis, believe me, if anyone could survive it's Max. Don't give up?'

Stannis nodded again, turning away, heading for his outer office. His face said he didn't believe it, but Felli wasn't giving up either.

36

A grim-faced Maxil Snr waved Mz Chan to a seat. 'Ho-San?'

Mz Chan chose to stand. 'When we broke in she was already dead, ser.' A tiny pause. 'There were no other signs of foul play but she left this. Tec swear it's safe, but I'd still advise a closed unit.'

'A suicide note?' Grandfather's back stayed straight but Felli watched his father sag against the padded chair back. *He* felt numb. Ho-San had faked her willingness to know Max better – so that she could plant a bomb and kill their cousin. Was prepared to kill, so many, even Father, to achieve that? It was inconceivable. Pure madness.

But she'd done it. He half listened to Mz Chan telling Grandfather and Father she hadn't opened Ho-San's last message but was still recommending a secured comp, a reinforced enclosure, "to be on the safe side".

Now she was talking about "residue". They'd identified the bomb. And a remote detonator, in Ho-San's desk. She must have set it off mere minutes after Felli left to go down to that self-same office. Had she meant to kill him too?

He raised his head. 'Why, Mz Chan? Why did she hate Max so much.'

'We don't know, ser. Perhaps her message will tell us. If not I promise we'll find out.' This time Mz Chan looked almost as upset as Felli felt. And angry. 'May I return to work, Founder,' she said stiffly, 'until you appoint my replacement.'

'Chan, you are not responsible for this.' Grandfather finally sighed. 'If we saw nothing, how could we expect you to. Carry on.'

Mz Chan swallowed, nodded curtly then departed.

Grandfather didn't speak again till the three Harpans were alone. 'There's no good time, but we need to see this sooner rather than later.' Grandfather's jaw tightened. 'In case there's anything else to deal with.'

Felli gulped. There couldn't be any more hidden bombs. Could there? But if Ho-san had set one bomb in the Mansion, under everyone's nose, they couldn't assume anywhere was safe, could they? Or anyone; accomplices, partners, whoever she'd exchanged those encrypted messages with they'd finally told him about. There were other *Family* who hadn't welcomed Max with open arms. *He* hadn't. If this vid had any clues… 'I'll watch it for you, Father. You don't need to.'

Father's eyes when he looked up were bright, with unshed tears. 'No, we'll watch together.'

+++

Watching through reinforced glassite was odd, but it was clear enough. Ho-San was wearing the same fashion statement Felli had seen last; she hadn't thought to change into something more dramatic, which he realised he'd half-expected. But there probably wasn't time. Or she'd known Security was too close.

She was sitting at her desk again, head high, hands clasped, like she was sitting for a portrait. She always looked so *sure*.

Her smile was the one she gave people she thought beneath her. Her words were calm, and measured. The only hint of anger was the pinching of her nostrils.

'Grandfather. And Father, if you're alive, but you're probably dead too, aren't you, so I'll assume it's you, Grandfather. And perhaps Felli, if I was fast enough. With Father and new-cousin out of the picture I should have been stepping up as rightful heir again, shouldn't I? But I see Mz Chan is on her way, which means you've found me out and all my plans have failed. Still, thanks to little brother I have at least managed to remove your new pet from the throne, so I suppose I haven't failed completely.'

Felli clutched the chair arms. 'I *told* her, about the search. Stars, I asked her to find out what was happening; that's why she set off the bomb?'

Grandfather paused the vid, shook his head. 'Felli, she'd already planted it. This is not your doing.'

'But.' Felli closed his mouth. They needed to hear the rest. 'Go on.'

+++

'When you come to your senses you'll see I was right. It's beyond comprehension, the degree to which you've pampered Maxil Junior. Giving him a medal, encouraging the whole planet to worship an upstart Mooner, one funnelling a fortune out there, from *our* coffers?

'I knew he was a threat as soon as you gave him Maiso's apartment on the eighth, so near yours. You wouldn't open it up when *I* asked, would you, Grandfather? *I* had to push someone out of the sixth. While you were grooming Maiso's son, favouring the direct line, cutting *me* out. As for parading him in front of Society, giving him everything Maiso left, instead of me? I couldn't have that, not when I'd made so many promises for my succession.' Ho-San's laugh was harsh. 'And in the end Maiso's brat's still beaten me, I won't be succeeding Father now, will I? But I'm taking dear Max with me, there's some satisfaction in that, eh?'

Maybe the patrician features sagged a fraction. 'Hopefully you'll still have Felli, if I blew the place before he reached it, so I don't suppose you'll lose too much sleep, will you, Grandfather? We're alike there, aren't we, we both do whatever needs to be done to keep the power we were born to?'

The vid went black, and it was Felli's turn to hold his father. Maxil Snr looked old, and frail. In a while Felli rose and poured Grandfather's brandy. No one argued when he poured himself one.

+++

Meanwhile...

New-Harp hovered in the grav-waves, half drunk on his new existence, half considering his choices. He supposed he could return to near-human, distantly aware they would be searching for him – that they might be hurting. Some would have emotional attachments.

But on Moon the Seed might understand, and Collar beckoned; he would rather start this new existence there, where others knew him. Trusted. Worshipped. Till he felt more able to protect them.

If this NewEarth that Maxil was so wary of was still a threat? Then let it save itself; he felt no urge to add it to *his* new-found purpose. Moon and World were his to guard now; never mind what fate decreed for others. But he couldn't stay on Moon forever, not and do this new-born duty.

37

Head up, shoulders back. Today he was Captain Harpan again. Flight Captain Maxil Xen Harpan, the VIII, long-lost offspring-grandson of the current Founder. Wearer of a medal for his part in running off the pirates, and "the Mooners' captain". Mere hours ago he'd been *on* Moon, the little planet he'd grown up on. Then he'd *wished* himself to World, straight into his... apartment, in the Mansion, flashing in unmeasurable seconds distances it should have taken days to travel, even in a pulsetec. He didn't really understand that yet, but knew he'd done it.

Course then he'd needed nearly all those intervening hours to think and talk coherently in human. Only then had Eda, bless her circuits, finally allowed Daichi and his team to rush inside; it looked like Eda was as keen to hide exactly what he had become as he was.

Then, of course, there was a muted sort of uproar. He was still "alive"; they'd thought he wasn't. By then he'd recalled what happened so he'd understood the questions, but it turned out those would need to wait on other secrets. In the end he'd barely had the time to change into this uniform and let Daichi bring him here, to join the Family in what Daichi called "The Mausoleum". Seemed like Worlders – Harpans anyway – put folk who died in fancy buildings, and he'd reappeared just in time for the interment.

He discovered that his human half felt more at ease now. Not that either version of him wanted to pretend respect or sorrow for the body in the casket sitting on its sombre platform but they rated him as Inner Family, so he'd been ushered past the crowd outside, while screens above had shown him a familiar stranger, one who followed other, distant, orders.

Past the honour guard inside, the politicians and the rows of less-mutated Harpans, most of whom had no idea what really happened, never would. To end up in a line where three who maybe did feel grief, however mixed, had stared at him in wide-eyed silence.

Some of these were why he had returned. He would respect *their* feelings, and their secrets, for the moment.

He was the last before the outer doors were shut. Now Ho-San and the four of them would form the focus of this bleak performance. Grandfather, Maxil Snr, stood farthest right, his Uncle Feldin, and then Felli, Feldin's teenage son, poor kid, then... Harp. Or as the watching crowds would say: the ruling Founder, then his heir and Ho-San's younger brother then "Moon's Captain Max". Who Ho-San tried to blow to bits, and only failed because her target wasn't only human any longer.

Why? Because she'd seen herself as next in line and thought his being found on Moon had blocked her from succession to the "throne". Because she hadn't known she'd never *been* in line. But not knowing, she'd assumed too much, and greed and arrogance had driven her to murder and collusion with the pirates, maybe others. Now she'd ended everything instead, and he was only here to support the living – mostly Felli.

Felli would be seventeen in a few days, but there was no trace today of the pampered youth Ho-San encouraged to distrust a new-found cousin. Felli was a statue at Harp's side, clenched fists the only outward sign of inner turmoil.

Human-Harp's expanded hearing, even keener now, picked up a murmur from the rear; Medam Dalla was describing Felli for the watching masses as "impressively mature, and coping bravely with the loss of his beloved sister". A stronger Human-Harp thought Felli still in shock, and hoped for his sake grief came later, to dilute the roiling fog of anger he could feel.

Maxil Snr and Feldin both did sad and stoic well, he thought, but then they'd had more practice. Daichi had updated him enroute. The story was an accident, of course. Ho-San had bought an antique pistol, a projectile, in a rush to try it hadn't stopped to get it tested. Sadly, when she'd got it to the Mansion's firing range and powered it up the thing had blown up in her face and she'd been dead before staff even got there. Understandably the Family had closed the casket on the ruined features.

"So young", Dalla was saying, "so sad". Trying to alert folk not to take such risks while not quite owning Ho-San had been criminally careless. An impossible attempt, but if anyone ever doubted Dalla was World's leading caster, this occasion surely underlined it.

Worlders called this a funeral. On Moon they'd call it a Seeing Off and it'd be a lot simpler, a gathering of those who cared enough, a few words and fill in the hole. Here, it meant a stone hall crammed with fancy clothes and sad – or trying-to-be – expressions. Most of whom, the cynic in him thought, cared less for Ho-San than for Maxil Snr's and Feldin's notice. Those he'd need to keep in line if humans here had a future.

What thoughts he had derailed; Maxil Snr was stepping forward. 'Family. Friends. Thank you for joining us today.' There was more but Harp tuned it out in favour of watching reactions. Did all these folk accept the lie or did the rumour mill already pick at contradictions?

If anybody here had doubts they weren't showing them, but then their worlds belonged to Harpans, and you didn't contradict your landlords, not and prosper.

Maxil Snr stepped closer to the casket, laid a steady hand upon the polished mepal surface of the fancy box, then stepped aside for Feldin to repeat the farewell gesture. Feldin's hand shook, but his face was stoic. Felli – Felli hadn't moved.

So Harp edged closer, dropped a hand on Felli's shoulder. Looked into the panicked eyes – too young for this still. Felli jerked a nod, stepped forward with him. When Harp brushed his free hand over Ho-San's coffin Felli did the same. They faced the truth together; Ho-San had been willing to include her father, and her brother, in the bombing, all to clear the way for her ascent to power. Instead she had revealed her treason, and her bomb *accelerated* Harp's already-close mutation into something more than human, and ironically saved him. Something those who knew would want explaining once this farce was over, cos they hadn't seen him, had they, since the bomb went off and he had vanished.

How the crip could he explain this calling, let alone the Seed, or Kraic?

When he and Felli stepped back a few others came forward. He noted Cousin Emika, in uniform. Did *she* know everything? How many had they trusted? Likely other so-called Inner Family; they never had revealed who was, who wasn't.

But he'd always know in future.

Then he spotted Medam Eleanora, grandma of another traitor, once a suspect and more recently an ally. She was one he'd saved, but wouldn't know. Or did she? Medam was inquisitive – polite description. She should be a threat, except all this had given her a long-lost grandson too, oh yeah, a new relationship she was displaying here. Her current need to lean on Stannis didn't stem from age, it was a public statement. Stannis was in favour now, not just as Eleanora's grandson – he had always been that after all – but as Harp's trusted aide, a post inside the Mansion. She was using Ho-San's funeral to underline her grandson's double rise to favour. Playing politics, another human vice that he would need to curb, to save them.

He almost laughed. Missus Destra used to call that statue by the hearth her "guardian angel". Was he meant to be an angel now? He didn't think so, more he'd gone from herding steers to herding humans, hopefully with those with sense, like Felli. Were there others out there too now? No, there *must* be others, surely?

Ah, the casket sank into its dais, so the burial was over. Maxil Snr led them all into the open air where crowds and 'casters waited. There were calls of sympathy and camras buzzing in the sky, though at a careful distance. Most folk though stood quiet, respectful of their ruling families and VIPs. It was a spectacle, but not a riot. Feldin walked with Maxil Snr toward a waiting transport.

Harp stuck close to Felli, one hand at his back to steer him to another. Felli likely couldn't see where he was going for the tears now falling.

No doubt there'd be vid of that, poor kid, and folk on World and Moon would see, and feel for the youth, not knowing that the tears weren't all for loss but for betrayal, that so-human curse. Well, hopefully he would do better.

Once he managed to explain things.

38

A pale vapour, without shape, appeared from nowhere, coalesced into a human-body ghost, and then... he just appeared. It should have been a trick. It wasn't, and the faces round him said they knew it. Thankfully Eda fast-forwarded the rest. Well, it lasted hours after all and not much happened. Onscreen the solid "Harp" stayed on his feet a moment then collapsed into a heap. The vid showed Eda checked his vitals then decided, on her own, to take no further action. Harp was grateful; maybe she'd worked out he was defenceless.

Hours later, as the chrono on the screen raced forward, Harp watched with the others as he raised himself and staggered, as he got control enough to answer Eda and allow Daichi and his people in, because of *course* Daichi had a sensor planted. Eda had repeatedly denied him entry? Ah, she'd claimed it was at Harp's instructions. Which it wasn't; he and she would have to have a conversation, this one unrecorded.

By the time she gave Daichi access he looked normal, on the outside anyway, so Daichi had prioritised, updated Harp about the funeral and left the bigger stuff for later.

But everything was there, for them to see. He wouldn't have too much to add then. He could do that, surely.

+++

He'd tried. It didn't look like he'd succeeded.

'You exploded, with the bomb.' Feldin eyed him doubtfully. 'Then somehow ended up in space, in *vacuum*. And without your body.'

'Didn't need one, cos I didn't have a human body out there,' Harp repeated doggedly. His head ached. 'Yes, I know it sounds impossible but it's what happened.'

Felli's turn again. 'You were blown up.' A grin. 'You really were. That's why the blast area was so small. I said you'd survive.'

Maxil Snr. Any earlier depression visibly receding. 'By becoming our legend.'

'I guess.' Harp wondered if the crazy woman on the ancient vid had had the faintest notion what she'd done to win their planets. Did he wish she hadn't? Only time would answer that one. In the meantime… 'I think Collar would have triggered the change but the bomb got there first.'

Felli was the only one who smiled. 'The volcano? During an eruption!'

'Yes. I think so, Felli.' Maybe Maxil looked more energised but Feldin just looked worried, while Daichi had regained his usual bland expression by the time Harp looked. Harp forced himself to think in human words, aware that was becoming harder. Staying here wasn't easy. Wasn't comfortable. Something else he'd need to work on. 'In space… I wasn't, I was…' vapour, like the vid; the cold of space, the heat of stars. 'I wasn't human.'

Maxil Snr dragged them back to practicalities. 'You've sealed the bargain.'

'I've begun.' Harp stared at Maxil. 'I will still be human.' With an effort. 'Or I can… dissolve… but then I can't communicate.'

A thoughtful Feldin: 'Where we couldn't hear you, like the way you mind-talk, as you call it, with the Kraic?'

'No.' Harp kept hoping talking would feel easier. If anything he thought it had got harder, but at least it looked like they believed him. 'With the Kraic, there are still some words, but… Sorry I can't…'

This time it was Maxil Snr who smiled. 'Under the circumstances I don't think any of us is complaining. You've saved stars-know-how-many lives, *and* paid off the Family debt. Congratulations.' Maxil even raised his glass. 'So what happens next?'

Harp didn't smile. 'I think somebody – I still don't know who or what – decided humans might become a nuisance,' he said grimly.

'Crip,' was Felli's comment. Even Daichi's mouth fell open. Felli's elders stared; his grandfather had lost the smile. Cos of course *he'd* hoped all this would make the *Family* more powerful. Instead the bloodline had produced a... *something* wasn't there for him at all, more like an independent witness, guardian. Judge? No wonder Maxil Snr didn't look so happy any more, though Harp felt sure the other man would try to find a loophole.

It occurred to Harp he had already stepped away from Maxil Snr. Maybe part of him still felt some loyalty, to some at least, but it was going to be a struggle, reconciling what his two forms saw, and what was valued.

'I think I'm supposed to bring us to heel,' he said bluntly, saw the fresh shock. 'Our blood was more receptive.' He watched Maxil Snr relax a fraction. That one had worked out its worlds might have advantage.

'But right now billions of your kind are pushing boundaries that someone won't put up with.'

Felli looked from him to Maxil, frown returning. Felli had caught up; this wasn't an adventure after all.

Harp realised that he was fading, maybe literally. 'If we become an interference in the waves... we humans have already damaged worlds. If we continue we'll condemn ourselves.' So easily. But Feldin might succeed, then Felli; guide these humans to a better future.

Still, he had to wonder; were there more like him, already out there? Or would others follow?

The walls felt like they were closing in, making him breathe harder. Part of him was sorry but it wasn't enough to stop him spinning apart. 'Must. Go.'

'Of course, Max,' Maxil Snr answered. Outward calm, but no doubt inner plotting.

+++

Collar's heart welcomed him back with a shiver of delight; he sank into its lava, drawing strength. Yes, this would be his refuge, for the centuries to come if need be. While he watched them and where possible protected.

Crip. Missus Destra used to say that statue was her

"guardian angel". Was *he* now an angel? Nah, more like he'd gone from herding steers to herding humans, into an uncertain future both for him and all *his* humans. Hopefully for generations *after* Felli.

Collar danced its pleasure to be chosen. Collar would protect, whenever honoured.

End?

Though elsewhere…

Project History: CLASSIFIED.
Personal addendum to report; Project Director to "Source".

"So you were right, ser, it now appears at least one unauthorised colony, established within OldEarth's final century, may have survived to this day. Further research indicates other lost, or hidden, fragments, from NewEarth's earlier history, might also exist, possibly as far back as the end of *our* first century. With your approval we propose moving our investigations to what we suspect was our earliest desertion. You will of course be aware such challenges to our early authority as were known have already been erased, to protect your predecessors' efforts to ensure our own survival, but I will of course keep you fully informed on any further discoveries."

So, the end. Really?

Read on for a sample of *Homeworld*, book three of *Worlds Apart,* and a look into its long-gone past, even though it's still *our* future.

While *Homeworld* can be read as standalone, it is also the third story in the *Worlds Apart* collective, following *Harpan's Worlds* and *Worlds Aligned*, all available from Elsewhen Press. Add the clues to build a wider picture…

So...New worlds, and evolution. Are the rest exempt? Were they ever? And how far back do the problems lurk? Perhaps it makes more sense to think of *Homeworld* as a picture of humanity's past, even though it hasn't happened. Yet.

So, let's see?

HOMEWORLD

From book three of *Worlds Apart*.

Meet Luc:

'Well now, if it ain't that pretty Marta, an' the little angel.' The oldie stretched a hand out but the "little angel" dodged the reaching fingers. Marta didn't slow at all. The old man shouted after them, 'Hey now, I only want me supper, girlie. Gotta real fine rat ta trade ya.'

'It's the off hours, fool. You come back later when I'm cooking.' Marta took Luc's hand and hurried to the nearest metal downshaft. Luc knew their real route was up but understood the misdirection; the oldie was a customer, no friend, and never to be trusted. Luc still smiled at him though, his foster mother said to always act as if he *didn't* know such men as this would scoop up careless children. And to stick real close to her "in case". She'd said rule two was even more important on today's adventure.

It was a long walk, as she'd warned, and holding Marta's hand as he had promised meant Luc had to scurry sometimes. They were venturing beyond the world he knew now anyway, these corridors were grimier, and more deserted, nothing like the bustle he was used to.

On another day he'd shoot a thousand questions, but today he needed all his breath for walking and in any case the pattering of Marta's footsteps on the metal floor kept chanting "Five today, I'm five, I'm five, I'm old enough to meet my *brother*." Marta had admitted that there might be something extra for his supper, but that paled to insignificance beside the chance to see his real live brother...

Matthew was a lot older than him. 'Fourteen now,' Marta had told him, 'Or maybe fifteen, more like Tolan.'

Tolan was grown up. Luc watched the boy the previous evening, wondered: would his brother be that big, that noisy?

Several cage-like stairways later they emerged in yet another draughty tunnel. 'See the scratched-out numbers, Luc? Sub Level One, we're almost there. Stay close now.' Marta led him on again, but slower now. These twisting metal byways weren't so different from the ones below except the sounds up here were clanks and hisses, mech instead of people. Luc began to take more notice. He was tired but still excited. Nervous too. The top tier of Sub-Level One was only one floor below Zero; almost in the real City. There might be a hundred strangers round each corner!

There didn't seem to be any people up here right now though, and the few they'd seen along Sub Two had hurried past, their gaze averted. Were they hiding, nervous 'cos of Matthew? 'Cos of course his brother was a Legal.

Luc had never seen anyone Legal before, that he knew of. He knew he and Marta weren't. She'd explained when he was little. The Legal Levels were called "Upside", and the people there were Legals. Most of 'em were "Lowers" but a few – the special ones – were "Uppies".

Ordinary riff like him and Marta hid out Downside in the warrens of the "empty" Sub-Levels. Luc still wasn't entirely sure what being Legal meant but he had listened hard when Marta told him there were men above who wore brown uniforms, called Mil, who hated all Illegals. She had glowered at him. 'Stay away. They'll cook you like my stew and eat you, if they catch you.' He had made a very solemn promise that he'd never, ever, stray above the second Level under.

But today he had done!

+++

Marta chose a metal niche she'd used before, large enough to conceal both of them from anyone passing that way. It had bolt holes where some long-pilfered mech had once been fixed into it and she used one as a spy hole so she could stay hidden till she saw if it was really Matthew. Footsteps made her stiffen and she felt Luc's hand clutch tighter, but when she squeezed back he stilled at once as she had told him. Was he scared? Why not, he might be little but he wasn't stupid. Three times each year since he'd been born and smuggled here she'd made this trip, at first to meet his father then just recently this brother, to collect the credits that were all that kept both Luc and her alive – till this year anyway. She felt a stab of satisfaction. Who'd have thought those fancy real cooking lessons she'd endured at school would help down here.

Footsteps echoed down the tunnel, louder now and faster. Was it him? She hated coming up here for those credits. It was risky, and reminded her too much of all the things that Luc would never have, that she had lost for ever. And Marta felt no warmth toward the older son. If her cooking ever earned enough they didn't *need* this…

It was Matthew. Marta stepped from hiding, keen to get this over. Luc came out behind her, without hesitation, staring at the darker, stockier youth who came toward them. Gripping her hand. 'Matthew.' Marta nodded stiffly. 'This is Luc.' She pushed him gently forward.

The youth halted. He looked surprised and then, oh no, revolted; as if Luc was something contagious.

But then Luc found his tongue. 'Are you really my brother?' Those hazel eyes gazed up. So hopefully.

There was an agonising pause, then suddenly the youth dropped down so he was level with the infant, albeit still frowning. 'Yeah, I guess.'

The smile lit Luc's face as if the sun he'd never seen had pierced the metal floors above. He stumbled forward till the two were almost touching. 'I brought Ted. D'you like to see him?' Certain of the answer, Luc tugged Ted, his tiny silver bear, out of its inner pocket. Marta had sewn its chain into the jacket's lining so he couldn't lose it but he usually kept it out of sight, obedient to Marta's warnings. Ted was mascot, absent family and treasured secret. 'Marta said our mother sent it, when I was a baby.'

Marta watched, forgotten for the moment. The youth stared at the trinket then took in the fragile-looking fair-haired infant, hazel eyes all bright and friendly, chattering away as if he'd known his brother for a lifetime. Marta watched the youth's distaste become confusion, then confusion change reluctantly to interest. This time Matthew lingered, basking in the child's admiration. When he straightened up and said that he was going Luc's smile faded. No, he didn't whine, or argue – kids down here knew better – but he looked so sad, and tried so hard to hide it, she felt sure...

The youth succumbed. 'I guess I'll see you next time, kid. Oh, here.' He tossed the precious pack of open-creds to Marta then retreated quickly, maybe with a hint of panic. At the corner he looked back though. Luc waved happily. His usually-surly brother raised a hand halfway then disappeared.

Marta let herself relax a notch. She'd had so many doubts, but Luc had wanted this so much, and, as usual, he'd melted all resistance. That smile had charmed a multitude already, even here, but – she frowned – he wasn't normally so trusting. She had trained him early to be careful of the dangers all around them. Still, it *was* his brother. That should count for something, surely.

+++

After that day Luc considered he had not one but three birthdays a year, for Marta took him with her to collect his 'llowance now. Even better, once she had the precious packet she would issue dire warnings then would leave him for an hour with Matthew. They would play at catch, or wrestling. Or talk about the magic of those Upside Levels.

'Matthew knows everything,' he told Marta over supper, after one such meeting. 'He knows about Upside, and credits, and Mil-isha, and, and everything.'

Marta smiled at him, chopping busily. The "stew girl" turned a rat into a banquet, so they boasted here in the enclave. Luc would beam with pride whenever someone praised her, and regard each greedy suitor as a rival till she had repulsed them.

Later, snuggled in his blanket, fed and warm and safe against the waist-high metal grating that did duty as her "counter" (Hot air from beneath them somewhere kept the food warm, very clever, and a pair of brawny brothers saw to it that no one tried to steal the pitch from Marta these days, in return for meals.) Luc lay staring at the condensation on the metal ceiling. He had always shared his day with Marta, especially his hour with Matthew. But Matthew had been very definite he shouldn't tell her they had *seen* Mil-isha.

Mil-isha was Matthew's bigger, Upside word for the brown-coat Mil. People had been saying it looked like the Mil were patrolling Sub-One more than they had. Luc had worried Marta would say he couldn't stay behind this time. She hadn't, but today the Mil had come while he was actually there, while *Matthew* was still there. Both boys had had to hide till they'd gone past.

Luc felt a glow of pride; he'd known the nearest, safest

place to make for, one of several that Marta showed him. He'd protected Matthew *and* himself from danger. So he'd done exactly as he ought to, hadn't he? As she'd have wanted? Everything was fine, and no, he shouldn't worry Marta with what only might have happened.

Only, after that scare Matthew didn't want to play so much. Luc censored that in his report to Marta too, he was seven now, after all. She'd given in to his repeated pleas to meet with Matthew on his own to get the credits, so she hadn't been in any danger. Nor had he. He was still small enough he knew a *dozen* different routes to get the credits safely back into her pockets; places now she'd never shown him.

But now Matthew flicked the packet in Luc's direction at once. 'Here, kid,' he'd say, already looking back the way he'd come, as if he was afraid that he'd been followed. Luc could usually catch the packet now, one-handed even. He had practiced daily; glowed when his success impressed his brother. But that might be the only game they played. Before long, Matthew was turning up without even a smile for his admirer. Luc considered tactics, and invented leading questions. 'What will you do when you're sixteen?' became a favourite. The Legals – odd idea – had to be *sixteen* to count as adults. But if he played that card it was more likely Matthew would forget to frown, and stay a little longer.

'Once I get accepted,' Matthew would begin, and Luc would soak up words that didn't always come with meanings. What *was* a soldier? Why did they wear un-i-forms? Why did they fight, and were they *always* fighting? Didn't they run out of people? Maybe, he opined, it would be better not to kill the en-emy at once, so there'd be enough left for the next battle?

Matthew gave one of his harsh barks of laughter. 'That's not how it works, kid, but then you don't know nothing.'

Luc accepted he was ignorant; aspired instead to imitate his brother's grown-up way of laughing. From the child the sudden exhalation came out lighter-hearted. Luc saw life as an adventure, and it would be years before he wondered if his lack of understanding then was due to Matthew's vagueness rather than Luc's inability to understand what he was told; if Matthew hadn't been so wise and knowing as he had pretended?

Luc never got to ask more questions. Matthew failed to make it to their next assignation. Luc waited in his latest air-vent hideout all that day and gave up only when he heard the sounds of others going past him on their way to Zero. That meant off-shift, when Illegals went to skim the Lowers who descended from their far-off, proper Levels to the bars and brothels at the edge of Upside Law on Zero. Matthew wouldn't come now there were witnesses. Luc trailed back to Marta, empty-handed. Did she think that something might have *happened* to Matthew?

'Let's not worry yet, eh, Luc?' She stood behind a now-extended counter, doling equal measures of the latest stew to customers who queued then spread around the makeshift trestles that had grown like weeds around her in these last two years. Even as she spoke she took a bag of greens as payment for a meal. 'That'll buy you supper now, love, and another one tomorrow. Deal?' She stowed the greens beneath the counter and went back to work.

She hadn't scolded. She'd said not to worry. Luc resolved to act his age (he'd heard that said to other children) and went to clear off empty dishes, even wiped them. But for once he wasn't the bright-eyed chatterbox her regulars were used to. Oh, he smiled when they teased him – always smile, that was business – but his eyes stayed solemn. And the next time, after Matthew didn't come again, he worked head down, and didn't answer when they teased him.

'What's up with Luc?' one woman questioned.

Marta spared a look in Luc's direction. 'His brother didn't come, again. That's the second time.'

'Poor kid,' someone murmured, 'he idolised that Upside brother, didn't he? Still, it were bound to happen sometime.'

Marta sighed, her eyes on Luc as he collected dishes. 'No use telling him that, is there.'

'So no more freeloading then, huh?'

Marta didn't answer. She hadn't said anything about that to Luc either.

But he'd been thinking about it. Matthew had said he was going to become a soldier. Soldiers were brave and went off to fight, and kill people. Soldiers, then, got killed. So maybe Matthew was... gone. And wouldn't *ever* be returning.

It took a while to get used to this conclusion, time alone and silent, bar the need to tell it all to Ted who always came and joined him for such private conversations. If Matthew was gone, so was the 'llowance. He still, he assured Ted, had a mother and a father up there, somewhere, but they couldn't bring it any longer, could they? Matthew said they were too old now. Marta had explained how he could never meet them anyway. They couldn't see him, and he couldn't see them either. They still existed, but the regular supply of credits didn't, any longer.

He spoke to Marta that same evening, before his courage gave out.

'I need to pay you for my food, now, don't I, like everyone else? Will this pay what I owe you?' "This" was Ted, stretched out along its chain in grubby fingers. A nearby tableful of women stopped their bantering to watch and listen.

Marta stirred the stew; didn't look up. 'Keep hold of him for now. Let's see how things work out.'

Luc stared up at her, then turned and went to get the broom, to sweep around the makeshift crates and trestles that were sometimes tables, sometimes benches. Once, he'd questioned sweeping then had listened carefully when Marta told him, 'No one wants us getting sick down here, do they? If we keep things clean we have more chance of staying healthy.'

Luc had decided if Marta got sick *he* would look after her. But if she needed medicines... ah, now he saw. Such things were very hard to come by, weren't they, and they'd cost a lot of meals and if Marta was too sick to cook 'em... It was better to be careful then. He'd swept more diligently after that, and put more effort into washing. Even when he wasn't very dirty!

Now, as he retreated, several of the women shook their heads at Marta. One spoke out for all. 'You've fed the kid for free, for months now, girl. Ain't like he's kinfolk, is it? You should take that bit of silver.'

Marta gave up stirring. 'How can I, Sil, when it's the only thing he has to prove that someone Upside cared about him.'

'Yeah? Well, what else has he got to pay with? Girl, he's eating half your profits, and it won't get better.' Pleased with her remark Sil spread the thought around the tables. No one argued. There were simple rules to living Downside and the simplest, if you wanted any allies, was you didn't ask for what you couldn't pay for, one way or another.

Marta's was the only protest. 'Luc'll earn his keep. Just look, he does already.'

Those who heard her shook their heads and dropped the subject, bar a few whose eyes began to follow Luc with speculation. Marta, seeing that, told Luc to hurry with the sweeping then come back and wipe the dishes. Solemn now, the child worked on. She saw him casting brooding glances round the other adults. Scared she'd sell him? There'd be buyers, she could count them by their faces. So could he, he wasn't ever stupid. How to reassure him? Marta did her best to let the child and everyone who watched them see he still belonged to her and that she found him useful; that she still gave him as much protection as she had before he lost his income.

It was late before her customers stopped coming that night but this time Luc didn't stop when he got tired. This time Marta knew better than to tell him to. Her Luc was stubborn, had a pride that many adults lacked down here. Even when the customers were gone she had to tell him, 'Off to bed now, Luc. We'll leave the rest until tomorrow.' It was clear, the line was drawn: he'd work until he dropped before he let her go on looking after him for nothing. Only, *could* she keep them fed and clothed without those extra credits?

For a whole week they didn't discuss it. Marta cooked, Luc swept and cleared, sometimes fell asleep before he'd finished eating, never asked for seconds any longer. Marta told him she was proud of him, and hid her worries. Then he vanished early one day when she wasn't looking.

By the time he returned it was off-shift and relief made her sharp. 'Where on earth have you *been,* scamp? I'm rushed off my feet tonight and we're running out of clean dishes.' Inwardly she breathed again. He wasn't hurt, or scared, although he *was* extremely dirty.

But he had that look, some secret bubbling up inside, just waiting for a chance to overflow and scald her. 'All right.' She turned from her pots. 'What have you been up to?' He was bouncing on the spot, his hands behind his back. She took a sideways step. He was concealing something, right enough, a small, flat packet wrapped in shiny, tell-tale yellow. Marta's mouth went dry. 'Luc, where in space did you find medicals?' Because medicals meant high security.

A beaming Luc held out the packet. 'In my tunnels.' He didn't mean the ordinary passages down here, he meant the air ducts and the narrowest maintenance shafts, an endless, bewildering maze full of traps, some set deliberately to kill off insect life and rodents. Luc checked the nearest regularly, for the pot, and she had always feared he went much further into them than other kids did. Now she knew it. More, she saw that he was also telling her he'd said goodbye to childhood, and would hear any protest as an insult.

So she took the tiny packet, hands unsteady. 'Do you know what you've got?'

'No,' he confessed, 'the words are too big. But I knew you would. You said meds are top price. They are meds, aren't they? Will they pay you for my upkeep for a while?'

'Yes, of course.' What else could she say.

At last he smiled. 'What are they for?' He looked so eager.

'They're purifiers. See this word, here, right across the label? They make water safer, kill the germs that live there?'

Luc studied the letters, mouthing out the sounds as Marta had taught him. He understood what germs were. She'd explained they were a sort of tiny enemy that lay in wait for people and attacked when they weren't looking, like the brutal Subbies did; that like the Subbie gangs they needed watching out for, dangerous and dirty and unhealthy. He also knew she boiled all *their* water, to make it safe. Was that why his face had fallen? Did he think she wouldn't want them? 'These are almost better than meds to some people, Luc. They can stop people *needing* meds.'

That perked him up again. 'So it's enough.' He hesitated. 'For a week?'

She almost laughed. She'd seen him often bargaining with other kids, occasionally with his elders, but he'd never tried with her before. She grinned at him. 'A month, Luc. I know just where to sell these; they'll fetch a whole month.'

Luc stood open-mouthed, but she wasn't finished. 'How risky was it getting them? I don't want you –'

'It's not easy, 'xackly, but I can do it again. I can get lots.' He saw her frown. 'I'm careful, Marta, honest. You know I am, when I wanna be.'

'I'm sure you are, but if you're going places that could trap you.'

'I'm not going *in* anywhere, only on *top* of them.' The words tumbled out now. 'There's a big storage depot. *Real* big. It's all sealed off, but I know all the hatches and the ceiling vents. I made a hook though, see?' He pulled a roll of twine – purloined from gods-knew where – out of a sagging pocket. One end had been tied into a loop, the other knotted to a bit of metal that he'd somehow worked into a four-way hook. The spikes looked sharp. 'It took a while, that's why I couldn't do it before.'

All week, between kitchen duties. Whenever she wasn't looking. Never say he lacked determination!

He let her take it. It was a miniature grappling hook, impressively business-like considering a seven-year-old made it. She bent to return it then yelped as it tugged away and clamped itself against the nearest pot. The metal was magnetic? Had he thought of all that, by himself? She stared at Luc. 'You made this, then used it to hook the packet and pull it up through a vent?' She shook her head but had to smile. Luc looked so serious, so anxious. 'Well, I suppose, if you're not actually going into these places…'

He shook his head emphatically. She chose to take that as a promise; thought he meant it, that he didn't want to leave her but he would if he felt guilty, wouldn't he? He'd vanish one day, and then chance knew what would happen to him. Truth was, she didn't want to lose him either, but if he was caught… she crouched, face stern. 'I don't want you to take too many risks. Deal?'

'I don't.' He actually looked indignant. 'There're lots of little parcels, see, that's why I thought of meds. They don't have to be big to be worth lots, and they're easy carrying, in case.'

He meant, of course, in case he had to run for it, and didn't only mean from Legals or Militia. Marta still hesitated. Truth was, life Downside wasn't safe, it never had been, only safe as they could make it. And there were far less palatable ways for such a pleasing child to make his living; some that lurked here at her benches, watching how she treated him and waiting for a chance to lure him from her. 'Luc,' she told him gently, 'Luc, love, you don't need to do this. You're always welcome here with me, you know that? All my kin are Upside too, like yours, so I can't ever see them either. But we have each other to rely on, yes? We need to stick together.' She would see that no one got the chance to steal him from her.

Luc's mouth twisted in thought. 'I'd like to stay here

with you, but I'm getting older, I should earn my keep now. Other kids already do.' He faced her squarely. 'I've been very lucky, haven't I? I've had a brother, and the credits, and had you to teach me things. But now it's time I earned a proper living.'

Marta hugged him, sniffing her acceptance of his words, his right to make decisions. His idea, so devious, so clever, was the safest option she could think of. There'd be danger, more as he grew older and became a bigger target. She would worry all the time she couldn't see him. But she'd hope and pray and fight to see him grow into the adult that he thought he was already. *That* was family.

They stuck together, pretty much the same, for twelve more years...

Thanks for reading, and it would be great if you could leave a review, or just a word or two. It really is helpful.

Terry

[Next; book 3, *Homeworld*; a beginning.]

Elsewhen Press
delivering outstanding new talents in speculative fiction

Visit the Elsewhen Press website at elsewhen.press for the latest information on all of our titles, authors and events; to read our blog; find out where to buy our books and ebooks; or to place an order.

Sign up for the Elsewhen Press InFlight Newsletter at
elsewhen.press/newsletter

BY TERRY JACKMAN

HARPAN'S WORLDS:
WORLDS APART

TERRY JACKMAN

If Harp could wish, he'd be invisible.

Orphaned as a child, failed by a broken system and raised on a struggling colony world, Harp's isolated existence turns upside down when his rancher boss hands him into military service in lieu of the taxes he cannot pay. Since Harp has spent his whole life being regarded with suspicion, and treated as less, why would he expect his latest environment to be any different? Except it is, so is it any wonder he decides to hide the 'quirks' that set him even more apart?

Space opera with a paranormal twist, Terry Jackman's novel explores prejudice, corruption, and the value of true friendship.

Terry Jackman is a mild-mannered married lady who lives in a quiet corner of the northwest of England, a little south of Manchester. Well, that's one version.
The other one may be a surprise to those who only know the first. [She doesn't necessarily tell everything.] Apart from once being the most qualified professional picture framer in the world, which accounted for over ten years of articles, guest appearances, seminars, study guides and exam papers both written and marked, she chaired a national committee for the Fine Art Trade Guild, and read 'slush' for the *Albedo One* SF magazine in Ireland. Currently she is the coordinator of all the British Science Fiction Association's writers' groups, called Orbits, and a freelance editor.

ISBN: 9781915304179 (epub, kindle) / 97819153041070 (320pp paperback)

Visit bit.ly/HarpansWorldsWorldsApart

YOU MIGHT ALSO LIKE

LOOPHOLE
IAN STEWART

Don't poke your nose down a wormhole – you never know what you'll find.

Two universes joined by a wormhole pair that forms a 'loophole', with an icemoon orbiting through the loophole, shared between two different planetary systems in the two universes.

A civilisation with uploaded minds in virtual reality served by artificial humans.

A ravening Horde of replicating machines that kill stars.

Real humans from a decrepit system of colony worlds.

A race of hyperintelligent but somewhat vague aliens.

Who will close the loophole… who will exploit it?

Ian Stewart is Emeritus Professor of Mathematics at the University of Warwick and a Fellow of the Royal Society. He has five honorary doctorates and is an honorary wizard of Unseen University. His more than 130 books include *Professor Stewart's Cabinet of Mathematical Curiosities* and the four-volume series *The Science of Discworld* with Terry Pratchett and Jack Cohen. His SF novels include the trilogy *Wheelers*, *Heaven*, and *Oracle* (with Jack Cohen), *The Living Labyrinth* and *Rock Star* (with Tim Poston), and *Jack of All Trades*. Short story collections are *Message from Earth* and *Pasts, Presents, Futures*. His *Flatland* sequel *Flatterland* has extensive fantasy elements. He has published 33 short stories in *Analog*, *Omni*, *Interzone*, and *Nature*, with 10 stories in *Nature*'s 'Futures' series. He was Guest of Honour at Novacon 29 in 1999 and Science Guest of Honour and Hugo Award Presenter at Worldcon 75 in Helsinki in 2017. He delivered the 1997 Christmas Lectures for BBC television. His awards include the Royal Society's Faraday Medal, the Gold Medal of the IMA, the Zeeman Medal, the Lewis Thomas Prize, the Euler Book Prize, the Premio Internazionale Cosmos, the Chancellor's Medal of the University of Warwick, and the Bloody Stupid Johnson Award for Innovative Uses of Mathematics.

ISBN: 9781915304506 (epub, kindle) / 97819153041407 (560pp paperback)

Visit bit.ly/Loophole-Ian-Stewart

YOU MIGHT ALSO LIKE

BIRDS OF PARADISE

RUDOLF KREMERS

Humanity received a technological upgrade from long-dead aliens. But there's no such thing as a free lunch.

Humanity had somehow muddled through the horrors of the 20th century and – surprisingly – managed to survive the first half of the 21st, despite numerous nuclear accidents, flings with neo-fascism and the sudden arrival of catastrophic climate change. It was agreed that spreading our chances across two planets offered better odds than staying rooted to little old Earth. Terraforming Mars was the future!

A subsequent research expedition led to humanity's biggest discovery: an alien spaceship, camouflaged to appear like an ordinary asteroid. Although the aliens had long since gone, probably millions of years ago, their technology was still very much alive, offering access to unlimited power.

Over the next hundred years humanity blossomed, reaching out to the solar system. By 2238, Mars had been successfully terraformed, countless smaller colonies had sprung up in its wake, built on our solar system's many moons, on major asteroids and in newly built habitats and installations.

Jemm Delaney is a Xeno-Archaeologist and her 16-year old son Clint a talented hacker. Together they make a great team. When she accepts a job to retrieve an alien artifact from a derelict space station, it looks like they will become rich. But with Corps, aliens, AIs and junkies involved, nothing is ever going to proceed smoothly.

If you're a fan of Julian May, Frank Herbert or James S.A. Corey, you will love *Birds of Paradise*.

ISBN: 9781915304308 (epub, kindle) / 97819153041209 (538pp paperback)

Visit bit.ly/BirdsOfParadise-Kremers

YOU MIGHT ALSO LIKE

Gardens of Earth
Book I of The Sundering Chronicles

Mark Iles

Imagine an alien life force that knows your deepest fear, and can use that against you.

Corporate greed supported by incompetent surveyors leads to the colonisation of a distant world, ominously dubbed 'Halloween', that turns out not to be uninhabited after all. The aliens, soon called Spooks by military units deployed to protect the colonists, can adopt the physical form of an opponent's deepest fear and then use it to kill them. The colony is massacred and as retaliation the orbiting human navy nuke the planet. In revenge, the Spooks invade Earth.

In a last-minute attempt to avert the war, Seethan Bodell, a marine combat pilot sent home from the front with PTSD, is given a top-secret research spacecraft, and a mission to travel into the past along with his co-pilot and secret lover Rose, to prevent the original landing on Halloween and stop the war from ever happening. But the mission goes wrong, causing a tragedy later known as The Sundering, decimating the world and tearing reality, while Seethan's ship is flung into the future. The Spooks win the war and claim ownership of Earth. He wakes, alone, in his ejector seat with no sign of either Rose or his vessel. When he realises that his technology no longer works, his desperation to find Rose becomes all the more urgent – her android body won't survive long in this new Earth.

Gardens of Earth is the first book of *The Sundering Chronicles*. The story tackles alien war, a future that may be considered either dystopian or utopian, depending on who you ask, and a protagonist coping with his demons in an unfamiliar and stressful environment – not to mention immediate threats from a pathological serial killer, the remnants of Earth's inhabitants now living in a sparse pre-industrial society under the watchful eye of the Spooks, and returning human colonists intent on reclaiming Earth. Underlying all this are issues of social justice, human and android rights, and love that transcends difference. In many senses this is classic science fiction, but the abilities of the Spooks provide an environment, and archetypal creatures within it, that are reminiscent of myth and magic fantasy. Truly cross-genre, *Gardens of Earth* is an exciting adventure, a heart-rending quest, and an eye-opening insight into the coping strategies of a veteran.

ISBN: 9781911409953 (epub, kindle) / 9781911409854 (264pp paperback)

Visit bit.ly/GardensOfEarth

ABOUT TERRY JACKMAN

Terry Jackman, variously teacher, tutor, Clarks shoe fitter, award-winning picture framer, lecturer, article-writer and/or committee chair [for the UK's Fine Art Trade Guild], joined the first BSFA online Orbit [writers' group] in 2005 and developed that for 16 years – 14 groups by then, scary thought – until a brain tumour and covid's arrival interrupted. So she gave up the day jobs, but she finally shared some stories.

Milton Keynes UK
Ingram Content Group UK Ltd.
UKHW030641230724
445892UK00002B/23